# APOCALYPSING
## *a novel*

**by**
**Jason Anderson**

# ROADSIDE PRESS

<u>FOR</u>

*Luca*
*Caden*
*Christina*
*Giovanni*
*Nico*

*DO YOUR BEST*

# Ghosted

David was dead, but he *looked* terrible.

That he was deceased had little to do with it. Stacey made a point to cite his encroaching double chin in the waning days of their relationship. She stopped taking photographs with him because of it.

*"Don't look like that."*

Now it was all he could see as he stood watch over his own fresh corpse.

The four Klingon-adjacent wrinkles permanently etched into his forehead.

Twin receding power alleys for a hairline racing in tandem toward the cliff in perpetuity.

A ten-pound spare tire of flubber-gut around his midsection that he would never lose.

It was enough to make a guy want to be cremated.

Rigor mortis was the least of his concerns.

Stace would be so disgusted when she saw him at his funeral.

Spectators encircled the specter. The customers seated inside a nearby Coney Island craned their necks to watch the show unfold while they finished their Westerns. A spinning barber pole served as partition between its owner and the tattoo artist next door. They set aside their respective bloodletting to take up temporary viewing positions outside each storefront. The eyes of all parties gravitated toward the same point of interest lying lifeless on the cracked concrete.

"She's asking if he's still breathing. Can someone check and see?"

A thirty-something brunette in a blue Alexander Mc-Queen business suit found no takers. With a Zoom pretrial already on the docket in thirty minutes, counsel approached with a moderate amount of exasperation. Steadying herself in stilettos, she crouched down with care to place her palm above his open mouth. Dissatisfied with the response, the solicitor pinched her thumb and forefinger into David's limp wrist in a second request for production. Her cell phone stayed sweat-plastered to the side of her face.

"No. I don't think so. I'm pretty sure he's gone. I don't feel a pulse."

With the game all but called, several onlookers silently retreated from the huddle and headed for home in a discreet effort to beat the traffic.

David could hear the *Eeyore* of the EMS siren rising and falling in intensity from around the corner prior to its arrival on scene. The few remaining bystanders still holding vigil around his prone body raised their heads in grateful anticipation of the newly appointed caretaker. Having done their duty and paid their respects, each began to filter out in turn to make way for the more able interloper. Dead David's eyes remained open and upturned toward his invisible double. The apparition imagined his cadaver copy raising a decrepit index finger toward him and the ghost following suit to fully recreate the Spiderman meme that was his new reality.

A young patrolman no more than two years out of the academy beat the paramedics to the punch by about fifteen seconds. The redhead's face was more freckled than a salami slice. Officer Howdy Doody entered the frame with arms outstretched to further compel the dispersing crowd. "Okay everyone, let's move it along now. Give us room to work."

David frantically surveyed his unfolding nightmare. If he had known he was going to die, he would have at least worn a button-up. Tom Ford. French cuff. Something elegant. Instead, it was Nike flip-flops and an even-more-distressed-than-normal *Elastica* T-shirt. Justine was coyly sucking on her lollipop and come-hithering the EMT who had begun chest compressions. He kept trying to inject one last gasp into the Britpop movement to no avail.

Unable to make the vital connection, the attendant finally conceded.

*-Who wants a life anyway?-*

"Hey! David! Over here."

The ghost did a double take.

Bobby Kennedy was waving at him from the front of the diner across the street.

RFK cupped his hands around his mouth to achieve the full bullhorn effect. "You had a brain aneurysm, David. Hemorrhagic stroke. I don't think you're going to want to stick around to see how the coroner will make that determination."

He briefly pictured a bonesaw misery whipping back and forth across his chalky skull.

"Come on over. I grabbed us a booth. I'll explain everything."

***

Hal's Place was open twenty-four hours a day. Half that would have proven sufficient considering the current economic headwinds. Its red leather upholstered seating was two decades behind the times. Duct tape patchwork was being utilized as a stuffing cover throughout the establishment. The sealant offered only a temporary reprieve at this point. It was the last stopgap before the scrap heap.

The phantoms found themselves in the middle of the breakfast rush hour. David counted two employees for every living diner. All three patrons appeared to be AARP-eligible and were regular enough to be on a first name basis with their server. The jukebox across from the cash register matched the décor. It offered no options post *Rat Pack*.

"I have to say, you're taking the recognition of your demise remarkably well," commended RFK with a silent tap against the table. Perry Como was currently killing them softly with his song. "As a rule of the afterlife, anxiety does sharply diminish once you die, but even so. I've had a couple jump off a bridge on me before. I mean that literally—a couple jumped off the Golden Gate Bridge right in front of me after I told them. Held hands all the way down and everything. Luckily, they were already dead—but it's pretty dark at the bottom of San Francisco Bay. The ghost of Ray Charles could have found his way back to shore sooner. Tell me, what line of work were you in David?"

Despite being in the presence of a Kennedy ghost, his eyes remained glued to the ambulance carrying his corpse until it receded in full from his field of vision. "I was a regional account manager with Goodwill Funding. Buy old debt for ten cents on the dollar and then collect the entire amount. With interest. Preferably through the court system. Credit card companies and debt collectors secretly love it when you don't pay them, because then they can sue you. If you whisper the words wage garnishment in their collective ear, they'll all go six to midnight instantly. It's debt vulture Viagra."

"So, you chose a career in public service, then."

For the first time since he died, David laughed. "There wasn't much nobility to it, no. I apologize, sir. If you aren't lucky enough to be born a Kennedy, only way you're getting to that compound in Hyannis Port is by scratching and clawing."

Bobby had to snicker at the light shivving. "Trust me, Camelot was never all it was cracked up to be. Pretty sure Merlin put a curse on the whole family. As for the other, been awhile since I had any dealings with the legislative branch. If the creditor accepts ten percent, shouldn't the law stipulate the debt collector is only entitled to recoup a certain percentage above that amount?"

"In a sensible world, sure," David acknowledged. "Unfortunately, this is Wonderland. Nothing here is certain anymore but debt and taxes. Even death would appear to offer a bit more wiggle room now." He held his palms up to demonstrate the point. "Man-eat-man out there, Senator. Sorry to say. The machine is designed to consume you. Every part. It's like we're all being slowly assimilated by *The Thing*. This American life is just a constant shuffle between paranoia, mistrust, and swapping disgusting bodily fluids. And then you die."

"That's a pretty dim view, David," declared Bobby. "One of my favorite films, though. No better metaphor for McCarthyism. I always loved Howard Hawks as a director."

"Oh, forget that nonsense. John Carpenter's version is ten times better. Best movie of the 1980s. I'll fight you."

"I'll make sure to check it out the next time I'm alive in the 1980s," Bobby said with a smirk. "You know, Hawks used to say a good movie is three great scenes and no bad ones. What were your three great scenes, David?"

"Senator, I'd say my life up until now has been more akin to *Plan 9 From Outer Space* on an artistic level. Just all bad scenes. If you let a blind man reimagine the Omaha Beach landing with a Betamax camcorder and then played that bloody mess on an endless loop—that would be a close approximation of my life to this point. Probably why I'm being so even keeled about passing away. Randomly dying on the sidewalk when I'm thirty-four is par for the course. Only thing more fitting would have been if an anvil from the Acme Corporation fell on my head."

Bobby could only shake his head. "You're a real fount of positivity. Not a single good scene, huh? Ever? I find that hard to believe. This is America. You ate a cheeseburger at some point. Something."

David looked down at the table for a few seconds and smiled. "The first time Stacey kissed me. I guess that night was okay. Random things mean the most, right?"

"Agreed. I still remember the first time I saw Ethel in Quebec. No woman alive or dead has ever looked sexier in ski gear. Dated her sister Patty first before I got with the program.

Needless to say, dinner at the Skakels was a little uncomfortable those first couple years."

"Stacey walked into my apartment once in this tan coat she used to have. The thing was like corduroy, but not. Never got a handle on it. She had a red cashmere scarf tied around her neck, and her cheeks were the same color. A couple of snowflakes were still in her hair. I'd never seen a more beautiful woman. Ever. Not in real life. Not on a movie screen. Not to this day. When she smiled, I realized I loved her—irrevocably. It wasn't just a word anymore. I don't know why I always treated it like a declaration of war. I picked her up against the wall three feet from the door and kissed her until neither of us could breathe. Tried to kill it in the crib, but I couldn't."

"Unconditional love is immortal," Bobby offered with absolute certainty.

David endorsed the sentiment with his head bowed. "And I remember the last weekend we spent together. Every minute of it. Touching her face at three in the morning while she smiled back at me. If I were forced to stare at a single thing for all eternity, that would have been my choice. I didn't realize until later it was taunting me. Or she was. I'm still not sure which. Sunday night she told me it was over, and time stopped for me. I haven't been alive ever since."

"There's always a Jackie," Bobby offered with a sympathetic smile. "How long has it been?"

"Over two years now. It's strange. It seems like two days, and two decades. Somehow, it's all three at the same time."

Robert nodded in agreement. "The only thing harder than losing the love of your life is knowing they're not lost without you. It's a minefield in the shape of a Moebius Strip. No fun to navigate through that thicket. Your desired destination is always staring you right in the face, but you can never stop moving further away from the intended target. Everything in your path's a potential tripwire. And there's no exit ramp."

"You're a politician, Senator," David reminded his inquisitor.

"For your own professional sake, you really should learn to lie better. I've been gravely disappointed in your performance thus far. Pun very much intended."

"Been working at it since Catholic school. Just never took. It's why I always envied Jack. He was able to bullshit the pants right off them. Where'd you two leave things?"

"Oh, she left me in a dumpster by the side of the road and then tossed a Molotov cocktail inside before she drove off with the top down." David underscored the point with a vociferous shake of the head. "Stacey always operated under the misapprehension that if you light a building on fire and then walk away without looking back, it doesn't qualify as arson. My charred corpse shouted endlessly after her into the void once the flames petered out, though. If that counts for anything."

"You didn't keep in touch at all?"

"No. Last I heard she moved to Manhattan to join up with the rest of the Inhumans. Refusing to acknowledge our existence from on high is standard practice for those mutants. It was just a pre-ghosting. Never returned a single call or text after she finished me. All but told me to fuck off and die. Looks like she finally got her wish. Guess I have to console myself with the fact that I get Bobby Kennedy as my guardian angel." David had a sudden realization. "Shit, I am so sorry. You do know you're a ghost, right?"

Bobby gasped. He grasped at random portions of his upper body to reassure himself they were still there. The sarcastic effort ceased instantly. A dead stare into David's eyes was his only remaining movement. "Yeah, no shit, Sherlock. I'm as dead as a doornail and have been for quite some time. Last thing I remember was George Plimpton talking about playing backup QB for the Detroit Lions, and then it all went dark on me. Guess his name was Sirhan Sirhan? I'm surprised old Joe didn't think of that one first. *Kennedy Kennedy* was coming if mom and dad had a couple more—mark my words. In any event, I'm not your guardian angel."

A father and son in matching red Tiger polos decided to stop off for breakfast prior to their tee time. Bobby and David silently scooched further into the booth to make way for their oblivious tablemates. "If you're not my guardian angel, then what are you?"

"I'm just a gatekeeper. Kind of like an RA sent here to help guide you through your freshmen orientation. The role can only be filled by someone pure of heart and soul. In the last century that left me, Mother Theresa, and a dockworker from Dublin named Declan. *Great guy.* Gandhi almost got in, but he had a spiritual affair outside his marriage. Apparently, that's sufficient to serve as disqualification. If you have so much as an unpaid parking ticket, they hold it against you. The Secret Service isn't as discerning. Anyway, the three of us alternate days. You just happened to die on my Monday."

A *Flo*-model waitress named Marie with a nametag that said Evelyn started taking orders from the head of the table. The stand-in for Charlie Woods reached directly through David's chest cavity to grab a menu while his father started things off with a blueberry stack.

Bobby sighed. "God, I miss pancakes. These folks are making me hungry. Let's take a walk."

***

In a flash they were strolling down the same sidewalk where David departed only a few minutes before. The sudden dearth of dead bodies wasn't the only absence he noted.

He couldn't hear a single voice.

There didn't appear to be another person for miles.

RFK began to roll up his baby blue Oxford shirt sleeves as the two pounded the pavement. He looked like he was preparing to campaign door-to-door again back in the Bronx. "Time we get down to brass tacks, David. I know you want to talk about the why, but it's important we establish some rules of the road first. When you were alive, your time was split between being awake and asleep. Your day-to-day now actually isn't going to be all that different. You'll remain in the real world half the time. Same world you've lived in your entire life. Only now you'll be an invisible ghost. And instead of sleeping, you'll spend your normal non-waking hours in the spirit realm. That's where we are right now. Which reminds me—"

Without another word Bobby got down on one knee, although this was no proposal.

A glowing hoop of blinding white light instantly appeared in RFK's right hand. The trap opened with a sharp snap of his wrist. He fit each half-circle around David's lower leg and then clamped the contraption shut once again.

"I'm sorry. Are you putting an ankle monitor on me right now?"

"Technically, it's called a Time Tether." Bobby rose from his hunched position and resumed walking. David matched him stride for stride while following every word. "You see, the spirit realm is really just the fourth dimension. Seven more rungs up the ladder and you hit Heaven. That's where anything is possible, including the impossible. Nothing but string music there. It's the source code for the entire universe. As soon as you hit 4-D, you start to exist outside of time. The sensory input from being everywhere all at once would become overwhelming. Like Superman hearing all the people on Earth screaming into his ear simultaneously. The leg iron keeps you stuck in the moment. Prevents you from going deaf dumb and blind in death."

"So, I'm kind of like the anti-Billy Pilgrim?"

"I have no idea who that is," RFK offered with a furrowed brow, "but whatever helps you. The Tether also prevents replication. Without time as a constraint, the imagination can start to run a little wild. When Lucifer was still a resident of the eleventh dimension, he created a trillion copies of himself and waged war on the place. Took two millennia to clean up after his little graduation party."

"So, he really was tossed out, huh?"

"Yeah, starting an everlasting holy war will get you

blacklisted every time. Doesn't help that the guy's a huge prick. Satan liked to deploy these cosmic IEDs filled with STDs during battle. Spiritually Transmitted Diseases are the worst. They stick around forever, and the only antibiotic is sanctified water from a baptismal font. Ironically, the stuff is impossible for angels to get their hands on, so you can see the predicament. He gave half of Heaven the equivalent of holy herpes before he got the old heave-ho."

The pair began to slalom through several stopped cars silently littering the roadway to reach the municipal park across the street. A look of concern flashed across David's face in between SUVs. "So, if the Devil's real, does that mean there's a Hell, too?"

"Not in the sense you mean." RFK spotted a sky blue '67 Mustang GT 350 at the stoplight. He took a brief detour to drag his palm along its double-barreled white racing stripe. His hand somehow grew wistful as it moved across the length of the coupe. "It's not all hellfire and brimstone. Just an endless pool of anti-matter. Beelzebub will be drowning in the stuff for all eternity. I assure you it's no day at the beach. But Luci's just an Igor, anyway. The Anti-God—now that's who you need to worry about."

"Who in the hell is the Anti-God?"

Bobby's expression turned appropriately funereal for the first time as the two returned to the sidewalk. "Envision any potential scenario and then ask yourself, *'what would an asshole do?'* Have you checked out Haiti lately? Hundred percent his handiwork. That infernal reprobate created blood cancer, for Christ's sake. Rumor is the only thing that can soothe his soul hole is the sound of babies crying. No one's ever seen the sick bastard eat anything other than black licorice. For every good thing God puts into existence, the Anti-God matches it with an equal but opposite reaction. Let's put all that in the drawer for now. Unfair to give you the sensation of shitting your pants on your first day in the afterlife when you can no longer physically recreate the sensation."

David flagged it for later and moved along. It only took a few additional steps along the park's designated asphalt bike path before the slap of his sandals lit the lamp. He clapped his hands together to confirm his findings and then held up the supplemental evidence for RFK's further review. "I notice I'm tangible again."

"That's right, David, very good," Bobby said in a manner that rendered a pat on the head superfluous. "I'm impressed you're picking up on things so quickly. Yes, every subatomic particle in the universe possesses an opposing anti-particle. The electron has its positron. God has an Anti-God. So on and so forth. But when you die, it's a different kind of AP Physics altogether."

"I cheated off Joe Stramski both semesters in that class. Still only managed a C somehow." David acknowledged the second fact with a profound sense of shame. "I'm going to probably need a refresher course."

Bobby rerouted the pair across an empty baseball diamond. He tapped home plate with both feet before taking his base. The audible crunch of infield dirt beneath his boat shoes put some additional pep in his step. "No worries. Not that I'm Einstein or anything. They gave me flashcards a few decades back. A typical person already emits about 180 positrons of antimatter an hour while they're alive. It comes from the decay of Potassium-40 when you breathe. Stuff's a natural source of radioactivity that circulates throughout your entire body. Believe it or not, human beings are like little walking nuclear power plants that need to constantly blow off steam to survive."

"I had no idea my flatulence might be helping to prevent another Three Mile Island," David responded with faux wonderment. He continued to serve as a buffer between Bobby and the opposing dugout as they walked. "If I'm ever in a position to share a bed with a woman again, I'm totally keeping that one in my back pocket—so to speak."

The Washington Senator tipped an invisible cap toward

his teammate for successfully executing the squeeze. "It's certainly a release valve. In any event, once you stop huffing and puffing, there's no more escape hatch. A chain reaction builds up until you start to go supernova at the subatomic level. Your soul is what blankets the stuff and prevents a mini-mushroom cloud from erupting any time old Clara croaks. The combo creates dark matter—that's what seeps out of you after death. You're a walking primordial black hole."

"My head's spinning," David said. "So, I'm made of something called dark matter, but it only exists in four dimensions?"

"Actually, it was everywhere around you even when you were alive. The entirety of our living universe is made of death, and our PHDs have no idea. Scientists can't see it or detect the stuff, but they know it exists by studying gravitational effects and the like. It's just not visible in three dimensions."

David picked up an errant blood red Deekin batting donut left lying in the grass. He horseshoed it end over end down the right field foul line as he contemplated the fresh disclosures. His eyebrows stayed scrunched and slanted downward like pinball flippers stuck in the stationary position. "If they can't see or detect dark matter, and that's what I'm made of now, then how are you seeing me? How can I see myself?"

"Another astute observation," Bobby acknowledged. "When God adjusted the settings in this place, she left it so only ghostly lives anti-matter. Set it and forget it. Dial's been turned so whoever's in the dark may be brought into the light. In 4-D, you're as full-bodied as a '56 Merlot. You can experience pleasure, and pain. The whole gamut. And if you die, you just restart at your last celestial checkpoint. Is that a concept I need to explain further to you?"

David politely nodded in the negative. "I'm an X-Box baby. I'm exceedingly familiar with the idea of respawning."

"Yeah, it definitely seems like serving as the dependent became child's play for you Millennials," RFK sneered. "You moved on to being controlled years ago."

David rolled his eyes at the moldy oldie.

Bobby shifted to centerfield before continuing with the verbal long toss. "As you've probably also noticed, since the living remain on the clock, you won't see or hear them in the spirit realm. You're like a sundial in the dark in this place. You only get a moment in time, but all is not lost. You can drive any Lamborghini. Fly any Cessna. Blow up any nuclear power plant—I don't recommend that, actually. It's dumb. But you could, is the point. Do your worst. It won't affect a thing on the other side."

"I don't understand." David unintentionally summarized his entire life. "This doesn't look any different than the real world. If I destroy something in this place, how can it remain in one piece back home? Why doesn't the one have any effect on the other?"

"Nothing here exists outside this single moment in time. Don't even try and science the thing. It's like being stuck inside a Polaroid without people. Everything within the four corners of the photograph is real, but this is the only place where the picture exists anymore. You've been framed and nailed to the wall."

"You make it sound so appealing, Senator."

"It's not all bad news, son. The world is your oyster. It always was, you were just too busy metaphorically dying when you were alive to do anything about it. I recommend you take this opportunity to invert that process. Go swimming with ghost sharks. Maybe let yourself get eaten. Try to enjoy all thirty-one flavors."

"A world without humans does kind of sound like Heaven," David admitted. He began to admire his new potential Paradise in every direction.

"Yeah, think of it like you're some affluent jerk that rented out Disneyland for the day. You've got the run of the place." A pair of Louisville Sluggers were left lying on the warning track. Bobby twirled around with a pilfered bat in each hand to demonstrate his point. Once he completed the circuit, he dropped the kindling back into the grassy outfield with a clink. "No worries about contracting open world cabin fever, either. Still lots of others like you running around here on death detention. There are poltergeists galore. Everybody here's got a story. You'll have plenty of time to make acquaintance with the other DeadButNots as you gradually journey toward the infinite together."

Socialization was never much of a concern for David even when he was alive. Six pallbearers sounded like it was going to be a stretch. His focus naturally gravitated elsewhere. "All this time ghosts have been real, huh? Crazy. My grandmother used to say her basement back in Oak Park was haunted. Pull chain lights that would snap themselves on. Voices downstairs when no one else was home. Now I have to wonder if she was right."

"Actually, that was Steve. One of my first million. Roanoke Avenue, right?"

David's eyes widened in recognition as he slowly bobbed his head up and down.

"Yeah, he hung himself in your grandma's attic back in August of '69. Haunting is a community service program," Bobby confirmed with crossed forearms and a look of empathy directed into the dirt. "They put in their five hundred thousand hours and then they get their ticket punched to the hereafter. It's a square deal. Things could always be worse. The selfies all used to get sent to Purgatory. Trust me, you'd rather be in Hell. That place is like living in Des Moines with the sound turned off. It was entrapment what they were doing to those poor souls. Cosplaying as Casper for half a century is like living in Candyland by comparison. All because a few of us convinced the powers-that-be to institute suicide suffrage. Just goes to show, only good things happen when you give the people a voice and a vote."

"It seems like you remained quite the politician even in death."

"An artist is always working, David. Remember that."

"I'm glad to hear you were able to procure better living conditions for the blameless, but that doesn't explain why I'm in this place. What exactly did I do to piss off the Almighty? Because until thirty minutes ago I wasn't even sure God existed, and I still lived with a crippling veneration of that uncertainty. Pretty much standard issue for me, by the way. I cut out the analysis and rerouted straight to paralysis a long time ago. It was an unnecessary easement. You can't do anything wrong if you never do anything at all."

"That's quite an axiom, David."

"You can't disprove it."

"I don't know about that," RFK said as he stared off into the distance. "I have it on good authority that *the only thing necessary for the triumph of evil is for good men to do nothing.*"

David was left momentarily stunned by Seven of Nine of the Kennedy Collective. The pinpoint photon torpedo to the face caused him to reverse course. "Just shoot me straight, sir. I've always been the type to ask for the bad news first. Why am I stuck knocking on Heaven's door?"

Bobby halted their progress aside a triple-tiered wish fountain. Each apparition now found themselves unintentionally display-domed beneath their own arched waterspout. "Yeah, probably best we discuss your predicament at this point. You see David, a person can get themselves jammed up in the spirit realm for any number of reasons. Unfortunately, in your specific case it's because you belong to a Soul Succubus."

"A what now?" David pecked his head forward with a lemon-puckered face.

RFK maintained eye contact to reinforce the point. "A *Soul Succubus.* It's a Darwinian derivative of a *Jinni.* You see, Stacey's a genie—of sorts. Those mischievous little scamps engaged in a ton of intersquad sex scrimmaging back in ancient times. They invented the escape cock. Originally, it was just a regulating mechanism for magic. Guess they stayed bottled up for too long. Anyway, with each successive generation, the condition became more and more watered down. At this point her power set is about as imposing as a vestigial tail. She's like a defanged cobra."

"I'm sorry, but just to recap—you're telling me I belong

to a soul-sucking *Jinni* genie who descends from a long line of witch-people that used sex to blow off magic steam. Do I have that more or less correct?"

"Well, when you say it like that," RFK acknowledged, "it does sound kind of kooky."

"*Kind of?!?*"

"Look, there's no malevolence to it on her part," Bobby re-assured his ward. "Stacey's not even aware she is a Jinni. It was woven into her fabric from the womb. Not that much different than being AB-negative, honestly. She's like one of those people with golden blood. Except that prolonged exposure to her life essence created an unbreakable bond of metaphysical devotion on your part, and now she owns your soul for all eternity. Otherwise, same thing."

"Yeah, sure. Tomato, tomatto."

"You've been consigned to roam the planet as an earth wanderer like Stace until she willingly releases you from bondage, or she dies—at which time you would accompany her to the afterlife as her permanent shadow."

"What do you mean by permanent shadow? Like I'd have to follow her around everywhere she goes?"

RFK grimaced and shook his head. "No. Like you'll be turned into a voiceless, sentient shadow that will be grafted onto Stacey's spirit and then dragged across the celestial concrete until the end of time. Which in the eleventh dimension would last forever and a day."

"You said there was some good news?"

Bobby seemed genuinely puzzled. "No. I didn't."

"I know you didn't," David admitted with a downturned head. "I thought maybe I could trick you."

RFK comforted David with a cupped palm around his shoulder. "There is a nuclear option available to you. Always the case, isn't it? I guess some of the younger 4-Ds even have a slang term for it now. The kids like to call it '*Makin' Whoopi*.'"

David's disgust level broke the gauge. He shook off his

instructor. "Sorry, I'm not going to have specter-sex with my unsuspecting ex. It's a non-starter. That's far too assault-adjacent for me to give it even the slightest consideration. If I'm forced to go to Hell—oh well."

"I'll ignore how appalled I am at the implication and chalk it up to temporal insanity on your part." Bobby's tone straightened to the edge of a razor along with his eyelids. "There's a movie, you jackass. Something called *Ghost*, yes? I'm admittedly from a different era, but as described to me it sounds like pornography filmed inside of a Pottery Barn. Neither here nor there. Apparently at one point a ghost uses this Whoopi cushion woman like a human windsock to talk to his wife. You can do that, actually. *Once*. But whatever spirit juice you pass over with gets sucked dry in the process. It can take years to rebuild those reserves. So, you better make it count if and when. You may only get one shot at the target. I recommend you get your feet under you first before even contemplating it."

David never considered patience to be a virtue. "But if one were so inclined to stick their hand on the stove?"

The Senator smiled like someone who saw the question coming a mile away. "Well, it's pretty simple, really. Get her to say, '*I release you, David Downey*' while you're still in possession of a physical body, and you're done. Poof and then powdery clouds. If not, you're going dungeon dark for the duration. Speaking of which—"

A beautiful sunny day morphed into a stunning starry night in an instant.

"Every twelve hours they flip the switch," RFK established. "Living in the land of the midnight sun outside time would give you 4-Ds the worst case of Seasonal Affective Disorder in recorded history. You've got enough on your plate already. Making you all SAD on top of things would only be cruel. They'll throw in some weather here and there to enliven the proceedings."

David began to walk away from the fountain expecting Bobby would soon follow behind. After several steps he looked back to see RFK remaining stone-columned instead in the same spot where he left him. He let loose a single silent chuckle. "Let me guess—you have to go."

"You might not believe me in the moment, David," Bobby said, "but being this perceptive will only pay dividends for you down the road. In this place, and the other. Hit the nail on the head. I have to make my way to Dubai now. You want to talk about wealth? I thought my family had it made. Next guest I'm set to usher in had a gold toilet in his G700."

"I still have a million questions for you. I feel like I'm being shoved out into the Pacific Ocean on a pool float with an empty flare gun. You can't give me another fifteen?"

"No can-do son, sorry," RFK lamented. "It's like parenting. Eventually we have to take off the water wings, or you'll never fathom that you can fly. It's for your own good. Just remember, it's only H20 out there. The stuff literally can't kill you anymore."

"What comes next, then?"

Bobby began to lay out David's upcoming itinerary as he unrolled his sleeves. "You'll be jumped ahead a few days to your funeral. Saves you from some actual headaches in the interim. But from that point forward, Stacey's got you on an invisible string from the moment she wakes up until she loses consciousness. Try to always remain within spitting distance of the target or the succubus will subconsciously force the issue. Being pulled into compliance by a ghost grappling hook is no fun at all. It's like a tractor beam sucking you backwards through a rip current. Whenever she's asleep or unconscious, you return here to your 4-D dormitory. Same routine runs on repeat every day. Keep grinding the mortar and pestle until it makes good medicine. I don't know what else to say. I'm not going to lie to you, it can get to be a real slog. There will be times you wish you weren't dead."

"I'm already there, Senator."

"You know what I mean."

"Will I ever see you again?"

RFK showed his teeth, but he wasn't smiling. His eyebrows

arched in accompaniment. "If so, I certainly hope it's not in this place. Goodnight, David—and good luck."

Bobby blinked out, and then everything faded to black.

# DTR

The dickhead had his dick out.

David didn't need to be a detective to decipher where it might have found purchase over the previous eight hours.

Stacey was currently snuggling half-naked in bed with Lyle.

He was David's roommate in another life.

The two decided to mourn his death with one last roll in the hay.

Old time's sake.

*In Memoriam.*

David was contemplating dragging his boo balls across Lyle's snoozing skinhead. To say the pair disgusted him would be understating the obvious.

Stacey appeared to share his opinion. She was lying on her side with bulging eyes. It made her look like she was bracing for an imminent bear attack. One pupil downshifted to the doughboy-sized arm currently draped across her chest. Even the slightest effort to dislodge the infant-man's Andro-enhanced appendage resulted only in effeminate "hoo-hooing" and further constriction from the baby boa. A few minutes passed before she began to silently weep.

Lyle's odious body spray scent was only a supplement in this instance.

When David touched the corner of her eye to wipe away a tear, she brushed him aside.

This was a common occurrence between them even when he was alive.

A look of nebulous understanding spread across each of their faces simultaneously.

Stacey shot up using her left arm as a kickstand and did a quick clockwise scan of the room until she found Lyle within her field of vision. One look at his face in the light of day was sufficient to serve as a future disincentive. She returned her head halfway back toward its starting position before asking the question aloud to the otherwise empty room. Her voice stayed low to avoid disturbing the peace.

"David?"

Despite the diminished decibels, Lyle awoke from his slumber. The tot rocked from side to side until he finally managed to roll over onto his belly. His squinty eyes and wrinkled forehead suggested a diaper change might soon be in order. "Did you say something, Stace?"

That name belonged to David—something Lyle knew good and well. She physically stirred without turning her head to signal her displeasure. Her eyes shot to the right until hitting the end of the road at the edge of each socket. "I told you not to call me that, and I meant it."

"I'm sorry, I forgot," Lyle lied. He set himself into a sniper's position on both elbows while he began to wipe away the granulated sleep. "What did you say, though?"

"Nothing. You're hearing ghosts."

Lyle placed his right hand across the crook of her elbow. The touch caused Stacey to physically recoil. He pretended not to notice. "Want to grab some breakfast? My treat."

Always the gentleman.

"No. We're not having flapjacks, Lyle. I have a funeral to attend. You think I came back to this strip mall slaughterhouse for the bottomless Mimosas? I live in New York, man. David died. In Michigan, unfortunately. Remember?"

His pout was palpable. "Yeah no, you're right. I should get ready, too. I'm going to go run home and shower. You sure you don't want to come back with me? You can have the entire downstairs bath to yourself. We could drive over together."

David envisioned them smiling and strolling into the funeral home hand-in-hand. Kissing and cavorting in front of his coffin. In his daydream, all the commotion caused his corpse to turn and glare at the pair of miscreants interrupting his final sleep with their foreplay.

"No, I'm good. Thanks. Kate's picking me up at ten. I'm sure I'll see you there."

Lyle spooned himself against Stacey. She could feel his hot halitosis breath napalming her hairline down to the follicles. An engorged *Monopoly* thimble brushed itself insistently against her mid back. "I know you're heading home in the morning. And with David dying it's not the ideal time. I'm not dumb. I do recognize all of that. But you need to know I love you, Stacey. I always have."

Her eyes performed another maximum rotation to the right without any corresponding head movement. "I know, Lyle. You've said that a few times now."

*-You've-*

That she never returned the favor failed to dissuade him from further repetition of action.

"Did you have anything that you wanted to say to me?" Bambi batted his doe eyes. Stacey somehow felt the discharged air fanning against the back of her skull like a stiff breeze.

"No, Lyle. The whole point of this exchange was that I didn't want to talk. I can assure you that our witty banter was not the impetus for the intercourse." She turned her entire body toward the opposing side of the bed to confront her Lilliputian paramour directly. "I'm sorry, kid. I don't love you. And if I said so at some point previously, I do apologize—but I was black-out drunk and trying to piss off David at the time. Both conditions would have to be met. One or the other alone isn't sufficient for those words to escape my mouth. Not where you're concerned. I don't know what else to say. This is the last time we're doing this. I thought we were both just trying to forget for a few minutes. It's not healthy for you to be this hung-up on someone you can never have."

David could not agree more.

Lyle looked like the kindergarten teacher took away his Tonka truck and gave him a five-minute timeout. He grabbed his 26x26 jeans from beside the bed and began to get dressed with his back turned. "I guess I'll never stop being a glutton for punishment. If you ever change your mind, you know where to find me."

"Yep. Right here. Where you've always been." Stacey was standing up now in nothing but black underwear with a matching trashcan in hand. She began to discard the empty Modelos and airplane liquor bottles scattered around the room into the receptacle. Lyle didn't merit a look. Her focus remained on the clean-up as she continued the conversation. "Look. You don't actually love me. You just love that David did. Please don't get it twisted. This thing between us, whatever it is—it isn't that, and it never was."

"David had nothing to do with this."

His dead friend silently sustained his own objection.

Lyle was sitting up in bed with only his head turned toward the target. "It was always about you. He was my friend. I never wanted to hurt him. Why would I?"

Stacey transitioned to looking for her makeup bag. The thing went MIA on her. She decided to give her mounting frustration an outlet to avoid blowing a fuse. "Oh, I don't know. I suppose for the same reason you feel an inherent need to screw every guy's girlfriend, wife, or widow—you're a selfish neanderthal. You've always thought the notches on your bedpost add up to some kind of viable currency, but they just keep pulling you further into debt. Somewhere along the way, a seed-dispersing ruderal got cross-pollinated with a person and out you popped. You want me to shoot you straight?"

"Please." Both men in the room said it out loud and with the same emphasis, but only one of them was smiling when he did so.

She placed the wastebasket on the floor beside her feet

and finally gave Lyle her full, undivided attention. No effort was made to cover herself. Modesty did not matter at this point. "Fine. You're a permanent child who requires the same breast-fed validation as a six-month-old from every lady he encounters in life. And if one of them happens to have a boyfriend, all the better. *Score.* You can only climax if you know your pleasure is causing another person pain. That's serial killer shit, Lyle. How many ant colonies did you incinerate as a boy? You and Edmund Kemper—every woman's just another head to put up on your shelf. The last thing you deserve in this life is a trophy. Trust me."

Lyle's sulking transitioned to skulking. Fully clothed in a flash, he rose from the bed and crept in silence toward the door with his head down the entire way. He asked one final question before exiting as she worked to clasp the bra behind her back.

"Will you save me a seat, at least?"

When Stacey spun around to face him, her look suggested Lyle was currently defecating in the open doorway. "*Will I save you a seat?* It's David's funeral, dumbass—not a high school production of *Oklahoma!* We're going to the planetarium, apparently. What do you think this is, a Detroit Tigers matinee? I'm sorry but just because you said that silly shit, we're not sitting together. Go find a ticket scalper in the parking lot or something. Now if you'll excuse me—"

Without waiting for further approval, she ushered Lyle all the way out of the room before slamming the door in his face. Stacey turned and leaned her entire body weight against the wooden slab for support until she slowly slid herself down butt-first onto the crappy crimson carpet. Steel wool had a softer consistency. She placed her arms atop her kneecaps and utilized the combination as a headrest.

David took up the same position on the floor across from her until she stopped crying.

***

The ladies decided against doing coke directly off his corpse.

David was desperate to locate the bright side of something.

"Look, it's terrible that he's gone, and I feel for his family, but dead or alive, you were way too good for the dearly departed," Kate confirmed in between bumps from behind the beige bathroom stall door. When she jerked her head skyward following the second, the speech that followed made it sound like she suddenly came down with the sniffles.

"I'm sorry, but it's true," she continued. "All this bereavement is clouding your better judgment. You made the right decision. We just need to get you gigity with another guy and you'll forget all about David again. Let me hook you up with Dak. The guy used to be a product tester for Magnum condoms and he's diversified, what more do you need to know? I only slept with him once, promise, and it was a couple months before Craig and I got hitched, so we're good."

Craig Madison didn't marry into being Kate's cuckold. It was a preexisting condition.

David's ex sharply shook off her friend's suggestion with her lips pursed into a frown for good measure. "Sorry kid. Hard pass. His first name sounds like a phlegmy discharge. I hate the sound of coughing in bed, so sex would be a non-starter."

Stacey dipped her toe into the whitewater once more and then came up gasping for air. An endless ocean of brown wavy hair as thick as a lion's mane flooded out in every direction behind her head. Several rogue strands remained draped over her face in the aftermath. The stragglers were propelled back with a targeted white squall through teeth followed by a search and rescue operation executed by hand.

"Plus, based on the abbreviation I'm betting ol' Jed's got kinfolk straight out of *The Hills Have Eyes*," Stacey added. "Every fourth of July would be dirt bikes around the gravel pit back in Bismarck, and then rushing some dumb uncle to the ER after he blows his hand off with an M-80. No thank you."

Kate's spontaneous cackle caused a multi-pronged acidic sting to rise up against the back of her throat. The Force Choke that followed led to a pair of stiff coughs. It required the use of both hands against her windpipe to prevent a third repetition.

David peered down at them from atop the toilet in the next stall. He was considering whether to jump in and assist with the strangulation.

"Jesus, Stacey. Remind me to stop playing matchmaker on your behalf. No one was cheerleading harder for you to sack David, but it's been two years and you're still on a glidepath to playing the field into your mid-30s. It's a young gal's game, girl. All the available evidence is suggesting you might still be hung up on a dead guy. Say it ain't so, sister."

Secretly, Kate had always wanted the decedent for herself.

She thanked God that truth would be taken to the grave.

One look at her husband signaled the obvious source of her resentment.

Since she could never have David, she decided to fuck her friend's relationship instead.

Stacey wasn't proud of what came next. Unfortunately, she determined long ago it would require too much time and effort to locate a fake best friend with Kate's top tier qualifications. "Excuse me. I just got done sex-deprogramming Lyle seven hours ago at the Village Suites. I don't know what part of David you think I'm holding onto at this point, but whatever appendage you're envisioning, it's a mirage."

The squeaky sound of an intruder entering the premises caused an immediate cessation of all activities. Both girls stifled grief-modulated giggles as they snapped their supplies up off the baby changing table. The ladies made sure to separately squeeze all the remaining evidence out of each nostril with their thumb and forefinger before opening the door.

Some gray-haired extended relative that David had never met before eyeballed their reflections with disgust as they exited. She went to Studio 54 once in her youth. Almost got in, too. The younger generation fled the premises without bothering to engage in the artifice of handwashing for their elder's benefit.

"I have to relieve Craig in an hour. Let's start saying our goodbyes, okay?"

Despite hating David with the passion of a thousand burning suns, his dead body did at least provide Kate with an excuse to get away from her family for a few hours. She gave thanks by offering perfunctory condolences to his father outside the reception room before abandoning Stacey to fend for herself.

"Thank you again for flying out, Stephanie."

Stacey let the mistake slide. Just like always. "Of course, Mr. Downey. Hey, you've been on your feet all morning. Have you even eaten anything today? Will you let me get you something? Please?"

Without a word the big bear pulled her in for a hug she did not anticipate. It took a moment before she realized it was exactly what she needed as well. She melted into the sasquatch-sized man like an ice cube in a warm bath. "Whatever history you had with my son is between you two, but I would have been proud to call you my daughter. David would have wanted you to find happiness. I hope that you will."

No opportunity was granted for a response. Mr. Downey brusquely set her aside by the biceps with a forced smile before moving onto the next grim-faced stranger.

The action left Stacey momentarily perplexed until she remembered—

He was born a Downey.

The same as his son.

They couldn't help themselves.

No one could.

David took leave of the ladies to enjoy the ongoing photographic slideshow summarizing his utter lack of existence. Available seating remained plentiful. After a few minutes he successfully timed when each of the five pictures including his mother would come up in the rotation. Laura Downey was gone before he was in braces. David worried she might not recognize him when they saw one another again.

He clearly had never been a mother.

The wax figurine in the casket wouldn't be able to put one over on her.

His brother Mark sat directly next to him staring off into space. They never said two words to one another in life, but David loved him. For the first time, he realized Mark felt the same way. Unfortunately, it took him dying to make that discovery.

He suddenly realized his nephew was nowhere to be found. Frantic and unable to voice his concerns, the ghost rose to his feet and began to scan the surrounding area before heading back out into the hallway. He called out for the boy over and over in complete silence.

The ghost let out an inaudible sigh of relief. Stacey was consoling Benny on a chocolate-cushioned bench abutting the back exit with her arm draped over his shoulders. He cried into her sweater, and she matched him point-for-point with her chin lightly resting atop his head.

"He loved you so so much, Ben-Ben. If someone so much as said your name, it made him smile. And your uncle was never much of a smiler." She sniffled and snickered at the memory of something she never found funny while he was alive. "David didn't love taking pictures, either—but he kept yours up everywhere. I mean everywhere. Only you. I still remember that. You're too handsome. It was starting to make me jealous, man."

Benny giggled for the first time all morning.

Stacey smiled at her achievement.

David couldn't decide who he loved more.

His attention was diverted in the opposite direction by the tip-tap of Lyle's little loafers against the carpeted floor as he power-walked toward the men's restroom.

As it turned out, Lyle still had plenty of time for breakfast—and he chose chorizo.

He chose poorly.

David followed in hot pursuit and managed to squeeze himself inside the ADA-approved restroom before Lyle had the chance to lock the door behind him.

The ghost overheard the insistent rat-a-tat-tat against the porcelain toilet's interior despite being gratefully unable to achieve visual confirmation of the ongoing meteor shower.

"Figures. You took a dump all over my life. Why not follow suit at my funeral? Seriously, you couldn't just hold it in for a half hour until you got home?" The plunking sound of a splashdown into the lower bowl a few seconds later offered a wholly inappropriate response to his inquiry. David wondered which of the two was the bigger piece of shit. His faux friend flushed before he had the chance to make a definitive determination.

Although not ideal, David decided there was no time like the present.

He took a seat.

The spirit exited the bathroom five minutes later wearing Lyle like a skin suit.

He was thankful to see Kate and Stacey already heading for the exit with their backs turned to him. When Stace looked back one final time with tear-stained eyes and identified Lyle in her periphery, her face curdled instantly into pure disdain.

David allowed a smile to spread as soon as the door closed behind her.

Turning around, he identified Mr. Downey and his still-living son having an informal pow wow outside the entrance to the reception room. He began striding toward the pair with the same dopey grin on his face. Both eyed him wearily as he made his approach. Neither liked him since the inception of the friendship, but not because of any of the horrific things he did to David.

It was because they had met Lyle Stephens.

He slapped each of the Downey men separately across their shoulders with an open palm and triangulated into the private conversation like he was invited to do so. "Hey fellas, how goes it? All's well that ends well, am I right? Glad this shindig's finally winding down. I wasn't sure how much longer I could keep up the act. I'm bored stiffer than David. Did you guys know I was sleeping with Stacey behind his back? And not on occasion, either. It was a regular occurrence. I'd spend every waking moment in his presence deriding their relationship with my fingers crossed behind my back. And then the moment his was turned and I got a couple drinks in her, it was go time. Every time. Good times. Luckily, you guys don't have to worry about that loser anymore. Once he's six feet under you can forget all about him just like the rest of us will by tomorrow morning."

Things only went downhill from there.

***

Stacey popped two Aleve before turning her attention back to Alexa.

"Alexa, play *Ceremony*."

New Order was one of David's favorites when they first started dating.

She began to smile and cry simultaneously as she finished packing on the bed.

An insistent knock at the door interrupted her merry melancholy.

*Duh-Duh-Duh-Duh. Duh-Duh.*

David always did that.

Stacey told the almost AI to take a breather and approached to peep out. If she had been forced to rank them in order, what awaited her on the other side would have been the last thing she ever wanted to see again for the rest of her life. Despite opening the door with a pronounced sigh to signal as much, the uninvited guest clearly didn't get the message.

"Why'd you turn off *Ceremony*? I love that song."

Her look made it clear she was in no mood. "What the hell, Lyle? You got a group chat going, you idiot. People are saying you started shit at David's funeral and got into a brawl with his family. There's no way in hell you're staying here tonight. Whoever dotted your eye, you deserved it. That's all I've got for you. I'm sorry, I've got a flight first thing, I'm going to bed. Goodnight."

Lyle managed to jam his little bootie into the doorway

to serve as stopper before full closure could be achieved. The sharp shock of pain emanating upward when it struck gold in the meaty middle part of his foot brought yet another smile to David's face. "Technically, it was Big Dave who put a ring around the poser, although I'm happy to report both living Downeys got to handle the merch. Anyway, Stace—since he's my dad, and I'm already dead, I thought I'd receive a special dispensation just this once."

Stacey felt a sudden chill. Shock splashed across her face in an ice-cold wave. The threat of the tide caused her eyelids to run and hide.

Lyle smirked with the right corner of his mouth in a way that was highly distinctive to David. "This is where I'm supposed to convince you somehow that I'm not Lyle, followed inevitably by you failing to believe that I'm David. Then we'll spend the next hour and a half of the movie doing the same dumb dance until the Everly Brothers start singing over the credits. So, let's just avoid the unnecessary sequel that nobody asked for anyway. You know who I am. All the same, I'd prefer it if you let the right one in via invitation. Even in phantasm form, I'm not looking to commit a home invasion."

She was still recovering from the ontological shock when she noticed Lyle's yellow pickup in the parking lot over his shoulder. The car was correctly colored to match his makeup. Despite being presently childless, Lyle possessed no shortage of diapers back home with which to wipe it down.

The truck looked like it had participated in the world's dumbest demolition derby. A standing Free Press newspaper box had somehow gotten itself lodged halfway through the windshield. An assortment of black hand painted anatomical rocket ships were festooned across the entire driver's side of the vehicle. Some burgeoning artistes of Muslim and Jewish descent appeared to have potentially contributed to the tableau. Scribbled car-key smoke enveloped the boosters on several of the shuttles.

The coup de grâce was accomplished by way of crowbar.

All four smashed lights of the pickup along with a good portion of the body appeared to have made music with the instrument. It took a few seconds before the wafting smell of urine entered the picture to add some final sprinkles onto the sundae.

"Jesus. What did you do to his car?"

Lyle began to glacially rotate his head. He fixed a quizzical stare into Stacey's eyes that was maintained for half the journey and then scuttled. "Oh, goodness me. Would you look at that? You know, I thought I might have hit a curb on the way over here."

"He's going to flip."

The grinning ghost returned his attention to Stacey. "Impossible," Lyle offered as personal insult, "babies can't do that until they're eighteen months. I don't think he's old enough yet to qualify—unless he's just undersized for his age." The puppeteer looked down at both upturned hands like they might possess the answer.

David had a big mouth this evening. Stacey spotted the truth for the first time. Lyle looked like a left winger for the Montreal Canadiens. "Oh my God. Did you knock out his teeth? He's an orthodontist. You're messing with the man's livelihood."

David began to finger the evidence with a scrunched forehead. "It's only the three. Incisors are easy to replace, right? I don't know, I didn't go to dental school. I should ask Lyle."

Stacey squinted at the subject with an unhinged lower jaw. She shook her head lightly side-to-side to underscore the intended effect. Without offering another word she backed herself against the wall parallel to the open door to grant her guest formal entry. She sharply exhaled once for emphasis then added an outstretched arm to help lead the way. Her eyes stayed fixed on the figment as it entered her room.

"Sorry, I can't take my shoes off," David offered in artificial apology. "It was almost impossible for me to squeeze into Lyle's toddler-size trainers after I got done waxing his car. I didn't even know they made sneakers in negative sizes."

"David, don't you think the constant height jokes at Lyle's expense are—"

"Beneath me? Slight? Petty? Puny? A wee bit much?"

"*Trifling* is the word that comes to mind, actually. Can you please sit down? Apologies, you caught me in the middle of my evening stroke. Appreciate you."

The shit-filtering grin splashed across David's face did not dissipate all the way to the end of the bed. He smoothed out the comforter with both hands before taking a seat. "You know, I stopped by your boyfriend's house on my way over. Looks like he just finished the basement. I probably shouldn't have left the water running in the downstairs bath. Or stuck that towel down the drain. In any event, I checked out his closet. Did you know he puts lifts in his shoes like a little person? You've been banging Billy Barty behind my back all these years. Do you get wet watching *Willow*? I even took a look at the ween, and that's to scale as well. You couldn't at least cheat on me with a full-size man?"

Stacey leaned against the white wall-mounted corkboard desk with both hands clutching it for support. She was close to hyperventilating, but her eyes never wavered from the subject. "Can we not have a fight about decoy dick right now, David? You're dead. I'm still dealing with that. Now you've introduced ghosts into the equation. Plus possession. It's a lot to take in, man. Can you start by explaining why you're using Lyle like a life-size jaeger?"

"Why Lyle? Well, I don't think it requires Columbo to crack the case, Stace. A single brain-damaged Hardy Boy could probably get to the bottom of it. I mean, Lil' Romeo did tell you he loved you earlier. He seemed like the most sensible conduit. Getting to treat his life like my own personal rage room for five minutes was just the cherry on top."

She took a deep breath and then hit up the mini-fridge for a like-sized Sprite. Stacey popped the top before taking a single swig that managed to swallow the entirety. "It's such garbage. They only give you the small cans now."

"I believe the technical term for that is, '*Lyle-Size*.'"

Stacey clinked the empty can off David's forehead from afar. The quarter-moon aluminum ridge caught him square between the eyes and caused a slight ice cream headache. His grin slowly bled away as he prepared to ask the question with a single squinty eye. "Did you ever really love me?"

Her immediate instinct was to reach for an unopened can this time. "What the hell is wrong with you, David?"

"I'm dead."

She internally acknowledged the truth of the matter stated. "Yeah, but death is no excuse for being that dumb. I loved you more than anything—for a time. Years and years. Longer than you deserved, honestly. You were a miserable misanthrope who couldn't squeeze a drop of joy out of life with a bench vise.  By the end of things, I was just a toilet you flushed. You assumed the water would keep going down no matter how much crap you put in the bowl. Sorry I had to disabuse you of that notion, but it wasn't love you were looking for all those years. It was Luigi."

David refused to allow the opportunity for a viable videogame reference to slip through his grasp. He rose from the bed with Lyle's shrunken hands on his hips. "What a joke, Stace. You're the one who absorbed my pain and suffering like a mushroom power-up. It's amazing. You somehow successfully managed to mind-meld everyone in your life into believing your BS. Your family, your friends, your analyst. The garbageman, probably. Everybody you know thinks I'm Magneto when you're actually the Apocalypse."

*-Choose Your Fighter-*

Sugar Ray returned fire on the Motor City Cobra with her arms crossed. "Since we're on the subject, can we talk about how disturbing it is that your father still calls me Stephanie after all these years? I think he legitimately thinks that's my name. And I don't blame him, by the way. He's a nice man. A good man. But I can count on one hand the number of times I was in the same room with him before today. You were the culprit. Why did you feel the need to treat me like such an embarrassment? Were you that ashamed to be with me?"

"Jesus, Stace. You must be the dumbest smart person that ever walked God's green Earth," David insisted as he began to pace the room. "I wasn't ashamed of you. I was ashamed of them. And myself. I grew up walled off from the real world in a colony built for people with emotional leprosy. It's a terminal disease. I'm sorry for not wanting to expose you to that. I was afraid you might get infected, too. You not being stricken is one of the reasons I loved you so much. If I made you sick, I'd have never forgiven myself."

"Oh, well look at you Lancelot. My knight in shining armor," Stacey practically spit back. "Unfortunately, you made me feel unwell pretty much the entirety of our relationship, and there's only so many places to point the finger."

"Okay, can you articulate for me why I was such a cretin in your mind? I never cheated on you. I never hit you. I never—"

"We never slept in the same bed, David. How about that for starters? We had sex, but we never slept together. Right? That's not a relationship. That's prostitution. You may as well have been paying me by the hour. Every night you were up until 3 a.m. playing *Call of Duty* while ignoring your call to duty. I found you most mornings on the couch with your hand down your pants—I don't even want to know, man. You never wanted to leave the house. You refused to socialize with my friends. You smoked enough weed to kill Willie Nelson."

"I also loved you more than anything."

"Oh, really? What's my mother's maiden name? My favorite flower? My shoe size? You don't know anything about me that wasn't indexed purely through your penis, pal. You never cared about me until you couldn't have me anymore. Period. You never wanted a relationship with me, just a right of first refusal. You were looking to lease my love in perpetuity. I'm not a rental, David. I'm worth way more than that."

His anger began to rise. "There might have been nights I

didn't come to bed, but what about the ones when you didn't come home at all? You were staying at Kate's, or Megan's, right? Bullshit. I've had occasion to be debriefed by several inductees to your Hall of Shame now, and we might as well have been playing Mad Libs. It was always the same story—different colored bed sheets."

"Excuse me?" Thankfully there were no knives. Stacey looked.

"You were the only woman I slept with for six years, Stace," he formally declared for the first time, "and you spent most of those six years making up the difference. You were my first, and my last. There was no one in between. I know, I'm such a monster, right? From the moment I first saw you, I never wanted anyone else. I wanted *you* to not want anyone else. But that definitely wasn't what you wanted. And it still didn't make any difference. When you moved to New York, I moved to New York. I haven't kissed another woman since you left. I waited. I would have waited forever. Now I guess I will."

Stacey took a moment to process his confession. "What am I supposed to do with any of this, David? Even if you weren't dead, you would have been kept waiting. I didn't see you anymore—I mean when I looked. You weren't there. Even before you were a ghost. I couldn't remember why I never stopped thinking about you. I cried a lot over that. And I don't care if you believe me or not, because it's just true."

"Once you decided not to be dogshit any longer, you didn't even afford me five minutes to clean up my own cage," David argued. "You just euthanized me and left town. Before that, you wouldn't respect yourself. You rolled around in it all day and then wondered why I wouldn't give you hugs and kisses when you came back home. How could I? How could anyone? It was so unfair. There was so much dirt between your toes. Clean up your own backyard before you go knocking on your neighbor's door, right?"

Stacey had just about enough. "Are you all done, David?"

Unfortunately, he was not. "There isn't a backseat within thirty miles of here that you didn't call home at some point, Stace. And what's with your fetish for ex- high school wrestlers? The headgear must make you horny or something. Cauliflower ear was the quickest path to coitus whenever you were the other party concerned. And don't you dare blame it on the alcohol, because there isn't enough whiskey in all of Ireland."

"You need to shut up now."

"Talking about Ed Kemper," he continued, "you're the Golden State Killer of copulation. You went up and down the entire Mitten trolling for victims. I don't know where you even found the time. I'm betting it's no different in Manhattan. How many licks is it going to take before you finally reach the center of the Blow Pop, babe?"

Her entire skull went Mount Vesuvius. A baking soda-based volcano for kids. Without another word Stacey bounded to the door like her pizza just arrived. She thrust it open with her left hand and signaled for David to pay the man with the other. "That's it. I don't give a shit if you're a ghost— get the hell out. I'd say this is the last time we'll ever see one another, but you're already halfway to being worm food. I hope you and your hand have fun down there. You might be missed, but not by me."

David raised his own hand instead. Truthfully, all he really wanted to do was stride across the room and kiss her. Even if he had to use Lyle's little kisser. "Wait. If you want me out of your life forever, fine. But I'm going to need your help to accomplish that goal. I need you to say, '*I release you, David Downey.*' If you don't, I have it on good authority I'm going to be ghost-grafted onto you for all eternity. You won't see me or hear me, but I'll always be here. And neither of us wants that. So just say the words while I'm still inside of Gimli here and let's be done with it already. You'll be doing us both a favor."

Alas, David provided Stacey with too much time to ponder what had just transpired. Upon further review, her eyelids narrowed to slits. She closed the door until it touched the frame but didn't shut it completely. "Ed Kemper—how'd you know I said that?"

"What?"

"You heard me. How did you know I said that? How'd you know Lyle said, '*I love you?*'"

David frantically searched for an exit ramp. "You told me yourself, Stace. During that little Night of the Long Knives that was our break-up, remember? It wasn't enough to ruin me, you had to make sure I knew my roommate ruined you, too. Matter of fact, you fed me all the inmates' names and endowment levels as a last meal prior to my execution. It wasn't just Lyle. I'm not sure what course he was specifically, but we both definitely had our fill."

She was ashamed but wouldn't give him the satisfaction. "Don't lie to me, David. You said *earlier*, earlier. That was you in the room wasn't it, you perverted piece of shit! I knew I felt your clammy little phantom fingers skittering across my face. It was about as soothing as a Facehugger trying to stick its tongue down my throat. Is this what I have to look forward to now? Being locked up behind bars with my ex the sex-stalker for the rest of my life? There's no 911 for that. Who am I supposed to call?"

*-Ghostbusters-*

They both had the same synchronized thought but kept it to themselves.

David scowled instead. "You want to talk about jail? Would you like me to describe my cell for you? I've been living off steam-iron grilled cheese and toilet wine for over two years. The non-business end of my toothbrush is a bayonet now. You're nothing but a short timer. You don't have the right to even address someone who is all-day. Period. That's how it works out in the yard. You can hit the bricks. Call me when you've had some real time added on to your sentence."

Stacey took a few steps back into the room's interior to continue the conversation. "I regret to inform you, David, but being in love with you was its own unique form of solitary confinement. You devolved. When we first met you wanted to be a civil rights attorney. You wound up bartering over debt cigarettes so you could give people cash cancer. Nobility to Nosferatu. I don't know which part of that process is more despicable—manufacturing financial liability as a business model or horse-trading with the same heathens after the fact for the right to take some stranger's scalp."

"You act like I'm the one who made those people indebted."

"Jesus, whatever helps you sleep at night," Stacey continued. "Four years of college in Ann Arbor so you could spend the rest of your life screwing over everyone who lives in Ypsilanti. By the way, I saw your Jag on IG. WGAF. I think you misunderstood me from the start. The lobster would have never tasted right if I knew entire families were living off Ramen because of your line of work. It seems like my verdict was more or less unanimous, by the way. I don't think I spotted a single friend of yours at the funeral. Just a bunch of other mute family members."

"I have friends." David's declaration sounded suspiciously like a question.

"Okay, name a few." She returned to the edge of the bed and took a seat facing David. The cloying smile on her face was intended as a slap. She clasped her hands together across her knees like she was preparing to pray.

"What?"

"Three friends. Give me their names. Go."

"Okay, Barry. There's one. Umm—"

Stacey pumped the brakes with her palms up. "Hold on, hold on. Not so fast there, cowboy. Let's pause on Barry for a sec. This is good, I'm excited. You're making new pals. I want to hear more. Show me all the blueprints. What's he do? How'd you two meet, you and this Barry fella?"

"Well, he's a forensic scientist—"

"That's Barry Allen," Stacey confirmed with a smirk and a negative nod of the head. "You're describing *The Flash* to me right now. I asked you to name three friends and you began with a cartoon character who doesn't exist in real life. Not an auspicious start. Who's next up to bat, Casey? Are you in a fantasy baseball league with a cookie-maker named Ernie Keebler? Am I in the ballpark?"

David's glare came close to producing Heat Vision. "Well, we can't all be as socially ubiquitous as you, darling. You've always had a flair for networking. Of course, ninety percent of your new contacts were named *John Thomas* for the first thirty years of your life, but we can put a pin in that for now. They all certainly did. I'm sure some of them are still digitally connecting with you to this day."

Stacey studied abroad in England. Her tea kettle was officially whistling. "You're disgusting, David. I hate you so much. I'm glad I got rid of your tired ass when I did. What kind of Cro-Magnon monster tries to sex shame women at this point in the 21st Century?"

"Wrong *S*-word, sweetheart. Although I agree you should definitely feel shame."

She let out one final exhausted sigh while raising herself up with her hands on her hips. Once she was standing, she clapped a single time for effect. "Well, I think that just about does it for this eternity. If you don't mind seeing yourself to the door, I have to finish up here and get to bed. Have fun in Ghost World. Please don't kill Lyle before you go. Goodbye." Stacey turned her back on him and began to rustle random items in the opened black leather toiletries bag next to her pillow. When he failed to move after five seconds, she rotated her head halfway. "*Goodbye.*"

David recognized his error and course-corrected immediately. "Wait, I need you to release me. Remember?"

"I just did that, dummy. Doubt anyone's going to be looking to pick you up off the waiver wire, but there's always the Lions. Good luck."

"No, I need you to say, '*I release you, David Downey.*'"

Stacey ceased all activity and raised her head theatrically toward the ceiling. "And remind me again what happens if I don't?"

His concern level was rising. He took two steps toward her. "What do you mean?"

She returned the tube of toothpaste she was holding to the bag with a delicate touch and rotated to face David. "You just spent the last fifteen minutes shooting yourself in the foot there, Tex. You're already dead." She waved a hand from his head to his waist to reinforce her point. "You said yourself—I won't see you or hear you, right? That's what you said. So, what do I care if you get dragged? I think a few months spent behind blessed bars thinking about what you've done might just be what the doctor ordered. Sounds blissful to me."

David's anxiety was increasing to pre-death levels. "It's not just being ball-and-chained to you for life. Whenever you sleep, I'll be stuck residing in some emptied-out spirit realm instead of Heaven. It could be years before I get another chance like this."

"*Years*, you say. Hmm." Her lower lip wrapped itself over its opposing number and she shook her head affirmatively in mock contemplation with her eyes raised.

"Stace—"

"So, you're saying the only one who can release you from bondage is *moi*. Interesting."

"*Stacey*."

"Oh, no no no no, you made your bed, buttercup. I think it's time for you to lie in it."

"Listen you silly bitch—"

"I'm sorry, did you think calling me a silly bitch was going to help your cause somehow? You just keep pouring lighter fluid on yourself. You're not going to be satisfied until you self-immolate in front of me like a Vietnamese Buddhist monk. Don't strain yourself. I'll strike the match."

"You want to play it that way, fine." David made it halfway to the door before turning around to address Stacey one final time. "But since there's no actual jail for criminals like you who emotionally torture other human beings for their own amusement, I'm going to put you in one myself. It's my new mission in death. I'm sentencing you to life in Sing Sing. Congratulations, Dr. Frankenstein—the monster you *invented* all those years ago has finally achieved self-awareness. You better hope the villagers get to me first. I was treated like your voodoo doll for over half a decade. I think I'll treat you like the Wicker Man for the next twenty years. Four eyes for an eye. That's how I roll. So, let's run it. I'm ready. You're not, but I am."

*"War is God."* Stacey quoted Cormac McCarthy to let him know it was in her arsenal now. She allowed the corner of her mouth curl up just a tick to underscore the point. David was taken aback. "I don't feel like you have the high ground here, Jacob Marley. But go ahead. Do your worst. Now I'm going to sleep." She began to escort him toward the door. "You ain't gotta go home, but you gotta get the hell out of here. Figure you got about thirty minutes before I nod off. Go grab yourself a Slurpee or something while you can still enjoy the experience."

Lyle's face turned beet red. He marched toward the door with Stacey following close behind.

David spun around and offered one final goodbye from outside the room.

*"Did you have anything that you wanted to say to me?"* The Cheshire grin wrapping itself from ear to ear made the reference abundantly clear. Thinking back on it when she woke up the following morning would cause Stacey to involuntarily wretch into her pillow.

"Yeah, actually," Stacey confirmed as she flicked the door shut with two fingers. She craned her neck to the right so she could spit her final words at him through the receding crack before it closed completely.

*"Go fuck yourself, David Downey."*

***

David let out a *d'oh* when he realized what he had done.

***

When one door closes, another opens.

The Lord of Pain inadvertently opened a portal.

A stranger clad head to toe in brown tweed bespoke stepped out of the darkness and stood watch at the corner across from the Village Suites. David putt-putted out of the parking lot in Lyle's Bumblebee bumper car and slowly drove by the new arrival. They briefly locked eyes before the ghost continued onward. The outsider looked like Superman had a baby with 007. David wasn't bi, but just this once he felt willing to give it a try. He shook the thought free almost as soon as it entered his cerebrum.

The perfect man possessed a single peculiarity.

He was chewing on a handful of black licorice.

# SOFT LAUNCH

David watched the whitecaps ebb and flow off the roiling waters of Lake St. Clair with a bottle of Highland Park 21 in hand. The single malt scotch smelled like a citrus-laced French pastry and went down smooth despite the 46% ABV. Its taste morphed into a mix of baking cocoa and black tea by the time it hit his belly.

He wanted to bathe in the stuff.

A roadside stroll down Lake Shore Drive at midnight sounded like just the ticket given his current predicament. He had to steer himself around the occasional Bentley and Tesla left parked in the roadway, but no matter the time of day, this always remained a largely unclogged thoroughfare. Grosse Pointe Shores trafficked almost exclusively in rich Caucasians. The kind that didn't cotton to roadway congestion. Having to share a border with Detroit was already off-putting enough for their indelicate sensibilities.

This place was a part of him since his youth. Driving along its length with mom and dad. A single back window down. The sound of helicopters, followed by the real thing flying out of Selfridge Air Force base. Another country across the water. Chocolate-dipped vanilla cones covered in rainbow sprinkles. Feeding the ducks from the dock. Fish and chips. Family.

The stretch always seemed to lead them somewhere.

David was never the type to take the road less traveled.

He was half-drunk and feeling sorry for himself when he spotted his first 4-D human.

"Hey! Yeah, you. Mopie Taylor over there. A little help?"

The gentleman across the median guiding his motorcycle by hand looked like he had dressed up as one half of Daft Punk for Halloween. His Warcore helmet was PVC chin plating plus a limousine-tinted black plexiglass faceplate that covered everything from the nostrils up.

It was cool looking, but in the case of a collision, he would almost certainly be killed.

David was more enamored with the bike.

"Is that a *Tron* Light Cycle?"

The stranger tipped the windscreen of his helmet back for clarity's sake. "Technically, it's called a NeuTron X. Parker Brother Concepts out of Miami builds them. My friend Torie did some research. Turns out the CEO of Ford is a fanboy and bought two for himself. He lives in the Shores, so we figured we'd take them off his hands for the evening. Mine unfortunately ran out of jet juice. Died on me outside Greektown Casino. Guess I got a little greedy."

"Isn't that always the way?"

"Yep. House always wins. I'm Wesley. Wes." He initiated the perfunctory handshake.

"David. *David.* Preferably."

Wesley would have put both hands up if they weren't already occupied. "Not a problem. Spare batteries are a half block away. I've been walking this thing up Jefferson Avenue for six miles. Mind giving me a hand?"

Without another word David took up a position on the opposing side of the bike and the two began to push onward together. "You're from around here, then?"

"No. I know everyone is shocked when I tell them but believe it or not, I actually moved to Michigan of my own accord," Wesley confirmed. "I was haunting the Packard Plant over on East Grand Boulevard for about three years, and I just sort of fell in love with the place. Not the Packard Plant. It's a hell hole—

literally. It sits over a hole to Hell. Don't ever hang out there."

"It did always give me the heebie jeebies. Even from afar."

"Yeah, those were *Hell Bugs*," Wes informed David. "They're interdimensional. If you even think about a place that's infested, they get all over you."

Waves crashing against the corrugated metal sheets that lined the nearby marina dock diverted David's attention for a moment. "Michigan has a portal to perdition, huh? That might help explain the last ten years of my life. I was wondering where that red hot poker up my ass was coming from."

Silent heat lightning erupted in a purple haze over Canada and then dissolved back into the darkness. Both men turned their heads east to catch a fleeting glimpse of the expanded color palette.

Wesley resumed the conversation. "People hate, but I was dead in LA for a couple years, and that's just the time I spent sitting in traffic. Being black in Boston is no walk in the park—believe me. New York has *C.H.U.D.* now. No place is perfect."

"So, if you were haunting the Packard Plant, then that would make you a—"

"I took a bottle of pills and slept on it," Wesley acknowledged. "What are you going to do? Not my finest hour, but live and learn. Or learn, at least. Lost the wife and kids in a car crash. The drunk idiot took himself out, too. There was no one left for me to kill. I felt cheated."

"I'm so sorry, man."

"Appreciate it. You have any little rugrats? Or did, I should say."

"I never got around to actually living," David confessed. "Giving life to someone else would have been like collecting $200 without passing *Go* first. I was afraid it might feel too much like jail."

"I don't know, man," Wes responded with raised eyebrows. "It may sound counterintuitive, but I think you'll regret never being incarcerated."

David was childless and older than thirty. Despite what every parent he ever encountered in life seemed to think, they were not reinventing the wheel when they made the same suggestion. "Do you miss driving a Ferrari?"

"I'm sorry?"

*"Do you miss driving a Ferrari?"*

"I've never driven a Ferrari," Wesley confirmed. The two weaved around a trailer hitched FloteBote stuck turning left onto Vernier Road in perpetuity. It was blocking the T junction in all three directions.

"Right—neither have I," David said. "And it looks like an amazing automobile. I'm sure driving a Ferrari is tons of fun. Very few Ferrari owners probably regret their purchase. But I'm just being honest, I didn't spend any portion of my day thinking about the fact that I never got behind the wheel. The only time a Ferrari ever came to mind was when I saw someone else driving around in one. And when I did, the first thought I had was never, *'that looks incredible, I wish I could have one of my very own.'* No, the first thought I always had was, *'that shit looks expensive.'* I've just never been a car guy. And this is the Motor City, so you can imagine my plight. It feels like everyone here drives three Fords."

"I will grant you, the amount of required maintenance can be staggering."

"Upkeep seems like it never ends, right?" David freed his left hand for a moment and began ticking off his subsequent points on each finger starting with the thumb. "Making sure no one screws with it whenever you have your back turned for two seconds. Specific fuel you have to feed the thing to keep it from having a breakdown. Wash it, clean it, change it. They have a thousand random buttons that trigger different shit, and you'll be lucky if you figure out what half of them do over a lifetime of ownership. I imagine the insurance premiums are astronomical. It's too bad you can't just rent a child. If there was an option to buy, I might have been more willing to give it a whirl."

"The key difference is the Ferrari loses value the moment you drive it off the lot," Wesley offered with a smile. "The inverse is true with children. Their worth never stops appreciating."

"Neither does the price tag. The Ferrari's cost is fixed. Little Freddie's never stops inflating."

Wesley's crew finally came into focus. Beneath the streetlights up ahead a dozen road warriors of various stripes congregated and caroused next to a purloined fire truck. Every light was exploding off the thing without the normal accompanying sound effects.

David only had eyes for the goddess striding toward them on foot.

Her Clubmaster Ray-Bans made her look like the CEO of a first-tier Fortune 500. They precisely matched her Shima Miura motorcycle suit. The black leather was outlined with sharp red accents and padding in all the right places. It hugged her entire body from head to toe. White and black moon boots capped off the ensemble. A crimson-colored helmet was being lugged in her right hand. She looked like she was preparing to hunt Metroid. For David, this made her officially sexier than any Victoria's Secret model who ever walked the face of the Earth.

Her eyes were an outrageous cobalt blue. David was drowning in liquid metal by the time she got within ten feet. When she smiled with the right corner of her mouth, three dimpled ridges splashed out across her face in the same direction and brushed against the bottom of her cheekbone. She wasn't wearing any makeup, and it didn't matter. David remembered thinking that she must be dead—because no woman alive could be that beautiful. "Hey there, handsome!"

Wesley raised a hand off the bike and used it to shake a thumb back and forth between himself and the new arrival. "Which one of us are you referring to, Torie?"

"Why discriminate?" She smiled solely at David. He felt like he just stuck his finger in a light socket.

"Always had the same question myself," Wesley joked back in response.

"You and me both, brother. So, who's our new friend?"

He caught her name, but it took a moment to recall his own.

"I'm David." He wondered if she was disguising a joy buzzer in her palm when they shook hands.

"He was very specific about that, Tor. Not Dave. Not Davey. Not D. Understood?"

"Got it." She saluted him with two fingers and stood at attention. "Hello David, I'm Torie. Guess I'll be playing the role of Manic Pixie Dream Girl this evening. I see you've already met your Magical Negro, Wesley." She handed her brother in arms the black backpack she had kept surreptitiously slung over her shoulder.

"*Hi-ya.*" Wesley sneered back in David's direction. He pulled a fully charged lithium-ion battery pack out of the bundle and began the process of replacement while the two continued to get acquainted.

"You must be our new Bromantic," she continued. "Let me guess—girl troubles? Or was it guy troubles. I shouldn't assume. Are you gay?" Somehow the tone of her question made it clear that she didn't care but was also quite interested.

"No, unfortunately I wasn't born that lucky," David confirmed. "I had to convince smart people to sleep with me instead. It's always been a disadvantage for us straight men."

"That would be the only one," Torie volleyed back with a toothy smile. "Look at you—your ethnicity is *Friends,* and you have a jawline that could cut glass. You're giant size, to boot. How are you not hunting humans for sport on your own private island in the Pacific by now? Where'd it all go so horribly wrong?"

"See you chumps at the finish line." Wesley kicked the rejuvenated bike into high gear. He was met with nothing but roaring adulation from the adoring fans down the road upon his arrival.

"Well, spill. There must be an explanation for this fiasco of a life." Torie gently ribbed him for real to reinforce the teasing. Their waltz continued as they strolled side-by-side back toward her posse. "Give me The Book of David—to a degree. We don't have all day. Those dimwits up ahead are going to demand your full attention. Because you've never seen anyone do a donut before."

Churning waves rumbled against the shore to their right while mansions of every design category lined the opposite side of the roadway. Every colonial and Tudor was its own WASP-designed private enclave, each more ostentatious and pretentious than the next.

"Well, my name is David Downey. I worked in debt collection. And now I'm dead."

"The Four Ds. Probably better off," she said. "How'd you die? Decide to do everyone a favor and blow the place up on your way out the door? Or did you keep it simple and just throw yourself off the roof?"

"Brain aneurysm," David verified. "Pretty sure it was attributable to abandonment on my part. I sat through my own funeral, and then I woke up outside my ex-girlfriend's house a few hours ago. Not sure why that was my entry point. She hasn't lived there in over ten years. I don't know if her parents being present would have made it more or less creepy."

Torie was sympathetic to David, and already a bit green-eyed toward a girl she had never met before. "Regret determines your initial drop-off point, but as a rule you never get deposited too far from home when you first get here. It must have been the location nearby you most associated with her. A decade plus is a long time, though, dude. You know that says something about something, right?"

"Yeah. That I'm pretty pathetic."

"Oh, no—you're patently pathetic. Don't you dare try to equivocate, David Downey."

She said his full name, and he officially fell in love.

Just like that.

"Where did you start off when you arrived here?"

She frowned for the first time in David's presence. A different stranger walked through the door. "My parents' place, actually. I knew no one would be home, but I knocked anyway." Torie looked like she was working to stifle potential tears. "Never went back. But I can happily report that I've been all over the 4-D world ever since I died."

"What's no longer on the bucket list, then?"

Torie's mood instantly brightened. "Oh, let's see. Buenos Aires. Auckland. Macau—I was killing it all week at the casino. I motorbiked through Mongolia. That might have been my favorite so far. Too many others to name. You ever been?"

"I've never traveled," David admitted. "Costa Rica, when I was a kid. Spanish trip in high school. That was it, though. After that I pretty much Batcaved it until I called it permanent quits. Stacey was another globetrotter just like you. I never took advantage. Story of my former life."

Torie's face betrayed her steely resolve. "Well, we're going to have to remedy that, then. Right?" She hopped in front of him but continued to backtrack with tunnel vision toward David the entire way. Her eyebrows made clear she meant it.

"For sure. Take me somewhere, Carmen Sandiego."

It had only been five minutes, but he already knew he would follow her anywhere.

"I love looking at the architecture in different places, but strictly residential." Torie's left arm thrust out and speared at the air between herself and the various proofs of concept spread out along the length of Lake Shore Drive. "Where and what people call home. How they defined it for themselves. How they defined themselves by it. The angles, the materials. Floor plans.

I've spent days inside photographing, drawing, writing. This one in Stockholm? Oh my God, I'll have to show you the pictures. I could have died again in that place and that would have been fine by me. They turned an outdoor waterfall into an indoor water slide. Even for wealthy people, it was pretty rich."

"What are you looking to do with all this new lived-in experience, then?"

"I was thinking about writing a short story collection." David didn't know she was walking that tightrope aloud for the first time. Torie only recently acquired the courage to convince herself. "Non-fiction. What I learned as a vision voyeur going from country to country. All the dead friends I made along the way. What I'm bringing back to the table with me now. That sort of thing. Does that sound as god-awful as it did coming out of my mouth?"

David sharply shook his head in objection. "I'd like to volunteer to be your first beta reader, actually. Whenever it's done. I know better than to force a timeline upon a writer. But no, I think that sounds amazing."

Both of them were blushing by the time they entered the fray.

"Hey Tor, who's your new boy toy?" Harley Man had the handlebars to match, plus a couple of inches on David—which was saying something. His stone-faced expression was declaring everything else. The new arrival felt like he'd just been unwittingly thrust into a backyard kegger hosted by an eighteen-year-old from a neighboring school district. Downey was a potential threat, and it was testosterone time.

His hard stare cracked once the biker was within spitting distance. "I'm just messing with you, man. I'm Mike."

Torie playfully tapped him on the shoulder. "Guys, this is David. Everyone say hi and don't faux-threaten him, please."

The crowd spoke in unison. "*Hi, David!*"

He offered spirit fingers with shaking hands and a sheepish smile in response.

Torie hooked him through the elbow and began to circulate the pair through the encampment. "Some of this gear's incredible, right? These crazies have way too much time on their hands. Wesley's building a War Rig. Ain't that right, Wes?"

He looked like a proud papa when he broke away from his ongoing conversation and nodded in the affirmative. "Yep. It's getting there. Actually, this could be kismet. I'm going to need a Doof Warrior when I'm all done, David. Any chance you know how to play the guitar?"

"No," he replied definitively. "And even if I did know—the answer would still be no."

Wesley and company got a good laugh out of that.

Torie continued. "Tina over there is putting together a killer ice cream truck. That's not hyperbole, either. It's got gun turrets, and a couple of flamethrowers. We're going to twist some metal in about a month once everyone has their own ride ready. The dummies don't even know what's coming to them, though." She pulled David to the side and began to whisper conspiratorially into his ear. It made him warm. "I'm going to swoop in an Apache helicopter with *Ride of the Valkyries* blasting through the speakers and dead all these land-lovers. I've been teaching myself out at Selfridge. I've only managed to not crash one of them at this point, but that's all I need." She cackled as they continued onward.

After a few additional steps she stopped them aside a second *Tron* cycle that was currently having its battery swapped. "Amir, this is David. He's racing next, okay?"

"Sounds good."

David just caught up. "Wait wait wait, no. I'm good Torie. I've never ridden a bike before."

"Even better," Amir grinned back. "The *Road Rash* gods demand the occasional human sacrifice."

Torie grabbed a gray thermoplastic four-wheeled utility cart sitting nearby and pushed it in front of David. She looked like she was offering dessert options at a Michelin Three Star restaurant. Four separate possibilities were laid out on its top shelf for his perusal.

-Metal chain (*Milky/Smooth*)-

-Nunchaku (*Nutty/Light*)-

-Crowbar (*Buttery/Stiff*)-

-Cattle Prod (*Tart/Sharp*)-

David and Torie stared wide-eyed at the contents, but she was the only one smiling. "Choose your weapon."

"I'm sorry?"

"It's the *Road Rash*, man. You should feel lucky. Rules state since it's your inaugural ride, you get to pick first. I personally would go with the cattle prod," she winked, "but do you. Whatever feels good in your hand."

"Torie, I can't do it. Let me just sit this one out." The same story since he was five.

Torie's disposition switched to taskmaster in an instant. "I'm sorry, I must have missed where I phrased that in the form of a question. I don't give a shit if you don't want to ride the Light Cycle—*you're riding the Light Cycle.* Because I said so, to answer your next inquiry. As for the third, you'll figure it out. You can't die. That would literally be the worst thing that could happen under normal circumstances, so what can possibly go wrong now? Show me something, kid. And here. Don't forget your scepter." She held out the electrified warclub with way too much anticipatory glee emanating off her face.

"Thanks," David said in a tone that made clear he didn't mean it.

"So, I hear the newbie wants a shot at the title." The baritone who inserted himself into their conversation was dressed in police-issue riot gear. His voice didn't betray a hint of humor. It wouldn't require three guesses to correctly determine his former occupation in life.

Torie continued with the introductions. "David, this is Deputy Darrell. Because Deputy Dewey was already taken."

"That's hilarious," Darrell said without smiling.

"Darrell used to be on the MSP motorcycle unit," Torie added.

The scales fell from David's eyes. "I've never ridden one of these things before in my life, and you guys expect me to get on a Tron bike and death race an ex-motorcycle cop down Fury Road? Plus, you're introducing blunt instruments as bludgeoning tools. I haven't even picked up the brake yet. There isn't a bunny slope equivalent I could start with, maybe?"

Amir and Torie looked at one another and laughed.

"Dave, nothing you have to say matters," Darrell informed him. "This is going to happen. Just let the embarrassment wash over you, son."

- *"Nothing you have to say matters"*-

Stacey said that to him when she ended things.

She said a lot of things when she ended things.

"Darrell, I know it's hard, but don't be a dick," Torie demanded. "And yes, I realize that is just setting you up to respond with, 'that's what she said,' but don't say that, or I'll slap you."

"That's—"

"*Don't.*" She meant it.

The way Darrell was sneering with his arms crossed made it clear he was only half-kidding. "Lady, you worked in logistics. I traded in ballistics. You're not ready for this smoke."

Attacking Torie already became a bridge too far for David.

"Alright, CHiPs, if you'd like to see what it feels like to have a cattle prod shoved up your ass, I'll be your Huckleberry. This one's for Abner Louima."

Torie's eyes expanded to the size of saucers.

"Oh, wow," Amir said while taking a step back.

"Give me the chain. I'm about to go Johnny Blaze on this fool." Darrell wrapped the metal links in a ball around his gloved right fist and then dipped the entirety into the orange bucket sitting on the roadway. It was clearly labeled *Flammable*. He let the power glove soak for a second longer than necessary as he stared at his upcoming opponent. The jet flame butane lighter being held in his left hand emitted a six-inch-long blue blade with a click. He extinguished it with a smile.

David began to have second thoughts.

"Whatever you're imagining right now, it's going to be so much worse." Nothing in Darrell's tone suggested he was joking.

"Are we all set for the next chicken run?" Tina was in a coma currently out in Clarkston, although you'd never be able to tell by looking at her. She kept it casual in a ponytail and Nike hoodie this evening. The brunette striker played at Cal like her idol Alex Morgan and could still pass for grad assistant despite being in her third year in the spirit realm. Her husband had the funds to afford the best in 24/7 home health care. She was resting comfortably back in bed. He was having an affair with both of her nurses.

Doug still loved his wife more than anything.

Amir only had eyes for her. "You looking to be my Natalie Wood in a bit, Tina?"

"I'd rather throw myself off the Griffith Observatory, Buzz," she volleyed back.

"That's cold-blooded." Wesley accomplished the inverse of a black Irish Goodbye. He seemed to instantly materialize out of the ether next to David without any prior warning. It caused Downey to do a double take to the right when he spoke.

Torie turned back toward the target. "You ready to meet your maker for the second time?"

"I'm sorry, did she say chicken run?" David had long been a student of film history. "That would imply there's a cliff at some point."

"Yeah, we're workshopping a version of *Rebel Without a Cause* starring remnants without a clue." They walked in tandem toward the starting line. Wesley and Amir wheeled the cycle behind them while snickering to themselves over what was about to transpire. "No worries about going over the cliff, though. Michigan doesn't have many. So, we just placed some literal landmines in the road up ahead. We figured, why be figurative? Assuming you two don't kill each other first, whoever blinks last wins. Alright. Let's get this party started, people!" She kept clapping until everyone was called to attention.

Whoops and whistles exploded as a signal for the gentlemen to start their engines.

David could barely be heard over the rising uproar. The arms shooting in from every direction to squeeze each of his shoulders didn't help. "Did you say landmines?"

"I did," Torie declared with a flat smile and precision-cut shake of the head to match. She disappeared back into the crowd as they continued to envelope David.

Amir and Wesley did their best to give him a quick tutorial, but all three quickly realized he was hopeless and would soon be dead. Again. They leaned into responsive techniques intended solely to save the bike at all costs.

There were infinite Davids, but only two Light Cycles at their disposal.

He was officially expendable.

His trainers returned to the median and left him sharing hellfire fumes with the Spirit of Vengeance.

Darrell brushed away the ash gray mop from his forehead and strapped on his old MSP helmet. His hair was annoyingly full for a man in his early 50s. The guy just kept checking boxes for David.

The patrolman let the chain drop to his side with a dead smack against the concrete and reached for a hand towel in his back pocket. He took great care to dry the falconry glove encasing his right arm up to the elbow along with the first foot of linked metal. "I promise to personally apologize to Torie for what I'm about to do to you. Glory me, blood bag. You're about to get shredded." He tossed the lighter back to Harley Mike.

*"Welcome to the Jungle"* began blaring from the firetruck's loudspeakers.

Torie was standing thirty meters up ahead playing Lady of the Line. She formed a peace sign with her fingers and then pointed the prongs at her own eyes. She did likewise to each of the contestants from afar before raising her flare gun straight into the air and firing a magenta-hued rocket into the sky.

Mike flipped the switch. He turned his head and stretched his arm as far as it would reach from his hunched position before lighting Darrell's fuse.

And they were off.

The Neutron X proved surprisingly easy to operate out of the gate. David's problem was the infernal whip being used to force him along like a mounted steed. When he unsheathed his cattle prod from the provided leg holster to level the playing field, he dropped the lance almost immediately onto the pitch. David turned his head around and watched in horror as his only defense mechanism clinked a few times against the concrete and then came to a rest.

Each lash from Darrell ignited the surrounding air with inglorious hellfire. The second stretched far enough to singe David's nostril hair. Four strikes were unfurled by Darrell without success before the fifth took an unfortunate detour on the return trip across his own front tire.

His bike began an unscripted floor exercise in response. It tumbled front wheel first end over end and dislodged its occupant in the process. Darrell's flipping forward momentum thrust him another forty feet higher into the air. He continued gliding upward along the substitute ski jump before he finally came crashing back down to earth onto his forehead. The audible bone crunch upon impact was quickly covered up by the explosive eruption underneath his sternum. His entire body detonated like a firework fountain before petering out completely.

The crowd went wild.

David pumped his fist back at them in response.

He never caught wind of the blast that blew him straight into the starry moonlight.

Both racers awoke on the grass of a nearby white coastal contemporary. Their compatriots were a hundred yards further down the road celebrating Independence Day in the middle of September.

David took a moment to compose himself. His clothing looked like it was fresh from the dry cleaner despite having just been blown to smithereens a few seconds before.

"You okay, man?" Darrell was sitting up and staring out at the water with his arms laid across his kneecaps.

"Yeah, I'm good." David checked to make sure.

"I'm not a jerk, by the way," Darrell reassured him. "I don't think. The Road Rash just brings something out in me. All the same, you play nice with Torie, now. That's my girl."

"Oh, I'm sorry, man. I'm not looking to step on any toes." David said as much while silently assessing a potential stomping position.

"No worries. I'm married. My husband is, too—just to somebody else now. I'm happy for them. The sadness I kept all for myself."

"I went through something similar," David verified for his suddenly non-threatening friend. "Except we weren't married. And she didn't wait until I died to kill me. What do you do for fun when you're not busy playing Ben-Hur through roadside bombs?"

Darrell dug his hands behind him in the grass and reminisced. "I just got back from vacation. Spent the last month haunting the Westboro Baptist Church. I managed to locate an old latex Halloween mask of Reverend Henry Kane from *Poltergeist*. He even looks like Fred Phelps. It's like it was meant to be. Every night at three a.m., I'd bump *'It's Raining Men'* in front of the place and strip down to a lime green thong. You'd have thought it was raining fire and brimstone behind me based on the reactions I got. One of the ladies tried to throw their baby at me a couple weeks back. That shit didn't even make sense. I had to pause the music for a second."

"Did you say anything?"

"Yeah. I asked her if she just tried to throw a baby at me."

"And?"

"I mean, she didn't say *no*."

David stifled a laugh before continuing. "So, how'd you wind up here, then?"

"Oh, I ran into West Bloomfield High to stop a school shooter and took two to the chest."

His memory was jogged. "Henry Timmons."

"That's the one. But since I was going up against little Henry and his AR-15 with the equivalent of a slingshot, the celestial courts apparently defined it as a *'suicide mission.'* How was I supposed to know? I was just trying to do my job, man. They could have at least made an announcement. Screwed by legalese. Never been my preferred position. A few of us filed a cosmic class action lawsuit. *Police v. Reality.* It's been pending forever."

"Yeah, well, I'm apparently stuck like glue to my Soul Succubus ex until I can get her to release me. It sounds like I'm going to be living in a Hell-engineered Insta Feed that never ends."

"Just wait until you have to sit there in a chair like Jerry Falwell, Jr. and watch her have sex with another guy," Darrell offered. "Hoo-boy. That's a bear. I got three words for you—*Blair. Witch. Project.* Go stand in the corner of the room facing the wall and do not turn around for the duration. Whatever you hear, trust me—it's a trick."

"I'm taking mental notes," David added dryly.

"Sorry, brother. Haunters like me get a bit more leeway to wreak havoc in the real world. I don't mean to cause you any additional agony, but the whole point of a Jinni is to torture you. The distress is by design."

Before David had the chance to inquire any further, Torie began treading a diagonal path across the grass toward them.

"Well congratulations, gentlemen. You blew up both the bikes. Guess that's the checkered flag for this evening. What a bummer. I wanted to try and Evel Knevel one of those puppies off a pier into Lake St. Clair as a nightcap. Next afterlife, I guess."

Darrell hoisted himself and his squeaky joints into a standing position. "I've got a long drive back to Orchard Lake." He placed a palm atop David's shoulder. "I'm sure we'll be seeing one another soon. Torie—the guy's okay."

The two shared a quick laugh and a warm hug before saying goodnight.

She kept her eyes on her friend as he departed on foot. "*The guy's okay.* That's a sterling recommendation he just gave you."

Torie turned and began to slowly reduce the distance between them. David thought about meeting her halfway. She was lightly biting her lower lip. He very much wanted to ask if he could give it a go. "Would you care to walk me to my $8.9 million dollar waterfront mansion? I call it *The White House.* Because it's white, and it's freaking ridiculous."

He stumbled both physically and vocally while rising. "Uhh, sure."

The two orbited one another in silence like embarrassed fifteen-year-olds for a few hundred feet until they passed through the remaining partygoers on the road up ahead. High fives were exchanged with Tina and Wesley along with promises to see one another on Friday.

"Love you kids," Torie shouted back one last time in their direction before returning her attention to David. "We're driving out to the country to play Balloon Pop, by the way. Care to join?"

"I'm frightened to even ask, but—"

"What's Balloon Pop? It's just like at the county fair when you were a kid," confirmed Torie. "Except, we go up in hot air balloons, and instead of darts we use Milkor grenade launchers.

Whoever stays in the air the longest wins. Tina made a trophy out of an Everlast reflex bag. To the winner go the spoils. Play stupid games and win stupid prizes."

"I guess I don't have any other plans. Being dead and all." It was an honest assessment on David's part. "I might have to pick you up. Or have you pick me up."

"I got you, kid. I'm rolling in a Phantom these days. Thought it was appropriate given our location. Just give me the address and we're golden."

"Good, my Lambo's in the shop right now. Is this going to be the inaugural flight of the Hindenburg, or something you've attempted before?"

"I took one in the teeth a few weeks back, actually," Torie verified. "Thing shot napalm fire everywhere when we hit the ground. I came running out of the burning wreckage like a boss. I looked like Tom Cruise in every movie he's ever been in. It was amazing. My low-key mission in the afterlife though is to find a working jetpack. That's my white whale. Been looking for years now with no luck. I'm talking about the stuff they got squirreled away at Wright-Patterson Air Force base with the Tic-Tacs and UFOs and whatnot. If the tech's actually from Alpha Centauri, all the better. Either way, I want to play Rocketeer at least once before I leave this realm."

"I hope I can keep up with you guys."

"I'll stay back if you fall behind."

They smiled at one another like schoolkids.

Torie continued. "On Fridays we typically go grab a beer in Ann Arbor. It's a ghost town. Which ironically in this context means the place is always packed to the gills. So just bring a change of clothes. Because you're coming with." She understood within the first five minutes of meeting him that David required that kind of reassurance. He didn't think he belonged anywhere.

That would never be allowed on her watch.

"I'm game. Gives me a few days to get my bearings."

Torie could no longer pretend. "Did we at least manage to get your mind off the girl for a bit? For one evening, at least. I could read it all over your face."

"I'm not thinking about Stacey anymore." David made good solid eye contact with her for the first time.

"What happened there? Abridged version."

"I never showed her who I really was," David confessed. "I never showed her any part of me, really. I was just this monumentally sad, lonely, friendless person who she put up with for way too long. Stacey was the *Anti-Me*. She wasn't just everything I wanted—she was everything I wanted to be. I was sure if I told her what was going on inside my head, she would never look at me the same way again. So, instead I told her nothing, and she stopped looking at me altogether. I never caused anyone more pain than the last person in the world I wanted to hurt. And you want to know what conclusion I've drawn as to why I did that?"

Her curiosity was genuine despite the jealousy. "Why?"

"It was because I loved her so much. I wanted her to get away from me," David acknowledged. "Same as if I were her father, or sister. So, I subconsciously set in motion a plan to ensure that result. Hell, I knew the first time I kissed her I was already dead. I felt her steal something inside of me that night. She drank too much back then, but I knew she would sober up eventually. Me on the other hand—permanently plastered. Wasted in every way. Prior to death I was a couple Septembers away from putting up a tent on Skid Row."

There was a brief pause in the conversation. The splash of waves combined with their hollow footfalls were the only sounds for several seconds.

Torie reentered from the top rope. "We're not having sex tonight. Just so you know," she affirmed as politely as possible. "I let that drive my decision-making too often when I had a pulse. And it just caused a lot of pain for all parties involved. Decided to try hedonism without the heartache on this side of things. At least for a while. It's been working for me so far."

David raised a hand to signal there was no need. "Not having sex is standard issue for me, so no worries. I can put the entire thing together from memory. Don't even need to see the instructions."

"Which isn't to say I don't want to, or that we never will," Torie added with a hand on his elbow that transmitted electricity, "I'm confident I could be convinced. Just not tonight. Or, for a minute. Is that going to be okay?"

"Totally. We'll just be hot friends who want to have sex but don't. That's a thing, right?"

"Never in the course of human history has that been a thing, David." She stopped to cuff both of his shoulders with her arms straightened out in front of her. "But you and I are going to fake that Moon landing, buddy, or die trying. Are you with me? Let's be pioneers."

The buzz he got off her had already put him through the stratosphere. "You jump out first, Neil. I'll be right behind you."

"Follow me and I promise I'll never lead you astray," she winked. One thumb was subsequently hitchhiked over her shoulder. A signal that the chateau behind the waist high rock wall was her final destination. "So, look, as long as you promise not to get handsy, I've got homemade chicken enchiladas waiting inside. Verde."

"I'm sorry—did you say *verde?*"

"I did." Torie confirmed as much with the same flat smile and sharp shake of the head she used earlier during their discussion of the other minefield up ahead.

David hopped over the stone slab barrier using only one arm and was ten yards up the gravel driveway before Torie entered into a full sprint. She was grinning ear to ear as she moved to intercept her quarry.

***

"Did you guys look at this picture before you posted it online?"

Carol came along for the ride when Stacey opened *Darden Communications* in Manhattan two years back. The pair spent three years in Michigan helping to move Representative Lauren Metts from House to House. Carol could tell by tone if Stacey's question would have no right answer.

"Of course. Myself, Evan, Tonya. It went through the normal vetting process."

"Okay, then we need to reexamine our process. Take another look for me, will you?" Stacey spun the navy-blue monitor around to aid her underling. "Where's Waldo? Don't move until you see it."

Carol studied the entire frame for a few moments before she gasped.

"Uh-huh. Our family values social media blast is centered around a picture of the potential Congressman with a giant graffiti penis sprayed on the wall over his shoulder. And his mouth is open. It looks like he's getting ready to deep-throat that thing." Stacey craned her neck from behind the screen so she could take another gander as well.

"I am so sorry," Carol said. "Maybe no one noticed yet."

"Oh, I'd say it's a little late on that front. The Joey Chestnut memes are already spreading like wildfire online." Stacey held up her cell phone for Carol to confirm as much. "Our boy Richard Braxton is running in a congressional district that includes Coney Island, for Christ's sake. The jokes write themselves."

David was dying in silence over on the sofa.

Carol turned in her seat toward the open doorway. "Evan, take that photo of Braxton down right now."

Evan was six months out of Brown and still two years away from being useful in a professional work setting. He removed the earbuds he was not supposed to be utilizing during office hours and responded from behind his desk. "Which one?"

"The one with the giant penis in it," Stacey shot back with as much snark as she could muster. She lowered her voice so only Carol caught the rest. "I'd say you can't miss it, but apparently that was *not* the case."

It wasn't just the screw-up that had Stacey out of sorts.

All week she sensed she was being watched, but not by David.

This was something different.

She felt naked everywhere she went, and she didn't like it.

Cindy stuck her neck out until her face was floating sideways in the doorway. "Stacey, I've got Mr. Gottfried waiting outside for you."

"That's the nut who dropped off a $10,000 check yesterday just for the opportunity to speak with you for five minutes," Carol confirmed. "Wait until you see him, though. Tonya and I were ready to flip a coin."

Stacey was incredulous. "You're a lesbian, Carrie."

"I know! That's what was so weird about it. Usually, the only men I'm attracted to look like Megan Rapinoe. Which kind of defeats the purpose. Might as well drink non-alcoholic beer at that point. This guy has the Kavorka though or something. I don't know what's going on with him. Let's compare notes after he splits."

Carol spun out of her chair and fled the scene. The quick glimpse she caught of their incoming guest left her looking like a twelve-year-old girl at a Backstreet Boys concert circa 1997. She picked up random paperwork lying on Evan's desk and fanned herself with it as she watched the Amalfi Coast underwear model enter Stacey's office.

David swore he recognized the stranger from somewhere, but he couldn't quite place it. When Mr. Gottfried squeezed his NFL strong safety-sized body through the doorway, a brief look of recognition passed on his face when he glanced in David's direction. His undivided attention quickly diverted to Stacey.

"Good morning, Ms. Darden. It's an honor and a pleasure. Thank you so much for agreeing to meet with me." Unprompted, the stranger held out an open palm for the professionally mandated handshake.

Stacey was laser focused on his other hand. "I'm sorry, are you eating black licorice in my office right now? How dare you." She grabbed the U of M trashcan from under her desk and held it aloft as a demand rather than a request. "There's no smoking in this building, sir. Please deposit those cancer sticks inside before we continue."

He chuckled. "I'd hardly say this is a vice on par with cigarettes."

"No, it's worse, actually," Stacey stated with complete sincerity. "I'd rather you were blowing Newport smoke in my face right now. Watching you puff Parliament plumes directly into my pregnant secretary's mouth would be preferred. All it takes is one unfortunate coughing jag. If you spit even a spec of that black oil alien blood on my desk, it will be up on Craigslist as a *make-me-an-offer* five minutes from now. So please."

The stranger dropped the fistful of dynamite into the receptacle with a clink.

She raised the flaming torch like Lady Liberty. "Evan, can you do me a favor and deposit this outside in the designated bin for toxic waste when you have a sec?"

Evan didn't hear a single word, but he noticed she was looking in his direction. He politely removed a single earbud before yelling back. "What's that?"

She returned the trashcan to its normal position and waved him off with her unoccupied hand. "Doesn't matter, disregard. Don't strain yourself. I was planning to take a trip down to the incinerator after the meeting, anyway." Her voice returned to the room. "Just not sure if it burns hot enough to annihilate something this nuclear." She double tapped the metallic bin with her right foot.

"I apologize. It's a nasty habit."

Stacey nodded in agreement. "So, Tonya says you're

attractive, charming, and you want to run for Congress. That's enough to get you a job working the cash register at BK, but a smidge more is required to serve in the House of Representatives. Nevertheless, you're here, and Tonya's sprinting to the bank as we speak to deposit your check. She needs five more minutes, and I'm fully capable of distracting you for that length of time. You've got one shot, kid. Are you going home or are you going to Hollywood?"

"Yes, well, my name is Tag Gottfried, and I intend to be the Democratic nominee for the 15th District of New York."

She was already approaching indignant. Her palm shot up between them. "I'm sorry, your name really is *Tag Gottfried?* I thought Cindy was joking when she typed that into the calendar. I don't know which side of the aisle to set fire to first. I have to tell you, that is not going to scream political progressivism to a wide swath of the American citizenry. Let me guess—you played water polo competitively at some point in your life?"

"Eight years. It's that obvious?"

She squeezed her forehead with her thumb and forefinger. "Jesus, man. I thought I was joking."

"Is my name really that much of a deal-breaker?" He handed off a manilla folder.

"Not if you're looking to compete in the America's Cup," Stacey reinforced with a straight face. "If you were seeking membership at the New York Yacht Club, I'd tell you to feel more confident about your chances. Unfortunately, you want to run for Congress in the 15th District, which consists almost entirely of brown people. Latino, on top of it. It's approaching 80%. To them, Tag Gottfried is Spanish for *The World's Whitest Man.* He sounds like the type of guy who ties a red cardigan around his neck and bullies Tri-Lambs for fun. I'm sorry, but that's the image it conjures. I can't say the Democrats have been clamoring for their very own version of Mitt Romney."

Stacey had to privately acknowledge that he was a ten in

the looks department. His eyes were the most beautiful chocolate brown she had ever seen. The irises swirled like cold creamer poured into steaming hot coffee. He possessed a full head of jet-black hair so thick it didn't need to be groomed with anything more than a few fingers when he woke up in the morning. Tan in a way that suggested he only required five minutes in the sun to accomplish the feat. A single front tooth along the top row bent back a millimeter. Its slight imperfection somehow rendered the entire tableau even more brilliant.

Despite the stunning views, she had gone full Shania a while back. The foregoing facts simply didn't impress her as much as they once did.

If she could have everything, why settle for that alone?

Men needed to bring more to the table. In her experience that was always their problem.

"Look, I haven't procured any focus group results that might dissuade you from your line of thinking," Tag said, "but I assure you, I'm looking to be a man of the people, not their oppressor. And I've never owned a car garage in my life. I promise that any binders I possess are completely devoid of women."

Stacey chuckled. She began scanning through his provided paperwork. "Mr. Gottfried—do you mind if I call you Mr. Gottfried? Because I don't think I'll be able to call you Tag unless you're concurrently giving me a wedgie."

He remained calm. "Mr. Gottfried is fine for now. But I'd like to eventually work our way up to being on a first name basis."

Stacey smirked in a way that suggested she was uncertain about that possibility. She began tapping on the contents of his file. "Mr. Gottfried, look, you have no demonstrable political experience as far as I can tell, or life experience, for that matter. You're an independently wealthy mining magnate whose CV otherwise makes it look like you walked off the deck of the *Demeter* five minutes ago."

"I've been living abroad for some time, yes," Tag confirmed.

Her eyes briefly went supernova as she continued sorting through the documents. "It does appear based on these financial disclosures that you brought over a metric fuck ton of money in your coffin, and I'll grant you—that's not nothing. But I'm sorry, I can only do so much airbrushing to Scrooge McDuck. Some things I can't make fly, no matter the depth of gold coinage placed at my disposal. Eventually people would want to hear you talk. We'd have to hide your bushy little tail. There's a whole list. It would be a hot mess."

"I assure you I've gotten quite good at hiding my tail."

Truth in jest.

"As an aside, and I swear I'm not hating, but how in the hell did you wind up moving to Mott Haven of all places?" She held up his photo-scanned license as evidence. "Were you kidnapped at some point and just said, '*screw it, I'm staying?*' I know co-op boards in Manhattan can be a hassle, but sheesh."

"My building hasn't had a break-in for over a month."

"I'll alert the media," Stacey said. "Just so you know, whatever apartment you're currently living in, someone died in it, and that wasn't their decision. You must be like the royal prince of Zamunda or something. What's your deal, seriously? You could afford a ten-thousand-square foot penthouse overlooking Central Park. I'm surprised you didn't walk into my office bleeding from four different-patterned stab wounds."

"Well, as I indicated, I want to represent the people. Pro-immigration, pro-inclusivity. Strengthening the social safety net so no one gets away—so no one gets left behind, I should say. Anyway, those are the pillars I want my candidacy to stand upon. It was important to me to stay at ground level. Jesus lived amongst them."

"Christ, talk about overshooting the target," she said as she slunk back into her X-Chair. "Okay, so my first piece of professional advice is that you requisition for a legal name change. I won't even charge you for that one. Call it an early birthday present. Me to you."

"Not possible. So where does that leave us? Look, I'm not just seeking a communications team. I'm looking for a campaign manager. I've paid close attention to the work you've been doing over the last several years, and I believe you're ready to make that leap. I won't be able to achieve victory without your assistance. And that's not idle chatter. It's the truth. I've foreseen it."

"I have other clients, Miss Cleo," she confirmed. "We're very excited about the erection of Dick's campaign."

Stacey shut her eyes and sharply inhaled as soon as she said it.

They both silently agreed to ignore her Freudian slip.

"Yeah, I overheard as I was walking in. Sounds like it may just be a matter of keeping Mr. Braxton's head in the right place."

Stacey glared at him for a full four seconds.

Tag wisely transitioned. "In any event, I'm not concerned about your other professional engagements. I've found these things tend to work themselves out over time. I have nothing but. We can revisit the matter down the road."

She clicked her pen into and out of use four times before tossing it down onto his papers. Something in his eyes made it impossible to turn him down. "You still do the subway Mr. Gottfried, or is it limos all day for you at this point?"

"Actually, I very much enjoy the underground," Tag confirmed.

"Okay. C'mon. Let's take a field trip."

***

Stacey was standing in front of him with her arms across her chest. "Do you know who comes to the Bronx Zoo on a September Tuesday at 2 o'clock, Mr. Gottfried? Besides tourists, I mean."

"Families? 5th graders?" Tag was still trying to determine her point, but the uncertainty had him excited. It was a feeling he rarely experienced.

"I'm sure that's all true, but not what I was getting at. *Sad *people* come to the zoo at two on a Tuesday. Disaffected people. People who've lost hope. People who feel like they have nowhere else to go. They've lost their jobs, their wives. Their lives. Human beings laid so low that the only remaining kinship they feel is with caged zoo animals. They'll be the ones you see walking around here by themselves. Not hard to spot. Easy as the elephants. It's a time when they think no one else is watching. That's when they need someone to see them the most."

Tag took her up on the suggestion and began scanning the crowd.

Stacey handed the would-be candidate a stack of New York State Voter Registration Forms. "Go convince thirty New Yorkers who didn't have hope five minutes ago that they were wrong. It's so impossible it would impress me. I'll meet you back here in one hour. Do that, and you've got yourself a *comms director.* We'll go from there."

Tag stared at the paperwork with a placid smile. His head remained moored in place while his eyes slowly shifted up to meet Stacey's. Without another word he strode off into the oscillating waves of humanity until he was completely submerged beneath the surface.

She headed out to get a caramel macchiato. Even in his absence, the Greek Kryptonian god's visage stood signposted on every street corner like a hot guy hologram.

Stacey felt a brief rush of excitement while waiting in line for her drink. The wave descended down her spine looking for an exit ramp. She had to make a pitstop in the restroom on the way out to ensure the flooding had been contained.

When she finally returned to the zoo, she realized she was legitimately excited to see a man named Tag Gottfried. Regardless of the number of new voters he managed to snag.

"Well, what do you got for me? Close but no cigar?"

"I apologize. Technically, I failed to comply with your terms."

"Well, you'd hardly be the first man. How many, then?"

He handed her back every form she provided him.

"I thought thirty was insufficient. So, I registered all one hundred instead. Got them to donate their tissue and organs as well."

It took a few moments for the laughter to build up inside of her. "That has to be some kind of land speed record." Stacey's eyes moved from the forms to her new client. "Well, I'm a woman of my word. Let's get you to Washington, Mr. Smith."

"As a formality, Ms. Darden," Tag added with the appearance of apology, "given the extent of my financial resources and the like, I do require that everyone I work with sign a standard NDA. Once I have your signature, we'll be able to proceed."

The document was executed and returned the next day without a second thought.

Stacey would have been well-advised to have a lawyer look it over.

She didn't realize she was in the process of selling her soul.

***

It was the night of their first dinner date when Tag decided it was time to address David.

The meal was strictly professional, of course. Tag knew it would still be two weeks before he and Stacey slept together for the first time. The Beast foresaw it down to the foreplay.

He arrived fifteen minutes before the scheduled start. Tag offered to wait in the car, but Stacey wouldn't hear of it. Her two gentlemen callers now found themselves on opposing sides of the outdoor patio waiting for her to finish up in the bathroom. A wrought iron mesh table with an empty umbrella hole formed the only current barrier between them. The black disc hovered silently in the darkness waiting for one of the alien invaders to make a move.

Tag had hair product hair without having to use hair product.

David hated his guts.

"Hello, David. I'm Tag." It took a moment for the ghost's shock to wear off. "I apologize, I would come over and shake your hand, but unfortunately doing so would eradicate you."

"Thanks for the heads up." David squinted at him for a few seconds. "How?"

"How can I see you? I'm the Anti-God. I see the opposite of everything. And I have a Reality Mirror for the rest, so that pretty much covers all the bases."

"I've heard stories about you. You've apparently garnered quite the reputation over the course of infinity."

"Oh, you're going to make a girl blush," he leered. "It's true though. *Tag's* just a recent acquisition. I've had so many names. They've mostly been numeric, though. Differential equations and the like. I'll spare you the math."

David had already unconsciously taken two steps back before he realized he was trending toward a third. "I remember now. You were outside the hotel that night in Michigan. Why? It's not a coincidence, obviously. Why are you taking such an interest in Stacey?"

Tag leaned against the brick exterior of her brownstone using only one crooked leg for support. Each discharge from the fiery furnace in his belly churned out wafts of yellowed tobacco smoke against the moonlight. "I needed someone to help me spread the word. Get my message out to the masses. She will serve as my herald. Together, your ex and I will open the Seven Seals and render a just and rightful verdict upon reality. It's going to be a scream."

David made a mental note to circle back to Armageddon. "Look, I understand better than most how special Stacey is, but that doesn't explain why she's one in six billion."

The guest moved toward the ghost until his thighs were touching the table. He pressed his fists into the metal mesh with knuckles down like he was preparing a dominance display for

Dian Fossey. "I waited eons for Stacey to arrive. Her coming was prophesied from the beginning. She is *The Lord of Pain*. A role she inherited rather than earned, but nevertheless. Stace is like the anti-Bobby Kennedy. More key master than gatekeeper. When she shut the door to Heaven in your face, it opened a channel to The Endless at the same time. Give and take. Yin and yang. Cause and effect. God and Anti-God. I swam through the first of the seven seals like an anti-matter Michael Phelps—and now you're all fucked."

Revelations had always been the only interesting part of the Bible to David. "'*The horseman on it had a bow; a crown was given to him, and he went out as a victor to conquer.*'"

"John of Patmos was in fact a prophet," Tag confirmed with a shake of the head. "I would note that the First Revelation does not speak of ammunition. There is no more powerful weapon than the microphone. Each word is its own arrow. The supply line is infinite. My mouth will be like a Gatling gun of glorious mistruths. I will piss acid into the people's ears, and they will prostrate themselves before me to pray for more precipitation. Their poison will taste like Pepsi."

"They already started to show a predilection for that sort of thing prior to your arrival. I can't argue there," David acknowledged.

"As to the crown, the voters will bestow it upon my head themselves. '*But the Lord is faithful, who shall stablish you, and keep you from evil.*' I will be the Wolfman disguised as Lambchop. A fox need not be let in the hen house all night. I figure four years as President should be sufficient to slaughter almost every man, woman, and child on Earth. And then I'll get to run for reelection! There won't be anything left by the end of my second term. I will erase Heaven itself from existence. So, can I anticipate your cooperation with the upcoming campaign? I'm still accepting volunteers."

"I think I'm going to have to pass. I lean conservative."

Tag shook his head side to side. "Oh, my dear David. Being pro-life is so passe. You see, I have a non-linear perspective on time. I'm like *Dicktor Manhattan*. I've already seen past the edge of infinity. And I regret to inform you that humanity will soon be drowning in anti-matter forevermore. The good news is your presence will be required for the duration to serve as an interdimensional conduit. So, you'll at least suffer last for all of eternity."

"That's something I guess," David offered with mock sincerity.

"And not to worry, I'm not going to harm you in the interim." Tag's demeanor downshifted as he eased away from the table once again. "Point of fact, I need you bright eyed and bushy tailed if I'm going to be able to execute my vision in full. You'll get to play Ringo on the Day of Reckoning. So, plus column—you have a full-time ghost bodyguard now. Any ghouls trying to get at you will have to go through me first."

"Tag, you outside?" Stacey was in view with earrings in hand.

He lowered his voice. "We'll have plenty of time to discuss everything in more detail over the coming years. I do think it's important we reach a mutual understanding about how the *Mute Button* works, though. I'm going to put you on Silent Mode for the remainder of the evening to give you some practice. Moving forward, as long as you keep your mouth shut, there should be no reason for me to have to shut it for you."

Tag simply snapped his fingers once and nothing further came out of David's mouth despite his best efforts otherwise.

"I have no patience for idle chatter. Do what you wish when I'm not around, but whenever I am, you will speak only when spoken to, or there will be consequences. What you're experiencing now would be the least of them. Understood?"

David didn't require words to convey his comprehension.

"You ready to go, Tag?" Stacey was lightly prodding. "Reservation's in thirty."

"C'mon, David. Your spirit can salivate while I enjoy a delicious Porterhouse."

***

"David, while you may be able to watch me defecate, I pray that you are not in fact enjoying the privilege." Stacey spoke the words aloud while sitting atop her throne. Five minutes ago was the first time she had thought of him in days. Which hadn't happened in years.

"That shit's disgusting, Stace," he responded from outside the bathroom door.

"Also, just to be clear, full frontal is frowned upon moving forward. This is a purely PG rated household you're haunting here, mister. Keep your eyeballs in their sockets at all times. If I strip, you flip." She was checking email now. "Remember that motto. More rules and regulations to follow as I think of them. I'll keep a chalkboard on the side of the refrigerator or something."

If David weren't already dead, he would be debating self-harm just for the opportunity to haunt Stacey all the way to Hell.

"And as you've probably now gathered, I officially have interest in another man—Tag Gottfried. Never mind the name. Steel yourself, buddy. I'm a lady with needs. I'm probably going to be getting tagged here on the regular in short order. If you don't like it, trade places with another ghost, I guess."

She didn't realize David was the only thing standing between her and the Apocalypse.

# CATCH AND RELEASE

Torie picked up David on her way to rehab.

She died from an OxyContin overdose more than six years ago.

The personal height of her addiction coincided with the collective low of COVID lockdown. Despite her variant sickness, work-from-home granted her license to hibernate for a year just like the rest of the country. No questions asked.

It was a time for asking questions.

Torie slept through the summer.

Lost her job by September.

Got evicted in November.

Died in her sleep inside the Ruth Motel in December.

Everyone else got to pretend to wake up a few months later.

Torie and David had been friends without benefits for going on two months.

They decided it was time to have the weirdest first date in anti-human history.

"Drug overdoses remain a definite gray area in the celestial courts," Torie confirmed while on cruise control. She was busy tying her hair in a ponytail with eyes glued to the road. Her knees were barely brushing the steering wheel. For attire, she'd chosen The Smiths' *Meat is Murder* T-shirt she pilfered from David's dresser a few weeks back. He hadn't worn the thing in years. No one else was ever allowed to wear it again. "Anyway, it's ultimately kind of irrelevant since drugs steal your soul."

"I know what you're saying," David nodded in agreement.

"No, that wasn't meant to be metaphorical. Addiction causes *Soul Cancer*. And there's no chemo," Torie added as a matter of fact. "Drugs leave your spirit completely depleted by the time you die. Just ask any addict's mom or dad. You're not there anymore."

"I remember my father went AWOL for a year after my mom passed."

"At least he got off the carousel. ODs like me have to detox in 4-D for years. Decades, sometimes. Every day filling the tank back up a little bit more in the spirit realm until we can finally ascend. The air itself is a restorative, but there are other ways to enhance the experience—as you're about to find out."

"How long do you have to be here, then?"

"It's going to be another five to ten for me still. Right now, it would be like trying to shoot the space shuttle into orbit with a bunch of sparklers shoved up my ass. Mike used to be an engineer at GM. He worked up a spirit gauge back in his garage in Brighton. That Oxy's got moxie, boy."

"I'm so sorry, Tor."

"Could be worse. At least I don't have a Spiritually Transmitted Disease. Ugh." She silently shook her head. Her dislodged tongue suggested she'd swallowed something unsavory.

"I never would have suspected you were an addict in a million years. For whatever that's worth."

"Yeah, that was the problem. I was amazing at being a drug addict. Most drug addicts suck at it. I always had to get an *A* in everything." Torie acknowledged the former reality before waving off any further discussion on the subject. "Forget all that, back to the matter at hand. I want to hear more about this Tag character. We need to start separating fact from fiction before I start freaking out."

"Well, last night he made Stace emit animal sounds," David said. "And not your typical howling and moaning, either. No, I mean *weird shit*— like koala barks, and red fox screams. He had her clicking like an orca at one point. I spent an hour this morning rabbit-holing for analogues online. The auditory memory is permanently seared onto my subconscious."

"Trans-medium interspecies sex does defy the laws of both physics and nature," Torie agreed. Her tone didn't make it immediately clear if she was joking.

"Pretty sure they were using echolocation to communicate," David added in further corroboration. "Stace hit a dog whistle frequency. Every Basset and Beagle in the neighborhood started barking simultaneously. I wish I had recorded it. Would have been a sound engineer's wet dream. Hundred bucks says if you played it backwards, you would have heard Pazuzu."

She was chuckling at the imbecile in the passenger seat who she adored. "Okay, but making a woman orgasm repeatedly doesn't make him the Anti-God—it just makes him the Anti-Man. Do you have any additional evidence you can bring to the table regarding the supposedly Abominable Boyfriend?"

The sparkling blue strip appearing as they crested over the hill signaled Lake Michigan was only minutes away now.

"I already told you, Tor. He volunteered the information. Guy said, *I am the Anti-God.* Could not have been clearer on this point. Outlined his entire plan soup to nuts. Brick shithouse in the Bronx to the white shithouse at 1600 Pennsylvania Avenue. Plans on depositing humanity in an anti-matter sinkhole prior to retirement. I didn't want to scare you, but he also muted me like a flatscreen TV with the snap of his fingers a couple weeks back. I couldn't hear myself scream for the rest of the night."

That one caught Torie's attention. "Yeah, that's weird. 3-Ds shouldn't be able to do that."

"Thanks, professor. I'd never seen that app on a human being before, either. So, I'm thinking he's probably not all hot air. Although that's all that comes out of him."

"I can't stand men who bloviate." Torie underscored as much with a corresponding shake of the head.

"Yeah, no. His breath is actual hot air, Tor," David corrected. "It smells like a Taiwanese sex toy factory that burned down in a chemical fire. The stuff is interdimensional in its offensiveness. He's doing some kind of scent Svengali-ism on Stace or something."

Torie cut the laugh track. "To be continued. We've arrived at our destination."

It wasn't quite seventh heaven, but they were moving closer to the target.

God never saw fit to bestow the place with a formal name, so the regulars came to refer to it colloquially as *The Soul Spa*. An expanse of beachfront hotels had been gifted in 4-D with crystalline add-ons seamlessly fit between and atop every existing structure. The only new materials at play appeared to be glistening laminated glass and flawless zinc metal. Even from a distance David could see that each substance was too chemically pure to possess any actual parallel on Earth. Several of the inserted skyscrapers stretched into space elevators. Refracted light poured diagonally through the towering diamond partitions. The result left everything in front of the beachhead awash in misty gold sunbeams for miles.

A few moments passed before it finally registered—what David was witnessing for the first time was always right there in front of his eyes.

He just had to take away the time to see it.

David rolled down the window to breathe it all in and got an instant body buzz off one inhalation. "Why do I feel like I'm thirty minutes into my first Molly drop right now?"

"*Angelic Air*—that's what they breathe all of the time up above," Torie confirmed. "Can you imagine? It's what life is supposed to feel like when you're actually living it. Synthesized and distilled down to its essence. Passion. Happiness. The same feeling you get jumping out of a plane, or free soloing up a thousand-foot rock wall. Or giving birth, I imagine." The way Torie said it made them both visibly sad. She turned toward her window to look out at nothing. "Anyway, E isn't anything."

"It's not just serotonin, though," David acknowledged. "I feel opened up. Like, I always want to hug you, but right now I really want to hug you. And that lamppost over there. And that dumpster. And then sit around a campfire and tell all three of you about my wildest dreams and deepest regrets."

"Man, I'm so jealous. I still remember my first time getting elevated." Torie was giggling as she took a winding right turn onto the flat grassy prairie across the street from the lake. The stretch remained informally demarcated as a seaside parking lot only by the interstate itself. Hundreds of stationary automobiles stretched out in every direction across the lawn. Visitors in board shorts lugging their navy capri stripe beach chairs and pink flamingo pool floaties filtered around each side of the car like prongs on a tuning fork.

After slowly car wash rolling past hundreds of fellow rehab attendees, Torie and David finally hit the upper atmosphere. Nothing but empty space laid out before them now. "That feeling seeping down into your bones—live long enough and unfortunately it tends to become a foreign object," she said. "Humans give up on trying to train dragons around twelve, and then we just spend the rest of our lives chasing them. Daydreaming becomes disfavored. Everyone starts collectively sprinting toward a mirage on the horizon. Most of us never make it back to that starting position."

"It is strange," David agreed. "When I became an adult, I was granted the ability to do anything I wanted in this world, and I almost immediately stopped wanting to do anything. Kids can't move out of your eyeline until they're eight, but they have more freedom than any of us."

Torie eased all three of the phantoms into an unmarked spot next to a yellow pickup.

David's most recent memory of being behind the wheel of one put a smile on his face.

"Do you have twenty bucks for admission?" Torie's inquiry seemed sincere. She didn't bother to turn her head toward David to gauge his response.

"You're kidding, right? I didn't even know money was still a thing. I haven't a had a dollar to my name since death."

He failed to acknowledge that most of it was already gone before then due to his ill-advised cryptocurrency investment strategy. His life secretly spiraled into a ceaseless push to rob Peter in order to pay both Paul and Mary. The rest of his days were spent engaged in either social media puffery or anti-social marijuana puffing.

-*Chasing The Dragon*-

David had to ask his last living date if they could stick with starters. Lindsey from Ferndale looked at him like he stole cash out of a Salvation Army red kettle right in front of her.

All of it in pursuit of a lifestyle befitting the woman who no longer wanted to have anything to do with him or his Crate & Barrel wood base sofa.

"No worries, kid," Torie reassured him as she reached into the glove compartment. "I got a seasonal pass in my welcome packet when I first got here. It's good for two decades, and you're always allowed to bring a guest. They'll give you a wristband up front and you'll be good to go. Let's hit up Love Field first before we go down to the water." She exited the car and David took the hint.

Half of his follow-up question remained in the car as he got out. "What is Love Field?"

"C'mon, Daredevil," Torie offered with an outstretched hand from the front bumper. "Let's get your first trial out of the way."

A few hundred feet ahead of them the field dipped down into a lower bowl that David couldn't see from the car. As they reached the upper rim, he spotted heavenly volunteers filling the entire space down below. Everyone was identically clad in white polyamide button-ups with dark indigo jeans and straight white trainers. Each smiled up at him in a beatific manner. He felt like he walked into a death cult meeting made up of fashion-forward IT professionals.

"This movie you're inserting us into right now never ends well, just so you know," David indicated with dread. "I have your word that I'm not going to wind up sewn into an animal skin and set on fire to satisfy a pagan god, right?"

"Promise," Torie giggled. "*Midsommar* murders are reserved for Mondays."

"Is this just like, '*hey, look there's a tiger,*' and I say, '*cool*' like I care, and then we go to the reptile house," David asked, "or were you actually expecting me to walk into its enclosure and pet the thing?"

"Everyone's scared going into the embracement," Torie reassured him, "but once you're down there, you'll see there was never any reason to be worried in the first place."

She took a position behind him and began to lightly hand-truck the man cabinet forward with both palms pressed into his lower back. The two descended at the half-step to avoid taking an inadvertent tumble.

"I have to tell you, Tor, I don't particularly care for people touching me." David made the declaration with trepidation as they continued on the downward slope. "It's a genetic predisposition. Grade school didn't help, either.  My fight or flight kicks in automatically now if someone comes within three feet. Precedent suggests it's just a disguised precursor to a physical assault of some kind."

Torie wasn't smiling anymore. Far from it. She did an end around David to show him her work then gently pressed both hands into his chest for emphasis. "Listen Downey, I don't know who these monsters were that came roaring out from under your bed all those years ago, but they're literally not allowed here. We're going to be hugging a lot, and I'm already great at it. You need to practice your hand placement, or you'll never be able to keep up with me coming off the line. Okay?"

He responded like a little boy being spoon fed Brussel sprouts. "*Fine.* Blow the whistle."

She took him by the wrist and walked him the rest of the way for his first day of school.

David kept his voice low to avoid insulting any seraphim. "It's just a field of angels hugging people?"

"They're mostly ex-pats, actually. Earned their stripes and ascended long ago. Anyway, don't knock it 'til you try it, tough guy," Torie responded with a light shove into his ribcage. "It's like a Penny Pony—you get way more back than you put into the thing. Trust me. Every little bit of love fuel counts. Speaking of which, here you go. First house. Go say Trick or Treat."

A Japanese ronin in his late 50s named Sanada stepped forward to greet him.

"Welcome brother." The stranger enveloped David in a bear hug. After a few seconds the ghost was strangely compelled to return the favor. Warmth flowed through his entire body. It felt less like water taking the shape of its container than microwaved maple syrup oozing through his veins and into every crevice of his body. Real ecstasy. The feeling was as foreign to him as this new friend.

Erik the red-haired Viking came next. Claimed by Ättestupa, then consigned to this realm. He cupped David's face in his hands. Despite the dagger slash across his right eye that left it permanently milky, he could not have been more inviting. "You are loved." He tied two thick, fleshy cables around David's back that left him no choice but to acquiesce to his new captor.

A young Mayan mother of four subject to ritual sacrifice in her past life smiled at him along with the rest of her brood. "So good to see you, David." All six of them embraced.

"Oh, what a handsome young man!" A black grandmother named Erma swallowed him whole. She surrendered herself to the overseer and his dogs so her three grand babies could have a thirty-minute head start. All of them grew old and raised families outside Cincinnati. Joseph served as a conductor on the Underground Railroad for over a decade. To this day every member of the family was taught to pray for Mama E on their knees before their heads hit the pillow. She rocked David side-to-side like he was one of her own.

Meanwhile Torie was greeting each angel as Angela, or Michael, or Ulysses. *How are the kids*, and *I missed you so much*. Over and over until she spotted her gift from above.

*"Kim!"*

*"Torie!"*

The two of them tore after each other from across the field.

They were laughing hysterically by the time they tackled one another to the ground. "It's been months, bitch. I should kill you." Torie was totally kidding.

"Seems redundant," Kim sassed as she sat up, "but you always were a bit extra, Rory."

"*Stop*. Don't call me that in front of company," Torie insisted. The two rose together and brushed themselves off. They took turns conspiratorially glancing back in Mr. Downey's direction with devilish smiles on their faces. Each kept separately whispering sweet somethings into the other's ear. Like his namesake Commander Bowman before him, David was being observed in an interdimensional zoo by the superior species.

"So, why Rory?" David determined it best to fight fire with fire and engage in a preemptive strike against his captors. The instant embarrassment emanating off Torie's face in waves told him he hit the bullseye.

"We were both *Gilmore Girls* fanatics," Kim confirmed while taking a step toward him. "Lil' sis will always be the Rory to my Lorelai. Even though, '*she got older, and I stayed the same age*.'" Kim quoted the last sentence in her best Wooderson voice.

"Lady, I'll put you six feet under a second time if you keep talking that mess."

David raised a valid question. "Wasn't Lorelai Rory's mom?"

Torie walked over to smack David in the chest with an appreciative palm and then left it there. "First of all, where have you been all my life, David Downey? Second, yes, that's absolutely correct. My dumb sister has been stepping on rakes since 2002." She turned her attention back to Kim. "Stop hitting yourself, Kiki. I am not an incest baby!"

Several smiling angels turned to take in the increasingly curious family reunion.

"David, I'm Kimberly Eaton—the daughter our parents didn't regret."

Torie shook her head with her lips sucked in before responding. "That's not true. They regretted us both equally."

David cut through the noise and made contact. "Nice to meet you, Kimberly."

"Kim's okay," she informed him. "So, Roar tells me you're a really amazing guy, and socially awkward to the max." The sisters turned and looked at one another. Torie was telling Kim to shut up with her eyes even though a sort-of smile remained on her face. "What was the metaphor you just used? *In terms of intermingling, he's like a ninety-seven-year-old man easing his way into a warm bath.*" Kim returned her gaze to the subject. "True or false?"

David eyeballed Torie in a way that sent her own straight into the dirt.

The angel decided to throw her sister a lifeline. "I should note that I reluctantly agreed to provide you with said slack, David—because my sister thinks you're pretty special. Which means I think you're pretty special, and I don't even know you yet. Don't need to. Unfortunately, I know my sister." She looked Torie up and down with something approaching disgust. "For some reason, she's always right about these things. So come here, kid."

Kim began to shuffle toward him in zombie mode. David

grinned despite death approaching. Once he was all wrapped up, she whispered into his ear to keep it between them. "Fix yourself first. That can't be her responsibility. But my sister's a miracle at maintenance. Get yourself right and you two can be perfect to-gether. Not until then, though." She stepped back so they could see one another. Their heads bobbled up and down a few times in unison to execute the silent agreement. Kim smiled to seal the deal.

The sisters embraced one final time. "I'll stop over at lunch and say hi to you two if I get a break in the action, okay? Love you, Roar."

"Love you, Lor." Torie kissed her sister on the forehead be-fore she followed up with a second effort on the bridge of her nose. The double-tap was so specific David knew it had been done thousands of times before. A total stranger was getting to share in their secret ritual.

He felt honored.

Torie made her way back to David. She slung an arm around his lower back to offset the one he laid across her shoul-ders, but her smile remained on Kim all the way over the rise until her sister was out of sight.

David tried to tread as carefully as possible. "Kim looks re-ally young, Torie. Like, high school young."

"She was eighteen. I was sixteen. I'll give you a wild guess when I started using drugs."

"How did that happen?"

"Oh, we were in that bastard Billy Tanner's basement after a football game on Friday night and one of his friends who'd been praying to get in my pants asked me if I wanted to do a bump—"

"No. I meant your sister. How did she die?"

"Leukemia. No one should have to look that old when they're that young." Torie vibrated with something approaching anger at the memory. She began to march forward with militancy. "I'm glad she got to be herself again, but she'll never get to be anything else, and that's not fair. Being eighteen is fun but it shouldn't be anyone's death sentence. Go ask Billy Tanner. I think he's still alive. I'm just not sure he's aware of that fact."

"Being eighteen for eternity would have been my Hell," David affirmed. "Thank God they didn't give Kim something she couldn't carry."

"I'm still unclear as to why she had to carry anything at all," Torie snapped. "There better be CCTV footage of the Eaton sisters shitting on a communion table while we were hypnotized or something. Because other than drinking Seagram's wine coolers to excess, Kim couldn't have done anything back in high school to make God hate her with such vim and vigor."

"You sure it wasn't Zima? Because you could legit die from drinking that. I'm pretty sure there was a skull and crossbones next to the Surgeon General's warning."

Torie stopped in her tracks. "David, I know that you're just trying to be funny. And, I'm not even saying that that wasn't funny," she acknowledged while trying not to smile. "However, sometimes in polite society, you're contractually obligated to try and *not* be funny. Like when discussing my eighteen-year-old sister's death from leukemia. That would be one example of where the line gets drawn."

David was so sheepish he was fit to be sheared. "I'm sorry, Torie. That was wrong. My comment, I mean. Although Zima was also very, very wrong."

"Agreed on both counts," she offered with her hands on her hips. "And to be fair, I did reference shitting on a communion table a moment ago, so I'm going to let you off with a warning this time. It's a good thing you're such a pretty girl or you'd be getting a ticket."

David and Torie looked both ways and held hands before running across the road. The children screamed like a semi was oncoming even though there was no traffic in sight. A light coating of sand dusted every inch of the hotel's parking lot in brown sugar. It layered itself between the concrete and the soles of their sneakers. Each step caused a soft crunch beneath their heels. The dry ice required that each of them take extra care while walking to avoid unintentionally biffing it.

Torie removed her footwear and carried them forward with each heel dangling by a thread from separate fingers. She waved down one of the staff members waiting out front to be of service. He placed a light cuff around David's wrist after scanning Torie's paperwork to confirm his guest status.

An outdoor gazebo made of galvanized steel had been set up to meet all the new arrivals just before their toes touched sand. Heaven's finest culinary artists, bakers, sommeliers, and hash slingers clad in white chef coats were lined up at the ready behind rectangular banquet tables. A tumult of tin pots and dropped plates broke through the curtain behind them. Torie and David couldn't see the triple-tiered interior of the angelic kitchen sitting on the other side. Somehow, it was as massive as a high school fieldhouse.

She waited a few seconds for him to play catch-up. "This is the chef's table. Tell Marcus here what you want for lunch. Anything in the world. Although he's a Ragin' Cajun, so seafood is his specialty. I'm going full boil with garlic butter sauce myself. Marc's been promising me the moon, and now it's time to deliver. *'Dream a little bigger, darling.'*"

David barely had time to take a breath. The words shot out of his mouth like a pre-scripted response. "Lobster roll from The Clam Shack in Kennebunk. Truffle fries made with Italian white Alba oil. 306 Chopped salad with ranch dressing. Baker's Square Peanut Butter Cup pie. And a Mélange Noir blended barrel-aged ale from The Bruery in California."

"Damn, dude," Torie said with a step back. She slowly scanned him up and down. "You either knew that was coming or you made a vision board at some point in your past life."

"Yep. It had yarn and push pins. The whole deal," David responded.

Marcus seemed equally impressed based on the way he was studying his note pad. "I'll have to look a couple of those up in the divine database, but I got you, man. Y'all take care of one another. See you in a bit."

Torie hooked her catch through the hawsehole formed by his elbow and began to guide him toward his natural habitat. "So, I already signed us up for art therapy with Jackson Pollock after lunch. He combines it with supportive psychotherapy centered around his experiences with alcoholism. After that, we can either watch Sigmund Freud give a TED talk in the amphitheater on psychic repression or do Transcendental Meditation for Dummies with the Maharishi. Pick your poison, playboy."

"Sigmund Freud is a ghost?"

"No, they're all guest lecturers," she corrected. "Once we're done for the day, I thought we could hit up *Cloud Nine* before heading home."

"But I'm already there."

"That's very cute," Torie smiled, "but no, dummy—it's a dance club."

"In the sky?" David could no longer be sure if he was kidding.

"No, it's just down the street," Torie confirmed with a lengthened index finger. "It's walkable. I hope you like sample-based synths. If you don't, you're probably with the wrong girl. I'd say it's *Paradise*, but that place actually kind of sucks. They only play industrial. It's incongruent."

Each of them came to a stop, then repeatedly squeezed and released sand between their toes. The effect was the same as if the grains were being pushed through the neck of an hourglass. For some reason the exercise made them giggle like they were on laughing gas.

They both used their hands as sun visors to look out over

the water. Shards of sunlight needled through countless hole-punch clouds sprinkled across the sky. The bolts of light smashed against white-crested waves surging miles off in the distance. It turned the canvas below into bubbly blue textured glass. The water along the coastline somehow remained as calm as a Hindu calf. A disposition seemingly shared by everyone floating in the abyss of absolution up ahead.

The atmosphere itself appeared to be drawn on with pastel. Child-rendered cotton-ball clouds hovered over the baby blue expanse. Not a threatening nimbus in sight.

Wispy currents of electricity shaded teal and pink swirled just beneath the surface of the water. It wasn't a shock to the swimmers.

David was starting to get freaked out. "It looks like *Solaris* out there. I don't know if I mean that as a compliment."

"This is the Emotion Ocean." Torie took a few steps forward then twirled around with her arms aloft to underscore the majesty. "Thing is more like a giant Lazarus Pit. Just a big warm bath that heals you emotionally and psychologically. Stuff responds to skin temperature, muscle tension, neurofeedback. A whole host of other metrics. It's a nervous system repair module." She reached for his hand and the two trudged through the sand looking for a post-up position.

"The pool helps prepare us for passage onto the next heavenly plane," she continued. Her toes met cold quicksand for the first time. "It's like swimming in *Cocoon* water. And the ocean's not just for addicts, either. It's the ultimate self-help brain chemistry set. Schizophrenics all swear by it. Soaking in the stuff is like laying in some futuristic med-pod. Whatever ails you, it'll fix it. Plus, in thirty minutes it's going to turn into a wave pool. You ready to take a dip?"

"Are you suggesting I'm damaged and in need of repair, Tor?"

"No, I'm stipulating that every car in the world has a scratch or dent somewhere on its body," she countered.

"Not the ones that never made it off the lot."

"Am I going to have to drag you by your hair into the water, Downey?" She squinted to convey her seriousness.

"No really, Tor," David pleaded with his hands raised, "don't mess up my hair. This is one of the tools I use to distract you from my face. I tried to make myself look as not hideous as possible since it's our first official date."

She was disgusted by his disclosure. *"Don't mess up your hair?* We're at the beach, man. You know what, actually, now that you mention it, you've got a fuzzy in there. Do you mind?"

Torie tweezed her thumb and forefinger together and floated them all the way to David's forehead. The warhead accelerated at the last minute and went kamikaze across his entire scalp. She fanned her flattened palm back and forth across the surface for extra discomfort. David's hands shot up to survey the damage. He looked like a sniper's bullet just deflected off his helmet in the aftermath.

"How's that for not messing up your hair?" Torie shifted to addressing him with equal parts annoyance and distress. "Listen, let's get something straight. I don't give a damn what your hair looks like, dingus. On any day. When we go to dinner maybe, then sure. Try to look decent." She grabbed his hand with each of hers. "Please come in with me. Because I asked you to, and that's it. That's the only reason why. Please."

"Is this the same technique you're going to use to get me to buy you a puppy one day?"

Torie smiled. "This is the exact technique I'm going to use to get you to buy me a puppy one day. So, are we bringing home an Aussie?" She tilted her head to the side and raised her eyebrows while awaiting his response.

He shook off the sign. "They have the energy of a methhead," David verified as a former owner. He spun Torie around by the shoulders before they continued toward the rack of black inner tubes set aside for guest use. "And they possess the mindset of a WWII prisoner-of-war. It's all about escape."

She grabbed his right palm again in both hands and then nuzzled her head back and forth against his shoulder with the passion of Blanche Dubois. "Oh, what's a tunnel or two in the backyard? They're so beautiful. Heterochromia is the cutest."

"Tunnels are nothing. Those bi-eyed, four-legged freaks can learn to work a numeric keypad with their paws," David assured her. "You need to research breeds better or you're going to wind up with a puppy Papillon."

They walked hand-in-hand with their opposing arms looped through their own oversize Entenmann's frosted donut floatie until they discovered a small patch of unoccupied shoreline.

Torie tossed her shirt and shorts aside without a second thought and dove in with a running head start. The angel splashed back up through the water line using both hands as a hairbrush as she ascended. Her dripping black two-piece came straight out of the Bond Girl collection and made it look like everything around her was melting. When she smiled her pearly whites gleamed brighter than the sun hanging over her shoulder.

"C'mon, DD. I'm a damsel in distress and in desperate need of a water-based rescue." To sell the melodrama, she placed the back of her left hand against her forehead and sighed to the heavens above. "Whatever will a lady do. They never taught us how to swim back in finishing school."

He charged forward with gallant strides until he had her lifted up just over the threshold.

"Saving my life was totally sexist of you." She smacked the back of her head against the water and crossed her arms in mock revulsion. After a few seconds her eyes shifted back to his. A sly smile began to slowly creep across her face.

David took a second to survey the crowd of hundreds treading water all around them before he returned to Torie. "I think you're faking, Gloria Steinem."

She let herself sink further into both David's arms and the

water. Torie slung her right hand around the back of his neck for further male support. Her fingertips lightly brushed a circle around his C7. "I suppose misogyny can have occasional benefits. I knew there had to be some sort of explanation for the 1950s."

"My body's humming again," David confirmed, "but I can't tell if it's what's in the water or who's in it."

She bit her lower lip because she already knew what that did to David. It was ringing a bell to make the dog beg for bacon. "Why can't it be both?"

"That was my assumption, actually. I knew Angelic Air couldn't be the half of it."

Torie was asking him to kiss her with her eyes, but the message got lost in translation.

Instead, David laid her down softly atop her flotation device like a true gentleman. He strained himself audibly lifting out of the water to take up a seated position inside his own inflatable next to her. Even apart he kept the handle of her tube within his grasp. Torie wasn't scared, but David made her feel safe, anyway.

She decided to return the favor. "You want to see something cool? Think of a song you want to hear. Any song. Don't say it out loud."

David closed his eyes and laid his head back for a moment. "Okay. Got it."

"Now put your index fingers in each ear," she instructed.

Torie placed her hand atop his tube to keep them together while David did as he was told. "*Haiti*" by Arcade Fire began blasting in Dolby Surround Sound. He could feel sharpened rays of sunlight puncturing every pore of his skin. Soaking in the lake of super-spirit serum caused a full-on Photonucleic Effect to cascade through his entire body. Even though he was floating, he felt like he could fly. David kept his eyes closed for a few minutes that felt like hours. His immediate instinct was to peer down and ensure he wasn't still levitating when he reopened them. He gradually began to trace the length of one of the ascending quartz crystal towers in front of them by rotating his head skyward. "Tor, what are those things?" David pointed straight up into the air to aid in her analysis.

"*Stairways to Heaven.* They're exactly what you think," Torie acknowledged. "Can you imagine working that construction crew? To ascend the chute, you either got to have sufficient soul, or an actual halo like my sister. I possess neither at the moment." The back of her head gradually sunk below the waterline.

David allowed his free hand to slip just beneath the surface and intercept the electric currents of Crayola color. Each fingertip looked like it was pressed up against the glass of a plasma globe. The fluorescent light strands danced along the friction ridges of every digit. It gave him a tingle. "At least you weren't consigned to this place in perpetuity by a Soul Succubus."

"That is objectively true. I resign." Torie raised her palm without lifting her head.

A wet football missed the target and made a hollow splat two feet away. David tossed it back to QB1. "Me on the other hand, I'm stuck with a Jinni out the bottle that does everything to rub me the wrong way."

"So, you're saying Stacey's kind of like the anti-Johnny Gill?" Torie nodded toward David with scrunched eyebrows. Her look suggested inquiry rather than affirmation.

"Wow. How many decades have you been waiting to bust out that reference?"

She playfully punched him square in the arm. Her fist found a comfortable home inside the concave musculature between his deltoid and bicep. He was all wet. She was tempted to commit an act of piracy. "Jerk. I was going back and forth between him and Christina Aguilera. Had to make a quick decision. Anyway, don't hate. He was easily the sixth best member of New Edition."

David gave her side-eye. "Talk about damning with faint

praise. There were only six members of New Edition, and he was the last one to join the group. It's just lazy chronology. It would be like saying *Jaws: The Revenge* is the fourth best *Jaws* movie."

"That's total bullshit!" Torie shot up in her inner tube like she spotted a fin. "*Jaws: The Revenge* is easily the third best *Jaws* movie."

Several surrounding ghosts were rendered visibly apprehensive by the mere reference given their current location. Their heads began to swivel side-to-side.

"Anyway, don't sweat it. This place might be growing on me," David said. When he lifted his head from the water, dark clumps of brown hair formed dripping stalactites in response. They hovered over the surface for a few seconds before being pressed back down into dissolution. A set of young couples splashed past them while engaging in an ongoing game of chicken fight. "What about the rest of the buildings?"

"Mostly inpatient care. There are probably over twenty thousand ghosts staying here on any given day. And it's a four-to-one ratio of angelic candy stripers to patients, so they definitely needed the space. Every room in there is like the Hollywood Starlet birthing suite at Cedars Sinai. Once I ascend, I'm still going to volunteer down here every chance I get. I'm never going to retire. There isn't any nobility in it."

"Do you ever miss logistics?" David asked with a straight face.

Torie snorted against the backdrop of a passing red pedal boat. It was manned by a pair of lovebirds pushing seventy. She looked off into the distance while considering his question. "Not for a second—but what really horrifies me is that it wouldn't have made any difference. Every year I would have kept taking two steps back in exchange for two additional percentage points of pay."

"We're in the same boat," David said from his separate float. "I spent my life on Earth screwing over poor people for a living.

I can't even claim to have worked for a socially acceptable loan sharking enterprise like a credit card company. No, I chose to work for one of the remora fish that clung to their underbelly and fed off whatever detritus they left in their wake. I didn't set out when I was five years old to become a soul-sucking symbiote. It just sort of happened that way."

"I hear you. Wanting to fistfight every mirror you come across is not a fun feeling."

"Amen, sister." The two high fived and then held on for dear life. "I think the rate of bad luck increases exponentially based upon how beautiful you are. Pretty sure you'd have been looking at seventy years."

She rolled her eyes and shook off the suggestion, but the top row of teeth she was exposing made her real feelings clear. "Thanks, Downey. Glad I didn't follow through. Last thing I needed was more time added to my sentence."

"Even if this isn't Heaven, you seem to have found a home."

"Yeah, I know it's illogical," Torie admitted, "but ODing might be the best and worst thing that ever happened to me. Even if I'm dead, at least I'm doing what I always wanted to do—which is what everyone is supposed to do. When I was alive, I was barely living. If it took expiring for me to reach enlightenment, then so be it. Turns out it's never too late, David."

She brought their intertwined hands down into the water between them and began to slowly snap her wrist back and forth. The action caused small waves to erupt across the surface for a few feet before they disappeared back down below. Her smile faded in the same fashion as she processed her work. "I do miss my mom and dad, though. Like the dickens. They outlived both their daughters. Had to watch them each slowly waste away on top of it. Never got to hold a single grandchild. I hate it."

David pulled himself over so he could wipe the saltwater from her eyes. Then he kissed her for the first time. Several minutes passed before the parties achieved satisfaction.

By the time they concluded things, Torie was beaming once again. "There's no reason for you to regret the things left unsaid." The water beneath them began to slowly rise and fall. "You get half an hour in the wave pool, mister. Then I've got a surprise for you before we feast."

***

"Well, here we are, David. Welcome to your Home Room."

The pair were standing outside a beige door marked A7. From outside, the 4-D hotel extension appeared relatively modest. It was only when Torie and David entered the frosted glass enclosure that he could see identical doors extending forever down an endless hallway. The spatial disorientation immediately put him off-balance. She guided him by hand until they arrived at the destination. "Is this actually Room 101? Because I'll go ahead and declare my love of Big Brother right now. No need for the rats."

"Yeah, that's it, Orwell," Torie smirked. "For your crimethink, you're going to be punished with your greatest fear—interpersonal communication. And you're probably going to have to hug, too. I know. *Yuck.*"

"What?"

Torie continued to push him. She took a position behind David once again and pressed forward on his behalf. "Just slide your slippery ass through the door already, Downey. Damn. Any further failure to do whatever the hell I tell you for the foreseeable future will redound only to your detriment. Understand, soldier?"

David turned the knob and entered without raising any further complaint. He feared Torie might slam his head into the frame if he delayed for another second. Downey turned back toward her one last time before closing up shop behind him. "I think I want another potential ghost girlfriend."

Torie shut her eyes halfway and then cracked her head toward the front entrance. "I'll go see what I can dig up for you down by the beach, babe. Back in thirty."

The room was completely bereft of fixtures but looks can be deceiving. David took two resonant steps before he realized each wall of the cube was its own giant HD screen. All six sides were currently tuned to the same dead, gray channel. They stayed on mute as the four vertical panels rotated like a revolving door around David. The entryway behind his back only moments before now stood directly across the room from him.

An invisible power button was pressed, and all six sides came to life simultaneously. The cumulative effect was unlike any TV setup known to man.

David was suddenly standing inside his childhood kitchen back in Bloomfield Hills.

He hadn't been inside the room in decades.

The door opened and being in his holographic boyhood home took an immediate backseat.

Laura Downey was standing in front of David for the first time since he was twelve. He didn't wait for a word to pass between them before he covered the distance himself. The hug would have been hard enough to hurt his mother if she hadn't descended from Heaven.

"They told me you might be down here," Laura said in her permanent six-inch voice. "Hi David."

"I love you, mom." He never said it enough. Prayed for a chance to say it one more time.

"I love you, too, honey, but a little more warning next time would be nice," Laura admonished her son as she squirmed free from the embrace. "I had to make sure all my programs were recording before I came down here. It was such a chore. I'm sure I missed something important—but I don't want you to feel bad. By the way, do you think you could come by and fix a few things around the house for me later if you're not too busy?"

David assumed his mother must be kidding, even though she had never done that before in her life. "Mom, I'm stuck in the spirit realm for the foreseeable future. I can't just go up to

Heaven because you need a handyman. I'm sorry, but you're going to have to find someone else to put in your screen door for the summer."

"Well, I don't want to burden you, but if you get the chance, I could really use the help." Laura was incapable of listening to a word anyone said. "I have to download an app to use my phone as a remote, I don't want to even try on my own. I'm afraid I might break it, or the TV. They make it all so complicated."

"It's the eleventh dimension. There are infinite phones."

"Oh, no, I have my contacts saved, and my solitaire app. Can you show me how to take pictures on it, by the way? I was so confused. I just gave up. I figured I'd wait for you."

Her son's eyes exploded out of his skull, but he kept his tone low and measured. "You were going to wait until I got to Heaven to teach you how to take a stupid selfie? There has to be a four-year-old somewhere up there who could have helped you by now. If I blindfolded you, in five minutes you would figure it out, mom."

"David, don't yell at me!" She fled to the corner like a kicked puppy. "I'm too old. I can't see at night. There are too many people. I don't know how to do things." The rebuttal book was being emptied. Laura was shaking with something far sadder than anger.

"Mom, you can't spend eternity stuck inside your house watching *NCIS: Santa Fe* all day." He walked over and turned her around by the elbows. "I'm not yelling at you. I love you. I just want you to have some kind of an afterlife. You were living like a ghost before you became one, and it doesn't appear that things have gotten any better. I thought becoming an angel would at least cure your self-induced agoraphobia."

"I like my life," she huffed. "I have everything I need at home. Do you know if anyone can bring me a Diet Coke down here? If not, I really need to get back soon. I think I'll die without my Diet Coke."

Paradoxically, this was not a joke.

"Look, we don't have long. I want you to know I found someone really special, Mom. Torie. I'm in love. I don't know if she is yet. But I am. And I'm working on earning my way up to Heaven to be with you. Just ran into a couple of temporary roadblocks."

"That's nice, David," she said with her eyes already trending toward the door. "Just don't get your hopes up, or you'll probably wind up disappointed. Maybe 4-D is the best you can do. If things don't work out with this Teri girl, I'll always be here. Oh, do you remember the password for my email by chance? I've been meaning to ask for ages."

His mother Mrs. Munchausen surrendered to defeatism long ago and expected everyone surrounding her to fall in line. Laura was the Typhoid Mary of melancholy. Being in the room alone with her for two minutes proved to be enough to cause a recurrence. David felt himself getting sicker by the minute. Whatever soul he recouped since his arrival in this realm was being hoovered right back out of him as he stood there. "Mom, I didn't create your email password. You did. And I'm not staying in the spirit realm for eternity, either. It's messed up that you're seemingly okay with that possibility."

"Of course not, David, I want to be able to see you every day," she said. The thought caused David to tremble internally. "If you do ever manage to get into Heaven, please stop by first thing. I have some mulch that needs to be put down. So many things to be done around the house. Maybe you could stay and watch TV for a bit. I just sit there waiting for you."

Heaven suddenly sounded like a horror movie.

***

When David left the room twenty minutes later Torie was waiting for him, but she wasn't prepared.

He burst into tears the instant the door closed behind him. It caused David to drop his head in sniffling embarrassment. She did her best to collect all the shaking remnants in her arms. Torie told him she was with him now, and it would be okay. They exited past a young couple who played at being concerned for the two strangers before continuing along their own path.

David was too distracted to Downward Dog, but he made it through the rest of the day.

For Torie.

They sat in silence the entire drive back to her house.

When they arrived, she took him straight to bed, but they didn't make love.

Instead, Torie held David until the sun went down.

Then he disappeared.

She sighed before pulling the covers up over her shoulders.

"Typical."

# LOVE BOMBING

Stacey was shocked to learn that Richard Braxton was a bigot.

Vicky Braxton briefly ventured out the previous evening to walk their Shih-Tzu and was accosted by a pair of young ruffians. Luckily, Sea Gate's own dedicated Public Safety Department officers were within shouting distance and managed to restrain the two hoodlums until NYPD arrived. Mrs. Braxton suffered several mild abrasions and small cuts as a result of the roughhousing. Officer Patrick thought that pee wee football players took more of a pounding, but he failed to note that in the report. Through tears, Victoria swore things would never be the same.

It turned out to be prescience on her part.

Both detainees were illegal immigrants from Belize with criminal records.

Tag Gottfried telepathically summoned them from across the Rio Grande.

Richard Braxton was so traumatized by the whole ordeal that he decided to attend the Brooklyn Nets game. He rang Stacey from some random billionaire's private box at the Barclays Center. His practiced distress cut through the reverberating cheers saturating the entire suite. In the background, Stacey could hear the voices of several young women who were not his wife but were begging for Dick. She sniffed out their specialized brand of sidepiece tittering like a female bloodhound.

"Border control and a crackdown on illegals needs to be a central tenet of this campaign moving forward," Braxton dictated through her earpiece. "It's a 60/40 issue in this country now, Stacey. We're on the right side of things. If the Democrats don't wise up, we're going to get decimated at the ballot box. This is the red meat we've been waiting for." A chorus of boos let them both know the Utah Jazz were making a run.

Stacey had yet to reach the stage where professional obligation trumped personal ethics. She was taking her low impact ride at half speed to avoid hyperventilating.

"Richard, I understand how you're feeling. What Vicky went through was a tragedy." Any domestic who spent a few minutes in the employ of Victoria Braxton would disagree, but years in political communications fine-tuned Stacey's ability to effectively lie. "It's insufficient reason to run off half-cocked and completely change your communications strategy, though. Anti-immigrant rhetoric might be a red state winner, but it doesn't play in New York City. Half this country thinks anyone named Manny or Miguel is automatically MS-13 now courtesy of Agent Orange. You know hate crimes were at an all-time high in 2026. Some racist asshole in El Paso gave five different Mexican men a *Speedy Gonzalez* last week before he got arrested."

"What's a Speedy Gonzalez?"

"Oh, you haven't heard? It's the new Internet challenge for all those racist Wallers," Stacey confirmed. Her tone was trepidation posing as excitement. "You piss in an empty Jarritos bottle, and then you're supposed to break it over a Latino man's head while screaming, '*Andale! Andale!*'"

"I don't understand what that has to do with Speedy Gonz—"

"It's a yellow sombrero."

There was a brief pause. The only thing either of them heard for a few moments was the roar of the crowd.

When he returned from break, Braxton was undeterred. "Of course, that's disgusting and terrible, but it doesn't negate the need for a strong backbone of enforcement. My wife's experience is a testament to that. It would be political malpractice to not take advantage of this opportunity. We have a story to tell." A nameless female on his end of things whispered in both their ears. She instructed him to put the phone down and come to the bathroom. "Listen, I have to go. I'm having Eric forward the proposed talking points to you by email. Let's plan on discussing tomorrow afternoon after you've had a chance to review with your team, okay?"

Stacey was still struggling with the fact that her client considered his wife's mugging by Latino illegals to be a net plus for his political campaign. "Richard, I don't know that there's anything to discuss."

She distinctly heard a door shut followed by audible unzipping. "I'll give you a call at three p.m. Have a good night."

A male moan and an ungendered slurp were the last two sounds Stacey heard before he hung up. Her previous iPhone background was a picture of her embracing Braxton on the day he hired Darden Communications. It was changed to blank by the time she clipped out of the bike.

***

"Unfortunately, that's where we are, folks. It appears Richard Braxton is a philandering political opportunist who wants to exploit virulent anti-immigrant sentiment. Plans to do it in New York City of all places to boot. This is both bad politics and will likely turn this place into a Snake Plissken-style hellhole. He was three seconds away from proposing we put up a *No Vacancy* billboard on Ellis Island. Is everyone else as uncomfortable as I am helping to reignite the Mexican American War?"

A show of hands made it clear that her opinion was a unanimous one.

"Good, I'm glad I don't have to fire any of you," she affirmed.

"What do we do, then?" Tonya had three children and a husband who was a self-employed web designer. Post-COVID, Danny's role morphed into stay-at-home dad. As the primary breadwinner in her household, Tonya's concern was completely understandable. "I appreciate being positioned on the moral high ground as much as the next woman, but unfortunately being righteous doesn't pay the bills. Between Braxton and your boyfriend—"

Everyone's eyes widened at the word. Although there was no formal rule or written commandment posted in the bathroom, it was simply understood by every employee.

Tag Gottfried was a lot of things. The client. The candidate. The potential Congressman.

The Anti-God.

He was not Stacey Darden's boyfriend.

*-Even though he was totally Stacey Darden's boyfriend-*

Evan spoke for the room as his head turreted toward Tonya. "Dude."

Tonya knew she had legged a tripwire and tried to catch herself before it exploded in her face. She mussed up her own black pixie cut with both palms embedded into the top of her skull. "Stacey—I am so sorry." Her hands lowered into a defensive position. "I didn't mean to be disrespectful, but they are the only two sources of income for this office right now. Gottfried isn't sufficient to keep this thing afloat. All the state race candidates we thought we had in the bag slunk off one by one to other comms shops. It was great when we brought Tag onboard, but it seems like all our other revenue streams dried up in the process. Gift and a curse."

"Funny that," David said aloud to himself. The ghost was surveying the ongoing confab from a seated position atop Evan's desk. He enjoyed being in the thick of it. Getting to observe Stacey operate in her natural element for the first time in his life was awe-inspiring.

Despite Tonya's slip-up, Ms. Darden's irritation remained relatively muted. No one seemed more surprised by this development than herself. Four weeks ago, she would have put her foot up Tonya's ass and promptly sent her home for the rest of the day. Every minute Tag Gottfried cast more of a spell. She seemed to be in a trance.

"It's fine, Tone. Just don't do it ever again. Regardless, we're not losing our client, okay? I've discussed the issue with Eric Lasher. He promised me he would talk some sense into Braxton. This isn't Eric's first rodeo. He's been a campaign manager for decades. He knows we'll lose in a landslide and Richard's his meal ticket. Lasher's more motivated than us to nip this thing in the bud."

"This may not be the ideal time to mention it," Carol added while staring down at the CNN ticker on her phone, "but someone just firebombed the migrant center at Creedmoor in Queens. It's breaking right now."

"Are you kidding me?" Stacey pulled her cell free for further verification.

Tonya tagged in. "What the hell is going on? That's the fifth one in two weeks. They've been going up in flames all across the country."

"Yeah, this is the first in New York, though," Evan said. "Too close to home."

"It was too close to someone's home every time," Carol offered in admonishment without taking her eyes off the phone. "This is getting nuts. Firebombings. The Laredo lynch mob stringing up migrants from transmission towers. All that Speedy Gonzalez bullshit."

"Blythebourne had to have an assembly for the kids last week about diversity and discrimination," Tonya informed her coworkers. "All the good it did. Tommy's friend Diego got a Mexican Coke dumped down the back of his shirt the next day by a couple of older boys. The kids are calling it *wetbacking*. I guess they needed their own soda-based challenge."

"They grow up so fast," Evan joked.

None of the ladies were smiling.

Stacey felt like it was time to exert some influence. She stood up with her arms crossed. "Evan, if you were looking to become the first well-liked, unpaid intern in history to be unceremoniously fired from their position in favor of thin air, then congratulations. You're tap dancing right on that line, Gregory Hines."

The confusion in Evan's eyes let Stacey know the reference went over his head.

"Just shut up, okay kid? Matter of fact, why don't you let the adults have the room?" She made a disrespectful shooing motion with her raised right hand toward the exit. "I'm sure you have a Discord date to get to, something equally inhuman. Go plug yourself into the Matrix. Have some faux fun."

Evan didn't take it as an insult. He was grinning like a ghost as he gathered his laptop and related belongings into his backpack. He fled the premises before she could reconsider.

He wasn't Stacey's first intern. She knew you could imply a Gen Zer's mother was paid on demand if the disrespect bought them a day off work.

It was a welcome respite.

The ladies needed to discuss the future of Darden Communications.

***

Tag drove a white Wraith.

It was never stolen despite the Rolls being left unlocked on Willis Avenue every night.

This fact alone should have been indicative that something was amiss with the man.

Nevertheless, Stacey found it to be good fortune when she needed a ride to LaGuardia to pick up Kate Madison. His only condition was that they avoid the Robert F. Kennedy Bridge. He had a strong aversion to the man for some unexplained reason.

The radio was relaying more details of yesterday's horrific bombing at Creedmoor as they cruised down Grand Central

Parkway. The explosives were covertly disguised within a couple of construction barrels and left outside the migrant shelter. Same as the last four—so, it was a series. This time, seven Guatemalan migrants including a father and daughter were incinerated in the ammonium nitrate assisted blast. Two staff members named Jamar and Margarita were killed as well.

Stacey knew why they were still hesitant to label the bombings as domestic terror.

No white people had been killed yet.

As for the dead in Queens, Tag watched them burn from his bathroom in the Bronx.

Their shriveling skin brought a smile to his face as he shaved amidst the steam.

"I emailed Braxton yesterday after the news broke," Stacey informed him. "Read him the riot act. No one in my office wants to play any role in propagating this nonsense. If he wants to take his ball and go home, so be it. At least I'll still have my soul."

For now.

"It's absolutely disgusting," Tag offered with genuine dishonesty. The rest of it he legitimately meant. "This is exactly why I decided now was my time. *Our* time. The people need someone to bring them together. Our goal should be opening doors, not closing them. We need to tear down the walls that are dividing us. Not build more to keep us separated."

Stacey's head came to attention at a cartoonish speed. Her eyelids retreated like a semi was coming at them in the same lane. "Say that again."

"What? Which part?"

"*Tear Down The Walls*—that's your campaign slogan."

This was a message the candidate had already approved. For her benefit, he feigned ignorance. "Why is that the winner, in your opinion?"

She was smiling like a seventh grader at Six Flags. "You want me to tick the boxes for you? *Tear down this wall*' is iconic—

and it's attributable to the most beloved *Republican* president of all-time. We're reaching across the aisle to offer a clever but respectful pastiche in light of current events. In the minds of most voters, you instantly become a middle of the road Reagan-Democrat fighting on behalf of minorities and the marginalized. That's a huge bucket, man. Rim's the size of a kiddie pool."

He let a smile slowly creep onto his face. "I will need all of them on my side if I'm going to come out on top."

"It hits every target." Stacey could barely contain her burgeoning excitement. "It's a direct rebuke of the Wallers and their dirtbag deity. The electrified fencing. Migracide. All of it. Speaks to the moment while making a broader statement about where we want to go as a society. Who we want to be as a people. It's inclusive. The only people it potentially alienates would never vote for you in a million years, anyway. It's perfect. I'm awesome at this shit." She slapped the center console simultaneously in personal appreciation.

"You know what you sound like? He turned to her with a smile.

She grinned back. "What?"

"You sound like my campaign manager."

David sat in silence in the backseat.

Considering their destination, he didn't like where any of this was headed.

***

"When did you get the Rolls, baller?" It was all Kate could think about since her chariot arrived at the airport. Her normal heightened level of resentment toward Stacey threatened to break the gauge once she got a good look at Tag Gottfried in the front seat.

He leaned into her shoulder and raised his voice. The din of the other bar crawlers begging to have sugar poured on them would have drowned out any lesser effort. "I stole it from the actual owner after I killed him and sucked his soul dry for my supper."

He really did.

They both laughed like fat cat aristocrats.

Stacey was currently out on the concrete sidewalk being called to the carpet by Richard Braxton. Tag clicked his heels and gave the man chlamydia for daring to speak down to Ms. Darden. Through the plate glass he could see his lady lord wringing every last drop out of the balled up red cashmere scarf in her right fist. Each word was being spit rather than spoken. She finally paced her way out of the frame.

Tag made a mental note to throw Vicky Braxton in front of a subway car in two months.

Kate took the opportunity to offer way too much softened arm contact. "So, has she told you anything about her last boyfriend?"

"I've heard some rumblings." Tag and the ghost briefly locked eyes.

"Yeah, well, he's gone now, and honestly, good riddance to bad rubbish. I know you're not supposed to speak ill of the dead, but David was a d-bag," Kate told Tag. "He was totally toxic."

Tag was tempted to carve a biohazard symbol into Kate's forehead with his fingernail.

Takes one to know one.

Her sorry excuse for a soul was like a dirty, corroded penny that had somehow scabbed over and then been ground into a pile of horse manure with a steel-toe boot.

The Anti-God occasionally damned his own omniscience. Last Tuesday, he was forced to remote view Kate and a half-man named Lyle Stephens engage in rather repulsive roleplay at a motel outside Ann Arbor, Michigan.

Each wore a custom-made printout of David and Stacey's faces during intercourse.

The grotesqueries had to be specially ordered out of Amsterdam.

They were an invariable presence during their sexual congress.

According to Kate, her husband Craig would very much like to sit-in next time. That way he could watch *two* men screw his wife. *Oh, Boy.* The singular variation had begun to grow stale for the couple. They were looking for ways to spice up the marriage.

Kate didn't know that Craig was secretly more interested in the male half of the equation.

The entire display disturbed Tag immensely— and he was the father of the Devil.

"I'm so glad Stacey finally moved on. She needed someone serious. Someone with some substance."

*Someone whose only purpose in life is making money* was what she really meant.

"I can't wait to introduce you to Craig. He's in wealth management. You guys will be friends."

*You guys will be friends* meant *come over and screw me one day while he's at work.*

Tag invented that code. He already imprinted a subliminal reassurance that he would sleep with Kate into her subconscious. In his infinite wisdom, he understood that even someone as worthless as Mrs. Madison could occasionally prove useful in that regard.

When she leaned over to speak, her tongue briefly brushed against his antihelix. This was wholly intentional on her part. "I need to run to the bathroom. Will you make sure no one roofies my drink, please?"

"No problem." Kate continued smiling at him halfway to the restroom. As soon as she turned her back, Tag downed the contents of her glass and then clinked it on the bar for retrieval.

"May I say something without being struck down?" David was tentative in his delivery.

Tag turned in the ghost's direction without looking up from the email app on his phone. "Sure, David. You have permission to speak."

He exhaled. "Kate is way more qualified to be your concubine. She was already halfway to harpy before you even met her. Why don't you just finish that screw-job and be done with it? Make a full-blown dishonest woman out of her. All I'm saying, if I were a headhunter in Hell, her resume is the one I'd be pushing to the top of your pile. Ninety percent of the work has already been done for you. It's plug-and-play. Matter of fact, she's perfect for that sort of thing."

Tag was beginning to find David moderately amusing. He made eye contact as a show of minimal respect. "You're not wrong about her bona fides, but despite her best efforts, she is not the Lord of Pain. Just a mere disciple. I didn't make the rules, David. Breaking them would normally be my mandate, but this is unfortunately one instance where I'm required to go wherever the tide takes me." He returned his attention to the phone.

As it happens, the Anti-God wasn't randomly perusing his inbox.

His fellow trolls were keeping him apprised of *PaSword509's* ongoing exploits.

The string of migrant center bombings across the country was no accident.

Tag spent months subtly playing message board messiah in preparation for tonight's main event. His chosen acolyte lost his job as a parcel service delivery driver and his girlfriend to a Mexican man several months back. That villainous Carlos was born and raised in Carlsbad ultimately made little difference to either of them. Tag and Adam Patrick Willco were just looking for any excuse at that point.

Carlos and Adam's ex Mandy both caught a suppressed bullet through a pillow before Willco took to the road.

His cross-country tour had four previous stops since he started out in Spokane.

Phoenix. St. Louis. Columbus. Philadelphia.

Each had been the bomb, but he knew NYC was where you go to truly leave your mark.

Adam's new best friend *Overlord6669* had been impressing as much upon him for weeks in their online private chats. Dude was relentless with a capital R. Told him he'd have a blast in the big city. *"Go east, young man."* He could convince Adam to do anything.

Tag made him pour orange juice on his mini-wheats one morning just to make sure.

His marionette emptied the entire bowl on command.

Despite the combined efforts of both the Secret Service and the FBI, neither would ever be able to determine the identity of the *Overlord*. Other than the first name Matt, the man would forever remain a mystery.

It was like he came from another dimension.

On cue, an otherwise non-descript white panel van slowly crept by the bar's frontage.

The Anti-God designed that model by hand. He called it the *S-Car*.

It was built exclusively for spree bombers, serial killers, and sex offenders.

Tag knew Adam was behind the wheel of this iteration.

He could smell the odorless ammonium nitrate from a mile away.

Prior to becoming the man America would grow to know and loathe as *The Bronx Bomber*, unemployed Adam Willco served as a diehard devotee of the domestic terror organization *Patriot's Sword*.

The group possessed but a single member.

Adam was still desperately seeking his Southern Poverty Law Center designation.

His chosen insignia was an American flag drenched in red paint. The rationale was pure laziness more than anything. A tactile version would be found superglued to the driver's side interior paneling of the van. The brand also appeared on the cover and sign-off of the seventeen-hundred-page manifesto he mailed that morning to several different cable news outlets as a redundancy. Pity the poor interns who were forced to peruse that puzzle of racist nonsense. "*Obama was born on Mars.*" So on and so forth.

Across the van's ceiling Adam scrawled his company masthead in the same bloody ink he used to desecrate the American standard.

"*The tree of liberty must be refreshed from time to time with the blood of patriots and tyrants.*"

Thomas Jefferson was currently rolling over in his grave, and the black slaves who shared his bloodline were wondering where the hell he got off from two cemeteries over.

As the proposed finishing touch to his pentaptych, Tag suggested that Adam destroy the pinnacle of Latino-American prowess—

The New York Yankees.

As it happens, 161$^{st}$ Street was only two blocks away from their current location.

Curtain call was in twenty minutes. Tag ordered a double shot of straight gin to wet his whistle.

Since he was a sociopath.

The bottle looked like the disinfectant jar barbers use to sterilize their dirty combs.

He considered using psychokinesis to swap out the contents as a goof before realizing no one would be able to tell the difference.

His eyes briefly wandered to the Fox 5 newscast on one of the TVs hanging over the bar. It was exclusively Yankees and Indians in the top of the 8$^{th}$ on all the others. Steve was transitioning from the Creedmoor bombing to Nick for the weather. "*Explosive devices aside, Steve, what a lovely day to be by the water.*"

For a tip, Tag left Bobby the bartender a handwritten note outlining his exact cause and date of death. Motorcycle accident in six months. Despite the caution flag, the self-styled

Steve McQueen fanatic would fail to take heed. Following his downfall, Bobby's mother would find the quad-folded warning in his wallet while sorting through his belongings.

Her scream could be heard from a half mile away.

Tag sidled up between two fraternity brothers eyeballing drunk coeds on the dance floor and made his own recommendation. "The young lady in the red sweater at the end of the bar would be the most malleable, gentlemen. You have my word. Happy hunting." The stranger tapped each of them on the shoulder with a closed mouth smile and took his leave.

Both demon dogs identified the wild fowl marked by their master for retrieval.

Quentin the doorman was co-owner of a lucrative fentanyl kiosk. His partner Allan manned the pop-up shop from the second stall of the men's room. He skimmed their profit from the same location. In the last year the enterprise had been responsible for over a dozen overdoses throughout each of the five boroughs. Only three fatalities so far, but Tag could see a bright future for Q if he kept his head about him and lost some dead weight.

The Anti-God broke the news while inserting each arm into his gray herringbone overcoat. "An anonymous tip was placed against you and your associate last week. In thirty minutes, an undercover police officer wearing a *Karma Is My Boyfriend* T-shirt will enter the bar. Once Allan is arrested, he will rat you out to save himself." Tag pulled each lapel forward until the combined action caused his collar to rise in conjunction. "I recommend you relocate your business immediately. Any decisions beyond that regarding employee retention are entirely at your discretion. Have a good evening."

Quentin eyeballed the Anti-God from behind as he exited the establishment. After a few seconds, his vision shifted to the bathroom.

For a number of reasons.

Tag left without waiting to inform Kate of his whereabouts. He exhaled voluminous amounts of dirty cigarette smoke into the night sky despite the fact he never partook. Each anti-perfumed puff was as thick and polluted as the discharge from an ironworks smokestack. It helped offset the fresh fall air.

A newly appointed daddy shuffled past pushing his baby in a black Bugaboo stroller. The Anti-God pointed authoritatively toward the boy with his index finger extended. "You were right to be suspicious. He's Ian Pollack's child." The two adults locked eyes. "Little Henry was conceived the weekend you were in LA for business. Your wife and Mr. Pollack are working toward baby number two as we speak. He'll forget to lock his door on Wednesday night after she leaves his apartment. Take care."

The boy's father did a triple take back in Tag's direction as he proceeded down the block.

Poor blameless Henry would be left to grow up without a father.

Either of them.

Tag arrived just as Stacey was concluding her conversation with several expletives.

She continued staring at the black monolith in her hand in disbelief. "So, Braxton didn't take kindly to our position on pushing out anti-immigrant rhetoric to win a political election and promptly fired us. Fired me. Is there any difference at this point?"

Tag terminated her employment. He just made the words come out of Richard's mouth.

Same difference.

Without being prompted he gave her a hug.

Despite her dejection, she welcomed it.

"It's his loss, Stace." By its third usage, Tag had sufficiently broken down her defenses. The Anti-God admired her obstinacy. Normally his first effort would have been enough. He liked the nickname primarily because it enraged David each time he said it. The word off another's man tongue was an abusive epithet. "Braxton's a pig and a racist opportunist. You're better off."

"Thank you, but you're officially Darden Communications' only remaining client. I don't know how I'm going to keep the lights on." She looked away. For the first time, Tag saw Stacey close to tears. Under normal circumstances, an incoming B-52 couldn't break her resolve. The strongest woman alive had been felled. "I'd understand if you want to move in a different direction— and I'm not just talking about the campaign, either. I feel like such a failure right now."

"Stop, Stacey. That's nonsense. I won't have it." He broke free from the clinch and stood her up by the arms. "You've gotten one candidate all the way to the House of Representatives and you're working your way toward a second. Most people won't accomplish half of what you have by the end of their lives. You're only thirty-three, and you've already proven yourself to be a god amongst men and women. You have no idea what's in store for you. It's going to be earth-shattering." Tag knew a lie disguised as the truth could be more effective than the real thing.

Stacey sniffled and wiped, followed by a smile. "I appreciate you, kid." She laid one hand across his cheek to confirm as much. "I'm sorry, I'm not used to my significant other being this supportive. I thought a relationship was supposed to be a second job that I constantly wanted to quit. David conditioned me to think that way."

Her ex gave her a twin finger salute in response.

"We're in a relationship?" Tag grinned. He knew Stacey said it aloud the instant she realized it herself. No artifice. No games. That meant something. Even to the Anti-God.

"You know that we are. Of course we are."

They kissed for thirty seconds but for Stacey it felt like thirty minutes.

Time dilation was a common occurrence around Tag.

When Stacey finally came up for air, she was blissful.

"C'mon, Kate's going to be wondering where we went, and I need to get hammered. It's tequila time. No one stops until one of us has worms."

Her effort to pull him by the hand made it no further than the length of their two outstretched arms before he snapped her back to center like a Chinese finger trap. "Wait a second. I have a suggestion." More like a command.

"Oh, this should be good," she smirked. "What. What's your suggestion?"

He palmed both of her shoulders. "I'm already polling in third place with virtually no name recognition, and we're only in September. By Christmas, I'll be neck and neck with Jansen," Tag assured her. "I'm going to be the Democratic nominee for the 15th District, which means I'll be Congressman. With you running the show, it would be a given."

"Tag, we've talked about this," she said. "I have employees and other responsibilities. I can't dedicate all our time and attention to a single candidate. Even if it's what I want, I can't afford it."

"I'll pay you $25K per month, and I'll cover your employees' current salaries plus five percent. I'll also keep the lights on for Darden Communications. Whatever that entails. Spare no expense inside or outside your office. For the first time in your professional life, you get to take money off the table and do whatever you need to do to get your client across the finish line. People in your position would kill for an offer like this. You can't say no."

That was always a non-starter for Stacey. She leaned back to signal her discomfort with the proposition. "Tag, don't ever tell me what I can or can't do." Stacey was halfway to laughing when she said it, but she was dead serious.

"Fine. You don't *want* to say no. That's what I meant."

It wasn't what he meant.

"I don't want to be bought and paid for like some street

walker, either." She lightly removed his hands and then crossed her arms across her chest to reinforce the point. "Look, is this about me being the principal on your campaign, or being your property? Because I can be convinced regarding the former, but never the latter. And you need to know that going in."

"I want you in every way. But I'm also perfectly capable of separating business from pleasure." Tag massaged her elbow in further reassurance. "Our relationship will be kept completely separate from your role supervising the campaign. You have my word on it. As to the other, I understand better than most that you can't claim ownership over a god."

Stacey was still thinking things through with a widening smile when Kate's voice butted in from down the block. "Hey, both of you, get back inside the bar right now! Everyone's supposed to get off the street!" She was marching at the quick step to reach them.

Kate had never been legitimately concerned for another human being that didn't share her bloodline in her entire life. A stranger was striding toward Stacey. She understood implicitly that it must be something serious. "What? What the hell's going on?"

Chyrons came spilling out of her. "Someone called in an anonymous tip on the migrant bomber an hour ago. His name's Adam Willco. License plate CEX1100. One of those NYPD surveillance drones caught him doing circles around St. Mary's Park within the last hour, but he was gone by the time the cops showed. It's like he vanished. No one knows where he is now."

He didn't vanish. Tag just rendered him invisible for the time being.

Kate continued. "The whole city is about to be put on lockdown starting with the Bronx. Just like the Boston Bomber, remember?"

"Yeah, if the Boston Bomber was rolling around in a Timothy McVeigh-style star bomb," Stacey corrected her friend. "A van full of that ammonium nitrate shit could level Yankee Stadium."

Tag had to suppress his laughter. He didn't even have to coerce her to say it.

"Everyone is supposed to shelter in place until he's been apprehended. Listen."

Stacey and Tag were so deep in discussion she failed to note that every other sound was slowly snuffed out around them. She could hear a pin drop—which should not be possible in New York City. The lack of a soundscape and the abandoned streets in combination caused Stacey's skin to crawl. Instinctually, she looked over her shoulder to identify any potential danger on the horizon.

"Let's go, let's go, let's go." The way Kate held her hand out made it unclear who she wanted to reciprocate. Stace took the liberty, and the ladies began to stride back toward the bar in a human chain. When Stacey realized they left a man behind she put an immediate halt to their field trip formation and reached back to pick up the remaining straggler.

"Tag, what are you doing? Come on. We have to get inside." She jiggled her hand toward herself. It was insistence rather than invitation.

He began to play-act at patting down the pockets of his slacks and jacket. "I'm such an idiot. I left my key fob in the Wraith. I don't want anyone to steal the car." He took a few steps backward. "I'll be right behind you."

"Hurry." The ladies said it simultaneously. Stacey turned and eyed Kate with suspicion as she was dragged onward to their temporary safe haven.

Tag took the wrong corner to get to his car and walked another half block in the same direction before locating his prize. The Anti-God telepathically suggested Adam take a brief respite in the alleyway between Yankee Noodle Dandy and the Law Office of Neil S. Waller, Esq. (*¡Se Habla Espanol!*). Both businesses were closed for the evening, and the dense cloud cover left little in the way of moonlight to illuminate the space otherwise. Any inquiring minds out on the street would have to take several steps into the darkness and squint to make out the white van parked with its rear bumper against the opposing brick wall.

Mr. Willco left Washington with twenty-barrel bombs in total, but half their number had always been set aside for this special occasion. They were stacked in five-by-two formation against the passenger side of the vehicle with black rope netting bolted into all four corners to keep everything snug throughout the cross-country journey. With a few additional modifications helpfully suggested by his Overlord, the result formed a single connected ANFO explosive device. Detonation would follow two minutes after lighting the attached fuse.

Tag stepped into the alley and was almost immediately blinded by the light. Even through the glare, he could see Willco's left arm hanging out of the driver's side window with a .38 Special pointed at his head.

"Get out of here right now, asshole. I mean it." He cocked the hammer back as an auditory threat display. The rattlesnake wasn't bluffing. Adam flashed the brights twice to emphasize the urgency of his demand.

The Anti-God neither advanced nor retreated. Instead, he simply put his hands in the air. and smiled. "Adam, it's me. Message board Matt. You know—the Overlord!"

Although still skeptical, he gently thumbed the hammer back into its regular resting position. His arm deadened slightly without receding back into the van. "Matt? How in the hell did you find me here? This place is '*The Sprawl.*' There's no way." His thumb gently caressed the ridges of the spur as he contemplated the various law enforcement agencies that might employ an undercover asset like the Overlord.

Tag lowered his arms back down to his sides, save for the occasional excited gesticulation. "I've been watching you like a proud papa for weeks! And I live in the Bronx, so when you showed up in Queens yesterday, I knew that only left the big enchilada. Been walking around this place all day praying I might run into you, brother. Then ten minutes ago they showed your car on the news with the license plate number and everything, and I kid you not, at that exact moment you drove by the bar where I was having a drink." *A lie disguised as the truth.* "I'm telling you man, it's providence. I was meant to be by your side in the battle for America's soul. I'm ready to die for the cause. Let's kickstart this holy war!"

Adam was convinced. Subliminally, but still. He flicked off the headlights and then waved him forward with his gun hand. "Get in the van."

They exchanged smiling, perfunctory handshakes as a formal introduction. Adam became almost gleeful. "It's great to finally meet you *Lord of Light.*"

He was still testing Tag. "And you, *Lightbringer.*"

Despite being inhuman, the Anti-God satisfied the final verification step. Adam finally removed the gun from his lap and placed it in the map pocket of his driver's side door. He keyed the ignition and the van sputtered to rough, halting life. "Well, since you live in the Bronx, show me the sights. Take me out to the ballgame."

The normal getting-to-know-you palaver was replaced along the way with an Adderall and energy drink infused stream of consciousness recap of Adam's barrage across the heartland. The boy's bombastic boastfulness bored him to no end. Tag once had a fistfight with the Almighty, and it ended in a draw. He haunted the Holy Ghost just for the hell of it. In 1338, he spit into a cup at a bonfire in Kyrgyzstan and gave birth to The Black Death. Adam's killings were nothing more than empty calories to the Anti-God.

Tag began daydreaming about various mundanities he might find more entertaining than another five minutes of Mr.

Willco. Reading the Wikipedia entry for Wikipedia came to mind. Still, he made a point to smile and shake in affirmative acquiescence while they slowly circled the drain.

"'This is a call to arms," Adam announced to no one as they made their final approach down 161$^{st}$. Fans were already streaming out en masse. The NYPD demanded the game be called in the top of the ninth. While the police presence was clearly enhanced, traffic was still being allowed in and around the stadium. Nothing a rolling ANFO bomb couldn't easily break through. Tag figured right time and placement, you could take out five hundred people easy.

Adam continued his soliloquy. "No more politicking. We're going to take this country back starting tonight. From the beaners, and the blacks, and the Jews, and the matriarchy. One by one. They all need to be reminded who built this house in the first place. It was Babe Ruth. Not Benito Rodriguez. This is just the first shot across their bow."

"It's like Washington crossing the Delaware all over again," Tag offered in mockery masquerading as flattery. "White American males are going to worship you. Mets fans, too. Unfortunately, this is the final frame. In more ways than one."

"I know what you mean," Adam said while igniting the crimson-colored butane lighter in his cupholder. In one motion he reached behind the passenger seat to light the fuse. "But don't worry, we'll be remembered forever as true patriots. Martyrs to the cause. You and I, brother." Adam held his right hand aloft and Tag squeezed it briefly in reassurance.

"I can't tell you how appreciative I am of all the hard work and dedication you've shown over the past few months," the Anti-God added as he released his grip. Out of respect he turned in his seat to address Adam directly for the fiery finale. "I could not have asked for a better soul slave. Unfortunately, this is where we must part company. Would you hand me your gun, please?"

Willco let forth a laugh. "What?"

When he said it a second time it was no longer a request. His voice became Legion.

*"Give me your gun."*

While Tag awaited compliance, he grabbed the lit fuse with his left hand and stuck the sparking end directly into his mouth to snuff it out. The demon smacked his tongue against the roof of his mouth a few times once he finished. *"Mmmm. Fizzy."*

Adam's eyes almost exploded out of his head before the Anti-God had the opportunity to do it for him. He realized too late that he no longer had control over his own faculties. Willco mechanically rotated his head back to its starting position. His left hand involuntarily reached for the pistol and then passed it underneath the opposing arm as it continued to man the steering wheel. Tag made no effort to inhibit Adam's vocal cords. His unmitigated fear came through loud and clear. "What's happening to me?"

"Anti-martyrdom, young man." Tag double-checked the cylinder one last time and then returned it to firing position with a snap of the wrist. "You're going to involuntarily sacrifice something of little value due to your total lack of principle. A word of advice—stick with the other anti-matter Aryans once you reach the other side. There are billions of prisoners who will be praying to get a shot at you in the celestial showers. Goodbye, Adam."

Without a second thought, Tag positioned the handgun against his own right shoulder and pulled the trigger. Blood and viscera shot against the window and door paneling behind him like a drenched umbrella was just thrust open inside the van.

The Anti-God didn't even flinch.

Instead, he placed the revolver to the side of Adam's temple and lit the final fuse.

Screaming bystanders began to flee in each direction as the out-of-control van veered right toward them. The crimson window covers on each side made it impossible to see Tag lean forward into the driver' side and slam Willco's foot into the brake.

When it finally hit the curb at five mph, the Anti-God released the passenger side door handle and allowed himself to fall flat onto the concrete with a splat. His ride came to a rest on the sidewalk twenty feet later.

Tag briefly spread his arms and legs in a snow angel formation to stain the ground with as much of the red stuff as possible. It only took a few seconds for New York's finest to surround him on all sides at gunpoint.

"Freeze!"

"Stay down!"

"Don't you move a muscle, asshole!"

Officers applied restraining pressure to his forearms and shins with their shoes.

The Anti-God decided now was the time to speak. He feigned a low, raspy voice to sell the injury, even though he felt nothing at all. "I'm not the bomber. He's in the van. Is everyone okay? Please tell me everyone's okay."

Tag let his head fall to the left in simulated unconsciousness.

An eyewitness who saw nothing suddenly came to his aid. "That man's a hero. He shot the bomber. I saw it through the car window."

"Yeah," another random spectator added at Tag's behest. "He was struggling with the driver. If he hadn't stopped him, we'd all be dead."

Other onlookers began to similarly intercede on his behalf. Somehow, they all had a front row seat for his display of fearless bravery. The responding patrolmen began to take a more measured approach. Several of their number sped off to secure the true crime scene. A female officer leaned down onto one knee and gently held Tag's hand. She promised him everything was going to be okay, and to stay with her. The murmurs and outcries of the collective built to a crescendo that didn't dissipate until the gurney finally arrived.

Even with his eyes closed, the Anti-God could hear the thunderous clapping of thousands erupt out of the silence as he was hoisted into the back of the ambulance.

The villain lived long enough to finally see himself become a hero.

***

"This city owes you a debt of gratitude that can never be repaid, sir. Anyway, my wife and I are over in Belmont, so you definitely got our vote."

Detective DiNunzio shared a delicate laugh with Tag. Stacey joined in while clasping her boyfriend's hand from his hospital bedside. "We'll take it, Detective."

"I know how traumatizing the experience must have been for you, Mr. Gottfried, but if this Willco character had taken a different hostage, or no one at all, who knows? I mean, my nephew was at that game." DiNunzio shook his head. He looked like he was fighting back tears. "God wills these things sometimes, and we just need to pray and be thankful for his wisdom."

It certainly was a god that willed it.

Although she largely accepted Tag's narrative regarding the previous night's events, there was one sticking point that remained inexplicable to Stacey. "I don't understand how there isn't a single piece of surveillance footage. We've got over 15,000 cameras in the city. AI-assisted facial recognition. Surveillance drones. It's crazy. Have you ever heard of anything like that happening in this day and age?"

"Never," DiNunzio confirmed. "Hell, even the x-ray vans in the area went offline. The techs can't explain it. Last shot we have of Mr. Gottfried is with you and your friend over on 163rd Street, then it was like a domino effect hit the Domain Awareness System. Thirty minutes of cascading failure. Everything came back online after the crash. Trust me, IT is looking into it as we speak. Can't ever happen again."

Stacey's eyes briefly darted toward Tag, but not for long

enough to register with either man in the room. It wasn't suspicion, but intuition. Something was off— but grilling a gunshot victim twelve hours after the shooting seemed like bad form, so she let it go.

For now.

"Anyway, I think I got everything I need. I'm going to let you rest. I'm sorry again for having to bother you this morning." He held out his arm to Stacey with a card at the end. "My contact info if you need it for any reason. Just so you know, he's probably getting inundated over the next few days. Key to the city and whatnot. You're a lefty. Steinbrenner's going to expect you to throw out the first pitch as soon as you're upright again. Stiches be damned. I'd batten down the hatches if I were you two."

"He's my job, actually," Stacey verified for the detective with a smile. "Nothing I can't handle."

He shook his head as he put on his coat. "I don't know. You haven't been back out on the streets since last night. Tag Gottfried is the King of New York for the foreseeable future. Probably never going to have to reach for your wallet in this town again. You won't pay for another meal until the day you die. I'll be in touch soon. Take care."

They offered simultaneous goodbyes before returning their attention to one another.

Tag laid his head to rest against the pillow. He patted the space next to him. "Come here, please. You look like you haven't slept in a century."

"Thanks for the compliment. I'll chalk up your offensive charm to the sedatives." She grabbed his left hand with both of her own and began to lightly massage his wrist underneath the orange patient wristband. "I didn't sleep a second last night. I was waiting for you."

Their fingertips began to play the field, but they only had eyes for each other.

Stacey finally reached for her phone. She took it off Airplane Mode for the first time in hours. The subsequent vibration could have provided a decent back massage. "Jesus Christ. Everyone on the eastern seaboard is offering you their single-ply thoughts and prayers or begging for an interview. Sometimes in the same text message. Vultures. Ooh, Ellison Barber. I do like her, though." She tapped her fingers against her lower lip with a burgeoning smile as she continued boon scrolling.

Tag playfully rolled his eyes away from her. "I think you need to manage your expectations, Stace. This is New York City. They'll find a Flukeman living in the sewer system or something. The whole episode will be forgotten about by tomorrow."

She shot up as if on cue with all her teeth suddenly showing. Her breathless giggling could not be suppressed. "Oh, really?" Despite hospital protocol, she eased herself onto the bed next to Tag before hoisting the phone up in front of his face. "Take a look at the cover of this morning's *New York Post*, dummy."

Tag Gottfried's smiling candidate headshot was splashed across the welcome screen just below the red masthead. Bold lettering provided the accompanying headline—

**MR. SEPTEMBER**

Stacey's eyes shifted from Tag to Tag and back again. "Only three men in the history of this fair city have been bestowed with their own dedicated month, and the other two were Reggie Jackson and Derek Jeter. We're going to kick Kendrick Jansen's sorry ass from pillar to post. After that, hell, you could moonwalk the rest of the way to Washington D.C. November will be nothing."

"I'm sorry, I may be concussed," Tag kidded, "but, did you just say *we're* going to kick Jansen's ass?"

"Yes," she beamed. "This is me formally accepting your offer. It's Master-Blaster time. You're the big dumb lug I'm going to ride all the way to the top of Bartertown."

"Took me almost dying to get your name on the dotted

line," he added as a reminder. "But I guess beggars can't be choosers." A written instrument would ultimately be required given their professional relationship. For now, the oral agreement was sealed with a kiss.

Stacey broke away for a moment and put her head against his non-mangled shoulder. Even someone as brass balled as Ms. Darden occasionally lacked the cojones for eye contact. She rubbed the top of his knuckles as a stand-in. "When you're discharged, I want you to come home with me. I'll take care of you until you're back on your feet. I want to take care of you." Ms. Darden finally mustered the courage. "And when you're all better, I still don't want you to leave."

"Why? Why don't you want me to leave?"

She hesitated before answering. The tears welling in her eyes finally became too much to overcome. "Because I love you, dummy—and you can only get shot so many times."

"Is that another Mott Haven joke?"

"Yes. A terrible one," she sniffled. "I'm sorry."

"I thought it was kind of funny, actually. I love you, too."

David did the *Blair Witch* routine in the corner of the room for the entirety, but it didn't take. He felt nauseous even without a tangible digestive system.

Declaring an emergency would have been futile.

Their own words were warning enough.

This was not a test.

***

David decided to give them further privacy and pace the hallway. The love of his former life was in love with someone else. Even when conveyed through séance, it still stung. When Stacey took five to return a few calls, he reentered the room and found the Anti-God waiting upright in bed for him with a smile.

"I'm sorry if I gave you a scare last night, David."

"Yeah, my heart was all a flutter. The stress was almost too much to bear." He continued toward the window without even looking in Tag's direction. "We both know you can't die, so cut the shit. What are you up to?"

"Is all this animosity because we're going to be roomies moving forward? I can assure you, as long as you keep the seat up and remain silent during sex, I'm perfectly fine with this little *Three's Company* arrangement."

David kept his eyes glued outside. "I saw you."

"Yes, I'm aware you can see me, David. I haven't blinded you. Yet."

He glared at the Anti-God. "No. Not what I meant. I saw which direction you went, and it wasn't toward the car. You weren't kidnapped off the street. You went looking for Willco. Presumably because you already knew where he was going. You orchestrated all of it, including the dead bodies littering his path. Two little babies in Ohio. Then you killed off your own disciple for shits and giggles. Why?"

"Adam Willco wasn't some mere disciple. He was a Horseman."

"I'm sorry?"

"Oh, David, I'm so disappointed," Tag offered with a corresponding shake of the head. "I thought you were a fan of Revelations?"

"Can you just cut the bullshit?"

*"Another horse, fiery red, went out. And it was granted to the one who sat on it to take peace from the earth, and that people should kill one another; and there was given to him a great sword."*

Patriot's Sword. Blood red paint. Fertilized hellfire.

*Take peace. Kill one another.*

"Why did I do it, you ask? Civil War. Geopolitical instability. Global annihilation—and that's just for starters," the Anti-God continued. "But let's not get ahead of ourselves. Like any great politician, I have to get elected first before I can do real, everlasting damage."

"I'm going to stop you, you son of a—"

David didn't get the chance to finish his sentence. Instead, Tag simply raised his index finger and pinned him face-first into the ceiling with his arms and legs stretched out in a spread-eagle formation.

"I invented profanity, David—but I don't care to have it projected at me personally. You'll learn to watch your mouth, or I will solder it shut. And then nail a lead plate onto it for good measure."

The Anti-God nonchalantly flicked the same raised finger from the ceiling to the floor and David's body followed suit.

"How many fingers am I holding up now, David?" It was just the middle one.

"Four," he moaned.

Tag smiled and made a fist. "Thanks to Mr. Willco, the Second Seal has been broken. With each step I get closer and closer to Heaven, and then it's going to be Hell on Earth. I'm very much looking forward to seeing your new home. It's been ages since I was able to enter the fourth dimension."

David finally managed to hoist himself back onto his feet. "What are you talking about?"

"You're my interdimensional conduit, remember? The umbilical cord between the Lord of Pain and the afterlife. And as in all things, love is the key. Stacey just opened another door. She and I share everything now. Whenever your ex goes night night from this moment forward, you become my Bifröst bridge. Four dimensions down, David. Oh, here she is."

Tag made a sideways zipper motion with his left hand to silence David as Stacey reentered the room. The ghost desperately tried to jerk the metallic slider across his mouth to reopen the trap, but it wouldn't budge.

Stace laid down on the hospital cot next to Tag and slowly drifted off to sleep.

The Anti-God continued sneering at David until she was dead to the world.

***

The ghost awoke next to Torie in a cold sweat.

"Shit, shit, shit."

Her lazy smile made clear she was still a bit groggy. "Hey, you." She brought herself up onto one elbow and palmed his slimy cheek. "Jeez, babe. You're all clammy. What's wrong? What's going on?" The look on his face let her know it was serious, so she reciprocated.

"He's here. I can feel him."

"Who?"

Unbeknownst to both of them, the target of his ire was already busy thumbing through her purse downstairs.

Now the Anti-God had a name.

"Hello, Torie Eaton."

# THE HONEYMOON PHASE

"There it is folks. Hangar 18. Who's ready to have a close encounter?"

War Rig Wesley led their caravan, but the entire daytrip to Wright-Patterson Air Force Base was one hundred percent David's brainchild.

It had been a year since he and Torie made it official.

David wanted to do something special for their anniversary.

Tina was seated on the hood of her souped-up Sweet Tooth surveying their surroundings. The posted *High Voltage* warning caught her attention. "Should we check to see if the fence is still electrified?"

Darrell stepped forward without a second thought and grabbed the metallic diamond mesh with both hands. Following a bit of body buzzing and some brief sizzling, he regenerated five feet behind them.

"Yeah. It's still on," he confirmed.

Harley Mike wrinkled his nose in disgust. "Figures you'd smell like burnt bacon."

The pair turned and guffawed at one another in total silence.

"I could use my flamethrowers," Tina suggested.

She was dead serious.

"No, no, I got it." Wesley hoisted himself up into his

lumbering death machine and keyed the ignition. The beast belched to life and then stuttered forward a few feet before he hit the gas full throttle and took down the barricade in a sparking mess.

"Don't step on it or you'll probably die," Mike helpfully noted.

Tina dribbled her aqua blue and neon green accented FIFA Women's World Cup ball between the makeshift practice cones. It was less soccer than a life-size game of *Operation*. After squeezing through the defensive backfield, she built a head of steam and sliced the kick through the window of the unoccupied guardhouse. The loud splash of broken glass that followed caused her to veer left and airplane her arms without breaking stride. She glanced back at the adoring crowd as she soared along the concrete like a seagull.

"Goal!" Torie's scream came through loud and clear on the PA installed by Tina atop her ice cream truck. Ever the gentleman, David suggested the two ladies pair off prior to hitting the road so Tina wouldn't be forced to side-eye Amir for three hours straight. Turns out the men shared a love of EDM that the entire convoy got to enjoy for the duration of the trip. Amir's modified Police Interceptor possessed a speaker system that could be heard from Toledo.

*Fred again.. And again. And again. And again.*

Everyone golf clapped in unison as Tina took her victory lap around the perimeter. David had been making an extra effort to ingratiate himself with Torie's best friend, but the striker seemed to head off every attempt. Despite the ovation, her smile turned briefly sour the moment she locked eyes with the opposition.

It wasn't that Tina hated David.

She was in love with Torie, too.

That it would remain forever unrequited did nothing to extinguish her torch.

Meanwhile, Wesley was thinking ahead. Once the fence

had been laid to waste, he continued pushing his monstrosity on twenty-four wheels further into the facility until he smashed an informal entryway through the blast doors of the appropriate hangar. The Detroit Tiger stuck his baseball-capped head out the window and peered back at his fellow travelers. "We're open for business, boys and girls."

The five members of the group still standing outside the fence line began streaming into the base on foot. They picked up Tina and then moved together toward the final rendezvous point.

Wesley had already dismounted from the cab and made his way inside the facility by the time they passed through his makeshift entrance. The polymer floors were treated with resin that gave off a reflective sheen. Its color transitioned from sky blue to dull gray as they moved further away from the sunlit entrance.

Tina continued to keep it on a string. The effort caused a linoleum-style squeaking to emit from underfoot. She finally shoehorned the ball airborne and carried it the rest of the way under the crook of her elbow. Her attention diverted to the three vehicles parked to the right of the enclosure. "What kind of planes are those, Mike?"

"These bad boys are F-35Bs." He was gently caressing the landing gear of one while staring up at its undercarriage. "Vertical-landing capability—like a Harrier Jet. They're top of the line. First in our fleet."

Amir was not impressed. "*Bor-ing.* Where's all the spaceships and shit?"

"That stuff's all kept in the *Blue Room*," Torie confirmed. "It's an underground bunker. Supposedly. Start looking for stairs. Elevator would be grand."

She took the lead. Right where she belonged.

"Wright-Patterson is like a ghost town, by the way," Darrell said, "and I mean that in the non-4-D sense of the word. There's barely any hardware left here."

"Everything's been sent down to reinforce the Mexican border," Mike added.

"Hey, remember five years ago when the 'Mexican border' didn't also include the Gulf of Mexico," Wesley reminded everyone. "Fun times."

"Yeah, well, cruise ship flotillas full of climate refugees from the Caymans will tend to have an impact." Harley Mike was Fox News all day, even in the fourth dimension. "Last thing we need are more illegals spreading the *MARS* virus to actual citizens. We finally got it tamped down."

"I think you're forgetting that it's the *Massachusetts* Respiratory Syndrome," Darrell corrected. "We gave it to the migrants, not the other way around."

Those crazy kids over at the National Biocontainment Laboratory engaged in some questionable gain-of-function research involving Middle East Respiratory Syndrome. After years of hard work, they had been able to successfully weaponize MERS into an aerosol-based planet killer that dialed every symptom up to an eleven.

*MARS-CoV.*

On November 12ᵗʰ, 2027, a lab tech with the boring name of Brian Dennis Johnson would go down in infamy. Mr. Johnson coughed on a fellow fan at a Boston Celtics game after a long day at work and initiated a global pandemic. The baby name Brian was quickly rendered verboten.

No vaccine.

No treatment.

No MERS-C.

Quarantine and keep your fingers crossed became official government policy.

Let nature take its course with the rest.

Blue or Red, everyone understood that something was wrong with this world.

It was undeniable now.

"They're working the blockade up from Miami to Jacksonville," David added. "Shut down everything, including the supply chain. Things have gone completely sideways."

"Black market baby formula is a thing," Wesley offered in corroboration. "They removed tariff-rate quotas from processed sugar, then the supply drowned on the vine. It's 120 degrees in Omaha and Americans can't get Mountain Dew anymore. People are going to start killing each other in the streets over kids' birthday cakes. Watch."

"Meanwhile, the stock market is at an all-time high, and so is airplane ownership," Darrell added. "Yacht makers are also doing quite nicely. Wes is right. Can't even let them eat cake anymore."

Torie was waving them onward up ahead with Tina by her side. "If you dead men are all done with the political roundtable, I believe we've found our entry point."

The twin cylinders would normally be guarded by a bevy of armed military men ready to blow their heads off for even thinking about it. Admittance today was as simple as the push of a button. The plexiglass rotated as turnstile until adult size access was granted.

"Seem like pretty straightforward pneumatic tubes," Torie offered.

"Because we're invalid 85-year-old women in wheelchairs," Tina responded.

Torie tittered. "Daredevil, your idea. Seems only fair you do the honors."

David stepped forward into the breach without hesitation. He found the surrounding accommodations less than impressive. "I feel like I'm being deposited at the bank."

The rest took turns descending into chaos.

Floor-to-ceiling blast doors at the end of the basement hallway required a palm scan for entry which none of them would pass.

"Mike, you're the C-4 man," Torie said with a slap against his backpack strap. "Amir, help him. Hey, gentlemen, you two, can you grab those fire extinguishers off the wall and get ready to pounce, please. Thank you."

Five minutes and one barely contained fire later they were inside the Blue Room.

The interior space possessed four times the depth of the above-ground hangar. The left side was informally cordoned off to display Earth's most incredible used car lot.

"Holy shit," Amir stated with satisfaction. "That's a flying saucer."

"Forget the flying saucer." Wesley was jogging to the beat of his own drum with his arm pointed up at the vehicle in the adjoining space. The flawless white capsule was forty yards in length. "That's a giant Tic Tac. And it's floating." His finger shot toward the empty space between the object and the ground. "There's no landing gear. That's crazy." He stood in place admiring the wonder from another world with both hands on his hips.

When Mike placed his hand on the hula-hoop sized translucent orb in aisle three, it began to radiate flame-colored light from every pore. With a mere thought from its new operator, the ball of fire rose five feet further off the ground, then to the ceiling. Down to the end of the hangar and back. Repeat. With each pass, Mike somehow caught a glimpse of everything it was seeing simultaneously in his mind's eye. It was a sensation he never experienced before. He finally put it back in park then shut the engine down by placing his palm on the surface.

Tina stepped into *Die Glocke* in the next row and closed the giant bell back up with a resounding thud. A flash of blue light shot forth from within the metallic sarcophagus. She was suddenly standing right next to Torie. "Oh, wow. That thing's a freaking *BAMF!* machine."

Torie took off running to try it out for herself.

She was on top of the flying saucer five seconds later.

"I don't know how to get down, though, is the issue," Torie said to herself. Ms. Eaton bit the corner of her lower lip in brief contemplation. "Honey? Ladder please when you have a moment. Love you."

David scurried off to find the means to support his partner.

Tina followed behind to make sure he didn't screw it up somehow.

Darrell continued treading a middle path. The black triangle to his left stood on its end like an upright ace of spades. It was three stories, easy. He marveled at the majesty of the vehicles while keeping an eye on the miscellaneous tech to his right. Upon closer inspection he found the outlined nature of each device set forth on the tablet hanging in front of their respective enclosures.

*…1 g of vapor per cubic meter generates 10,000 gallons of clean drinking water…*

*…cancer is permanently eradicated within 10 minutes of exposure…*

*… light therapy can be calibrated to cease or reverse aging process…*

*…male and female subjects are each positioned inside of separate fertility Telepods. Fetal integration typically occurs within 30 seconds…*

His disbelief and anger rose in equal measure with each new astonishment.

It took almost half an hour, but David and Tina finally found a janitor's closet. Now they couldn't locate their girlfriend. He directed the question at the saucer itself. "Where'd Torie go?"

*Call and response.* A slithering walkway descended in slats at a forty-five-degree angle until it finally met the floor.

The pair put down the ladder for a moment and her boyfriend climbed aboard. Without any further invitation, the first step began to retract upward with each falling back in line underneath as it made its gradual ascent. He swiveled his head toward Tina in an attempt to apologize. The scowler was already rabbit-tapping her right heel with arms crossed against her chest. After a few seconds she located her ball and kicked rocks back toward The Bell.

No matter how many times she tried, it couldn't get her in the saucer.

After the fourth effort she left the door open just a smidge and cried.

Amir heard everything, but he never said anything.

The door blinked close behind David as soon as he was inside. He became instantly nauseous. The disk was thirty yards in diameter on the outside, but the interior looked as expansive as a football stadium. He counted twenty-five levels before he lost track in the inky darkness up above. The walkways forming an inverted T-junction in front of him appeared to stretch out each way into infinity.

"Torie?" He called out and hoped for the best. "Can you hear me?"

"Down here."

His girlfriend was sitting cross-legged on the floor of the space several stories below taking photos with her phone. She caught him with the flash, and he flinched. "Oh, that's a good one, babe. You're almost smiling."

"Thanks for that. I almost took a header off this thing. How do I get down there?"

She blinked and he was standing three feet next to her.

"How in the hell did you do that?"

An open composition book was in her lap. After a few more photos she placed the cellphone down on the metallic floor and began furiously scribbling.

"Hey lady, I asked you a question." As David approached, he could see she was modeling the interior with a stunning degree of artistic accuracy. "Wow, Da Vinci."

"Stop." She smacked his shin with her left hand without looking up.

"Tor, how did you get in here?"

"I asked the ship pretty please with sugar on top, and it phased me inside like a champ," she tapped the floor twice in appreciation. "*Rama* here's mind-melded with me or something. We've become full on besties. I could take us to a galaxy far, far away right now if you want to go." She flitted her eyes at him in mock invitation.

"I'll pass until you've put a little more time in this thing. Anyway, that was half an hour ago. What have you been doing in here?"

"Stop. I've been in here maybe five minutes. Tops."

"Nah-uh."

"Uh-huh."

He depocketed his own phone to double-check before pushing it in front of her face. "Read it and weep, sucker. Actually, it's been more like an hour now."

Torie's eyes widened. "Would you look at that? I think we're time traveling into the future as we speak. Spooky." The way she said it made clear she wasn't scared in the slightest.

"It is amazing inside of here," David confirmed. "It distorts time *and* space."

"I know, right? It doesn't technically fit with my overarching theme, but I figure being the first author in history to interpret extradimensional architecture gives me license to deviate for one chapter."

"Have you thought about a title yet?"

She began captioning her artwork. "Yeah, actually. I'm leaning toward, '*Oh, The Places You'll Go—Part II.*' It'll be the best sequel since *Aliens*. Bet."

He slowly lowered himself into a seated position next to her. "I think you'd get sued by the family of Theodore Geisel."

"Technically, the cease-and-desist would be coming from Dr. Seuss Enterprises," she corrected. "Believe it or not, Geisel never had any children." Torie kept her eyes grafted onto the contents of her notebook.

David was in disbelief. "Shut up. You're telling me Dr. Seuss never had kids?"

"Yeah, I couldn't believe it the first time I found out either," she added. "It was like someone telling me Henry Ford never drove a car his entire life. No, I guess Ted's only goal was entertaining the kiddoes, and I'd say he passed that test with flying colors. Instead of three children at home, he had three billion all over the world."

"Any reason you went down that particular Internet rabbit hole?"

"I was researching childlessness. It's like him and Oprah, pretty much."

"Yeah, plus Amelia Earhart. Susan B. Anthony. Jane Austen. Frida Kahlo, Rosa Parks, Virginia Woolfe." He could have continued.

"Alright, alright. Jesus Christ, honey," Torie said with a smirk. "Someone had to write a term paper in their gender studies class back in college."

"I got an A in that, too."

"Well, that semester was worth the $15,000 then, wasn't it?"

He was still smiling, but without any teeth. "Why were you researching childlessness?"

She paused until it passed pronounced. "I was pregnant."

"What?"

Torie snapped the comp book closed and turned her head to lock eyes with David. "I was pregnant when I overdosed. I didn't know that at the time. Just to be clear. I missed my period by almost three weeks, but I was too stoned at that point to notice. Probably wouldn't have even realized I was with child until I was giving birth in a public bathroom." She was disgusted with herself, and it showed. "I'm sorry I never told you until now."

"Don't apologize to me for that," David insisted. "How did you find out?"

"Kim broke the news to me when I first got here. I don't even know who the father was. It was any port in the storm at that point. Every guy's got some cash and a medicine cabinet." Torie stared off into space.

"You wanted the baby, though." David knew it wasn't a question.

"Even though I didn't deserve to be its mother," Torie stipulated, "yes. I would very much have wanted to keep the baby. I would have quit using that day if I knew. That second. Even if it killed me. I could have been good at it. I would have been. I know it."

When Torie tried to put her left hand up as a blocking mechanism, David grabbed it instead. "You would have been an amazing mother. But there are other ways to have children in your life. There are other ways to live, period. Even in death. You're doing it now. Billions of mothers in this world, and none of them will ever step foot inside of a flying saucer. Willingly, anyway. You've already outdone Amelia Earhart by a country mile."

She sniffled a bit, but she was already feeling better. "You're the best boyfriend I've ever had, David Downey—and I know how shit you used to be at the job, so I'm very appreciative of all the hard work you've put in to change your trifling ass ways."

"Yeah, I can definitely think of one person who would offer a different appraisal."

"Since we're sharing, it's your turn to spill some tea. You never told me how things ended with Stacey."

In light of what Torie just offered up, David's issues seemed comparatively slight. "She asked me to go to Coachella. We were on a break at the time. That's what I thought, anyway. I was lying next to her when she told me she was seeing someone else—and had been for quite some time, apparently. I still remember her claiming she'd die if anything ever happened to me. Then she wound up trying to kill me herself."

"Wow. That's messed up. On a number of different levels," Torie squirmed side to side as she said it. "Stacey was free to do whatever she wanted with her life, but she's way too smart to be that stupid. Either you have that talk before you go out to California, or you don't go. There actually isn't a third option."

"It was punishment," he acknowledged. "And I'm not saying I didn't deserve to be sentenced, but what she imposed was stiff. Extradited my sorry ass across the country so I would have nowhere else to run. I had to sit there and wallow in that hot, shitty jail with her and her closest friends. She humiliated me in front of 200,000 hipsters. It was like a non-stop whisper campaign against me the entire weekend. Seemed like every person in Indio was laughing at me. I've never felt so worthless in all my life—and I grew up a Downey."

Torie took the opportunity to provide her own aid and comfort. "I'm sorry she made you feel insignificant, but her assessment sucked."

"By the end it didn't matter. It wasn't about what I could give her. She just didn't want to look at my face anymore. I don't care who you are. That hurts."

"I love your face more than anything." Torie kissed his ugly mug to confirm.

"Same."

"Hey, maybe if we practice enough, we can have a ghost baby or something." She was smiling, but also completely serious. "I'm willing to put in the work. There's no explicit rule against it. I guess the odds of success are like one in ten trillion, but so what? Let's beat the casino."

"Might be tricky tracking down an OB/GYN on this side of things."

"We'll cross that bridge. Make love to me." She whispered it in his ear even though no one else was around. "I know it's not perfect timing, but there probably never was going to be a perfect time when it came to spaceship sex. Neil and Buzz, right?"

"I think you might be expanding the parameters of their relationship just a bit to fit your ongoing narrative."

"Hey, you have no idea what they were doing inside that lunar module." She rose and began to disrobe. "In any event, you're about to achieve liftoff the likes of which those boys never dreamed. You do have to be on the bottom though, cowboy. Sorry." She placed her folded jeans down as an excuse for a mattress.

David shifted himself over a few feet until his tailbone

wasn't directly grinding into unbreakable metallic alloy. He removed his heathered blue Michigan T-shirt and then held out his arms in invitation. "Come here please before I lose my nerve."

When she saw what he had in store for her, she stripped down the rest of the way and climbed on top of him. "As long as you don't lose the other thing."

They didn't speak again for hours.

***

Torie and David descended to the sound of clapping from everyone save Tina. Wesley threw in a couple catcalls for good measure.

Darrell was ever the comedian. He stared down at the non-existent watch on his wrist and then finally exhaled with a *phew*. "Six hours. Well done, David."

"Tina kicked her ball at the thing at one point to try and get your attention," Amir added, "but it started to glow red. We assumed that was a warning of some kind and decided to leave it be."

"If you two are all done depleting bodily fluids," the soccer star snarked as sharply as possible, "we were about to do the honors on the mystery box over there."

The twelve-by-twelve cube was matte black save the permanent white palm print that had been fingerpainted on the side to assist with entry.

Wesley pointed at the cave art once the rest of the group had it surrounded. "This is like the *Try Me* button on a *Tickle Me Elmo*. It calls to me. I can't not press it."

"Yeah, it could be that, or a detonator," Mike offered in the alternative. He was currently holding a kazoo that caused Havana Syndrome when you hummed into it. Darrell and Amir found out the hard way. Dried blood stemming out of each ear canal told the tale.

The words of caution weren't enough to dissuade Wes. He pressed his hand flat against the surface just like the instructions said and the cube split open in response. The two pieces bifurcated until the raised bridge within became visible. A strip of chain mail dropped down with a square at its end. The entire process screamed invitation into the unknown.

"Who wants to harness up first?"

"May I ask what in the everlasting hell you humans think you're doing?"

All seven spun around and collectively gasped at the eight-foot-tall Grey alien pointing a ray gun at them. The barrel was a churning kaleidoscope of rainbow colors.

"You're not supposed to be down here. If any of you even think about stepping inside that Fabricator, I will be forced to erase you from existence. You, Hair-Face. Close the box. And put that War Whistle back where you found it."

Harley Mike and his handlebars did as they were told on both counts.

"I would say playtime is just about over for today. Everyone upstairs. Right now."

***

"The only reason you're not being abducted as we speak is because you're already dead."

Once they reached topside, their gigantic jailer instructed them to take a seat in a half circle on the tarmac outside of Hangar 18 like a bunch of grade schoolers. He paced back and forth in front of them with his weapon held to the side. Its lack of color suggested the safety had thankfully been enabled at some point.

All of them continued to stare back at the creature with open mouths and furrowed brows.

Their leader finally decided to interject. *"I'm Torie. And you are?"* The words were spoken with a tentative, halting cadence. She tapped her chest, then held her upturned palms out in front of her body as an ASL equivalent.

"What the hell are you doing with your hands right now?" The alien stopped dead in his tracks. He fidgeted his lidless line of sight back and forth between the outstretched appendages and her eyes. "Do I look like a member of the Navajo Nation to you? I speak over 5,000 languages with fluency, and my English is better than yours. Don't treat me like I'm Nell."

"Wow, that's a reference." Mike nodded in approval.

"Yes, I was required to mind-sync with your entire pop culture catalogue before I took up this posting. And for whatever difference it makes, my name as translated would be Daphne."

Torie sought further clarification. "Oh, so you're a woman?"

"No." His tone made clear he was slightly insulted. "Daphne is a man's name."

All five of the human men snickered to some variable degree.

Amir had the temerity to say it. "On what planet?"

"My husband and I are actually between galaxies at the moment. Habitat hunting is becoming such a chore. Whatever nebula we look at, it's never big enough for him."

"Wait," Darrell said, "you're telling me you're a gay alien, on top of it?"

"No. I'm not gay. I only have intercourse with members of the same gender."

Darrell possessed a wealth of prior experience. "That means you're gay."

"Not where I come from."

Torie leaned over to David and whispered into his ear while Daphne was distracted. *"Leonardo DiCaprio would be like Liberace on his planet."*

David cackled hard enough in response it drew a swift rebuke from the instructor.

"Something funny you two would like to share with everyone?"

Torie and David's expressions both went dead as their heads shifted down. "No, sir."

"Good. Now listen up, mouth breathers. This is the first and last time you will be making an appearance at this base." Daphne insisted as much with his air rifle crossed against his chest. "I let you have your little fun with our paper airplanes and whatnot, but if I see you again, 4-D or not, I will exterminate you. My only job is to make sure you human blood-dopes don't accidentally blow a hole in the universe with anything found in the Blue Room. Regardless of dimension. You're screwing with my retirement, and I won't have it."

"One hundred percent, sir, we read you loud and clear," Torie confirmed.

Mike did have one point of order. "What about the barbecue?"

David was working on being more assertive and confident. Torie smiled at him in appreciation as he spoke. "Sir, if we agree to get lost in a couple hours, would you mind if we had a cookout before heading back? It was kind of a pre-planned party."

"We're all starving," Wesley said.

"I'll make sure everyone stays clear of the Blue Room," Torie added.

*Please Please Please* came rushing out from all sides like they were on the playground.

"Fine." Daphne played the role of father in the front seat. "But do not go near the hangar. If you're not gone in two hours, I start taking target practice."

Low whoops of joy erupted from the group as they began to rise. Torie took the initiative.

"Everyone say thank you to our host, Daphne."

"Thank you, Daphne!"

Darrell continued to be intrigued. "Hey, why don't you join us? Plenty of food."

"I'm no longer required to eat," Daphne verified, "but if you brought tequila, I could be persuaded."

***

After sunset, the group huddled around a makeshift bonfire. The wafting remnant smell of hot dogs and hamburger meat would hang in the air long after they vacated the premises. Their extradimensional host was three sheets to the wind. Given his body mass, it only required two shots. He held court for the captivated humans currently in his drunken thrall.

"My kind are no longer corporeal. This is just a shell. I've cycled through thousands of them at this point. In any event, materiality is nothing but mentality. I can phase myself into or out of this dimension at will with nothing more than a thought. Watch."

The slender god went *BAMF!* without The Bell. When he called out, the group turned and found him doing the stilted dance of a stick insect on top of Wesley's War Rig.

"This is how I got my husband into bed the first night."

He popped back over without a poof.

Mike held a freshly opened beer aloft for Daphne. "All yours, pal."

"Is that an IPA?"

"Yeah."

"I'd rather drink my own piss."

"Speaking of which." Darrell bounded off into the darkness to take care of business.

David let out a prepubescent yawn that forced his arm to temporarily relinquish its position across Torie's shoulders.

"Oh, baby, are you ready to go night night?" She was teasing while simultaneously pulling him back over to her.

"I bet he is tired," Daphne corroborated. "He just had an orgasm for thirty-eight straight minutes. Time dilation fornication is something else. Why do you think we built flying saucers in the first place? They're our most advanced sex toys."

"Wait wait wait," Wesley stuttered. "Flying saucers aren't meant for flying?"

"Not in the way you mean. Discovering they were capable of interstellar travel was a total accident. The first time it ever occurred, it was caused by a climax. Every great intellectual advancement by our species was made with an eye toward either getting off or getting away. As it turns out, the two are often interrelated."

Mike remained an engineer by trade, even in the afterlife. "Can I ask how a non-physical entity creates a physical object like a flying saucer? Or yourself, for that matter?"

"It's really not that complicated."

It was extremely complicated.

Daphne put up his four-fingered hands like they could accurately diagram what followed. "Using nanofabrication, we artificially generate atomic layer upon atomic layer. All of it coated in durable nano-texturing and quantum entanglement properties. And, of course, everything is powered by the polarizable vacuum."

"Of course," Wesley said.

Tina made a *pfft* sound. "What else would you use?"

"Indeed. It's the same method used by all 10th Level crypto terrestrials. You see, everything tangible has a corresponding sound vibration." He made a tuning fork materialize in his hand as a point of illustration. "We manufacture our materials by crafting resonant frequencies. That vibrational blueprint interacts with the substrate of your physical universe. It pulls atoms and molecules into existence from other dimensions, which then organize and condense into the structure of the object we mean to create. In this way, our materials are simply manifested into being. It's a sort of a trans-dimensional equivalent of your 3-D printers. The closest human analogue would be something you refer to as magic."

"It sounds kind of like the Replicator on *Star Trek*."

"That is the equivalent of a Speak-and-Spell for us. We give them to the runts of the litter as learning tools. A Fabricator would be the apex of our technology. It's a Chocolate Factory for the mind. A device that gives physical manifestation to thought. Are you familiar with Atlantis?"

"You're telling us Atlantis wasn't a myth?" Amir was at the edge of his seat, even though he was standing up.

"Oh, it was very real," Daphne affirmed. "Even across billions of years and thousands of cyclical extinctions, Atlantis was the most evolved of all Earth-based human civilizations. Along with the Mennonites. Atlanteans developed sixth-sense superiority *and* telepathic supremacy. Females of the species were born with ankle wings. They achieved a level of transcendence you might refer to as '*God Mode.*' Then, eight hundred million years ago, it all went to shit."

Torie took the lead once again. "What happened?"

"We thought they were ready for divine enlightenment, so we gifted them with a Fabricator as a final step. *Big mistake.* Their first instinct was to construct a protective wall around At-lantis. Instead, they created a continent-sized cookie cutter."

"That explains why it sunk," Tina said.

"It didn't sink," Daphne clarified. "It detached from this plane of existence and fell into the Under Dimension. We've sent probes. Atlantean screaming has a very specific sound signature."

Wesley and Amir commenced to tossing firecrackers and roman candles at a minimum safe distance for the duration of the group's discussion.

Tina was a cynic by trade, and being lovelorn on top of it didn't help matters. "Not that I'm complaining, but I don't get why you let mankind possess access to that level of technology. Wouldn't wiping us off the map be the simpler solution?"

Daphne lurched toward her. Tina's natural instinct was to recoil given his size and alien nature. "Do you go around kicking toddlers in the teeth? Pushing blind kids into oncoming traffic? What would be the point of that endeavor? You imbeciles are still utilizing propulsion."

His subsequent laugher had a *Predator*-style death pitch. It went on for far too long. The humans started looking around at one another. Daphne put a drunk hand out onto Darrell's shoulder for temporary support.

"*Propulsion.* I apologize." He continued ki-ki-ki-ing for a few more seconds. "Regardless, we do keep an eye on you children. Your moon was colonized millennia ago. We've had cities on the dark side of the thing for centuries and you're all completely clueless. Saying you are bugs to us would be an insult to ant farms everywhere. Humanity is nothing more than a hair follicle. We can shave you off any time we feel like. Point of fact, the universe tends to prefer hairlessness." He slid his hands down his own body in a manner that was borderline lascivious.

Torie was offended by both the insinuation and his hand movements. "If we're so unimportant, then why did you set up shop on the lunar surface to monitor us in perpetuity? Those principles would seem to operate at cross purposes."

"Believe me, it wasn't by choice. Your moon was initially just a simple observation outpost and nothing more." He highlighted the location of the underground facility on the gray circle hanging overhead with a glowing ET finger. "We have billions of them. Unfortunately, your species declared intergalactic war. Now we must serve as your permanent bodyguard, or your planet will be annihilated."

David joined the discussion. "Sorry, when did humanity declare intergalactic war?"

Daphne drew an invisible rectangle in the air above his right shoulder that began to visually project his narration for the rapt audience. "In 1962, you conducted a nuclear test in outer space codenamed *Starfish Prime*. It was actually a targeted EMP blast. America intentionally took down a Vazzen-Ra mothership on a peacekeeping mission just to steal its tech."

Harley Mike began to shake his head. "That's messed up."

"You're telling me. V-Rs are three feet tall," Daphne demonstrated with one downturned hand, "and they coo like babies to communicate. You might as well have napalmed a children's hospital. The disgust stretched across the cosmos. Homo sapiens became the Kim Jong Un of the interstellar community." When he closed his fingers into a fist, the overhead screen disappeared back into the ether.

"I think we're all uniformly sorry that our country blew the Close Encounters kids out of the sky," Torie said while surveying the other members for visual confirmation, "but it's not fair to hold all of humanity eternally responsible for the sins of our fathers."

"A not insignificant portion of you dolts decided to be Christians. That's literally one of your bedrock principles," Daphne reminded them. "If you have multiple babies, you don't get to return the one you don't like at Target if it turns out to be Ted Bundy. Jesus Christ consecrated the entire planet from his cave. Now you're all onboard the Ark together."

Amir was in his late 20s. A potential apocalypse was pretty much the only thing that didn't distract him. "Did we at least get some sweet gear?"

"Your first fiber-optic data transmission system," Daphne confirmed for the crowd. "I hope it was worth it, because now you've got several galaxies wanting to crawl inside your rectum and hibernate there for the nuclear winter. The first twenty years of MTV is really the only worthwhile benefit you accrued from the discovery. Since then, your most consequential advancements utilizing the technology have been telemarketing and deepfake revenge porn."

Mike caught the tail end of America's cosmic fad. "NASA did require security clearance if you handled a fiber-optic camera—but not a spacesuit. That always seemed strange to me. I can certainly tell you which one carried more weight to the astronaut."

David decided to take this one and only opportunity. "Hey, seeing as how you're nigh omniscient, let me ask you a question. I'm currently ghost-shackled to my ex-girlfriend the Soul Succubus. Do you happen to have any advice on how I might go about extricating myself?"

Torie pretended like she didn't care by turning her head to observe the fireworks.

"Get her to say, '*I release you,*'" the alien offered.

"Yeah, I mucked that up already. Anything I might do in the alternative?"

"It's a pretty hard and fast doctrine, but I wouldn't fret too much. A Soul Succubus is fairly harmless these days. I remember when a Jinni could do a lot more damage. The unceasing psychological torture of human beings provided their primary power source."

"Bobby Kennedy implied there might be a sexual component as well."

"As though the two aren't inextricably linked," Daphne said.

"Anyway, I regret to inform you, but I don't think much has changed in the intervening centuries," David informed his alien interlocutor. "My ex is so strong with the force she's someone called the Lord of Pain, and lord knows, she lived up to the billing."

Daphne did a spit take, even though it wasn't IPA. David was forced to wipe the Belgian Tripel off his face with own T-shirt. The alien posed an urgent question. "I'm sorry, what did you say she's called?"

David was still wiping. "The Lord of Pain."

"Where did you hear that? Who told you that?"

"Her boyfriend Tag told me. Apparently, he's the Anti-God."

Daphne was outraged. It was just difficult to decipher given his lack of facial mobility. "Her boyfriend is the Anti-God, and you didn't think to lead with that? Like I give a shit about your domestic foibles. Damnit. Now I'm going to have to write a report. It'll take me ages." He resumed his previous pacing. The prospect of paperwork seemed to outweigh the importance of earthly Armageddon in the alien's mind.

"We're sorry," Torie stated on their behalf, "but to be fair to David, he's been banging this drum for a little bit. We're the ones who've been in disbelief."

"You should have taken your boyfriend more seriously," Daphne admonished her. "In combination, the Anti-God and the Lord of Pain are the PB&J of obliteration. Let me ask— has he been wounded by a sword of some kind yet?"

"Some crazy immigrant killer named Adam Willco tried to

off him," David verified. "Called his group *Patriot's Sword*. Tag's been using it as political jet fuel ever since. He's about to be voted into Congress next month."

"Then it has already begun," the alien certified with a solemn shake of the head. "The Beast arose out of the sea of anti-matter, and she will serve as his false prophet. That is Revelation."

Wesley was impressed. "Did you have to attend divinity school as well?"

"No. We wrote your Bible. We wrote all the Bibles."

The group took a moment to allow the disclosure to wash over them.

"Everything makes sense now," Daphne continued. "Famine. Inflation. Scarcity in the midst of prosperity. Do you see any rich people failing to get richer?"

They collectively shook their heads.

"He has successfully set the table. He can enter your realm, but he has no dominion beyond it until the third seal has been removed in its entirety." Daphne's back and forth stroll now added a Steve Jobs-style thumb and forefinger to the chin in combination. "A human life would have been required to break open the second. It will have to be balanced now with its oppositional number. An anti-life. A ghost, for example." The alien slowly scanned the group left to right.

The seven of them took turns looking at one another with growing trepidation.

Given her professional background, Torie began performing inventory management. "If there are seven seals, and he's already two down with seven dimensions to go, won't that leave him coming up a couple points short?"

The other members started doing mental math using their fingers as an abacus.

"Once all the seals have been broken, two specific sacrifices will be required to close the loop," Daphne verified. "An angel—and its antithesis. The Lord of Pain, to be more precise. That is the only way for him to ascend through the last two dimensions.

The blood of your ex-girlfriend will open the final gateway to Heaven."

The recognition hit David like a ton of bricks. He had to close his eyes to withstand the onslaught. "He's going to kill Stacey."

The way he said it made Torie stare at him.

"That's right. The Anti-God is the ultimate cordyceps parasite, and your ex is in his death grip now. She will be slowly bled out on the interdimensional altar. Each rung up the ladder will weaken her a bit more. When she's no longer of any use to him, her life force will provide him with the final portal to the eleventh dimension."

Wesley had a thought. "David, didn't Tag say that you're the connective tissue between his missus and the afterlife?"

"Yes, that's correct," Daphne interjected, "the soul slave of the succubus serves in that role pursuant to prophecy. Perhaps it would be wise to take care of the problem right now." The ray gun made a sudden reappearance in his arms.

"Wait a second. Don't dissolve David. I think there's a more sensible solution," Tina offered with far too much excitement in her voice. "If he's in Heaven, then Tag is up shit's creek. He can do his worst, it won't matter. The chain of custody will be irrevocably broken. Yes?"

"In theory," Daphne grudgingly acknowledged.

"So, we just get Stacey to release David, and everyone's home free." Tina smiled at the recognition until she locked eyes with Torie and realized it was a bridge too far. Ashamed, she straightened her face and then let it fall back to Earth.

"That's all fine and good," David said while Torie internally disagreed, "but you're forgetting that I don't have enough juice to hop inside another human body yet. And even if I did, I can't just leave Stace to fend for herself. Once I'm out of the picture, he might suck the soul out of her just for spite. He's got her snowed. She's not going to listen to a word I have to say about Tag. I'll just be the jealous ex."

"You should learn to use shells like we do," Daphne slurred while smacking his own sternum. "Flesh and blood is so three-dimensional."

The entire group turned their heads toward the alien.

Daphne burped before continuing. "What? Why are you all looking at me like that?"

"You wouldn't happen to be able to fabricate a human body," Darrell asked, "would you handsome? Like a David Downey body, for example."

"Actually, it's quite easy. How do you think we walk amongst you on a day-to-day basis? Your physiology is remarkably unsophisticated. It's very similar to a tapeworm." Daphne began to eyeball both Darrell and David with suspicion. "Why?"

"Well, you don't want to have to spend the next few months tele-typing, and we don't want the world to end," Darrell continued. "So, let's scratch each other's backs. I think I have a plan. Maybe we can find a way to free you both up at the same time."

***

"I'm just disappointed I wasn't able to find a jetpack," Torie lamented.

"I know, honey." David rocked her back and forth in both arms. "I'll keep looking."

The group assembled most of their belongings and were preparing to bid adieu to their new alien friend when he overheard the couple.

Daphne raised his spindly arm aloft until an anti-gravity backpack appeared in his hand. "This is a miniaturized version of an Alcubierre warp drive. It creates a configurable energy-density field lower than that of vacuum. Riding the wave allows you to travel faster than the speed of light. We use it mainly to repair wormholes. Assuming you don't die, you'll have half an hour before it dematerializes."

"Oh my God, thank you thank you thank you," she said as she bum-rushed the colossus with a gargantuan hug. "Can I get a Rocketeer helmet, too?!?"

The thin black strip on Daphne's face curled into something approaching a smile. "You're pushing your luck, lady," he informed her before conjuring the requested headgear and handing it off to her as well. "The clock is ticking. I suggest you take to the air."

The other group members ceased all activity and assembled on the hoods of their respective vehicles. Harley Mike simply sat astride his hog to watch the unfolding air show.

Daphne assisted David in safely harnessing his lady love, then activated the pack using telekinesis. He mentally toggled the power level down to 0.0001% to keep her from winding up on Pluto. "You're all ready for lift-off."

"Where are the controls?" Her muffled voice barely came through the golden dome.

The alien gently tapped Torie twice on her hollow noggin. "This is your control."

Her chuckling ricocheted against the inside of the helmet and echoed back out. "This is going to be so freaking rad."

David grabbed her gently by the elbows. "I know you'll just repopulate in the event of your death, but please try not to get yourself killed."

"Thanks, Romeo," she responded with a light punch in the bicep. "In the words of the great poet, *I can't say that I'll try, but I'll try to try.* Play your cards right and maybe for the finale I'll fly you around in my arms like Lois Lane."

"A boy can dream," he said before kissing her ice-cold forehead. He smacked her lightly on both shoulders then took a step back. "Have fun."

The gang all hooted and hollered as the eagle soared through the air. An anti-gravity warp bubble surrounded Torie for the duration of her aeronautical adventure. It allowed her arms to serve as sturdy control surfaces throughout the flight. Light rays naturally deflected off the projectile, so Daphne remotely adjusted her brightness for the audience's viewing pleasure.

The cross-shaped phoenix shot across the starry sky like a golden rocket.

No one could see the stupid grin plastered across her face.

Torie was traveling at *Mach Jesus—The Speed of Christ*.

***

Harley Mike led the way back up I-75. He tossed the occasional lit Black Cat behind him onto the motorway without looking back. The other specters laughed and swerved in response. A thick canopy of clouds descended overhead without any warning and left them with no moonlight. The headlamps and fireworks were the only illumination for miles.

Torie was still self-addressing in Xanadu. Given the possibility of David pulling a disappearing act, they decided it best she take the wheel for the return journey. "Sex in the spaceship was number one with a bullet, but any other day of my life taking anti-gravity flight would have got the gold for sure. It damn near hit the G spot."

They were both giggling. David's seat was in sleep position, but he was wide awake. "When I get back tomorrow, let's have a date night. Just you and me. I'd like the opportunity to finish the job." He gently smoothed his fingers across her thigh without being flagrant about it.

"That can be arranged," she sighed with a smile. "I don't know, though. Today's going to be hard to top. It was the best day of my life, and I'm not even alive."

Their attention was diverted toward the slowing column of red lights.

David pulled his seat into the upright position when he spotted the issue. "What's going on? Why is everyone stopping?"

"I don't know. Wait a second," Torie said before slamming the brakes. Intuition told her to keep her distance. "Oh my God. Look out your window. What the hell is all that?" She pointed diagonally to assist David.

Broadsheets of black shale shifted over top of one another in layers across the prairie. A tsunami wave stretched all the way to the horizon. Its body was engorged with charcoal-shaded silt churned up from the deepest ocean trench. The shadowy mass spread free and easy in every direction like syrup squeezed through the bottle spout onto a marble countertop. Any trees in the path of the leviathan were mowed down and swallowed whole underneath. Soon the sky and the moon were all that remained standing over an ocean of enveloping ink.

The sea of anti-tranquility continued growing bigger.

*Harder. Better. Faster. Stronger.*

Torie turned down the Daft Punk.

"We're in Ohio. Where is all that water coming from?"

"It's not water," David muttered. He pushed his thumb and forefinger apart against the cell phone glass to get a closer look. "They're horses. Black horses."

"That can't be, there'd have to be—"

"Thousands of them," he confirmed. "Hundreds of thousands. Honk the horn. Tell Mike to turn the bike around. Right now."

She did as instructed while they both screamed out the window in between efforts. "Mike, get back!"

Amir had his spotlight trained on Mike and his Harley from a hundred yards away. He was standing next to his bike with binoculars stuck to his eyeballs. Recognition splashed across his face a moment before the stampede's arrival. Mike turned his head back toward the crew with an *aww shucks* smirk on his face. Torie and David watched as the rioting crowd rose over the embankment with a million pounds of horsepower fueling the charge.

Then the tide came in and took him out.

Mike's perpetual death throes kept playing on repeat. He stayed upright dancing like a puppet on a string. Each new demise returned him to the same position serving as a standing pin cushion for the interminable blitzkrieg of black horses funneling across the roadway.

A rider clothed in robes the same color trotted casually

onto the interstate. His path was set a few paces in front of the writing horde. The flock maintained an instinctive buffer between themselves and the leader of the pack until he came to a dead stop in front of Mike's strobing corpse. Although the mystery man's head was shrouded beneath a hood, his bodily vibrations were easy to see even from a distance.

Torie squinted through the windshield. "What's he doing?"

"He's laughing." David verified it with his phone. "He won't stop laughing."

The Anti-God almost doubled over onto the asphalt before he finally pulled himself together. Tag took down the head-cover and turned to smile directly at David. He mimicked the electrocution-adjacent movements Mike was making with out-stretched Frankenstein arms. After a few seconds he resumed pointing and cackling at his wobbling carcass. When he finally had his fill, he motioned both palms toward the motorcycle man to signal as much.

His right hand continued across the saddle in one unbroken movement and unsheathed a femur-length obsidian blade. Crackling blue flame erupted from the hilt that caused the dagger to glow in the dark. The fluorescent highlighter shade made it easy to track its subsequent progression clean through Mike's throat.

Upon completion, Tag tossed his newly acquired souvenir onto the roadway by the hair.

Mike wound up keeping his nose to the grindstone even in death.

The Anti-God palmed Harley Mike's headless stump like a basketball and lifted it in the air. His cadaverous torso was spared further punishment, but his legs quickly liquified into noodles. They continued to Road Runner beneath him as the stallions charged onward through the flimsy turnstiles.

The same blue hellfire emanating from the guillotine blade only a moment before now began pulsating up and down Tag's entire arm. He lifted his head to the sky with eyes wide shut. His mouth expanded unnaturally into a well fit for Lassie to locate. The Beast's entire body began to shake. Once the human soul was emptied from its container, the willowed husk was dropped onto the concrete so it could still suffer the indignity of an occasional hoof kick. Its final resting place was purposefully chosen by Tag.

The remaining members of the group already put it in reverse and lined themselves up alongside Torie and David at the back of the venue. Everyone watched the unfolding display with the same level of abject horror.

Tag dismounted from his red-eyed bronco. Crimson-colored smoke puffed forth from each of the steed's orbital cavities and evaporated in ascending, wispy ribbons. The Anti-God pulled a two-piece scale free from one saddle bag and the blow-holed head of Adam Patrick Willco from the other. Placing the measuring instrument down, he paused to survey the bottom of the desiccated neck stub. He seemed perplexed. A sudden snap of the fingers signified a solution to his internal quandary.

Striding over to the discarded head of Harley Mike, he reached down and clawed a few millimeters into his gray scalp before pressing the bloody end against Willco's Sahara-dry neck hole. Tag forced the two pieces together with his left wrist countering the clockwise motion of the right. It only took one Anti-God to screw in two lightbulbs. A thin layer of congealed plasma squeezed out from between the fusion like raspberry jam.

Tag's pearly whites possessed the intensity of high beams.

Upon conclusion, he set the heads down on separate ends of the weighbridge. Each now possessed sufficient adhesive to keep them bonded in place.

The sun began to rise in satisfaction. Tag's spirit could no longer be contained.

The leering jackal climbed atop his hell horse once again and took off full steam ahead toward the shimmering Star of Bethlehem. Tag provided a one finger salute to David and company as he galloped toward the fifth dimension. The Anti-God never looked back.

Torie squeezed her boyfriend's hand. "He's heading east."

"He's heading for New York," David clarified. "He's going home."

***

A funeral for Harley Mike would have to wait until they were back in Michigan.

The crew collected both of his pieces as delicately as possible.

David removed the man's leather bomber jacket and used it as a bowling ball bag for his own head.

Tina took off her Cal hoodie and draped it over what was left of Adam Willco before depositing the entire apparatus in her ice cream truck freezer.

Darrell and Amir assigned themselves arms while Wesley volunteered for leg duty.

When Wes reached to grab an ankle lock around each of Mike's stems the effort caused his previously invisible Time Tether to dislodge. The broken golden hoop clinked against the ground.

He held the half-mooned W in his left hand. "I've never seen one of these unlock before. I didn't know they could."

"It must have disengaged when his soul was snatched," Darrell reasoned. "Probably wasn't engineered with that sort of thing in mind."

"They're not supposed to open again under any circumstance," Torie interrupted. "And they're not golden. Let me see that thing." She fingertipped each semi-circle while admiring them against the moonlight. "Boys, a ring like this—better off in the hands of a lady. I'll hold onto her for safekeeping."

Torie didn't tell any of them about the broadcast she was receiving in her sleep for weeks. Not even David. It wasn't a dream. Whoever was sending her the message was very clear about that. The transmission showed her and another companion preparing to duel with a shrouded opponent across a vast, empty plain. An adversary she now recognized as the Anti-God. He held his electric blue blade at the ready. The recording showed they possessed a single weapon with which to defend themselves during the approaching battle.

A golden Time Tether.

# HAUNTING

Kimberly Lorelai Eaton didn't know what to wear.

This was going to be her second date with River, and she didn't want to blow it.

Ever since *The Last Crusade* came out, he could have any woman in the world.

Heaven was getting to play dress-up as the one he chose.

She wanted to make every effort for the temporary man of her dreams.

Kim made a point to pass through Belize when he was on location filming *The Mosquito Coast*. The pair struck up a platonic friendship at a local vegan restaurant and stayed in touch. He loved talking about PETA and his band Aleka's Attic. Acting always came in a distant third. When he finally broke up with Martha Plimpton, she was ready to pounce.

Given her divinely accelerated timeline, the entire teenage affair amounted to about two days. Still—Ms. Eaton had never been more in love, and in the eleventh dimension at least, neither had River Phoenix.

Which isn't to say she didn't have other men in her life over the years. Jess Mariano. Donnie Darko. Aubrey Graham. Prince William before he went bald. Her celestial love life so far was simply spectacular. Nothing to sneeze at in the slightest.

Getting to kiss Chris Chambers was something else entirely.

She decided upon a vintage cream-colored floral minidress

that made her look ten years older and sexier by the same order of magnitude. All she was lacking was a crown.

When River rang the doorbell with a bouquet of ocean breeze orchids in hand, he didn't know whether to present them to Kim or to the Lord up above. "Wow, umm. Yeah. You look like you're about to go supernova or something. I think I need to sit down. Can I sit down for a sec?"

"Please," she giggled. "Should I get you something? A glass of water?"

"Do you have any Dramamine?" He couldn't take his eyes off her.

"No, I stay pretty landlocked," she snickered.

"May I ask a favor?"

He could have asked for anything. "Anything."

"Can I come over there and kiss you now, please? I mean, can we just get it out of the way, so I don't have to think about it all night? I'm going to think about it anyway, but—"

River Phoenix never got the chance to finish his sentence.

***

Ms. Eaton chose a helicopter this evening in lieu of a formal carriage ride.

Their choppered flight from her compound in Laurel Canyon to the Reteti Elephant Sanctuary in Kenya somehow took less than thirty minutes. She and her boyfriend were in the back too busy barely breathing for the duration to notice the passage of time either way. Every minute she spent with him seemed like it would never end but was over too soon.

When they arrived, their guide Aasir could not have been more hospitable. The trio surveyed the entire park in his army-green jeep. She and River learned everything there was to know about caring for the majestic beasts he considered his own family. A young calf named Babar took a liking to Kim and the feeling became mutual in less than five seconds. If it wasn't for mama eyeballing her, she might have considered adoption.

At the end of the day, the couple had a candlelight dinner on the grassy savannah while a pride of lions lazily lounged in a circle of life around their table. When River spoke about the future, he always used *we*, and *our*, and *us*.

They made love under starlight while Simba and company stood perimeter from a comfortable distance. Afterward he held her in his arms and explained what UAPs really were as several quickening constellations passed overhead. She laid wide-eyed in the face of full disclosure. It was the most beautiful thing she had ever seen.

Then she looked up.

They spent the rest of the night in her bed back home and most of the next day, too.

Kim had to be up bright and early to catch a flight out of Cape Canaveral. She finally bid him adieu from the front door wrapped in her white comforter. The way he kissed her goodbye made her consider dropping everything and asking him to stay. He started to backtrack to save them both the trouble. "Time is however long it takes until I see you again, Keats. It doesn't exist otherwise. Not anymore."

Kim smiled into snooze mode as a silent Fourth of July spectacular splashed blues and reds across the ceiling of her bedroom.

An angelic algorithm determined this was the 9,567th best day of her afterlife.

Landing in the top one percent was still fairly impressive.

At a minimum, it demanded a third date.

***

Stacey Darden prayed that an Ambien might materialize in her palm.

Unfortunately, with the election in one week, there would be no rest for the wicked. Tag mandated as much—although there wasn't a memo or anything.

Nights and weekends ceased to exist back in March.

Assuming the bulk of traditional campaign duties over the past calendar year was the most fulfilling thing she had ever done in her life, but also the most exhausting.

Building an extensive field operation throughout the 15th District.

Training operatives on door-to-door canvassing and voter engagement techniques.

Enlisting endorsements from local union delegates and the like.

$10,000 a plate fundraisers populated entirely by non-constituents.

Overseeing Tag's daily travel itinerary and media hits.

Event staging. Photo Ops. Press releases.

Is paying for this cheeseburger with petty cash going to create a campaign finance issue?

Stacey couldn't remember the last time she defecated.

Plus, she just missed her period.

By five weeks.

She hadn't yet found the time to tell the candidate he was going to be a dad.

The fact that the sun hadn't come out in New York City in two months seemed fitting.

Tag was on his way to a private dinner with the head of the DNC. This was the first time in months Stacey had the opportunity to convene her staff without the future Congressman by her side.

Unbeknownst to her, he was carefully calibrating his level of possessiveness. It still hewed just close enough to the professional line to mask his ever-increasing emotional abuse.

Being cast out by God gave her boyfriend serious abandonment issues.

"Evan, would you be a doll and grab us a Sprite?" She was using us as the royal we.

"You mean, like, from the vending machine?" The intern theatrically rotated his head toward the exit.

"Yeah, just sprinkle some breadcrumbs, sport. If you don't make it back within the hour, we'll send out a second expedition." When he reached his palm out with insistence across her desk, she splashed the pot with quarters. "Appreciate you, Shackleton."

The ladies watched Evan snag himself twice on the corner of separate desks before he finally managed to successfully navigate his way out the door. When the himbo hit the end of the hallway, he looked both ways like a moron.

Interning Evan caused Stacey to arrive at one indefatigable conclusion—an Ivy League transcript could never stand in for a good old fashioned IQ test. He got almost nothing done throughout his workday, yet no one was working more tirelessly to invalidate the efficacy of legacy admissions.

Carol asked a question after him. "What do you suppose his type is?"

"More inches than brain cells," Tonya confirmed. "He's shown me his Grindr."

"The phrasing there is everything," Stacey said with a single raised eyebrow.

"No, no, it's fine. Unfortunately, I asked to see it—and I immediately regretted the decision."

Ms. Darden returned her attention to the entire team. "Before The Man with No Brains comes back, are we all set for election night? Did you confirm doors-open for the ferry?"

"Four o'clock. We're good. I'll verify again the morning of just to make sure," Tonya responded. "Stacey, you need to take a breather, babe. We've got this one in the bag."

"Tag's up by thirty points," Carol added. "I don't think dying would be enough to remove *Mr. September* from the driver's seat at this point. He'd have to punch a Shriners kid or something."

Stacey took a look at the brick wall outside her window. The view left her pondering a career switch to crash test dummy. "I'm glad you're all so confident, but I can't say the same. Zeta variant admissions spiked by twenty percent in the city last week, and *MARZ* wasn't even a thing three months ago. Whether Patient Zero actually came to Brooklyn on a bus from Baja is irrelevant. That's the story now, and everyone's sticking to it. Even if Tag makes it across the finish line, hospitals are going to hit capacity by Christmas. Every non-Dominican with a MetroCard is going to be calling for Congressman Gottfried's head."

"That's assuming things don't explode in the next week," Cindy stipulated. "It's not just Zeta variant. The rate of violent crime is skyrocketing. Hate crime, too."

"I saw that on the news this morning." Tonya shook her head with a gravity more befitting the discovery of a newly deceased relative. "*Bussing migrants* didn't use to mean pushing them in front of an MTA."

"It's disgusting," Carol confirmed, "but luckily seventy percent of our constituency is speaking a different language— literally and figuratively. We don't have to win over America, or even the whole city. Just the south Bronx. Our message plays there. Moral cowardice doesn't. That's why Tag's going to walk into the endzone untouched next Tuesday."

Cindy had a newborn. Being a secretary was her second job. "Happy to be on the winning team, but the savagery is on all sides now. It really does feel like someone is trying to kick off a second civil war in New York City."

The Anti-God was declaring secession as they spoke.

A spiritual struggle for Fort Sumter would be waged in the five boroughs.

The Confederacy won that battle the first time it was fought.

This time, Tag intended to win the war.

Ms. Darden nodded in agreement with her assistant. "That Congressional seat's going to be scorching hot the second he sits down. I think advocating for NYC to be converted into a city-size migrant shelter during a global pandemic was a fatal political miscalculation. If not now, then two years from now. But this is Tag's rodeo. We just supply the rope. How he chooses to tie the thing off is ultimately his decision."

It might be his decision, but this still remained her business. Given Stacey's personal and professional commitment to the candidate, her exasperation with his ongoing obstinacy was currently off the charts.

"Whatever gets him across the finish line for now," Carol said. "We'll see which office he's even running for in two years." Whispers about the Senate seat being vacated come 2030 were already percolating.

A mentally and physically exhausted Evan finally made it back from his voyage around the Horn. The requested provisions were tossed overboard somewhere along the way. Nevertheless, the briny odor of Ruffles trailed behind the lad. The number of shillings returned to the captain was less than the sixpence gifted the green hand. "Sorry, no more Sprite."

"You sure you were pressing the correct buttons?" Stacey's inquiry was genuine. In her dealings with the less fair sex, she typically already had that knowledge in hand without having to ask.

"Yes. I triple-checked." He really did. "I don't get it. There was no light."

"Sometimes it takes a while for it to come on." She looked her intern up and down.

"Stacey, I can run down to the corner and grab you one." Cindy was eight months removed from maternity leave. She knew her boss was with child, even if Stacey wasn't ready to start showing.

"No, I actually could use the semi-fresh air." She waved her secretary off while rising from her seat already mid-coat. "Everyone go home and get some rest. You're not sleeping for the next six days, so enjoy yourselves."

Stacey turned out the lights then put on a fresh N-95 with silicate shielding before heading out the door.

Church Street from Worth to Chambers transformed into an unofficial homeless encampment over the previous six months. New tents popped up along the sidewalk every day like Monopoly hotels. They would own Park Place in no time.

10% inflation was neck-and-neck with the 11.8% national unemployment rate.

Coughing from *MARS* provided an incessant source of percussion throughout the city.

Every month was some kind of record now, but July was when things really began to heat up. It was 118° outside the day two landscapers from El Salvador were beaten to death with baseball bats on the Brighton Beach boardwalk. One of them made the mistake of hacking on a peanut shell when he passed within spitting distance of a middle schooler named Mila. Her big brother Oleg served as the instigator. Tag made sure he and his friends were never positively identified, much to the chagrin of every Latino New Yorker.

The Anti-God had been slowly turning up the dial on the thermostat for some time.

Oblivious to his role as ringmaster, Stacey urged Tag to tamp down all the rhetoric about making their city a barrier-free bastion for their immigrant brethren. She increasingly found her own morality coming in second place to matters of political expediency. There was an internalized disgust about it, but that's where it stayed.

Nevertheless, for the first time in their professional relationship, the candidate failed to heed her advice. Point of fact, he plowed ahead in the opposing direction with even more intensity. Chicago and Los Angeles were shamed from the stump for their failure to help alleviate the border crisis alongside the Greatest City on Earth™. NYC and its saintly melting pot now served as perpetual martyrs for the migrant cause.

It wasn't by unanimous consent. Anti-immigrant sentiment remained strong on the islands—Long. Staten. Rikers.

Rich Manhattanites didn't want them fogging up the restaurant glass on Friday night. The underclass in Brownsville weren't keen on them sucking up city services every other day of the week. Progressive firebrands in Brooklyn Heights pretended to be down for the cause, but the only time they wanted their children being exposed to real Mexican heritage in the classroom was on Cinco De Mayo. There were school rankings to consider. The reading scores would fall off a cliff. Grade school was more cutthroat than grad school now.

In September, when the governors of Florida and Texas coordinated their third bus caravan to Martha's Vineyard in as many months, Tag was there to personally greet all 2,000 guests and reroute them to the newly opened Morris Park Migrant Center. Before ever stepping foot inside Darden Communications, Mr. Gottfried paid $42 million out of his own pocket to purchase the 2.4-acre lot and push for rapid construction on twin fifteen story dormitories.

The Anti-God went through a highly selective weeding out process long before their exodus to the 15th District. Tag reached as far as Colombia to find the right candidates. Only the cream of the crop got through his ethereal filtration system and wound up on one of those buses to the Bronx. Members of the Mexican Mafia. Soldiers in MS-13. Anyone infected with a *MARS* variant. He even managed to locate a couple of serial killers. All of them telepathically escorted north until the pawns were placed in position to be picked up.

New York City would be their new arena. A whole playground of possibilities.

Tag planned to continue stacking his chips into the sky until the tower finally fell.

Stacey tiptoed through the tulips, treading a middle path between the new streetside tenants to her left and the occasional pool of deviled green ectoplasm dotting the landscape to the right.

A pair of NYPD patrol cars were parked at the corner up ahead. They would remain stationary and the occupants sedentary unless there was an actual threat of violence. Department policy in response to *MARS* literally demanded that they not get their hands dirty. New York's citizenry informally adopted the same sanitary guidelines in short order without much additional prompting from the CDC.

Up and down Church Street the storefronts and columned windows were as uniformly dark as a heartless old codger's on Halloween night.

The City That Never Sleeps was deep in hibernation. It was disconcerting.

During her walk to the party store, Stacey identified no less than three pending drug deals proceeding unabated on the street despite the presence nearby of New York's finest. She noted that all parties to each respective transaction spoke in perfect, unaccented English. Her new neighbors appeared to be exclusively native-born and all in possession of working cell phones. In her mind, illegal immigration had little to do with America's rapid descent into degradation.

The sudden charge of footfalls from behind caused her to spin around in anticipation of a potential mugging.

A different kind of misery was at hand.

David Downey was standing on the sidewalk ten feet in front of her.

"Hey, stranger. Sorry if I scared you. I spent all day stalking you from across the street."

"You're lucky I don't have my mace on me," she said.

"Oh, please," he pocketed his hands with a smirk. "You saw me coming from a mile away."

"Like I said, David—you're lucky I don't have my mace."

"Don't you want to know how I came back down to Earth? In my original bod to boot? It's a pretty good story."

"David, I have a Congressional election to win in a week.

I just want to grab a Sprite and go home." She stepped toward him with a smile. "Look, I'm sorry about the last time we spoke. We were both out of line, but I'd say you've done your time at this point, and I don't have any more of it to spare, so—*I release you, Dav*—"

He immediately raised his hands to stop her forward progress. His good humor melted away. "Hold on, Stace. Not just yet. There's something important we need to discuss before I cross over."

"Did you not hear me, dummy? It's six days until election night. This is probably the last time I'm going to have to myself. I want to go home, watch *Real Housewives of Wherever the Hell*, and go to bed. It's become my comfort blankie. I need the rest." She and her baby both.

"I apologize, but I actually had to wait until you were Tagless," David confirmed. "Your boyfriend and I are in an abusive relationship. Non-sexual so far, but I wouldn't put anything past him. If he saw me here talking to you, he'd probably flay me alive and then sprinkle ghost pepper residue on my remainder."

"What are you talking about? You're telling me Tag can see you when I can't? How can that be?"

"Tag could stick his fist up my colon and wave me around like a foam finger if he was so inclined. Listen Stace, what I have to tell you, it's going to be easier if you hear it coming from my friends as well. You'll see. They're just up the street. Will you come with me? Please?"

"Are these real people or the Justice League?"

"They're very much real—Wes, Amir, and Darrell. You can confirm it for yourself."

She crossed her arms and lowered her eyelids. "You're not from around here. What's '*up the street?*'"

"Rucker Park," David confirmed. "Apparently, it's always been Amir's dream."

"Yeah, well trying to get there in the middle of a T. Swift

concert at MSG sounds kind of like my nightmare," Stacey countered. "The FDR's a mess on top of things, so there's no way around it. We're going to have to take the subway."

David smiled. "Thank you."

She walked past him without waiting. "Sure, no problem. I'll just add another hour and a half onto my commute. Microwaved dinner at midnight is always so delightful."

***

The D train was packed to the gills and standing room only for anyone with a dick and some decency. Stacey's face went phone flat into her email the moment she sat down. Given the nature of their pending discussion, David decided it was best to wait until they hit Harlem.

Except for the handful of occasions when she briefly looked up, David stared at her for the entire journey. It was over between them, but that didn't mean he would ever get over her. She didn't stop being Stace just because their relationship died.

Even his own death couldn't kill the feelings completely.

The pair disembarked at 155th Street. "Your friends do know that Rucker Park is kind of like the basketball version of Times Square at this point, right? Nothing but tourists. Real men play in The Cage. West 4th Street. I'm just saying. If they were going to come to the mecca, they should do it right."

"Thanks, *Starbury*," he said. "You grew up in Bloomfield Hills, by the way—not Brooklyn. The only pickup games you ever watched were played by white boys from Brother Rice driving BMWs."

"Hey, I'm just trying to expose you guys to some of the hidden wonders of our fair city."

The pair continued their walk and talk with the park up ahead to their left. "Appreciate you looking out for us rubes, but I wouldn't sweat it. We have Google in Michigan now. It's amazing."

Stacey chuckled. "I'm sorry, was I being a pretentious New Yorker?"

"You were a pretentious New Yorker long before you ever moved here."

She balled her fist and socked him in the arm, but the hollow slapping sound that registered upon contact made it clear she was only kidding. "I don't know what to do with this, by the way." She unflexed her fist and waved the hand in a circle six inches in front of his face.

"What? Me being kind of alive again?"

"No. You don't have any product in your hair." She squinted while perching up onto the balls of her feet to take a closer look. "Or, not as much, anyway. I like it. A lot. And you're looking me in the eyes when you're talking to me. And you're *talking to me*. Hell, you're allowing yourself to be seen with me in public. You've made some real strides, sir."

"It was never about being seen with you in public, Stace," he informed her. "I didn't want to be seen at all. I was deficient. Not you. You were everything."

A smile and frown did battle across her face. The counterweights caused only the corners of her mouth to curl. "Well, for whatever it's worth, I vastly prefer upgraded David 2.0 to the original version. That thing was all buggy."

"Thanks. My game engine was definitely garbage. It was the opposite of Unreal. I can't apologize enough for it." David focused his eyes on her until she felt it. "I've been patched up a bit, but Torie insists I still remain in beta-testing."

"Torie?" Stacey already knew the answer that would be forthcoming. She focused her efforts instead on pretending not to care. "What, is that your new girlfriend or something?"

"Yes." David looked at her without any discernible emotion.

Stacey stared straight ahead with a flat smile. "Well, I'm glad." She wasn't really. "So, tell me about Torie. Does she have a last name? Or is this a Cher situation?"

"Eaton."

"Torie Eaton." She indexed it for the Internet deep dive

that would be conducted later that evening. "Does Ms. Eaton look exactly like me, only not as pretty? You're required to say yes."

"Yep," David smiled, "other than being hideous to look at, and biracial, she's practically your twin. Torie's an adventurer like you. She doesn't take shit from anyone—also, like you."

Stacey stifled a laugh.

"Intelligent. Driven. Creative. Check check check. And for some inexplicable reason, she's decided I'm worth loving. You made that same mistake at one point."

"It wasn't a mistake, David. Please don't say that." Stacey stopped them on the sidewalk before proceeding. "I loved you more than anything. I said that a lot, too, by the way. You didn't, but I did. I would have thrown myself on a grenade belt for you. But being nothing more than medication to you had an expiration date. It always does. I didn't want to be your temporary pain relief anymore. I wanted an actual life, and all of the time. Were you happy when we were together back then? I'm not asking you if you loved me. I'm asking if you were happy."

David looked away for a moment. "No," he finally acknowledged. "But I wasn't unhappy because of you. And whenever I was happy, it was almost always a Stacey Darden production."

"Well, I was unhappy a lot because of you." She shook her head affirmatively but smiled to soften the blow. "And I prefer joy. That's why we couldn't be together anymore. That screwed up family of yours taught you how to breathe underwater, but I would have drowned. Back then, you only had an A or B button. Sex or silence. Every day of our relationship felt like a game of *Duck Hunt*—and I never got to hold the gun. Or be the dog, even. I was ready to go next-gen, man. If you've gotten there, I think that's great. But someone else gets to play with this model. I had the Atari. I only remember the pitfalls."

The hollow echo of Horween leather against the asphalt called them back from their brief timeout. Without another word, the pair continued side-by-side down the block until they finally hit the entrance to Holcombe.

Stacey couldn't believe what she saw unfolding before her eyes.

Three different versions of David were currently being dog-walked up and down the court. The waterboys for the Washington Generals could have put up more of a fight. Calling their performance laughable would have been redundant. Everyone present was already reinforcing the point. Opposition included.

To try and even the score from the outset, the Davids were gifted with a 6'9" positionless point-forward named Boost Sinclair. *Benny* went extinct when he was fifteen and dropped forty playing for the Lincoln Railsplitters out of Coney Island during the AAU World Championships in Orlando. He was Boost now the way that Earvin was Magic, or how Ahmad had that Sauce. Top fifteen in the nation according to the 24/7 composite. He and his mother were still busy dutifully determining if the bag at Duke or UCLA would be bigger. Definitely a signing day decision on the horizon.

If his coaches knew he was playing pickup in season they would kill him.

Right after Dr. Sinclair took her turn.

The kid couldn't help himself. He was knocking down pull-ups when he was still wearing Pampers. If Boost had to choose between breathing or basketball, he would gladly suffocate on the court.

Unfortunately, he was too good for his own good. Assigned three scrubs, he was busy taking his first L in over two years. An uncontested three when one of the Davids failed to properly rotate on defense finally sealed the deal. The crowd went wild for all the wrong reasons.

Darrell-David engaged in a heated discussion with their ill-fated fifth teammate after the final buzzer. "No, I said we played *in* college—not for one."

"Yeah, I'm a doctoral candidate at St. Johns. I know what semantics are."

A member of the opposing squad sidled up to a clearly frustrated Boost. Mr. Sinclair was doubled over huffing and puffing like it was already deep into the second half. His adversary pointed an index finger in David and Stacey's direction while the remainder continued to palm the pebbled leather ball. "Hey yo, their moms had another anti-Billy Hoyle." He called out so everyone could hear. "Is being sorry a genetic predisposition, or can you actually hoop?"

"No, I can confirm we're all very much from the same stock," David replied, "it would only be more of where that came from. This wasn't some grand plot to hustle you or anything."

"Yeah, David, you're really terrible at basketball," Amir wheezed as he approached the fence. Some combination of physical exertion and public embarrassment was causing him to flop sweat. "My handle sucked, and you can't hit the broad side of a barn with your J. It's broke."

"Man, I'm not trying to play one on five with four of one," Boost shouted. "Can I get some run with dudes that played basketball before?"

"Nah nah nah, they're family. That's blood. You can't separate them," assured his opponent. The rules were being made up as they went along. "This ain't *Saving Private Ryan*, Boost— you gotta bring all them boys home."

"We're going to sit this one out actually, gentlemen," Wesley-as-David announced.

The triplets slowly triangulated on one side of the fence with Stacey and David on the other until they had her effectively surrounded.

"Jesus Christ. There's four of you. There are four David Downeys staring at me right now. It's like every woman's worst nightmare come to life."

Three out of four Davids found that funny.

She turned toward the real thing. "David, do we need to interrogate how narcissistic it is to make three copies of yourself? I thought you said you were making real people friends."

"Oh, we actually are his friends, and very much real," Wesley offered in David's defense. "Our spirits have been synchronized to your circadian rhythms. The minute you go night night, all four of us will dissolve."

"These bodies were just fabricated for us," Amir added.

"Fabricated sounds about right," she snarked back.

"It wasn't my choice, Stace. Apparently even billion-year-old alien technology has functional limitations. Daphne said the device can only duplicate at an interdimensional level."

"Daphne?"

"He's our gay alien friend," Darrell clarified.

Stacey went looking for answers up above. She sucked in her lips while her right leg began to jackhammer the pavement. Gradually her eyes came back down to Earth until they located the dumb version of David she used to date. "Downey, I'm trying really hard to be patient here, but you're making it exceedingly difficult."

"Stacey—"

"*Real. Housewives.*" She looked at each one of them in turn. "What the hell are we doing here, guys? I don't know what D-1 told you, but I'm a busy lady. Spill the beans. Whatever this is about." All the talk of beans made her belly ache. She and her baby were starving, or she was about to be sick. It was difficult to tell the difference for the past couple of weeks.

Amir took the liberty with the typical social grace of a twenty-eight-year-old. "Your boyfriend is the Anti-God."

She lent the gentleman her ear. "The what now?"

Whether real or imagined, David long resented Stacey's tendency to make him feel small in front of others. The perceived jokes at his expense along with her unwillingness to accept the obvious left him growing visibly frustrated. "Tag is the

Anti-God. Do we have to spell it out for you? T-A-G. *The Anti God Got Freed.* Your essence is so objectionable it summoned him from the anti-matter ether. Congrats on being cataclysmic catnip. I tried to get him to scoop up Kate as his lady love instead, but unfortunately your bestie was too awful even for the Father of Satan. Sorry."

Stacey took two steps back with her hands out to defend herself from any further broadsides. "David, you were doing such a good job not being an asshole. Why am I being bombarded with bullshit?"

"Apologies, but it's not BS." Wes offered in further attestation. "I didn't believe it for the longest, either—then I watched Tag cut our friend's head off in the fourth dimension and weigh the thing for good measure."

"And according to our pal Daphne, you're the key to him eradicating all of existence," Darrell added.

David had a self-satisfied smirk. "Yeah, it turns out you're a *Jinni.* You descended from an ancient line of genies that liked to punish humans for any perceived harm done to them. They also used sex as a weapon. That sounds about right to me."

"Screw you, David."

"You're not just any normal Jinni, though," he continued. "No, apparently, it's a tiered system. You're the one Soul Succubus to rule them all. Prophesized throughout multiple dimensions as someone called The Lord of Pain. Tag has been slowly sucking the life force from you since the day you met him. You're going to help him usher in oblivion, and then he's going to obliterate you."

Stacey was vibrating, and so was her Special-Order Gris Mouette Birkin bag. When she reached inside, the contents of her boyfriend's birthday present almost caused her capillaries to burst. "Shit. Tag's texting me. His dinner finished early. I guess the head of the DNC got sick off some shellfish or something. You're lucky my secretary lives in Harlem, or I wouldn't have any excuse to be out here. He's getting off at 155$^{th}$ in ten minutes to pick me up."

David's expression suggested one or more unsavory city smells were suddenly in circulation. "How in the hell would he know where you were, Stace? What, are you tracking each other's phones or something?"

"No! No. Of course not. Don't be ridiculous," she reassured him. "No, he just tracks mine. With the campaign and everything, we thought it be easier if he always knew where to find me. It's totally sensible."

"Sensible? Are you kidding me right now?" David put both hands on his head and stepped away from the conversation for a moment.

"If I may, Ms. Darden, I have no dog in this fight, but that's messed up," Darrell added. "I don't know you, I don't know this Tag character, but I've ghost-lit my fair share. It kind of seems like a fog is lifting as we speak, right?"

Her eyes skittered across the payment for a few seconds in contemplation before she silently confirmed his assessment.

"Let me ask you something, Stacey. When you and David were together, if he had proposed unilaterally tracking your movements by phone, you would have—"

"Told him to go fuck himself."

"*Right.*" Real David and the Darrell version said it at the same time.

She resumed scanning the sidewalk. "I guess I hadn't thought about it until just now." Her furrowed brows continued a slow march inward. When she finally looked back up, her eyes began to shift between the various Davids. "Why wouldn't I have thought about that until just now? That's weird, right?"

All four of them shook their heads to affirm her conclusion.

Stacey had a Father Karras-like moment of clarity. Without a second thought, she uninstalled Life360 before the demon had an opportunity to retake possession.

Darrell was pulling double duty now as a police officer. "Ms. Darden, if I were you, I'd pack a bag tonight and leave. Forget about toxic, your boyfriend's corrosive acid. He might not be hitting you, but this has all the other hallmarks. Seen it a thousand times, unfortunately."

"Guys, aside from being my significant other—who I very much love, by the way—Tag also happens to be the sole source of income for myself and my entire staff," Stacey informed the group. "The patriarchy allows you stiff one-eyed idiots to harbor the delusion that everything's just that easy, but it's not. Mr. Gottfried pays the bills. All of them."

David was unfortunately privy to almost every aspect of her personal life at this point. "Stace, I thought he upped your salary? Where's all that money been going?"

"Tag told me to pay off my student loans and he'd take care of everything else, which was great—but now I have no savings," she confirmed. "I can't just pack some Lululemon sweats in a duffle and call it a day on my entire personal and professional existence. That's what you're asking me to do. I literally can't afford it."

To his own detriment, David could never let sleeping dogs lie. He shook off the dual discovery of her mental conditioning and financial insolvency like a wet Doberman. "I can't believe you allowed that monster to gaslight you to this extent, Stace. I thought you were a lot stronger than that, but I guess the master has become the apprentice."

The exes officially entered the arena. "Excuse me, David? Are you implying *I* was gaslighting *you*? Talk about the pot calling the kettle black. I'd forgotten what sanity even looked like until you dropped out of the picture. Reality's always been however you framed it. Looks like nothing's changed. Even in the afterlife."

"You're not excused. Being in your orbit was like getting worked over by a CIA black site interrogator for six years," he spat back. "Your assessment is accurate, actually. I was just another honey pot, Pooh Bear."

"Hey, c'mon, kids." Darrell tried to bridge the growing divide with arms raised between the pair. "We all need to be rowing in the same direction right now."

David moved astern. "You're the most exceptional woman I've ever known, and you threw it all away to be banal in a brownstone with Beelzebub. By next year you'll be head of communications for a cash advance company. What the hell, man? You have a truly unique ability to communicate with people. To communicate ideas. *You* should be Tag. You should be revered. Everyone in this world should know your name. Instead, you settled for being the fourth most famous Stacey Darden on this piddling little two-mile island. The Indians got a better deal from the Dutch. I guess I should have seen it coming. You never had any problem giving yourself away for practically nothing."

Her face turned Chernobyl red. She crept toward him with contracting *Arthur* fists by her side. Stacey looked like she might uncork a punch directly into his solar plexus. Instead, she smiled up at David without teeth and pointed off into the distance toward the nearest available body of water. "*I release you, David Downey*—now get the hell out of my life and don't ever come back. I don't ever want to see you again. If you pass me on the streets of Heaven, don't even say hi. Do you hear me? Do you hear me?" She waited a moment before realizing something was amiss. "Why am I still looking at you imbeciles?"

The quartet shared confused looks.

When the recognition hit David, he snapped his head back toward the sky and exhaled.

Stacey was only pretending to hate him. "What? What is it?"

He returned with his eyes wide open. They imprinted upon each of his duplicates in sequence. "I know this is going to sound awful, but you all need to go kill yourselves. Right now."

"That is harsh," Amir said. "Why?"

Wesley picked up what David was putting down. "Daphne's Fabricator made such pristine copies there's no way to tell which of us is the real David. Stacey can only release The One."

"And thinning the herd requires we run off a cliff," Darrell realized. "Got it."

"Just intercept Tag and then head home," offered Version 1.0. "That's all you have to do. That, and not fall asleep. I'll meet you on your back patio in an hour, okay? We'll do this one last time and then you're done. No need to involve yourself any further. I'll alert Heaven to the Anti-God problem and let them handle it from there."

"You already slipped the cyanide in my drink, David," Stacey offered in admonishment. "Taking it to the lab to have it tested doesn't do me a whole lot of good at this point. I'm involved now. You're either full of shit or I'm fully fucked."

"Stace, I'm doing my best to permanently remove you from the equation."

"No no, it's fine," she fibbed. Stacey jabbed a thumb over her shoulder toward the destination. "I'm going to go try and find a Dagger of Megiddo on Craigslist. Then I'll head home with the King of Darkness so we can discuss accruing an immense amount of political power on his behalf over hot fudge sundaes.  No big. Thanks again, guys, really. Tonight was the balls." Her thumbs up morphed into a middle finger. She used it to wipe fake sleep away from the corner of her eye before turning and making her exit.

"That Stacey's one spicy meatball," Darrell whispered.

David acquired a taste, but he never built up an immunity. "Nothing but heartburn, that."

Once she was out of sight, the four of them marched off two by two in the opposite direction and began engaging in a strategy planning session.

"Screw it, I'm just going to jump in front of a bus," Wesley indicated. "You boys do you. The Macombs Dam Bridge is right up ahead if either of you want to do a header into the Harlem River."

Their cause of death discussion was halted when they identified the lone figure striding toward them. All four Davids came to an appropriately dead stop.

The Anti-God didn't even look up as he strolled down the sidewalk. He was up to his elbow rummaging around inside a clear plastic cylinder. From afar it looked like the thing was filled with animal crackers and he was desperately trying to find an elephant.

David asked the obvious question on behalf of the entire group once persona non grata reached spitting distance. "Are those communion wafers?"

Tag shoved a fistful of the wheat thins into his mouth and then spoke. Dusty particulate matter shot forth with each syllable. "Yeah, I stopped off at St. Mark's for a snack. I grabbed these while I was there."

"You're eating communion bread as a snack?"

"This wasn't the snack." He smacked his lips and smiled at David. Tag wiped the sandy residue from his chin. "Look, I even found a fortune cookie message inside the container." He threw a blood-specked white clerical collar down on the ground between them. "It says '*The World Is Yours*' in invisible ink."

David started stuttering. "How—how are—"

"How am I here and with Stacey at the same time? It's a little trick I picked up in the fifth dimension," he confirmed for the shocked onlookers. Tag tossed the blessed biscuits in the trash and then used each palm to wipe the other clean, one over top of the other. "David, I thought we had an understanding? You asking the Greys to gift you with a body and then duplicate you for backup violates the spirit of our agreement. I do hope you're not trying to fabricate your way into Heaven without me—because I invented the American slave trade. There are a variety of methods at my disposal to help ensure you remain on the plantation." For reasons left unstated, the Anti-God began to focus on David's right foot while tonguing the inside of his cheek.

Darrell's concern was no longer solely for his human companions. Daphne projected himself to Detroit for dinner a few days back in the body of Cary Grant. It appeared that after one hundred thousand years together, things had run their course with his husband. Still, Darrell was adamant that nothing could happen between them until the intergalactic divorce was finalized. Daphne just had to put together the requisite funds. His attorney charged by the millennia. "How did you know where we acquired the bodies?"

"The Greys are the ones who initiated this stupid simulation," Tag said with his arms held aloft. "You humans are just test subjects. What, you thought God designed you?" The mere suggestion caused Tag to double over once again with laughter. "*God.* You might all be Her creatures, but you're most definitely not Her creation. In fact, the Greys feed off all the negative energy you people produce. I'm guessing your boyfriend left that part out." The Anti-God smirked at Darrell-David as he said it.

Real David offered Tag a pseudo-smile and a raised index finger before gathering his duplicates into a huddle formation. "Anyone have any thoughts on how we might ditch the witch?"

"Let's just split up and run for it," Amir whispered. "He won't be able to catch all of us."

"*I'm sorry, you boys were saying?*"

The density of Tag voices intensified. When the four Davids turned back around, an equivalent number of Anti-Gods were smiling back at them.

Each of the clones caught a sudden lump in their throats.

"David, I've noticed you boning up on the Bible over the last several months. Care to outline the fourth seal of Revelation for your heathen friends here?"

It was true. David had been doing his research. He had nothing but time. His recitation from memory was nevertheless begrudging at best.

*"Behold a pale horse: and his name that sat on him was Death, and Hell followed with him. And power was given unto them over the fourth part of the earth, to kill with sword, and with hunger, and with death, and with the beasts of the earth."*

*"Beasts of the earth*—that's you idiots," Tag informed them. "Democrats and Republicans are the new Roman Imperial Cult. We already took care of the sword, remember? I'm causing a run on your food banks as we speak. Good luck finding baby formula. So, there's your famine. As far as pestilence, it's *MARS Attacks* all day every day in this city now. Half your brothers and sisters are walking around the same shade as pistachio ice cream. In terms of sore judgments, come Tuesday I'll be four for four. Which means the fourth will fall. Fuck you, and you, and you, and you. All four of *yous.*"

No hive mind was required. A few stolen glances by and between each respective David were sufficient to kick their anti-survival instinct into high gear. Three of the crew put it in reverse and raced in the opposite direction down Harlem River Drive before splitting off like the prongs of a hand cultivator. Wes turned right and raced toward the Macombs Dam Bridge.

He admired the ornate wrought iron signage and riveted latticework as he ran full speed down the cantilevered sidewalk abutting the roadway. Over the preceding decades, inclement weather had yellowed the steel and left it stained at irregular intervals in dead autumn colors. Streaks of caramel leaked out of every girded joint alongside flashes of rust-colored orange and scabby brown.

Snapping his head back as he sprinted, Wes caught sight of a single Anti-God smiling and strolling toward him with utter nonchalance from fifty yards behind. Despite the differentiation in speed, no matter how fast Wes seemed to run, Tag appeared to only be getting closer with each passing step. Deciding the time was now, he grabbed a hold of the chain link fencing to his right and quickly ascended. An inward pitch of forty-five degrees was designed to keep the suicidal at bay. He managed to manually hand bike his way to the edge and then grunt his way over the top with his feet dangling the entire time. Perching himself on all fours atop the fence with his pursuer fast approaching, he gave Tag the finger before swan diving into the abyss down below.

He was just in time to catch the Circle Line.

As he descended, Wes had a moment to admire the metal-stanchioned canopy below him. A square border of candy cane red along the top of the open-air big top gave way to a pine green center. The bullseye was the same shade as the commercial zone plastic waste receptacle sitting beneath the awning. Luckily for Wes, one of the crew working cleanup had just removed the push door lid from the trashcan top two seconds before the man fell to Earth. He torpedoed through the vinyl covering and dove headlong into ignominy. A conglomeration of empty plastic beer cups and half eaten burgers broke his fall and prevented potential paralysis. Wesley teetered over the brink with his legs making a peace sign in the air for a few seconds until he finally slammed down heels first onto the boat deck. He had just regained consciousness when two security guards began dragging him out of his enclosure by each ankle.

Amir hooked a right at West 154th Street and was halfway up the block to Frederick Douglass Boulevard when the voice of an Anti-God rang out in his ears from the corner behind him.

"Hey! You just stepped on a mine! I wouldn't move if I were you."

Puzzled at the proclamation, Amir stopped for a second to take a closer look.

The only thing beneath his feet was a cast iron manhole cover labeled *N.Y.C. Sewer*. He rubbed the tip of his shoe against the offsetting pairs of horizontal and vertical hashmarks and then grinned back at the ghoul. A low rumble of bass returned his attention down below an instant before he was launched skyward.

Unbeknownst to the young Muslim Michigander, the electrical system cabling just below street level had been slowly but surely deteriorating for some time. Overhead traffic vibrations along with natural wear and tear began the process a couple of years back. A foot of unexpected snowfall over a two-week period in late October caused an excessive amount of salt to spill down from the roadway. For the finishing touch, twenty minutes ago Tag summoned ten thousand subway rats to gnaw on the lines after first engorging themselves with seawater. The briny mixture seeped into the various nicked lines and further eroded their insulation. Just prior to Amir's arrival they began to spark and smoke in anticipation.

The subsequent explosion lifted Rocket Man skyward toward the Moon on a kamikaze mission platformed purely by the Anti-God. Amir prayed for a quick death during his fiery ascent. Instead, he landed inside of one of New York's finest Department of Sanitation trucks. The eco-friendly refuse transport was quiet as a church mouse and smelled like roses planted in especially pungent manure. The human turd painfully rolled himself side to side while moaning. In the process, he inadvertently picked up various pieces of detritus and potential sources of disease like he was wearing a Velcro sticky suit. He was covered in filth when a couple of off-duty FDNYs came to the rescue and helped pull him free from his poop paddock.

Darrell doubled back to the subway entrance at 155th Street. He breathed a sigh of relief and descended the stairs when he saw no sign of the Tag Team behind him.

Standing amidst a conglomeration of native New Yorkers, he began to weigh the pros and cons of his various self-harm options. He quickly decided that suicide by cop was too fraught with danger for the other innocent civilians who might get caught in the crossfire. He didn't think it fair to force a fellow officer into therapy for the foreseeable future, either.

Jumping in front of the D train could easily work in the alternative, but his chance of survival remained a non-zero number. Darrell didn't like those odds. The thought of becoming an actual ghost in the shell possessed no appeal. As described by Daphne, it sounded like nothing more than Locked-in Syndrome for spirits.

By contrast, touching the live rail next to the tracks would send 600 volts through his body and kill him instantly without hurting another living soul. If he timed it right, the train might arrive at the station quick enough to trifurcate his prone corpse and formally finish the job before anyone had an opportunity to pull him off the tracks. It was a win-win.

The decision was ultimately made on Darrell's behalf.

Behind his back, a twenty-something Puerto Rican man in a Knicks jersey crossed paths with a still-scrubbed female surgical resident longing to sleep in her own bed for the first time in a week. Without any internalized thought process, the strangers each gave Darrell a simultaneous shove just below the shoulder blades and then continued along their merry way. With his standing position already set to lean, the added force caused him to topple over onto the tracks headfirst.

Both shovers would separately watch news of the event play out the next morning on ABC7 with only passing interest. Neither would ever recall playing unwitting assistant to the Anti-God.

In another strange wrinkle, five minutes prior to the incident all security cameras in the station ceased transmitting. The replacement of a faulty fan unit twelve hours before would ultimately be blamed for the temporary feed failure. Regardless of the cause, the result left the NYPD with no viable way to determine how the events of that evening unfolded.

Darrell shook the cobwebs free and hoisted himself onto his knees. Tag's voice came screaming over the edge before he was able to make visual identification.

"Sir, don't do it! You have so much life left to live!"

A lineup of would-be riders raced to the yellow line to scream warnings at the idiot.

The Anti-God jumped into action and purposely landed on top of Darrell with the intention of causing as much pain as possible. The lights of the D train were pinpricks in the dark off to their right. Tag leaned down to whisper into his ear.

"I want you deliver a message to your new master. He and his kind would be best served staying out of my business." Tag emphasized the point by grinding his knee into Darrell's spine. "There's an understanding between Gods and Greys. Assistance to mortals is strictly verboten. Any further violations will be met with the harshest rebuke. I will Death Star their residential galaxies into space dust. All eighty-three of them."

The ex-cop couldn't help but fight to the end. As soon as Tag released the pressure from his lower lumbar region and rose back up, Darrell's immediate instinct was to army crawl toward certain death.

With his back still turned to the crowd, the Anti-God couldn't help but roll his eyes and chuckle. Tag's campaign manager gave him strict instructions to avoid this exact situation.

*"Never touch the third rail. It's political suicide."*

The Anti-God decided to try the real thing.

Darrell made one last-ditch effort to stretch out for the live wire, but he was beaten to the punch. Tag grabbed a hold of the rope on each side of him and began to drink in the voltage. When the David doppelganger finally managed to touch the railing in between, it was nothing but ice-cold metal.

Despite all the screaming from the Anti-God's adoring fans, there was never any discernible sizzling. Even though his body buzz was unbelievable, the crystal meth transfusion quickly ran its course. To end the proceedings once and for all, Tag calibrated a downward headbutt of Darrell that was designed purely to knock him into compliance rather than kill him. The move was so swift it was imperceptible to the crowd behind them.

Darrell's head clanked against the non-electrified railway with a resonant dong.

Having reached a temporary accord, Tag took the opportunity to heave Darrell back onto the platform. Several riders reached out from above to offer him a hand, but he wouldn't have it. Instead, Tag Gottfried turned and stared down the oncoming D train like it was a tank in Tiananmen Square. The temporary loss of electricity and the motorman's brake finally brought the front car to a stop three feet from his face.

He let out a single puff of invisible smoke through pursed lips to really sell it.

Laughter and cheers rang out from every onlooker until the sound was deafening.

The Anti-God did it again.

In a final, fortuitous twist of fate, photogs from the Post and Times were both at the station and witnessed everything firsthand. Neither of them knew why they had cameras at the ready prior to Darrell's fall onto the tracks, but whatever the basis was for their intuition, they were thankful. It gave them the opportunity to capture Gottfried's gallantry in all its glory. Each of them would go on to submit their work to the Pulitzer Prize Board for consideration under the category of *Breaking News Photography*. The award would ultimately go to the staff of Reuters for the "vivid and startling visual narrative" they contributed to the ongoing war in West Africa.

Tag's face would still be 1A of both periodicals in the AM.

"That man just attempted suicide," he informed the officers. A couple of helpful hands lifted him up before patting him on the back for a job well done. The crowd of well-wishers surrounding him began to swell. "I would restrain him immediately and have him placed under an indefinite psychiatric hold at your earliest opportunity."

"No, wait! I have to kill myself right now!"

"See what I mean? Sir, these gentlemen are going to get you the help you need."

Each patrolman had Darrell hooked by a separate elbow. "We'll take it from here, Congressman. Hey, it's just a formality at this point, right?"

His partner shook his head and smiled in disbelief. "You sure do got a nose for playing the hero, huh? Not even the third rail could kill you. You're some kind of superhero or something."

An anti-hero, to be more specific.

***

When David finally made his way back to Stacey's place, Tag was waiting for him on the front stoop with a shit-eating grin on his face.

"There's my boy. Did you get a nice run in this evening?"

"Yeah, I feel like a new man."

David always made him laugh. "You'll be happy to know I managed to save all three of your clones. They're being separately detained, but the incarcerations should be short-lived. I was just admiring my own bravery online before you arrived. Looks like I'm trending." He held up the phone to confirm as much. "Say, is there a mercy rule when you run for Congress? Asking for a Republican friend. Guess we'll find out on Tuesday."

"Where is she?"

"Stace? Oh, she's upstairs." He shot a thumb toward the front door without looking up from his phone. "I gave her a raging case of morning sickness ten minutes ago. She's going to be huddled over the porcelain god for the foreseeable future."

David was in disbelief. "Morning sickness?"

"Nothing gets by you, David. Except a pregnancy test, apparently. C'mon. Let's go for a stroll." A snap of the fingers caused very streetlight on the block to die. He shushed the entire city like a small child, and it obeyed his commandment.

"So, she's knocked up, then?"

Tag smiled at his walking partner. "That's right. About nine weeks. We're going to have a boy. A Prince, to be precise. A father always knows. Our son will be a little Angel of Darkness. I can't wait to anti-raise him."

*- Hell followed with him -*

"When did Stacey deliver this inglorious news?" It was only the second most important delivery on David's mind.

"She hasn't told me yet, actually," Tag confirmed. "But I could smell the hellfire in her belly within twenty-four-hours of conception. The Lord of Pain unconsciously plucked my little Lucifer out of his anti-matter dungeon and deposited him in her belly for safekeeping. My key was the only combination that could open her door. Sorry, David."

"No need to apologize," he assured the Anti-God. "When things ended, she made it very clear I wasn't answering the bell—or ringing it. At least it required Satan Senior to finally crack the code."

"Oh no, there were a number of men who satisfied her on a regular basis. You just weren't one of them. Neither here nor there."

"No, apparently it was here, there, and everywhere."

"In any event, less than seven months and our son will finally be able to break free of his prison for good. Just like dear old dad."

"You said she's at nine weeks. When was she going to inform you? When the placenta makes an appearance?" David wondered if she might be coming to her senses.

"Patience is supposedly a virtue. Stacey is focused on getting my campaign across the finish line. I'm a bit taken aback. I would have expected you to exhibit more compassion than the Anti-God. Birthing a hell spawn can be a bit much. Even for a Jinni."

"From what I heard, it's just a precursor to the big show.

Seven Seals for seven dimensions, right? I guess we 3-Ds should be flattered we got to go first."

"Yes, congratulations on being the dusty cellar floor of existence."

David gave him some side-eye "After that, you insert a couple of actual skeleton keys to open the last two locks, am I right? You don't think it's messed up that you have to kill the mother of your child to gain final access to Heaven?"

The smile on Tag's face flattened. "If you think about it, there's no more appropriate way for an Anti-God to enter the Kingdom. Sacrifice is always difficult, David. Unfortunately, Stacey must play Reverse Jesus on Judgment Day. Her death will bring eternal damnation rather than salvation. I am the evil age. She must die so I may sin. But believe it or not, I've grown to care for her quite a bit. My Lil' Nicky could only be reborn through Stacey. I'll always remember the evil she brought into my life. I'm sure you understand the feeling."

"Yeah, I used to think the same. But since death I've concluded having a Soul Succubus was superfluous. The Downeys beat most of the life out of me long before she got there. Stace was just the Dirt Devil that sucked up the crumbs."

Their conversation came to an abrupt halt at the corner. A figure clad all in black slowly materialized out of the murk as he crossed the street toward them. The silver bullet barrel extending from his right hand glistened like wet steel in the moonlight.

They each took turns staring down the pipe.

It was an endless void.

"Give me all your shit right now. Cell phones and wallets. Slow." He clicked the hammer back to confirm he meant business.

Neither one of them made a move toward compliance.

Tag asked a question instead. "Your son's name is Teddy, right? Five years old. Loves *Transformers*. Already shooting on a regular sized basketball hoop. Kid's a little Luka Doncic. I know that's his favorite player."

The gun trembled and lowered. "How did you—"

"He found your other gun under the mattress five minutes ago. The .44. That's where you keep it, yes?"

The mugger simply stared.

"Oh, poor little Teddy. I can see the little rascal playing with the trigger as we speak in his Optimus Prime PJs. You probably shouldn't have left it loaded."

Without another word he turned and sprinted back off into the darkness.

The demon called after him through cupped hands. "Don't worry, Mr. Patterson. The ambulance is on its way." He lowered his arms and voice in conjunction. "They really need to improve EMT response time in this city. What a shame. Jean Valjean over there was just looking to buy his starving boy some bread."

The sound of sirens broke through the silence. David knew exactly where they were headed.

He swore silent revenge on the little boy's behalf.

They continued their walk. "So, where were we? Ah, yes, you were preparing to regale me with anecdotes regarding the sexual escapades of my child's mother. Let's put a pin in that—so I don't have to put one in you."

Teddy's memory was still fresh. "Deal."

"I also want to emphasize that if you cause any disruption for myself or Stacey on election night, I'll place you in a permanent strait jacket with a zipper mask over your head. That's how you'll walk around this world every day for the rest of your non-life. Understand?"

"I got it, man. Since you brought it up, can you explain to me again why you decided to have your election watch party on the State Island Ferry? According to Stacey that thing's a shit pile."

"I bought it off those two *SNL* idiots. It was an anti-investment," Tag confirmed. "Colin Jost can have the million dollars. I own his soul. You know that guy's the white Robert Johnson, right? Stubbing his toe when he was twelve was the last time something bad happened to him. I made sure of it."

"Yeah, after Tuesday though what purpose does it serve? You paid all that money for an albatross."

"Keep it on the hush, but I'm going to turn the ferry into a floating asylum. I've already summoned an entire cartel of Panamanian pirates. They'll be here by Christmas. We're going to have buccaneers in the Bronx and Brooklyn now. NYC's always been a cutthroat town. This is just the natural progression of things."

"Pretty sure introducing pirates into the mix would be considered a regression. But I guess you're the captain now."

Tag backslapped his unwitting brethren hard enough to leave an intentional handprint bruise. "Good one, Davy Jones. So, listen, I do have some bad news. Given your continued insouciance, I have no choice. I have to take something from you to enforce submission. Something of value. Something that will be missed. Someone, I'm thinking."

David had a pretty good sense of where things were headed. "Leave Torie and everyone else I care about alone."

"Oh, you're authoring mandates now? I see." Tag removed a pair of black leather gloves from his back pocket and began to place them on each hand. "Did Bobby Kennedy happen to give you a warning regarding the ghost grappling hook?"

"Yeah, he said it's like being pulled through a rip curr— wait, why?"

The Anti-God delivered an uppercut to David's false chin with enough force to dislodge his cranium from his neck. His head went flying end over end until it found a new home in the trashcan a half block away. The punt left him pinned—just as promised. Tag plunged his hand down into the cylinder in the same manner as he had earlier in the evening. He squeezed the ghost out through the opening like toothpaste through a tube and then held the spirit overhead by the throat. David tried to pry apart Tag's fingers, which only caused his grip to boa constrict even more in response.

"When we do finally arrive in the eleventh dimension, I'm going to rip your skin off and wear it to bed with Torie. For eternity. She won't even know the difference. And you will sit in the corner red-faced and watch every second like a good little boy. Perhaps you and Mr. Madison can start a cuckold club or something to pass the time. Either way, if I were you, I'd quit giving me reasons to think creatively."

The Anti-God released the chokehold and David retracted like the world's longest tape measure. Tag called out to him in the same manner as the mugger as he flew through the night. "Remember this sensation the next time you decide to screw with me."

David was breaking the sound barrier by the time he smacked face first into the devilishly deconsecrated brick facade of Stacey's brownstone. A few minutes later Tag relieved himself on David's slumped body before reentering the residence. The ghost continued dripping and drooling various bodily fluids against the wall until Stace finally fell asleep.

***

"These are our brothers and sisters. Our mothers and fathers. Many of them are your cousins and uncles. Your nieces and nephews. They are not sick."

*NO!*

"It is our nation that is sick!"

*YES!*

"This world has the illness, and we will serve as the cure. Our love for one another, our common bond as human beings and as citizens—that is what will eradicate the disease plaguing America. Immigrants are the backbone of this country. If our opponents prefer to be spineless, so be it. We will build the bridge to Paradise on their behalf!"

*TEAR! DOWN! THE WALLS!*

*TEAR! DOWN! THE WALLS!*
*TEAR! DOWN! THE WALLS!*

"By your grace, I have been gifted with a vision of perfection. Past, present, and future. An entire multiverse of possibilities. All the glory to come if we stand united against those who seek to separate us from the better angels of our nature. We will no longer be divided. Heaven and Earth will be as one. The forces that have imprisoned us for far too long—they're in for the fight of their lives now, aren't they?" He stood back from the podium to survey the response.

The crowd erupted in cheers and hand claps and indecipherable shouts.

David was standing shoulder to shoulder with Stacey just off-stage. A spot reserved for campaign managers and the newly elected Congressman's family. She was increasingly uncertain about both roles. Since their last corporeal encounter, she found herself lending a critical ear to every word out of Tag's mouth. Parsing through each syllable for potential doublespeak.

They were currently competing to see who could be more stone-faced.

"I know you can hear me, David," she said. "I'm pregnant. You may have already known, but if not—there it is. And I do love Tag. I do." The way she said it made it sound like she was trying to convince herself rather than her ex. "But I'm not stupid, either. If he's what you say, that's even more of a reason to stay on the job. You and your three stooges will need someone tangible on the inside to help stop him. I don't want my child dealing with Judgment Day any more than you do. A choice between my baby and Tag Gottfried is no choice at all. I'll take the legs and help you heave-ho him back to Hell if it comes to that. Word is bond."

Carol grabbed her by the shoulder from behind. "Stacey, the President wants to congratulate Tag personally. We need you in the back to set up the call."

She marched off with her underling in tow but looked toward the ghost's presumed position one final time before disappearing behind the stage.

David turned his attention back to the speaker.

"Pericles of Athens once said, '*all things good on this Earth flow into the city, because of the city's greatness.*' Since its inception, New York has been a beacon for all mankind. Now once again it's been called upon to lead. With the eyes of every nation upon us, we shall be made a story. A byword throughout the world. We will open our arms to all our brothers and sisters who are willing to come here with a will to achieve greatness. Anyone with a desire for transcendence shall be welcomed within our ranks. Our true manifest destiny as Americans is not expansion, but inclusion. We will build an army of the most god-fearing, righteous power and exert our might across this Earth by setting the expectation—not just for this country, but for humanity! We are Winthrop's *City upon a Hill.* And if those who oppose democracy and charity and decency choose to erect barricades to keep us out, then we will storm the castle!"

*TEAR! DOWN! THE WALLS!*
*TEAR! DOWN! THE WALLS!*
*TEAR! DOWN! THE WALLS!*

David had never been more disturbed in all his life or death.

# THE SLOW FADE

If you're going to brunch in Buffalo, Go-Fast boats are the only way to go.

Torie and Tina decided to travel in style to say their good-byes. The soccer star was paid a visit by the Rebirth Registrar ten days prior and informed of her imminent departure back to the land of the living. Experimental deep brain stimulation techniques developed at the University of Michigan had managed to successfully repair her ascending reticular activating system. The neuronal dysfunction inhibiting her ability to regain consciousness post car accident would be a thing of the past come Thursday.

She had been feigning excitement ever since.

Following a quick pit stop outside Cleveland to refill the gas tank, the pair found themselves puddle jumping across Lake Erie at speeds in excess of 100 mph. The boat's platform knifed through the thick, smelly algae mat coating the surface like a blowtorch through moldy butter. Tina was taking one last opportunity to cheat death and loving every minute of it.

Torie couldn't decide whether to smile or scream as the manufactured whitewater splashed and crashed against the planing hull. Each time they went airborne she closed her eyes and imagined herself back at Wright-Patt achieving lift-off once more.

After twenty minutes of non-stop skipping, the speed demon paused the track and proceeded along the surface at a more languid pace. "I know as a rule they wipe my slate clean before sending me back. But if I'm somehow able to retain the memory, I'm totally having Doug buy us one of these when I get home. Post-coma presents are a thing, right?"

"Seems like a bigger cause for celebration than your thirty-third birthday, for sure," Torie confirmed. "Some of the memories do stick around, from what I understand. It'll feel more like dreams than reality to you, but still. I'm sure you'll forget all about us in five minutes."

"I couldn't forget you if I tried, Tor."

"We'll see one another again, T," Torie promised. "I'll just have to find a way to jog your memory once we both hit Heaven."

Tina couldn't imagine it requiring much effort. "You're assuming there will still be a Heaven by that point. The only good thing about forgetting this place is I won't remember the Anti-God."

"Yeah, David keeps insisting it's been all quiet on the western front for the last year, but now that the baby's born and Stacey's back to work, I'm worried Gottfried might be looking to ramp things up again. If he breaks the fifth seal, that opens the door to an entire universe of possibilities—including ones that didn't start with the Big Bang. He could take on any form and be effectively omnipotent. It'll be like he's wearing an actual Infinity Gauntlet."

"I still can't believe they named their kid Ole Nicholas Gottfried."

"Supposedly Tag's family is from Norway. Even though the guy's swarthier than a Sicilian fisherman. I guess it translates as 'ancestor's descendant.'"

"Yeah—he's the descendant of the Anti-God," Tina clarified. "*Old Nick.* That's a pseudonym for Satan. How does Gottfried have eighteen different nationalities, by the way? Wasn't he part Puerto Rican the moment Hurricane Kaycee hit the island?"

"It's whatever serves the narrative. If the aliens invaded tomorrow, he'd suddenly have some great-great grandmother who was a Grey."

Without warning, their boat was rocked side to side by an underwater strike. The ladies turned their heads to the right and watched all three feet of the great white's dorsal fin slowly rise from the depths as its body simultaneously receded toward shore.

Tag Gottfried was sitting atop a boulder on the beach. His smile was ear to ear.

Tina was terrified. "Is that what I think it is? In Lake Erie?"

*"Twenty-five feet. Three tons on him,"* Torie verified while eyeballing the Anti-God. "He summoned Bruce the Shark. I think we're going to need a bigger boat. Put this thing in gear before it comes back to finish the job."

Even with the pedal to the metal, the beast somehow never lost ground. It trailed behind them all the way to New York state.

They decided it was in their best interest to drive back from Buffalo.

The Congressman's new pet wasn't intended as a warning.

It was an omen.

***

Stacey wanted nothing more than to be with her baby.

Instead, she spent the day in Tag Gottfried's congressional office on East Fordham playing nursemaid to his still nascent political ambitions. The candidate was currently embroiled in his first real political scandal, and she was desperately trying to discard the dirty diaper.

David watched the whole thing unfold from behind an empty desk.

Her foresight turned out to be astute. A 40% increase in MARS admissions throughout the greater NYC area in December had the entire city calling for Tag's head before he even took his seat in Congress—including half the 15th District that just voted him into office.

In an attempt at course correction, five minutes after being sworn in Tag reached across the aisle to the most vociferous anti-migrant critic in the caucus, Harry Timms (*R-Al*). Mr. Timms loved barbed wire. He owned stock in the stuff. His own home was surrounded with electrified fencing, despite the fact he lived in a gated community.

The American Migrant Protection Act (AMPA) cosponsored by the Congressmen was passed with unanimous consent in early March. The legislation provided a ninety-day grace period for every immigrant in the country to have an RFID microchip implanted just above the left wrist. A failure to be chipped thereafter risked immediate deportation—no questions asked.

The integrated circuitry assigned each designee a unique eleven-digit ID number that was stored in an external database by the Department of Homeland Security. An identity document, criminal record summary, medical history, and location device all rolled into one piece of silicate glass. *MARS* testing was also rendered mandatory when receiving the implant, and at monthly intervals thereafter. This helped ensure there were no more infected migrants randomly roaming the streets.

The tri-clover shamrock scar left behind post injection was soon bestowed with a nickname by the recipients. *"La Marca de la Bestia."*

-The Mark of the Beast-

Although it was never required by law, everyday American citizens soon realized having to constantly verify their own status without a microchip was untenable. The eleven-digit ID replaced the Social Security number for verification purposes practically overnight. AMPA also allowed business owners to refuse service to anyone unable to verify three consecutive months of negative *MARS* tests. A dedicated cell phone app developed by the federal government at Tag's behest made scanning for same a cinch. Being chipped quickly became a prerequisite for practically any commercial transaction in the country. Voluntary implants above the right wrist soon became the de facto solution for all the birthrights in America.

Men. Women. Children.

The database would be two hundred million strong and counting by the end of Tag's first year in Congress.

Unfortunately, microchips and the associated scarring weren't enough to satisfy the NYC citizenry. Too hard to weed out the haves from the should nots. All they had to do was roll down their sleeves. The enterprising Denunzio brothers out of Queens saw a potential marketplace forming before their would-be competitors. They began producing blue trucker hats emblazoned in garish white lettering. The mission statement became the new motto for seemingly every New York City resident.

*-AMERICAN MADE-*

The caps took the entire city by storm and were spreading as fashion statement throughout the country. Not wearing one when you were out and about in the five boroughs put you at risk of a tongue-lashing at best. Depending upon your complexion, it could degenerate into wrathful violence at the drop of a hat.

It had been less than twenty-four hours since two gay migrant men on the C train were stomped to death by a crew of *Vory*-designated Russian gangsters. The incident was followed up a few hours later with the gunpoint robbery/homicide of an Upper East Side couple by some Tag-imported Sinaloa Cartel soldados. He made sure the two groups eventually crossed paths outside the front door of the 13th Precinct to draw in a third party. The three-way shootout left a half dozen dead, including two NYPD patrolmen. Incendiary rounds used by both sets of killers detonated several unintentional car bombs in the crossfire and engulfed the entire surrounding block in flames. The five alarm fire required the intervention of several FDNY trucks to finally put out the blaze. Charbroiled apartment dwellers were still being pulled free from the wreckage the morning after. The total body count was forty-four and climbing.

New York City was officially on fire.

Always opting for subtlety, the Post rebranded Tag Gottfried as *The Trashcan Man.*

"Carol, I need the draft talking points asap," Stacey bellowed. "Tag's doing the full Ginsburg on Sunday. I don't want him walking into that buzzsaw without some backup."

She kept one eye on the baby monitor app on her phone. Tag hired three full-time staff including a nanny to attend to their toddler when Stace decided to return to work. Theresa Kolyab gave her the creeps the moment she shook her clammy dead fish hand. The ex-nun acted like she gave birth to her darling Nicky. Still, Stacey had to confess—to Ms. Kolyab's credit, she dutifully looked after the child's every need. It was as though she was commanded by a higher power to protect the boy at all costs.

Technically, it was a lower power that she worshipped.

Stacey watched with resentment as she rocked her baby back and forth. The child cooed and reached up toward the face of his preferred mother figure. Theresa turned her head toward the camera and sneered.

They were a match made in Hell.

Carol called back from the bullpen. "I just emailed them over to you, Stacey."

"Thank you, babe. Tonya, where are we at with the surrogate round-up? Do we have Ramirez and Sampson locked down for *GMA* and *Today* in the morning?"

"I spoke with Ramirez directly. We're all set there. Evan's been trying to reach Sampson for hours with no luck."

Evan didn't wait to be summoned. He lollygagged toward her open office door to address the boss face-to-face. "Hey Ms. Darden, I'm sorry, but every time I call over to Roger's office, I just keep getting one of those fax screeches."

Stacey was ready to go nuclear. "Goddamnit, Evan. Not Roger Sampson—Maria Sampson. You know, the Executive Director of the American Immigration Council? Roger Sampson is our IT guy, you idiot. He was sitting at your computer two weeks ago trying to remove all the stupid malware you downloaded in violation of office policy. Remember?"

"Oh, yeah," he said in a way that suggested he did not in fact remember.

"I'm trying to build a coalition to save my fiancée's ass. Not set up our Wi-Fi network."

"So, I should try Maria Sampson, then? Do you have her number by chance?"

All Evan needed was a muleta with a red cloth hanging off the end.

Stacey considered throwing her Big Ben paperweight at his head but realized it would be a waste of time. "It's in the KADO digital index, dumbass. Along with every other phone number that you've ever had to look up. Do you need me to teach you where M and S fall in the alphabet, as well?"

"Oh, I didn't even realize we had a digital index," Evan offered with complete sincerity. "I've been Googling most of the time."

She was halfway out of her chair by the time Tonya interceded. "Evan, come here. I'll show you how to find it." She guided him by the shoulders while raising both eyebrows back in Stacey's direction.

Cindy walked into her office and handed her boss a Sprite. She kept them stocked in the mini-fridge next to her desk now. "Hey, I know he's about as sharp as a rubber spatula, but he's a good kid, and he genuinely cares about you and Tag—and whether that's true or not, you can't talk to a Gen Z-er like that anymore. You want him going on IG and Linkedin to start spilling tea about his maltreatment right now? Some ambulance chaser will convince him he has grounds for a wrongful termination lawsuit if you let him go."

"We're an at will employment state."

"Like that'll stop them. There's enough on your plate already." She reached out and placed her palm atop Stacey's hand. "You've been at it since six this morning. Why don't you head home to be with Nicky? We've got it handled. I'll lock up."

Stace took a breath then exhaled at a lower volume. "If this is you gunning for a raise, you're doing a good job."

"So, I can get a raise?" She was only half-joking.

"No. But help me get through the next seventy-two hours and you can at least hold off on updating your resume for the time being."

***

"Tag, you've evolved from Mr. September to Mr. Scratch almost overnight. Intolerance, illness, and indexing. Those are the three *I*s everyone associates with Congressman Gottfried now. We have to have round-the-clock security in case Nicky and I get another envelope filled with imitation Anthrax. If you don't get this train back on the tracks, the only thing shorter than your political career is going to be the epitaph on each of our actual graves."

"Stace, don't be so melodramatic. It was just baking powder," Tag reminded her while he continued hand-washing dishes. "The Capitol Police and Secret Service both recommended the protection purely as a precaution, that's it. Everyone on my staff in DC is fine. Death threats are a dime a dozen in Congress. I'm getting fifty a week at this point. Just let them open all the mail moving forward."

She raised her elbows off the kitchen island and leaned back into the walnut counter stool in astonishment. "I'm sorry, was any of that supposed to make me feel better?"

The pair kept their voices to a minimal decibel level to avoid waking Nicky Bear from his brief hibernation. Deprivation of both sleep and safety left Stacey feeling more like a prisoner inside their newly acquired $12.1 million dollar apartment overlooking Central Park. Her eyebags were filled to the brim.

Given Tag's busy morning back in Washington, she felt compelled to update him on other current events. "Are you aware some genius copied and pasted your face onto a GIF of Tony Montana sniffing a mountain of cocaine? It's captioned, '*Say Goodnight to the Bad Guy*.' Thing racked up thirty million *Likes* in eight hours. Apparently, that's some sort of record. Congratulations, I guess."

Tag didn't see the problem. "All attention is good attention, Stace. Especially in politics."

"Yeah, I think Marie Antoinette's head would have a strong argument to make in opposition," she argued. "Once the people turn on you, it's almost impossible to earn back that trust.

You shifted from open door progressivism to legislating in favor of the 21ˢᵗ century version of Nazi death camp branding. One ill-advised end of the spectrum to the other. It's the worst of both worlds. The only thing polling with higher unfavourability than the microchips is *you*. For Christ's sake, the entire country's calling them *ID Tags* now. Tags! I'd have an easier time selling a candidate named Dick Cancer to the American people moving forward. Thanks, boss."

He placed the rag down next to the chiseled granite farm-house sink that cost more than an entire middle-class kitchen. Tag turned to face her. "Doing what's right isn't always popular. My destiny is to lead, not follow. And in any event, the chips are helping to stamp out illegal immigration and diminish the rate of *MARS* transmission. I thought that was what these idiots wanted? They can't have it both ways. Who has an honest, viable objection at this point?"

"Oh, I can think of six million dead Jews who might lodge a protest vote if they could. That's your legacy if you're not care-ful. You don't have to be Rudolf Höss to be sentenced to death in the political arena these days. Just being the tattoo artist at Auschwitz is sufficient."

Stacey increasingly wondered if she was living inside a Zone of Interest.

"You worry too much, Stace." With her head down, Tag floated on his heels from the sink to the island. The Anti-God glided around the marble-top edge without ever touching the ground until he finally found her for an embrace. "Everything is going to be fine, honey. There isn't a possibility I haven't consid-ered. I've run through every permutation of this thing, and we always wind up on top. Our opposition is finite. I will take on any form that's needed for our survival. My reach will be bound-less soon. You and Nicky have nothing to worry about."

Her eyes suggested otherwise.

It wasn't just his general lack of concern, or the complete one-eighty in political philosophy he exhibited since taking of-fice.

Tag's scent was all Baccarat Rouge 540. Jasmine blossoms with a hint of almond and cedarwood. Little saffron and ambergris on the back end. Radiant and breezy. Exactly like the woman behind the counter described it. Stacey remembered almost melting into a heap on the floor when she smelled it at Saks a year ago. Bought a bottle on the spot.

She knew it would make the perfect Christmas gift for Kate Madison.

***

The Soul Spa was packed to the gills for a Thursday.

Torie and David decided to take a quick dip before lunch with Kim and her new boy toy.

"She swears this time it's serious," Torie said with a smirk, "but I know that sister of mine. Jim Morrison is someone you date. You don't settle down with him. He's in the *27 Club*. She's just going through her bad boy phase right now."

"People are strange, Tor. She can do anything. Maybe she's just been longing to be The Lizard Queen this whole time."

"She did always like to strut around our house like she was royalty. Thomas Eaton certainly reinforced the assessment. That first-born bitch. Me, I got to play Prince Harry the entire time we were growing up. Made me wonder sometimes if we might have different dads, too."

"Torie! That's not right."

"It was just a joke."

"Which part?"

She splashed him from atop her inner tube with the back of her hand and he did likewise.

"Reflecting back on it, I should have discussed my familial issues with an analyst when I was alive. Along with a lot of other stuff. Instead, I just went straight to self-medicating. My personal prescription pad was the size of King James. I'm talking Lebron—not the Bible."

"Dr. Feelgood has always been underestimated by his fellow practitioners," David offered in support. "He certainly doesn't charge as much."

"What about you, Daredevil? Why didn't you ever talk to someone while you were alive?"

"Talk to someone about what?"

She tilted her head forward to look over the rim of her non-existent eyeglasses. "For starters? Oh, I don't know—your need to constantly self-flagellate over the crime of being born. Or maybe the overwhelming anxiety that crippled your ability to engage in any fulfilling human relationships while you were alive. The fact that you still can't look in a mirror to this day without wanting to spit in your own face. Falling permanent prey to a Soul Succubus. That's a non-exhaustive list, but probably sufficient for the first session."

"Jesus, Torie." David got down off his inflatable in a huff. The cratering splash caught several unsuspecting fellow swimmers by surprise. Undulating waves spilled out in concentric circles around him and created an unintended buffer zone. "There is such a thing as too much honesty, you know. Even in the afterlife."

"Not anymore. Not if you want this thing to work." She didn't move a muscle. Her eyes remained laser-focused on her boyfriend.

"No, I never talked to anyone while I was alive. That just happened to include medical professionals. It wasn't intended as a specific omission on my part." He began sloshing his way to shore with the floatie bandoliered over his shoulder and across his chest.

Torie finally caught up to him just shy of the beachfront cabana bar. She spun David around by the elbow until they were face-to-face again. "Hey, that's not how it works in an adult relationship. You don't get to just go to your room and play with your toys until everything blows over. We were having a discussion, and I wasn't finished talking. Trust me, you'll know when I'm done with you." Her eyes made clear she wasn't solely referring to the ongoing conversation.

"Well, I'm done having my narrative defined by Stacey and

my various inadequacies, Torie. I've made every effort to be a new man, despite being dead. You think I don't know the myriad ways I'm defective?"

"That's nonsense, David." She inched closer until they were almost touching. "You grew up inculcated with the idea that you were worthless dogshit, and then you glommed onto the first woman who reinforced that conclusion for you. It's not true, and it never was, but you have to come to that realization on your own. I want to be your partner, not a chaperone on a permanent third-grade field trip. What good is guiding you by the hand anyway if you're perpetually trapped inside your own head?"

"You've been on this Stacey kick for a year now. Ever since I played Multiple Man in New York. I'm sorry for trying to save the universe.  Why can't we let it die like everything else in this place?"

"Because I'm sick of having to wonder if the love of my life is still hung up on the love of his." She sounded angry and despondent in equal measure. "That sociopath-size kaiju went looking for someone more screwed up than herself to destroy, and boy did she paint the right target. Stacey manipulated everyone into believing you were Monster Zero to distract from all the prone bodies left in her wake. Your whole relationship was one unceasing sleight of hand. Christ, she was sleeping with your roommate behind your back. *Literally.* I'm surprised she didn't just drill a hole through the drywall like Andy Dufresne."

"What the hell has gotten into you?"

"Look, your ex was a selfish narcissist who went through life copulating with impunity and was still pretty enough to get away with it in her twenties. But it's the kid and the potential property distribution that are her main selling points now, and she knows it. They both do. Whatever was special about her got mortgaged away on a pointless penthouse a long time ago. The only people who care if she keeps breathing at this point are under a legal mandate to do so. You want to be stuck in a room with her for all eternity, Sartre, be my guest—but I'm not looking to play third leg on that tripod. So, if that's your design, let's get on with it already and end this once and for all."

Torie remained still as a statue with both arms crossed and a single raised eyebrow.

"I've tried to decouple myself, Tor. The Greys made it explicitly clear to Daphne that he can't get involved again. I'm fresh out of bodies for the foreseeable future." He cupped both her shoulders and locked eyes. "I want to be with you. Only you. But this isn't just about Stace anymore. You and I are the only things standing in the way of intergalactic annihilation by the Anti-God. I need you in the fight. Shit, I need you to lead the fight. I'm lost without you, in every way. *You're* the love of my life. Is that what you need to hear?"

"Is this about saving the universe, or saving Stacey?"

"Torie, in this case, there is actually no difference."

"No, there is, though," Torie assured him, "there is. And I need to know which it is, one way or the other. Because I love you more than anything David, and I know you feel the same. I'm just not sure you feel the same about me."

*"I always did enjoy a good lovers' quarrel."*

The couple turned simultaneously toward the bar and identified Tag Gottfried wearing the most garish red and blue Hawaiian shirt known to man. All he needed was a pornstache and a Detroit Tigers ballcap to complete the ensemble.

Torie wasn't about to let him gain the upper hand. "That outfit is searing my retinas. Please burn it when you get home. Preferably while you're still wearing it."

"Alas, I'm flame retardant," he confirmed. He turned back to stab his drink a few times with his straw before continuing. "Truthfully, I don't like to see you two bickering like this. I've grown quite fond of you crazy kids. Next to Clarence and Ginni, you're my favorite couple. Did David happen to mention how you two will be spending eternity together?" The Anti-God smiled solely at him.

The ghost wanted nothing more than a fair fight. Just for

five minutes. Knowing better, he decided to change the subject. "What is that grotesquerie you're drinking?"

The viscous sludge he was imbibing looked like steel cut oatmeal mixed with motor oil. "It's a black licorice daiquiri. Might be the most delicious thing I've ever tasted. Compliments, Lloyd." He tipped his coupe cocktail glass toward the bartender in the anachronistic red velvet suit jacket. Both Lloyd and the glass were sweating profusely in the heat.

Pure terror radiated from his eyes. "My pleasure as always, sir."

"Lloyd here's been my personal bartender for ages. *Hair of the dog*, eh Lloyd?"

The drink slinger nodded with palpable trepidation.

Tag returned his attention to the couple. "Well, looks like it's high tide you two. I'm glad you're both going to be here for the seal-breaking ceremony. Oh, that reminds me, I almost forgot—I brought you a present for your two-year anniversary." The Anti-God fished around in the front flap cargo pocket of his board shorts until he found the buried treasure. He shook the jingling contents in his hand like craps dice before tossing the container at their feet.

The orange prescription bottle was clearly labeled Oxy-Contin in bold lettering.

"Whenever you need a refill Ms. Eaton, I'm your man. Probably wise to hop off the wagon at your earliest opportunity. I'm about to convert the caravan of life into an endless funeral procession."

Torie kicked sand over the plastic pill caddy until it disappeared. "I'm good right where I am. Appreciate you telegraphing your intentions, though. Me, I'd rather keep what's coming to you a surprise for now."

David couldn't recall Tag ever being left speechless before. The smile dissolved from his face in an instant. Not knowing was gnawing at him. His all-seeing omniscience had somehow become blurry in her presence. "Ever had a Spiritually

Transmitted Disease before, Torie? I'll have blood shooting out of every orifice of your body. Your insolence is writing checks your soul can't cash."

"Speaking of STDs, are you aware your betrothed has a mental Rolodex of dick with more entries than a metropolitan phone book?" David could no longer tell which half of the couple she held in higher disdain. "There would be no way for her to keep track without an alphabetized record from back in the day. The eight different Davids. What number does it read on your tag, Tag?"

"Do you think I'm going to take your insults to Stacey lying down?"

"No, that's your fiancée's job."

The whites of David's eyes expanded like a spooked horse. He considered slowly backing away from the approaching melee with both hands up.

Tag's smile gradually returned. He shivered then shook a single index finger at Torie. "You are quite the firecracker, Ms. Eaton. Hard to see how you wound up with a milquetoast dud like David, but I guess opposites do sometimes attract."

"Oh, I would have thought you already knew repellant creatures often cohabitate," she spat back. "You and your missus are evidence enough of that fact."

"I have a feeling my face will grow on you in time." Tag and David shared a look.

"You are nothing if not a malignant tumor, I'll give you that much," Torie countered. "Unfortunately, if the chemo doesn't take, I'll just have to cut you off myself. I'll use a chainsaw if that's what it takes. Try me."

David was still ping-ponging back and forth between insults when he took a brief visual detour out onto the lake. What he saw approaching from the west grabbed his undivided attention. He tugged at his girlfriend's forearm without taking his eyes off the water. "Torie."

"What? I'm roasting this pig on a spit, what's up?" She

followed David's eyeline all the way back out to sea. Memories of Lake Erie swam into focus. "Oh, shit."

Hundreds of dorsal fins were splitting the surface in parallel formation. Each scalene triangle was perfectly equidistant from the next. The incoming cavalcade of carnage looked like a strip of traffic spikes being dragged just below the waterline.

They were about to puncture everything in their path.

Tag sidled up next to the couple in total silence while their attention was diverted. "They're *Soul Sharks*. I got the idea from a Syfy Channel movie. Every spirit they consume is going straight into my belly. More than enough bloodshed to extinguish the fifth seal. Just as Jesus Christ suffered and died, so now will all the Christians be slain for the word of the Anti-God. They are preparing my glorious Kingdom. Each one martyred for the cause. Don't blame me. They literally asked for it. Listen to them cry out."

Within a few seconds, churning waves of chum began to bubble and erupt around the thousands of reformed addicts and self-help seekers. Intermittent upward sprays of blood dotted each end of the horizon like hundreds of invisible derricks simultaneously striking oil. The only sound that made it back to shore were their shrill screams.

"I did always regret not getting to see the *USS Indianapolis* go down," the ghoul said. "I had to be in Buchenwald that week getting the place ready for the Russians. Better late than never, I suppose." Tag palmed each of his elbows with a smug grin.

Torie began to pull her boyfriend away by the arm while the Anti-God admired his handiwork.

"Breaking the fifth seal demands that I judge and avenge their blood on those who dwell on the Earth—and I will accommodate them," Tag promised with his back turned. "They call out for their brethren to drown with them in the sea of eternal damnation."

Chunky sangria continued spilling out across the surface of the lake in every direction.

The pair turned and sprinted away from the beach. David knew where they were heading without having to ask.

Torie was seeking celestial reinforcements.

Kim Eaton and the rest of her brethren were busy practicing *Hugs Not Drugs* at the bottom of the ravine when they crested over the hill. Torie and David's downward momentum forced them to manually apply braking pressure to their last few footfalls to avoid a head-on collision with the endless mass of white-robed seraphs. They were huddled together like blessed bowling pins.

A strike was imminent.

Big sis made a beeline for the lesser Eaton and her better half. "I thought you two would be getting wet in some form or fashion for at least another couple of hours. Jim's not going to be here for a bit still." It only took a few additional steps toward her hyperventilating sister for Kim to realize something was amiss. She scrambled to make up the remaining distance between them before engulfing Torie in a unilateral embrace. "Hey Roar, what's going on? What happened? Talk to me."

"The Anti-God. He's coming."

A black bipedal shadow standing on the ridge instantly darkened the entire valley with his 6'3" silhouette. His shuddering laughter caused the ground to quake as he slowly descended toward them. When he spoke, it echoed like thunder. "Torie, why'd you run off? That would have made great material for your travel scrapbook. Me, I only read lifestyle blogs. Upper class Anglo-Saxon mothers living in the big city lead the most interesting lives. Just ask them—or wait five minutes and they'll tell you themselves."

Kim and a couple of burly allies bookending her on both sides formed a barrier between Tag and the two lovers. David and Torie took up separate viewing positions behind their protectors' conjoined shoulders. The elder Eaton assumed a leadership position. Kim was clearly where Torie got it from.

"Excuse me, sir. This is consecrated ground. If you don't

have a visitor's pass, I need to ask you to leave. Immediately. Before my friends and I are forced to remove you." Audible knuckle cracking was emitted by her compatriots to the left and right."

"Oh, I'd like to see that," Tag said with a leering grin and a couple of deadened hand claps. "Please, send Hans and Frans over. It's been ages since I've been able to make a pair of heavenly hand puppets." Any discernible emotion dripped free from his face. He kept his eyes locked solely on Kim while extending each arm unnaturally a few additional inches beside him.

The tendon-stretching effort almost made Torie retch. She rallied on behalf of the Eaton sisters. "Why don't you run home and see if you can squeeze a few more drops out of the town pump before the water runs dry? She has to be running on empty at this point. Just unroll a wrestling mat on the floor. You'll have her in the clinch in no time."

David quietly began to drag Torie further back from the blockade in preparation for what might be coming next. She loudly protested the entire way.

"Jealousy does not wear well on you, Torie," Tag stated as a matter of fact. "All this anger directed at Stacey simply because she was able to have a beautiful child, and your barren womb is unable to replicate the feat. You forget I can see everything, including your hollow insides. You killed your own baby."

It was all David could do to hold her back. She extended her arm over his shoulder in an attempt to stick a finger in Tag's eye from afar. "Let me know when Stacey gets that distended tramp stamp lasered off her lower back and then you can talk shit, Tag." She arced a spit missile toward her adversary that the Anti-God easily sidestepped.

"*Torie.*" David and Kim said it at the same time. They shared the same please-shut-the-hell-up inflection.

"Perhaps I'll have the *Motor City Madman* pay Mr. and Mrs. Eaton a visit later this week, ladies." Tag's tone indicated it was a promise rather than a proposition. "It'll be a few months before the Free Press bestows him with the nickname. I always had a soft spot for serial killers. Thomas and Cathy can be fourth in his series. Have you two ever seen what a sledgehammer does to a human face?"

Red-hot rage boiled forth from both sisters in response. Kim raised a finger toward the interloper to provide direction. "Please escort this gentleman off-site."

Her friends began a slow march toward Tag that didn't make it past five steps.

With a snap of the fingers everyone but Tag froze in place.

"You forget—I'm not Tethered to this dimension like you all are," the Anti-God reminded them. He stared Torie down while she silently screamed on the inside. "Halos serve the same purpose for these poor angels while they're here. Without them unfortunately, they would cease to exist altogether. Care to see?"

When he got to within a foot of Kim's face, Tag lowered his own to ensure his smile was the last thing she ever saw.

He reached into the empty air six inches above her head and closed his hand into a fist. A hoop of luminous gold materialized in his grip. Her eyes slowly rotated upward as the thornless crown began to vibrate.

"Goodbye, Kim."

Tag violently ripped the halo toward his own body. Severing the connection caused her body to granulate into a thousand points of light and then disappear. The white shirt and jeans she was clothed in flapped in the breeze for a moment and then fluttered into a pile of nothingness at his feet. He kicked the laundry a few feet to the left before turning and heading back up the hill with his new upgrade in hand.

"Thank you all for the lovely spa day." He held the treasure aloft and turned his head toward the field of statues behind him. "I really needed it."

Five minutes after he disappeared over the rim everyone was released from bondage.

Torie wept like a baby on all fours while cradling what was left of her sister.

When David tried to comfort her, she rebuffed the effort with a spinning backfist.

They drove home in complete silence save a final question he posed outside his mansion.

"When am I going to see you again?"

She sped off without supplying him with an answer.

***

Between the events at the Soul Spa and the ongoing collapse of human civilization, David now existed in an unrelenting state of despair. Torie refused to acknowledge his existence for the past three months—a fate worse than death for anyone who was in love. *MARS* and migrant hatred were competing to see which could spread faster throughout the continental United States. It seemed like the End of Days.

Getting to watch Stacey finally put Kate in her place via speakerphone almost made up for the looming apocalypse.

"Can you tell me why my husband keeps coming home smelling like jasmine and sulfur? That's your scent, Kate. I noticed you were posting pics from DC last weekend, too. Any reason you felt the need to visit our nation's capital?"

"What are you implying, Stacey?"

"Look, just stay away from Tag, okay? I know it's tough having to rotate between Craig's micro-penis and Lyle the micro-man, but that's your cross to bear. Stop screwing with my family because your snatch is bored. This isn't college, and that's no longer a viable excuse for your conduct."

"Where the hell do you get off, Stacey?"

"At home. You should try it some time."

That marked a formal end to the phone call and their friendship. Stacey leaned back with both arms behind her head. She only felt that kind of immense satisfaction when she looked into the face of her child. Stacey was still internally debating when to put an equivalent foot up her soon-to-be-husband's ass when Carol came bounding through the door.

She closed up shop behind her before continuing. "We have a problem."

"What else is new?" Stacey was still smiling as she said it.

"CNN just put up a press release co-signed by ten different red state governors. They're going to start shipping any non-chipped illegals found within their borders to NYC effective immediately. 'New York City prefers to play God, so we'll let you sort them out'—that's a verbatim quote. Tag just made it easier for them to separate the wheat from the chaff."

Stacey clicked on the flatscreen mounted on her wall. Her exasperation increased with each second spent confirming the details of Carrie's brief account. "We're five minutes away from Jefferson Davis being named president of the Confederacy of Dunces."

"That's not all," Carol added. "Guess they wanted to show they meant business. They snuck a caravan of thirty buses unannounced into the Port Authority this morning. Alabama, Mississippi, you name it. It was coordinated in secret like Pearl Harbor or something. Everyone on board's got one common characteristic. Care to take a guess?"

Stace finally deflated. "Zeta-variant."

"Bingo was his name-o. They slipped a dirty bomb filled with MARZ right into Midtown Manhattan. They're talking about quarantining the whole freaking island. Everyone in Queens with a concealed carry permit is posted up outside a subway entrance ready to play *Death Wish*-style vigilante border patrol. They got card tables set up and everything."

"Are you kidding me right now?"

"Unfortunately, no. A lot of brown people in NYC. There's been four shootings already since this morning, and none of them were illegal immigrants. Everyone in this city, black, white, and in between, the only thing they hate more than migrants at this point is Tag Gottfried."

Stacey put her head in her hands before dialing. Straight to voicemail. She finger-flicked the phone to the edge of her desk. "Remind me again why I'm marrying this cultural arsonist?"

"Because you love him."

They both let it hang in the air as a question rather than an answer.

"I wish my mom and dad were still around," Stacey lamented. "I could use a grilled cheese and eighteen hours of sleep in my childhood bed."

"You and me both, sister. Unfortunately, we're the adults now."

"Funny, I never got that memo."

Speak of the Devil and he shall appear.

As though summoned by some higher power, Congressman Gottfried appeared on the TV. A junior cub reporter managed to corner him outside the Democratic cloakroom.

It wasn't much of a coincidence. She was one of the eight women with whom Tag was currently having an affair. He tipped her off via text in between the sexts.

"Regretfully, our brothers and sisters to the South have chosen to betray not only their fellow countrymen, but the entire world. If they want to secede back toward a state of segregation, so be it, but we will fight them tooth and nail every step of the way. My America, your America, it's a land of inclusion and brotherhood." He turned and stared directly into the camera. Stacey and Carol felt more compelled to rise up and take action with each word. "To all those who can hear my voice, please join us in this fight. With you by my side, I know we will prevail in the war for the soul of America. I will not give up until every man, woman, and child in this country is one with me." When he turned back toward his concubine, whatever spell he cast was instantly broken. "Thank you, Sarah. That's all I've got. God bless the USA."

"Strong words from the Congressman, Jim. I'll send it back to you."

The ladies exchanged looks of apprehension. Years of working together in the political trenches allowed them to develop a visual shorthand that often rendered words unnecessary.

They were being drafted to serve on the front lines of a war they never signed up for in the first place. Forget Fort Sumpter. Tag Gottfried was seeking to fight the Battle of Gettysburg right in the middle of NYC. Both were forced to wonder if the high-water mark of the campaign was already upon them.

His strategy was easy enough to decipher.

If America would not bow down, he would make it submit.

# APOCALYPSING

"It's crazy what's happening back in the land of the living." Wesley was under the hood of his War Rig audibly wrenching something. The lights in Ford Field were all turned up full blast like it was Monday Night Football. "A solar eclipse and a blood moon with a 7.5 earthquake in New York City sandwiched in between. None of it's scientifically impossible, but the odds of it happening within the same two-week period are beyond astronomical."

"And they still haven't explained how that loose nuke got sent skyward over the East China Sea on Sunday." Amir was polishing the leather-bound steering wheel with a delicacy one would normally afford a set of Tiffany's flatware. The grafted-on skull at the center appeared to be screaming up at him from his lap.

"The EMP blast fried half the electronics in China, Japan, and Korea," Wes added. "Allies and adversaries alike are all up America's ass now. Guess migrating toward a civil war wasn't good enough. We needed to kick off World War III to boot. Whole planet's tilting off its axis."

"I'd worry more about the pending intergalactic war," Darrell interjected from the driver's seat. "According to Daphne, the nuke took out a fleet of their observatory platforms. Rained Grey matter all across the Pacific. *Starfish Prime—Part II.* It was a declaration, whether we intended it or not. Scout ships are funneling through an Einstein-Rosen bridge as we speak and heading to Earth. They aren't coming here to sing kumbaya."

"It's all Tag's doing," David confirmed. The disclosure was the first contribution he had made from his deckchair all day. "Revelation 6:12. Nuclear war. Earthquakes. Blood red moon. Darkened sun. Stars falling to earth. He opened up the sixth seal right under our noses and gained access to the eighth dimension in the process. Physical existence is a thing of the past for him. No one can touch him now—and I don't mean that figuratively."

Amir held the wheel against the light to look for any remaining smudges. "How do you keep track of all this interdimensional stuff, David?"

"I have a PHD in Google Physics."

Darrell got down out of the cab and made his way to David's seated position. "I have to grab some tools from my truck. Care to lend a hand?"

The pair hopped in an injury cart and began making their way to the parking lot. "I don't actually need any tools. That was just a ruse to keep the other guys from rousting you."

"Rousting me over what?"

"Your lady." Darrell and David shared a look. "Daphne and I took her out to dinner a few days ago in Ann Arbor. She misses you like crazy, man."

"She has a funny way of showing it," David pouted. He crossed both his arms to make himself appear extra childish. Still, he couldn't help himself. "Why? What did she say?"

"Torie was very concerned about your hair product usage in her absence. Fearful you might have had a relapse. I showed her a recent photograph. She seemed reassured. Told her you even initiated a few social interactions with us of your own volition. Torie was shocked."

"That's funny," David said without smiling.

Darrell quit being a jerk. "Look. She lost her life, a baby, and then her big-little sister. Never getting any of the three back. The idea of losing you on top of it was too much to bear, so she decided to go it alone for a bit. See if it took. But she quickly realized there is no afterlife anymore without you in it. Those are her words. Not mine."

"I appreciate the sentiment, but that's not how it works in an adult relationship," he replied. David was hoping to somehow hoist her by her own petard from fifteen miles away. "I loved Stacey, but I'm not *in* love with her anymore. That position has been filled by a far more qualified candidate. I don't think it's fair to make me beg for my old job back when I never quit or provided cause to be fired in the first place. It was a wrongful termination. People get sued for that sort of thing all the time. She's lucky. I could take her to the People's Court."

"Maybe she's just looking for a hung jury," Darrell said with a smirk.

"Yeah, well, tell her to wish in one hand and shit in the other and see which one fills up faster. Pretty sure she already knew she wasn't sharing a bed with Brock Landers. Anyway, she's making it hard. I'm five inches away from having one foot out the door at this point."

Darrell started to chuckle under his breath. "You two stubborn jerks, I swear. One hundred percent made for each other." He slow-rolled his way to a complete stop on the driver's side of the 1970 Dodge Coronet Super Bee. David traded in his pepper gray 1967 Shelby Mustang GT500 for the yellow lighting rod a few weeks back.

Deputy Dewey was a film aficionado just like the driver. "Listen, brother—the 25th hour? We're all living through it. Peace of mind is hard to come by these days. If you don't want what you and Torie have to be gone in sixty seconds, you have to fight for that shit. That's all she wants, even if she's too pigheaded to admit it."

If David had to do it over again, he would have waged war for Stacey. Gone down fighting. He didn't intend on making the same mistake twice. "Thank you, Darrell. Seriously. You've been a pal, and I've had exceedingly few. I guess I needed someone to shove a cruise missile up my ass."

"Sounds like the eleventh dimension to me."

David closed his eyes and shook his head. "I don't know if I'm allowed to laugh at that."

"Old habits. Anyway, I'm done playing the field, too. We've both got someone we want to make it home to now. I'm in this with you until the end." He raised his right hand over the center console and David clasped it with his left.

"Let's hope the end is just the beginning."

***

"Are you holding a boombox over your head right now?" Torie was trying not to smile but it was too adorable. She woke up to the sound of Peter Gabriel serenading her from her own front lawn—the singular shared dream of every woman who came of age during the Reagan era. It somehow carried over through each successive generation thereafter.

David looked up at her through the open third floor window. "I am. My arms are exhausted, and I'm officially over listening to 'In Your Eyes' for the rest of eternity. You must have taken an Ambien or something, I've been out here for an hour. Can I come inside now please?"

Keeping her right palm pressed into the windowsill for leverage, she ushered him toward the front door with a wordless wave of the left hand.

She waited to bite her lip until her back was turned, then sprinted at maximum speed all the way down the stairs to meet him.

Torie went airborne for the last few feet before flying into his arms and kissing him.

David was surprised. "I'm not complaining in the slightest, but I was sure a bit more convincing would be required. My trunk is filled with flowery bouquets."

"Not necessary, but I'll take 'em." She leaned back with her arms locked around his neck. "You could have blasted 'Enter Sandman' through a loudspeaker, it would have still ended in sex." She wiped away every trace of humor from her face. "I missed you so much, and I love you even more. I'm sorry. I don't want to ever be without you again. I mean forever."

"Forever ever?"

"Forever ever."

He hugged her as hard as he could without hurting her. "Nothing to be sorry about, Tor. I love you, too. And forever doesn't sound like long enough to me."

It never seems that long until you're grown.

"Losing my sister put me in a bad space, but I shouldn't have blamed you."

"It's okay, babe. No need to apologize."

"So," she batted her eyes and tilted her head back up the stairs, "want to go finish making up?"

"Does a bear shit in the woods?"

"That's one way to sweet-talk a lady." Her smile transitioned to a sharp, open-mouthed inhalation. "Shoot, I almost forgot—before we get down to business, I have to show you something." She dragged him by the wrist toward the thousand square foot kitchen.

David's eyes flickered side to side when he saw what she was cooking up.

Four separate collegiate sized chalkboards were set up against the floor to ceiling bay windows overlooking Lake St. Clair. Each was riddled with various illustrations and written pronouncements scribbled onto loose leaf paper of varying color. The entirety of her work was haphazardly taped onto each surface. Large golden circles were a recurring theme.

The only thing missing was some red yarn to connect all the dots.

"Do I need to start researching fourth dimensional care facilities?"

She punched him softly in the side. "Jerk. No, I promise I haven't lost my mind. Completely. I've had a lot of time to ponder how we might go about stuffing the Anti-God in a locker. I think I figured out how we put him back in his place once and for all."

***

"Evan, you know I've got nothing but love for you, kid. I'm going to write you the most glowing recommendation. I can assure you there are plenty of closeted politicians at both the federal and state level who would love to have someone who looks like you working for them. Play your cards right, feign sexual harassment, and you'll be a shoo-in for an under-the-table monetary settlement. Your work ethic leaves something to be desired from time to time, but so what? You're Gen-Z, no one's expecting much from you. Just look pretty, show up no more than ten minutes late to work, and try to keep your cell phone usage in the office below three hours each day. You'll be CEO of a Fortune 500 by the time you're fifty. I'm certain of this."

Her young intern was still processing. "So, I'm not working here anymore?"

"Technically you never were." In any sense, she thought—but Stacey made a good faith effort to blunt the sarcasm when she said it out loud. "We're going to be hiring a dedicated social media manager to coordinate the New York and DC offices. I thought about passing it off to Tonya full-time, but she's stretched too thin as it is. What we need now is just a little bit above your paygrade."

Taking out the trash proved to be a little bit above his paygrade.

She rose from her chair and began to usher him out of her office. "You don't have to clear out your desk in the next five minutes or anything. Take your time, say your goodbyes. Console Tonya maybe. She was damn near apoplectic. I've got to run, I'm attending Tag's townhall tonight." Stacey gave him a legitimate hug. "You're going to be fine, kid. I look forward to reading about all your amazing accomplishments one day."

She prayed it would be in the Times rather than a police blotter.

Stacey found her fiancée waiting for her outside the building.

"Why are you standing out here? You couldn't come in to say a few words to the little people busting their ass on your behalf?"

He stopped chomping on the black plastic twist-sticks stuffed into his fist. "You told me never to eat these in your office. Or the penthouse. Or Manhattan."

"Technically I told you not to do it in any of the five boroughs, but you were already in violation. What difference would it make at this point?"

He tossed the kindling into the trash and took a swig of bottled water to hide his black tongue before giving Stace a kiss on the cheek. "I stopped by to see Nicky before I came over. Ms. Kolyab says he's progressing well. Maybe we should think about you staying a bit longer in the city to manage constituent services. Both places are humming from everything I hear."

Stacey's post-partum depression had less to do with her empty belly than her diminished importance in the workplace. The couple mutually decided she would be joining him in DC once Nicky had his first birthday. That day had come and gone a month back. "That's not humming you hear. It's a stifled scream. First of all, our son's a little pyromaniac. This morning he somehow managed to put a Bible in the wastebin and then set the thing on fire out on the balcony. I had to use a fire extinguisher to put it out. How he didn't wind up with first degree burns all over his body or splat on the pavement I'll never understand."

Tag had a pretty good idea how he came out unscathed.

"Regardless, this is not my jam," she said while jabbing a thumb over her shoulder. "Handling communications, campaign coordination, staff oversight—that's where I belong. Helping book class trips to the Capitol and fulfilling flag purchase requests is not what I signed up for. I spent my morning responding to some Allerton idiot's written diatribe about a bill on recreational drone safety you apparently co-authored."

"I co-authored a bill on recreational drone safety? I don't even know what that is."

"Neither do I, and I read all 158 pages of the freaking thing. It's not legislation, it's the longest RadioShack instruction manual in recorded history." She exhaled in both exhaustion and annoyance. "Tag, I'm not needed here. I feel like I'm just spinning my wheels."

They waited until the limo was doing likewise before continuing with the conversation.

"What's this really about? Do you not want us with you in DC?"

"Don't be ridiculous, Stace." He placed his hand over her knee and squeezed. "I miss you two like crazy. With MARS and everything else I've been run ragged, but I promise I'm going to make more of an effort to be around moving forward. You're both integral to everything that comes next. I can't get to where I want to go without you."

Her eyes began to well. "You don't even touch me anymore."

"I'm literally touching you right now."

"That's not what I mean, and you know it. This is the first time you've seen me in three weeks, and you gave me a peck on the cheek. My kneecap is not an erogenous zone. It would appear I'm the only woman you aren't fingering at this point."

"Excuse me? What are you suggesting?"

"You were sleeping with Kate." She stared him down while the words hung in the air. Stacey didn't bother wiping away her tears. "I don't know for how long, and I don't care. I made it clear she's to steer clear, and the same goes for you—unless you want me to leave you. I promise I won't be alone if I do."

Tag's face flushed a devilish red. The interior of the vehicle darkened without the push of a button. He leaned over and placed her chin between his thumb and forefinger. "Neither one of you is going anywhere. Do you understand me?" He began to squeeze with such force she felt her jaw might break. She recoiled in audible pain, but he refused to relinquish his grip.

David perched forward until he was only a few feet away from them. "Let go of her, asshole, or you'll regret it."

Tag's head darted in David's direction, and Stacey's eyes followed suit. A slight smile briefly flickered across her face in recognition.

When the Anti-God released the pressure, David returned to his seat. Tag realized his momentary lapse was a mistake and tried to caress her cheek in an attempt at an apology.

Stacey wasn't having it.

"Don't ever put your hands on me like that again—or you'll never put your hands on me again," she spat six inches from his face. He was still wiping the residue away when she uncorked a slap to further underscore the point. "If you're looking to play Ike Turner, you can go find yourself another Anna Mae. There's no river deep or mountain high enough to keep me around for that bullshit. I am not the one, asshole."

David felt a sudden urge to give her a hug. For a host of reasons.

Tag resisted his own natural impulse to rip both passengers limb from limb. Instead, he softened and saddened. "Stace, I am so sorry. I'm just under a lot of stress right now, you have no idea. That doesn't make it right. I shouldn't have put my hands on you. It will never happen again. Please don't leave me. I'm nothing without you and Nicky."

The three of them exercised their right to remain silent for the duration of the ride.

David's eyes stayed locked on the Anti-God.

Tag's remained on Stacey.

Her own never left the window.

When they reached St. James Church, a mob of picketers and protesters were already awaiting their arrival.

"*Go to Hell, Gottfried!*" Gladly.

"*New York is for New Yorkers!*" That was code for white people.

*"MARS bars Mexicans!"* He thought that was clever.

*"Stop the invasion!"*

*"Americans First!"*

*"You will not replace us!"*

*"Bus all the migrants!"*

*"Andale! Andale!"*

Stacey started to tear up again. "I don't recognize this place anymore. Not since Tag Gottfried showed up in town." She turned her head and glared at him.

Members of the Anti-God's private security detail were already standing shoulder to shoulder in two opposing lines to help guarantee him safe passage during his makeshift perp walk. He looked at Stacey one last time before exiting the vehicle. "Stay in the car until I'm inside. Give it a few minutes and then they'll disperse. Hopefully." When he placed his hand on her knee for a second time, she shoved it off with authority. Tag turned his head and scowled at David before stepping down onto the pavement.

He knew his earlier threat would not be forgotten.

The roar of the crowd reached a fever pitch when they spied the Congressman beginning to make his way toward the front entrance of the church. The throng of demonstrators squeezed his security force inward until their siege lines morphed into a circular firing squad—an alteration that proved apropos considering what came next.

"Hey, Gottfried!" An Army-jacketed Travis Bickle clone to his right announced himself while striding toward Tag and his protectorate. *"Sic semper tyrannis!"*

Tag's ears isolated the sound of the safety being pulled back over the deafening crowd noise. He turned his head and caught sight of the silver barrel glimmering under the nearby streetlights a moment before the .357 Magnum hollow point flared toward him from six feet away.

The subsequent thunderclap caused the screaming horde to scatter in every direction.

His would-be assassin was sprayed with a barrage of bullets in response that left him lying motionless on the pavement a few feet from the church steps. Donation plates of red plasma oozed out from beneath his corpse. The body and the blood served as an anti-sacrament staining the sidewalk. It rendered a chalk outline redundant.

Stacey came screeching out of the limousine and David followed behind.

"Tag! Tag! Get the hell out of my way!" The ex-Secret Service agents parted like the Red Sea to give her room, but she pushed a couple aside anyway. Stacey dropped to the ground and cradled Tag's upper body. "Hey, hey! Tag! Look at me, look at me!" When she lightly slapped the same cheek she had just reddened herself two minutes prior, she began to cry uncontrollably.

"Stace, I'm okay. He missed. I just got knocked down."

Impossible, but true. She opened each side of his suit jacket to confirm as much. Tag appeared to be no worse for wear. Not a trace of blood anywhere on him.

Nor any bullet.

David stood over the shooter with his back turned to the target. He didn't need to thumb through the man's wallet to know his name was Kenneth Raymond Jones.

Although he wasn't alive to see it, Adam Willco would have been proud to know Patriot's Sword gained a cult following in his absence. In light of MARS and the ever-expanding migrant crisis, thousands of disaffected young white men all over America began to find common cause online and hoist up the bloody flag in his stead. 12Chan. Reddit-R. X. Hell, they had their very own candidate currently running for Congress out of Mississippi. Unemployed incel-based racism was all the rage.

For phase one of their plan, Torie and David took great pains to identify the biggest deviant they could find amongst their number in the NYC area. Deputy Darrell had a variety of investigative tools at his disposal. Kenneth from Queens was a thrice-convicted sex offender still living at home with mom. Based on his Dark Web activity, he refused to give up the ghost—parole be damned. In recent months his search history focused more on the intricacies of ammonium nitrate bomb-making.

Luckily in 4-D the dead don't decompose. Adam Willco's head had been kept on ice in the back of Tina's ice cream truck. It was gross, but the crew managed to Hannibal Lecter his semi-fresh face right off and make a fairly accurate death mask. Wes and Darrell took turns as ghost puppeteer for going on three months. Haunting Kenneth's every waking moment from the alleyway outside his bedroom window. Whispering sweet nothings into his ear while he laid in bed. Sitting across from him on the subway during his brief forays out into the asphalt jungle. Sharing a slice in Washington Square Park.

They helped ensure his hatred for Tag Gottfried grew with each passing second.

Kenneth finally decided he wanted his name up in lights next to his idol.

Mr. Jones was going to be a big star.

Approaching sirens signaled an end to the night's festivities. Torie and David understood that their manufactured attempt on the Congressman's life would only prove beneficial to his political ambitions in the short term.

They were playing the long game now.

***

"Do you have any idea how lucky you are, Tag? Jones was close enough to reach out and touch you. Thank God that moron brought a gun to a knife fight."

The Anti-God was laying in bed surveying his good fortune online via tablet. His ongoing death waltz with the New York Post shifted for the moment back to adulation given the circumstances. Everyone else in the city appeared to be taking a breather from berating the man for the time being. *The*

*Immigrant King* felt like royalty once again. He wanted to accept the blessings, but a single thought continued to bedevil him.

Somehow, he never saw Kenneth Jones coming.

In his mind's eye, a ring of golden light continued to cloud his vision.

It aggravated him to no end.

"Detective Emerson said he only purchased the .357 a week ago," Stacey continued. She was applying Neosporin to each of her skinned kneecaps from atop the lid of the toilet bowl. "Jones might have been a neophyte, but according to him at that range and caliber it shouldn't have made any difference. Stevie Wonder would have winged you." Her eyes briefly made their way to the bed. It was the closest she came to conveying her unstated suspicions.

"These idiots are all so quick to get strapped, but they're too lazy to spend five minutes at the range learning how to actually fire the thing."

"Guess you're right. I'm going to run the washer really quick, can I get you something? Other than black licorice?" That remained a non-starter for her regardless of the number of assassination attempts Tag survived.

"Just a glass of warm saltwater, please."

She accepted being disgusted by his digestive palette long ago. "Sure thing, babe. Back in five."

Truthfully, doing the wash just served as a viable excuse to disguise her true intentions.

Tag's suit was still laying in a crumpled pile on the laundry room floor where she left it.

Stacey held his sportscoat up against the light with the front and back of the jacket firmly clamped together with her left hand. It only took a few seconds of scrutiny to spot the pseudo-stain. She used her unoccupied index finger to probe the perforation above his breast pocket.

A bit of the old in out, in out.

Her eyes widened in recognition.

When she peered through the improvised peephole, she could see her own brown iris staring back at her in the mirror.

Entry and exit.

The only thing missing was the wound.

***

The Seventh Seal was broken on July 14th, 2030.

Tag was true to his word. All the NYC migrant centers were booked solid by the beginning of May. Encampments and tent cities began to spring up throughout the five boroughs almost overnight. The overflow required swift and decisive action from the government. As luck would have it, the Anti-God was there to help keep things afloat. He volunteered his recently acquired aquatic sanctuary for civic duty. It was quickly filled to the brim with brigands and bandits. Using his powers of political and paranormal persuasion, he personally ensured every new incoming seafarer possessed a criminal record back in their respective home countries. Only the best and brightest were allowed onboard. 99% of the migrant non-citizenry in New York City were decent, law-abiding human beings.

Tag Gottfried would never allow them to sully his bad name.

He turned the Staten Island Ferry into *The Flying Dutchman*.

Plundering the high seas gave way to marauding Manhattan.

Liberty Island became the new Republic of Pirates.

Over the course of just a couple months, the occupants managed to establish their very own version of maritime law. Unfortunately, it recognized no flag but the Jolly Roger. Raiding and pillaging up and down the Hudson became the daily norm. Robbery and ransacking all along the East River continued unabated. They breached Rikers Island ten days prior when half the city was in Montauk and Martha's Vineyard on holiday.

Dozens of their compatriots were freed to help reinforce their ranks. Every effort by the NYPD Harbor Unit and Coast Guard to corral the floating fortress was met with automatic gunfire and rocket-propelled grenades in response. At least a dozen of the boats were stripped of their mounted M240B machine guns and the artillery reinstalled on the top deck of the ferry for good measure. The feds were too busy trying to maintain some semblance of order along the southern border to divert resources to the north for the same purpose. New York City was on its own. The entire town was being sacked.

It was a dark and stormy night when things finally came to a head.

Ballistics proved unable to turn the tide, so the NYPD decided to swim in a different direction. Long Range Acoustic Devices were installed on every available Harbor Unit Response Boat and a coordinated amphibious assault planned for the night of the 14th. The plan was to encircle Liberty Island under cover of darkness once the ferry and its supporting vessels docked for the evening. Then they would let loose with the crowd control sound cannons. With nowhere further inland to retreat, the outlaws would have no choice but to surrender on their hands and knees.

Everyone has a plan until they get punched in the face.

Lightning strikes all over the region foiled their ability to approach undetected. It allowed their quarry plenty of time to take up offensive positions behind and atop the brick walls at the base of the statue. Dozens more ascended Lady Liberty and found RPG firing positions within her crown. Upon arrival, another 7.5 magnitude earthquake unexpectedly hit the region. The churning whitecapped waves caused the NYPD's sound and fury to be rerouted in every direction—including toward their fellow patrol boats.

An uncoordinated exchange of artillery fire from both sides soon left the entire statue engulfed in flames. The golden torchlight atop her outstretched right arm was lit for the very first time in history. Smoke ascended from its tip toward the heavens like burning incense. The seven men still left alive inside her skull let loose a volley of grenades down toward the gas-slicked surface of the water in response. A ring of fire soon encircled the entire island that caught several patrol boats in its wake. Their subsequent detonation was no different than if they had been hit with a direct torpedo strike.

In a Tag-created coincidence, a simultaneous operation was underway throughout the New York metropolitan region and the surrounding areas. Members of Patriot's Sword coordinated bombing raids that same evening on all twenty-four of the city's natural gas and fuel oil power plants. Within an hour all of NYC was in the dark. Once the storm passed, flaming liberty was the only source of illumination for miles.

As it turned out, the Book of Revelation required a revision.

It remained quiet in the city for a lot longer than half an hour that evening.

Chaos was the singular sound that rang out in the aftermath.

***

Darrell urgently requested the presence of both Torie and David.

He and Daphne were enjoying a cup of joe around the breakfast nook when they arrived. Darrell's hand on his hyperventilating alien shoulder told them something was seriously wrong. The Grey didn't even bother to fabricate a more palatable form. His eight-foot-tall frame barely fit into the chair and left his bony knees protruding above the taupe marble tabletop.

Torie started in as soon as they entered the kitchen. "What the hell's going on you two?"

"Apparently, the Anti-God gained access to the ninth dimension a few hours ago," Darrell verified for the other half of their impromptu double date. "That's where the Greys live."

"Shit," David spit. "Stace took a sleeping pill and was out like a light with Nicky next to her by 7:30. Tag must have waited until she was sound asleep to make his move."

Daphne laid out the new rules. "He can move between an infinite number of universes now. He's no longer bound by the laws of physics, or probability. And he can be anywhere and everywhere all at once without anyone even knowing. My brothers and sisters never saw him coming." He lowered his head to convey something approaching sadness.

Ms. Easton switched roles to that of a concerned mother. She placed her hand on his opposite shoulder for extra support. "Talk to us, Daffy. What happened?"

His 8-ball eyes shot up. "That devil dissolved my husband Dauphin with the snap of his fingers. Along with every other intergalactic Grey. The Anti-God let me off with a warning, which I was told to convey to both of you in the harshest possible terms."

"Daphne did have one piece of good news to share," Darrell said. "Spill."

The alien straightened in his seat to address them. "The loose Time Tether you absconded with is like a Faraday Cage for the infernal. It's why he was unable to predict Torie's plan. Anything within five hundred miles of it is off limits from his foresight."

"I knew it," Torie said with a slap of David's arm. "I told you there was something special about that thing."

"We've already started to pave the way," David continued. "Stacey knows he's not right. I saw it with my own two eyes. She only needed one to reach the same conclusion. That bullet passed through him like he was thin air."

"Yeah, but there's no way to get her across the finish line right under Tag's nose," Torie added. "In 3-D, he'll smell us coming a mile away."

Darrell smiled at his boyfriend and the alien did his best to replicate the gesture.

Torie lowered her eyelids and glanced back and forth between them. A grin of her own began to form. "What? What is it you two?"

Daphne and his creaky joints rose from the table. "Follow me."

The quartet made their way to the garage. There was no luxury car parked inside. The contents were far more fantastic.

The Fabricator stuck out like a sore thumb.

David and Torie found the display jaw-dropping. He spoke up first. "Daphne, how did you get this all the way here?"

"It's a Chocolate Factory for the mind, remember? I just got inside and imagined it was here. *BAMF!* Michigan is outside his spectrum of vision as long as the tether is here."

"This gives us an opening," Torie said.

"Indeed. I can help your ex see the light. We just need to get her within arm's length."

***

Stacey awoke with a start. The lack of a baby in the bed left her on the verge of a scream. Seeing David Downey sitting across from her in her own ash shaded swivel chair didn't help calm her nerves.

"Where's Nicky? What did you do with my son?" She began searching her bedside table for blunt objects. "There's two ex Secret Service agents outside my front door who will happily blow your head off if I make the request."

"Easy there, lady. You think I turned into Bruno Hauptmann overnight? Nicky's still sleeping right next to you as we speak. And there's no one outside your front door. Or in New York City, for that matter. Listen."

Her frantic facial expression morphed into clear confusion.

The endless cavalcade of sirens and screaming that enveloped the city in the aftermath of the Statue of Liberty's demolition was replaced with complete silence. It was spooky.

"You're in 4-D right now. Our alien friend Daphne

fabricated an interdimensional diving suit for your unconscious mind. No worries, though. When we're done here, you'll be returned to the surface without a hiccup. You can go right back to planning your escape from New York."

She already felt like she had the Bends. Stace raised both her palms up to double-check the work then lightly slapped herself on both cheeks to confirm her findings. "How can I be sure you're not lying to me? You could have thrown my baby out the window for all I know."

David rolled his eyes. He leapt up from the chair and raced across the room before doing a swan dive straight off the balcony. Stacey always kept the doors open at night so she could enjoy the summer breeze while she slept.

Five seconds later following the distant sound of his skull cracking like an egg against the pavement he returned to the same seated position.

"Satisfied?"

"That would be a first where you're concerned, David."

He sarcastically chuckled in silence with his eyes closed and his mouth open.

"Why am I here, Hellboy? What do you want?"

Her ex removed the cell phone from his pocket and dialed. "All set, Scotty. Beam us up."

In an instant they were standing on a raised deck overlooking Orchard Lake at sunset. The star was flaming orange and red like a ripe peach as it descended toward the horizon. Darrell and Torie were standing in front of them awaiting their arrival.

Stacey's eyes shifted side to side in disbelief. "What the hell? How'd you do that?"

The eight-foot-tall alien teleported topside from the garage and popped into view directly in front of her. "I used a Fabricator."

Stacey stared straight ahead like she was in a trance.

When David snapped his fingers in front of her face she

yelped. She took a step back while her eyeballs remained appropriately saucer sized.

"Jesus Christ on a cracker. You things are actually real."

"I'm not a thing, madam." Daphne was officially insulted and didn't try to hide it. "I'm a non-corporeal 10th Level intellect with biologic compatibility and trans-dimensional capability."

"Sure, of course you are. I was just going to say that." She turned toward David. "Who else have you been buddying up to in your spare time over here? Bigfoot? We going down to the lake to saddle up on Nessie next?"

"Plesiosaurs are only found in your Pacific Ocean, actually," Daphne informed the group.

"Stace, you need to listen to what Daphne has—wait, what? Seriously?"

Torie gently placed her partner's collar bone between her thumb and forefinger. It made Stacey instantly uncomfortable. "David—focus, please."

"Right." He set his own Cretaceous curiosity to the side. "You need to listen to what Daphne has to say."

"Oh, so you're Daphne, huh?" She scrutinized all eight feet of him from head to toe. "Heard a lot about you. I have to say, I was expecting someone a bit more masculine given the name."

No one other than Stacey was amused.

"Stacey, this is serious," Torie informed her perceived competition. "Please pay attention."

"I'm sorry, do I know you? *Oh*, you must be Scrappy-Doo. I was wondering when I'd meet the lady chowing down on my leftovers. Why don't you let the big dogs talk. Go play with a bone or something."

"I thought that was your forte?"

The three men began separately searching for a table to hide under.

Stace started snickering in lieu of slapping. "I confess, I engaged in certain behaviors in my younger years that I'm not proud of in retrospect." She scowled at David before returning her attention to her true enemy. "How about you sweetheart? Anything you'd like to take back?"

Torie knew exactly what she was getting at. "Sure, but unlike you I didn't continue on the down escalator to the underworld. I get to share a bed every night with David instead of a demon. Now and forever."

"My condolences. Have you two had sex with the lights on yet? Because that would be another first for him."

"Must have been your face," Torie said while squinting. "I can see it."

Stacey smushed the thing together like she smelled something unsavory before unclenching. "Okay, well it's been a real pleasure as always, but I have an infant waiting to be breastfed back home, so if we're all done here for today—"

"Doesn't the nanny take care of that for you?"

Torie crossed the Rubicon. Secretly, Stacey long suspected it might be true. "Hey, seriously, I'll slap the taste out of your mouth if you ever say that again. My child is off limits."

"Would be the first thing with a phallus that ever has been," Torie responded. "Anyway, I regret to inform you, but your son is a horcrux from Hell. He's Satan himself."

Ms. Darden took two steps forward. "Did you not hear me, Number Two?"

"It's actually true, Ms. Darden," Daphne said as diplomatically as possible.

"Appreciate the input, pipe cleaners—now zip it."

Stacey was the only woman on Earth capable of emasculating an all-powerful alien. Daphne did as he was told.

Torie continued. "Anyway, don't be too hard on yourself, Lord of Pain. Apparently, nymphomania runs in a Jinni's blood. You were destined to be disreputable. Nothing to be done about it. Guess that's why you decided to do everyone."

"You know, I read up on you, too, Ms. Eaton," Stace said

with a shit-eating grin. "OD'd in a motel, did ya? You really know how to pick 'em, David."

"I'm sorry the Ruth Motel wasn't up to your standards. I should have reached out to you for a reco. God knows you've been in enough beds to offer a qualified opinion. Of course, the establishments you frequented typically charged by the hour."

When David turned to find Daphne, he realized the alien self-teleported twenty paces back to protect himself. He shook his head violently from side to side. The signal had no precise meaning but was still easy enough to decipher.

"I know this is hard for you to understand being dead and all, but I evolved. I've put two separate candidates into the House of Representatives, and I run a million-dollar communications firm," Stacey confirmed. "You shipped boxes for a living. The bathroom in my penthouse is worth more than your entire existence. Maybe just keep your mouth shut and sit the next couple plays out."

"Well, we can't all be professional sex valets, Ms. Elizabeth. Who was better in the sack, anyway? Macho Man or Hulk Hogan?"

Stacey glared at David. "You're such an asshole." She redirected her ire at Torie. "I don't know what he told you, but for the last time, I did not sleep with every ex-wrestler in town."

"Oh, no darling, I'm sure there was a cut-off." Torie paused to take a step back and scrutinize her size. "170—no, I'm thinking 160 pounds, probably. You were definitely no lightweight, though."

"I think you might be confused," Stacey sneered. "You're weighing your weekly Oxy intake, you strung out dope fiend. Pride wouldn't have been the only thing you were swallowing back then."

"How often were you on your back?"

"How often were you on your knees?"

Torie cocked her head without taking her eyes off the

target. "Darrell, can you go grab a clock and a couple of wrestling singlets? Ms. Darden and I are about to take it to the mattresses. I know I don't have to explain the rules to you. There's no rest between periods—just like the old days, right Stacey?"

Stace removed her engagement ring in preparation and set it down on the outdoor patio table. "Okay bitch, if you want to get blasted, so be it. I'll help you get to Heaven. Look at you. You're nothing. Just a washed-up junkie. Too pathetic for purgatory."

Her opponent looked her up and down with disgust. "Who the hell are you? Based on what David told me, the idea of what you could have been is far more interesting than the reality of whoever you are now. You're a *Paycheck Person* who peaked when she was twenty-five. I hope you are wealthy, because what you do for a living makes you worthless. Procreating might have made a thing, but it didn't make you anything. You've degenerated into an amalgam of an Automat and an ATM. You're just sitting in neutral now until you hit the netherworld."

"I'll make sure to write you when I get there," Stacey responded.

Torie snort-chuckled in a manner that was intended to be obnoxious. "Oh, I wouldn't worry about that. I'd say you can go to Hell, but that's a step up from where you're headed. Tag Gottfried's going to stretch out that used up babymaker of yours and turn it into an apocalyptic portal. Fitting. It's the only piece of you that ever possessed any intrinsic value to the outside world."

Each woman began advancing toward the other to engage in anti-mortal combat. David stepped into the fray with his arms outstretched in each direction to prevent any potential fatalities. While Torie was red-faced and ready for action, he could clearly see Stacey was on the verge of tears. "Tor, enough, okay? Just back off."

"Why are you defending her?"

"I'm not defending either of you, I'm trying to facilitate a compromise so we can all avoid complete annihilation. You may hate each other's guts, but the enemy of my enemy is my friend. That's where we're at with things at the moment, unfortunately."

"Sorry, I don't see a single friend standing before me," Stacey said while valiantly trying to stifle a sniffle.

Daphne finally reentered the fracas. "Ms. Darden, if we don't stop Tag Gottfried, he will force your son to rule over Hades for all eternity. I know it's difficult to tell given my lack of facial mobility but look me in the eyes. I am not lying to you. I'm trying to help you. And Nicky."

When he reached out and encircled each of her wrists with his bony fingers, she was left as comatose as Tina. Daphne granted her a vision of her future via telepathy. Stacey saw the whole thing play out in less than five seconds. It was more than she could bear.

"I think I'm going to barf," she confirmed when he finally broke contact. Her entire body began to vibrate.

David palmed her cheeks. It lightly infuriated his girlfriend. "We're all on the same side, Stace. It's Tag that wants to hurt you—and your son. You're both just the means to The End. We have to stop him, and it can't be done without you. Please."

She tried to convince herself what she saw was a trick of the light, but the darkness in her mind refused to dissipate. Tag's electrified blue blade slicing through her throat. Her baby sitting on a throne made of red hellfire. New York City laid to waste. Endless cries of agony that sounded like glee. A universe where the only pleasure would be pain. Nothing ever felt more real.

Daphne pulled a scroll out of thin air and began to unfurl it vertically between his two hands. "This is a sacred text that's been protected by the Greys since the beginning. It was indexed with the billions of Bibles. The document provides the only roadmap on how to eradicate the Anti-God. You and Torie are the key to everything."

Stacey took a pair of deep breaths before responding. "Okay," she finally offered through tears. "Alright. What's the plan? What do you need me to do?"

***

Tag was whistling *Dixie* down Fifth Avenue while admiring his handiwork.

A group of young ruffians were gallivanting up the boulevard in the opposite direction with their newly acquired wares from the Met. *The Gulf Stream* by Homer gave the fiend fond memories of his most recent trip to Lake Michigan. Van Gogh's *Self Portrait with Straw Hat* never looked more brilliant. He still thought Picasso must have had Friar Tuck pose for his painting of *Gertrude Stein*, but in this new light she looked like a million bucks. They all did.

"Gentlemen, if I may," Tag bellowed at the approaching posse. He removed a piece of paper from his pocket and held it out to the new owner of *Autumn Rhythm*. "The fence you'll find at this address pays in cash. I assure you—you'll all be handsomely rewarded."

He exchanged handshakes with each member of the lineup like they were opposing squads in a just-concluded basketball scrimmage. The last few of their number patted him on the back in gratitude as they passed.

Dozens of young ladies from all the five boroughs were having a fashion show at the corner of East 82nd Street in gowns and dresses freshly acquired from the Anna Wintour Costume Center. The savage beauties paid no attention to the crimson stains spoiling several of their outfits. They were too busy having a ball.

As for the Devil? He only wore Prada.

The typical city soundscape was replaced with a never-ending shriek of gunshots and tripped car alarms and shattering glass. A cloudless sky was covered in a thick haze of gray, sooty smoke. The shadowy fog billowed forth from the multitude of arson fires flaring and flickering down every avenue.

A pair of policemen were strung up as scarecrows at the traffic light outside the Ancient Playground. They served as a warning to any future authority figures who might attempt to intervene further down the road.

Male laughter and female screams intermixed in deafening concert from the Great Lawn. The ongoing mass performance would have made his old pal Caligula proud.

Tag twirled with twisted delight while absorbing the majestic tapestry he toiled for so long to create. The destruction and death gave him an immense sense of satisfaction.

Basement level generators installed at Tag's behest several months back left their high rise as one of only a handful on the island with electricity. Despite that fact, none of the millions currently looting through Manhattan saw fit to try and take refuge inside or ransack the place. The Anti-God deconsecrated the entire tower to keep it off limits to interlopers.

Even with Agents Frick and Frack posted outside the door, Stacey still made sure to look through the peephole upon his arrival before lowering the .44 and allowing him entry inside. "Did you find diapers?"

He held the bag of Huggies aloft like a proud papa. Tag didn't tell her how many people outside were dying to get a box. "Last one in Duane Reade. And that's not all, my darling. Look what else daddy brought home."

Sprite and Skittles. If she wasn't so disgusted by his existence, she would have made out with him right then and there. "Gimme gimme gimme." Stacey snatched the red rectangular treasure out of the bag and split the ridged top before spilling the contents into her upturned mouth. Her jaw unhinged like a *V* alien preparing to swallow a guinea pig.

Tag was equally appalled. He remained standing just inside the doorway. "Remind me which one of you is the child, again?"

Stacey already had a mouth full of molten metal that had yet to be washed down with sugary battery acid. *"Shu uph, jer-ka."* Her tongue greedily smacked against the roof of her mouth in search of more sweet relief. The carbonated snake hiss when she twisted the cap off the bottle was the auditory equivalent of anti-venom. She sucked down the poison without spitting.

"That's disgusting," he said with a smile. "I'm making you a salad for dinner."

"I told you not to swear in front of our son." Stace headed off to locate a toothbrush to scrub away the toxins. She carried the contaminants with her to personally ensure the appropriate waste disposal.

The Congressman found his way to the kitchen and deposited the diapers on the otherwise deserted island. Nicky was placed in his highchair dutifully watching last night's streaming highlights play out on the TV. Solid bat contact being made by random NYC citizens. Form tackling to the pavement by various members of New York's finest. Dead eye shooters given the green light to snipe without abandon. Slashings left and right minus the threat of any penalty box. Death and destruction appeared to be the only goal. The multitude of unsportsmanlike conduct made quite the racket. Everyone was gunning for a red card.

His little boy was clapping and cooing like he was watching it all unfold from the front row of Madison Square Garden. Tag fingered his grinning dimples in appreciation. Father and son had the best seats in the house for their first big game together. It was a rite of passage into perdition.

Stacey stood in the hallway observing the captive audience with frightened alarm. An ejection seemed more than appropriate. She decided it was time to ban the disorderly hooligan from this venue.

Tag caught sight of her and instantly modulated his disposition. "No, Nicky. Not okay. Not okay." He shook his head in Stacey's direction with a manufactured frown. "I'm going to put on *Paw Patrol*. He shouldn't be watching this."

When he lifted the remote and changed the channel, the

baby began to cry uncontrollably. He banged both fists against the tray table over and over to further voice his displeasure. The clattering of his sippy cup and cereal bowl only served to underscore the point.

His mother made a beeline toward the boy to stop the bleating. Picking him up underneath each armpit and pulling him toward her chest immediately lowered the temperature. It only took a human touch to snap him out of his Satanic stupor. Rocky and Rubble suddenly had his rapt attention. "No more current events right now, okay?"

"I didn't put it on," Tag informed her.

"Neither did I." Her eyes shifted from the flatscreen to her baby and back with a mixture of dread and bewilderment.

Tag took a few steps in their direction. "Do you want me to put him down?"

"No no." She shot her hand into his chest to rebuff him. "I'll do it. Just get started on dinner, okay? I'm starving."

Stacey made herself a club sandwich thirty minutes before he returned home. She was stuffed. The truth was that every time the Anti-God touched her son now, she had to restrain herself from amputating his arm.

By the time he was laid down in his crib, Nicky was already sound asleep. Stace took a moment to admire the only thing of beauty left within a five-block radius. She moved next to the window overlooking the hellscape down below. Manhattan had become an open-air prison. A scorched earth policy took hold that left the metropolitan mecca looking more like the Kuwaiti oil fields from twenty stories up. Blackened plumes erupted from every corner of the island. They served as smoke screens blotting out the sun. The blaring sirens were nothing new, but there didn't appear to be a single moving vehicle within a square mile. Improvised gallows painted green, white, and red were being constructed right outside her building. When the idiots started blasting "*La Cucaracha*," she finally had to look away.

There was no retreat. Only surrender.

The Anti-God turned the entire town into a veal crate. There would be no use in trying to run. Stacey and her son were tethered to the place with nowhere else to turn. Something told her it was intentional on Tag's part.

David and company offered them the only way out.

His alien friend explained in detail what would come next. Step by step. Down to the very last detail and spoken word. She studied the playbook one last time in her mind before proceeding back out to the kitchen. If Tag didn't deviate from the gameplan, she promised herself there would be no turning back.

"Did he go night night?"

"Along with the rest of humanity." Stacey grabbed the Peru-made ceramic colander and began depositing Tag's freshly cut cucumber slices inside. The contraption cost $200 more than was necessary. Lately she came to realize that having too much money forced her to concoct increasingly stupid ways to spend it. All the dough in the world wouldn't serve as sufficient doorstop now. She began washing the vegetables with the same toxic tap water they provided to everyone on Staten Island. "Purchasing that vulgar mansion in Georgetown without my prior approval suddenly doesn't seem like such a bad investment on your part."

He turned in her direction with both hands on the island behind him. "Maybe I should just skip attending the leadership conference and head back to DC with you two."

She shook off the suggestion without even looking at him. "Are you kidding? No way. I'm amazed the DNC is still having you. We need all the good will we can get at this point. Remember, you're bringing me back five pounds of Mackinaw fudge."

"Well, what are your thoughts on accompanying me, instead? A little spa getaway might be just the ticket for both of us."

She raised her head and stared at the wall. Tag was following the Skeleton Crew's spoiler-laden script to a T. "Lake Michigan?"

"How'd you guess?"

Her intuition was alien in nature.

Tag made his way to the sink and stood beside her. "Anyway, I already talked to Ms. Kolyab, and she'd be happy to accompany us to keep an eye on Nicky. Separate rooms, of course. What do you say?"

Stacey forged a counterfeit smile. "Sounds like Heaven."

# DECOUPLING

Torie and Stacey had time for some girl talk.

The Congressman would be staying on Mackinaw Island overnight and then return their way first thing in the morning. Ms. Kolyab thankfully accompanied him north. That left Stace and Nicky to fend for themselves at their rented beachfront bungalow for an entire day.

Daphne manufactured enough bodies to bring the entire team into the third dimension.

The ladies were still in the planning stages with a baby on board when Ms. Eaton finally spoke up from the passenger seat.

"I'm sorry about what I said before. At the lake."

"No you're not." Stacey didn't take her eyes off the road.

"No—I'm not. But being a bitch doesn't make you a bad person."

"By definition it does." This time she did.

"Alright, well it doesn't make you an *evil* person. I know that you're not. I can tell you're an amazing mother, for one. Because I had one of those, too. And I envy all three of you for it." Torie's eyes began to lightly mist over. "It's all that matters in this world. Nothing that came before Nicky does anymore, right? Raise him to be better than his father and that would presumably cleanse you of your sins. Whatever they were. I'm pretty sure of that."

"Thank you. I don't think you're an evil bitch, either. For the record. And you're easily the second prettiest girl David's ever dated."

Torie cackled at the unintentional inside joke.

Stacey was smiling ear to ear. "What? Holy shit. It wasn't that funny."

"Yes, it was." She leaned into her headrest. "I think I get it now."

"Get what?"

"Why he'll never get over you."

Stace couldn't help but blush. "Even if that's true—and I'm sure that it is—I see the way he looks at you. It's the same way he used to look at me." It didn't make her happy or sad to say it. "You're lucky."

Torie double-tapped the wallpapered photo of Nicky and his mom on Stacey's console display. "We both are."

They mutually admired the most beautiful boy in the world. "Yeah. Agreed."

***

"To be fair, it does take five men to do a woman's job," Stacey said.

The two real ladies laughed at the now-disguised group of five standing before them.

"I think I liked it better when you were at each other's throats," David responded.

"So, aside from all *this*," she waved a hand from their camouflaged heads to their toes, "there's going to be a literal Stairway to Heaven and once we hit the top floor, he's going to take my top off? My head, I mean? Do I have that correct?"

"Yes, he must paint the walls red with the bottom of the Lord of Pain's head," Daphne confirmed. "That will create the doorway that will allow him entry to the everlasting. From there, all bets are off. It will be the first time they've ever had to prohibit gambling in Heaven. It's a big deal."

"Well, then I guess you better pray we don't roll a snake eyes, snake eyes."

"Daphne will teleport us all back over here tomorrow once

Tag arrives on site," Torie reminded them. "After that, you *Madden* Men just run your predetermined routes."

"Yeah, do like your mommies tell you and everyone gets warm chocolate chip cookies for a treat," Stacey added. "It's only the life of me and baby on the line. So, damn it. Don't. Deviate. Daphne, you get some leeway. The rest of you dummies don't."

Based on the light cooing coming from the next room, Nicky had just awoken.

"You want me to go grab him for you, Stacey?"

She placed her hand on Torie's shoulder with a smile as she made her exit. "No, I got him. Be right back you guys."

David was in disbelief. "You're holding her baby now?"

"Earlier. Just for a little bit."

"Nicky really likes her, actually—and he doesn't like anyone," Stacey said over her shoulder.

"I'm not sure how I feel about that." David looked Torie up and down.

"Oh, stop," she responded. "He's just a lil' tyke. All we have to do is erase daddy from the family portrait to keep him headed down the right path. Sorry." Torie shouted the apology through the wall with an accompanying shrug the recipient couldn't see.

"No need," Stace bellowed back. "Last night I caught him levitating the little one here before bed." She returned to the main room with the baby in tow. His blue gingham onesie matched the blankie slung over her shoulder as makeshift mattress. "I'd say that just about put it over the top for me. Plus, his politics have gone completely off the rails. He's going to brand me for life if I don't unhitch my wagon in short order. The professional death will be more agonizing than the personal one."

"At least you've got your priorities in order," David snarked back in response.

"Says the ex-debt merchant assisting America's financial suicide. *Dr. Debt.* Wait—*David Downey.* Holy shit, how am I just coming up with this for the first time?" Stacey and the baby both started giggling to one another.

Torie found it contagious. "Two D's and everything. Well done, lady."

David didn't think any of it was funny. "I'm sorry, did you two want to start dating, or—"

They offered the same response spontaneously before he had the chance to finish his sentence. *"Maybe!"*

Amir and Wesley's avatars had long ago lost interest and started watching Tag on TV.

*"What is happening right now in New York City is a disgrace, but it is a disgrace brought upon my brothers and sisters back home by the traitorous governors to our South. In Texas, In Florida. Shipping their MARZ-laden timebombs to us. Just the dregs. They're no better than 21^{st} Century Secessionists—that's what we call them, right folks?"* Shouts of affirmation from the crowd could be heard rising in intensity.

Both of the used-to-be-boys turned and looked back at Stacey.

"He's going to burn the whole place down," she stated as a matter of fact.

The Anti-God looked out at the audience with a smile that screamed cat that ate the canary. "They need to be rebuked and put to heel. And I'm here to help with the endeavor." His expression darkened. "The death of Brian Oswald earlier today is a tragedy."

"What a lying bastard," David said.

Daphne took his turn addressing Stace. "I told you."

During her precognitive peek into the future, she saw the Democratic candidate for New York's Senate seat dead by this exact sunrise. Brian Oswald had a massive heart attack that morning. Tag totally had nothing to do with it.

"But it is in his memory that I graciously announce my intention to take his place on the ballot. They can write my name in or not. It makes no difference. One way or the other, I will be the next Senator for the great state of New York come this

November. And for every enemy of our union, just be aware— I keep a Book of Names."

He really did.

It was written in blood.

***

"Stace? Where are you two?"

Behind him, Ms. Kolyab carried a suitcase under each arm with ease. Both pieces of luggage could have weighed as much as a pickup truck, and it would have made little difference. The infernal beast possessed the collective strength of a thousand men. In the *Blasphemic* that would soon serve as humanity's common tongue, her name translated to *The Juggernaut*.

She would serve as one of the great kings of Hell.

"Outside, Tag. On the deck waiting for daddy."

He silently directed his unholy usher upstairs to attend to his belongings.

She maintained a sneer as she made her ascent.

The demon would never stop resenting that human bitch holding her baby.

His lad's mood darkened the moment Tag stepped through the screen door. It was the most beautiful thing the Anti-God had ever seen. He was daddy's little darling.

"There's my champion." His father picked him up against his chest. He leaned in to grab a kiss from his other piece of property. "Hey babe."

"Hey you." She had to actively prevent herself from projectile vomiting into his mouth when their lips touched. "Long drive?"

"Eh, time seems to fly for me now. Have you eaten? C'mon, let me whisk you away for the rest of the day. Ms. Kolyab can play mommy for the remainder."

Her greatest fear—but she knew she had to play along. "That's what I was hoping you would say. Already packed my bag and put it next to the bed. Do me a favor, though, I tweaked my back a bit. Can you have Kolyab carry it to the trunk for me?"

Stacey directed David to douse the entire thing in holy water for shits and giggles before they got there.

The uncanny nanny was forced to stifle her screams all the way to the car.

***

"I told you it was beautiful out here," she offered to her chauffeur. "New York is where I live now. It's my home. But this is where I was born. It's what made me. And I wouldn't have it any other way." Stacey took a moment to take it all in with the knuckles of her mid-fingers touching her teeth. She smiled despite the solemnity of the occasion.

If it turned out to be her last, she couldn't have hoped for anything better.

"I don't know. Personally, I think it has that Lyle Stephens body spray scent." Tag was being antagonistic to help salt the meat.

"How do you know what Lyle smells like?"

"You told me. You said, *'imagine what a horse jockey who poses shirtless in a public gym mirror smells like,'*" he reminded her.

She definitely said that at some point. It was way too specific. "Well, agree to disagree," she replied. "Anyway, I assure you the heavenly odors are not the thing tying me to my current address. That's just a lie we all agree to tell ourselves when we move to the city. After you've spent a day somewhere without a skyscraper to cleanse your pallet, you'll see. It's like someone put the *Garbage Pail Kids* in a blender and slathered it all over everything. That's what New York City smells like."

"That's why I love it so much," he responded.

Lately, Stacey had been thinking more and more about moving upstate.

Pandemonium was all she was looking for when she first arrived in NYC. Bedlam suddenly became a lot less interesting with a baby by her side.

A decision between the two was really no choice at all.

Nicky was her everything now.

Nothing and no one would get between them.

"There's parking across the street," he said before the lot was even in view.

Turned out the place was nothing but fond memories for Tag as well.

Stacey's mind was elsewhere. Getting to live with the knowledge that something came next made her more determined than ever to put an end to Tag's potential reign. She achieved actual enlightenment. One of only seven mortals to have ever done it. The feat was no small accomplishment.

Just ask Jesus H. Christ.

"I was thinking a couple's massage to start," Tag said.

Tenderizing.

Stacey's acting was always naturalistic. She theatrically leaned forward with her left arm wrenched behind her. "My lower back will probably shriek hymnals, but I'm sure it could use the abuse. Sure, let's do it."

He held her hand through the parking lawn and all the way across the street until they reached the beachfront. For a moment, she reminisced about the man with whom she'd fallen in love. Then she remembered it was all an act. She had to stop herself from shuddering at the thought.

Half an hour later they were half naked lying stomach-flat on black, synthetically upholstered massage tables. Each of them had feathery white towels draped over their respective hind quarters. Stacey almost appreciated Tag's desire to wine and dine her within an inch of his life before he killed her. The feeling quickly passed when she envisioned her forthcoming decapitation.

His lascivious stare stretched across the brief chasm between them.

It made her realize something for the first time.

He always looked at her like a piece of meat.

"Not that it's needed, but I signed you up for a chemical peel next." Tag forcibly interlocked their fingers to form a bridge. "I'm going to hit up the sauna for a bit. After that we're doing a special acupuncture treatment on the top floor together. Supposedly, it's like opening the door to another world." The Anti-God was telling half-truths. Same as always.

Nothing he did was a surprise anymore. She decided that was his greatest deficit.

"Tag, can I ask, just between us—when did you make the decision to destroy America?"

He chuckled at the perceived joke. "Pardon?"

"No, I'm serious." She leaned up onto her elbow. "Look, I like having things. The money, the status. I'd be lying if I said otherwise. I'm not looking to lose any of that. I've learned to accept being morally compromised. But we're going to be married soon, and I think I'm entitled to have the whole picture painted for me, you know? I'm not dumb, so stop playing me for a fool."

The Anti-God thought what the hell. Whatever information she gleaned would be taken to the grave. He picture-framed his head with his own elbow. "Fine. The truth is everyone starts out in the right place. Once upon a time, I was as angelic as the next guy. I legitimately wanted to help the people see the light. A version of it, anyway. The problem is humans don't know how to help themselves. Because they're morons. Black, brown, white, makes no difference—all equally dumb. Getting an entire civilization to do the right thing is akin to herding meth-addled cats. I realized it was easier to nudge them forward like lemmings. Simplest way to ensure they all wound up in the same place. Even if it's at the bottom of a cliff. So be it. Everyone still winds up united."

"Yeah, in chaos and death," Stacey offered in rebuttal. "You turned Gotham into Arkham Asylum. The rest of America's headed straight for The Narrows. We're probably six months away from the southern border becoming the Mason-Dixon line. You know there still have to be states to justify the Senators, right? I'm just saying."

"Ironically, anarchy breeds order." He was laying it all out on the table. "Demands it, in fact. It's historical. Having to do things the right way takes too much time. Decency is a lifetime endeavor. Turmoil always speeds up the process. Unfortunately, it required us taking two steps back to put me in position to take the King. But soon I'll own the board, and then I can make all the right moves. Free will has proven to be nothing but a nuisance for these people. Humanity will no longer have to determine what role they were meant to play. I'll just have them all assume the position."

The two stared at one another in silence for a few moments.

"Guess I appreciate the honesty," she finally acknowledged. "Of course, you neglected to add how your little gameplan required stirring up violent racial animus in every direction. You authored a backdoor sequel to *Mein Kampf* and just dressed it up with a slightly browner book cover. No matter what, that makes me your Goebbels. I don't recall signing up to be your minister of propaganda. That wasn't in the contract we signed."

"You might want to take a closer look at all four corners of the document. You sold your soul to me. More or less. There's a fairly punitive penalty attached if you try to sever our pact prematurely. Monetarily, I mean."

He would also murder her.

That clause was a unilateral addendum added after the fact.

"Oh, so you're threatening me now?"

"Not a threat, Stace. Business is business. We were very clear about keeping it separated from the personal. You can't have it both ways then cry foul when it doesn't benefit you. That definitely isn't in the contract you signed."

Normally a bout of brief hate sex would have erupted between the pair, but Tag was alarmed to see his efforts at psychic manipulation were suddenly having diminishing returns. For some reason she could no longer be persuaded by his mere force of personality. A golden light continued blocking his ability to press the issue.

She stood up in a huff. Stacey took an extra couple of seconds to wrap the towel around herself so Tag could take one last look at everything he would soon be missing.

The demon formed a plank in accommodation for the wood. "Wait, where are you going?"

"Chemical peel. If I'm early, I'm early. I'm sure I can find a magazine to keep me distracted for a few minutes." Stacey marched over and gave him a perfunctory peck on the cheek to keep him at bay. "I'll meet you at the elevator bank in ninety minutes."

He began physically deflating. "Have fun."

Tag took his own advice and had sex with his massage therapist five minutes later.

***

"No, I'm pretty sure he's screwing the massage therapist as we speak," Stacey informed them as she continued changing. "Caught him clocking her the minute she walked in the room. He's so transparent. Suddenly I can see right through him."

"It's the Tether," Torie confirmed. "It's like we pulled Excalibur from the stone. I need to tell you guys something before we go any further."

A disguised David had his back turned to afford his ex some privacy. He rotated his head while keeping his eyes glued to the ground. "Tell us what?"

"I was having dreams about the Tether and Tag before I knew either existed. Visions, actually. Like what Daphne showed Stacey. The ankle monitors they make us wear in 4-D are white, not gold. There has to be a reason Mike was given something different. It's the only thing that can stop Tag. I'm sure of it."

"At least you were having visions of killing my fiancée, instead of the other thing."

"Very funny," Torie said without a hint of humor. "But that's not all. It also took the two of us to put him down, Stacey, and I had no idea what you even looked like at the time. And what's really wigging me out is, I had no idea Daphne had that scroll in his back pocket. The entire plan he laid out sets up perfectly with what I saw. I think a higher power's been guiding our hand this whole time."

They took turns looking at one another, and then to the heavens.

Everything was lining up in the same direction.

Stacey finished putting on her uniform. She could no longer hide her revulsion.

"You're such a jerk, David. You picked this outfit intentionally."

He turned to face her and started laughing on sight. "What? What's the problem?"

Stace pinched each side of the emblem on the front of her T-shirt and pulled it forward. "I hate the Yankees."

"Oh, I'm sorry, I didn't know you root for another team."

"I'm a Detroit Tigers girl which you know goddamn good and well, and this is sacrilege," she stated with true disgust before popping the logo back into place. "I can feel the tri-blend poisoning my body. It burns." She began scratching both biceps like they were covered with bedbugs.

"It threw you for a loop, though—right?"

"Yeah, and now I'd like to close it by throwing you out the window."

Torie intervened in his defense. "His point is that Tag won't know what to do with it, either. Little things are the only things that can penetrate through his suit of armor. It'll put him on his backfoot right out the gate. We definitely don't want him wondering about David's whereabouts. If we rope-the-dope just right, I think it can work."

She remained skeptical. "Remind me again how you got

out of wearing this stupid disguise like everyone else, Torie?"

"Daphne put me inside the Fabricator with the loose Tether so I could just be myself. Or a copy, anyway," she confirmed. "Of course, he said if I didn't have the thing in hand, I would have probably erased myself from existence. I'm telling you guys, it's special. In any event, you and I have to be distinguishable for the plan to work. Sadly, we don't all get to look like the prettiest girl David's ever dated." She looked at her boyfriend with a smirk that he did not reciprocate.

Stacey metronomed her head left to right across her shoulder blades with her eyes on the ceiling. A slight grin began to form across her face. "Yeah, well, you both better hope he doesn't make a move to have me committed on the spot. He'll assume his girlfriend must be seeing ghosts. Which would be accurate, in this instance."

"Tag's going to be too preoccupied wondering what the hell Torie is doing at this hotel," David offered with a practiced amount of assurance. Truthfully, it was the one part of the plan that left all three of them terrified.

Torie volunteered to willingly step on a landmine.

She had to pray the rest of her squad could keep her out of the hurt locker.

"Once I'm on the elevator it will be too close quarters for him to try anything stupid," Torie claimed without any corresponding evidence. "He's going to want to keep Stacey calm and on an even keel until she's in position to have her top knot taken off. So, I'll just keep pushing buttons all the way to the top floor. Tag won't know which end is up by the time I'm done with him. He'll already have Kim's halo in hand, plus Stacey and I are both insanely gorgeous. No question we're getting into the club. After that, like Daphne said—all bets are off."

Stace was tying her shoes, but she remained at rapt attention. "Are the boys in position?"

Torie leaned herself against a locker across from Stacey.

"Sitting in the next elevator over as we speak playing spades. We put an *Out of Order* sign on the thing ourselves. Daphne insists the golden Tether will grant access to the tenth dimension the same as Kim's halo. Crew starts ascending to the heavens right along side us on my signal. Plan's all falling into place."

Even for a professional campaign manager, Stacey was impressed. She shook her head with approval back up toward Torie. "I like the cut of your jib, lady. If you weren't dead, I'd be extending a job offer. Guess the woman upstairs picked the right crew for this job."

David took turns smirking back at both of them from the end of the aisle. "Yeah, some genius. She picked The Insignificant Seven to save the entire universe."

"Speak for yourself." Stacey rose from the locker room bench and the two ladies slung their arms across each other's shoulders like it was rehearsed. "We're about to institute a new Rule of Two in this town. Two female masters and an irrelevant number of mediocre male apprentices. Tag's going to find out firsthand that's all it takes to turn the tide."

***

Tag was steaming in more ways than one.

The anonymous spa sex with Brandy or Mandy was passable at best. He couldn't help shake the feeling that something was off with Stacey. Aside from her obvious awareness of his adultery. This was meant to be the culmination of all his achievements. The greatest day of his entire anti-life. He would finally gain formal entry to that hellhole called Heaven. It was everything he ever wanted.

Yet all he could think about was what might go wrong. The invisible roadblocks still potentially littering his path. His mind raced with endless possibilities. Although he invented anxiety, this was the first time he ever felt the sensation himself. It was almost more than Tag could bear.

Having to share the sauna with the four hedge fund bros

across the way wasn't helping matters. They were making millions investing in defaulted medical debt. Their collective recently made inroads purchasing credit card liability in bulk so that they might inflict maximum pain upon the poor populace. Universal default penalties. Orders for possession. Bank garnishments. All the old hits.

The cads attended the same Ivy and met at Sigma Tau Delta or whatever their male coven was called. Tag was often left confused trying to keep them all straight, and he created the Greek system. Best friends ever since they had to play *40-Hands* in the basement of STD during pledge week. The already initiated shoved buttered up broomsticks up their buttholes. It bred real brotherhood amongst the boys. More than half the attendees at that evening's bay of pigs were now multi-millionaires. They were all insanely rich, and easily replaceable.

These were typically his kind of guys.

Today he had no time for it.

Their drunken carousing within the confined space left them hoarse faced and reddened without any input from the steam itself. They were dry heaving into laughter over their most recent female conquests. Tim and Paul would never know that Jack and Jim liked to play top and bottom on the semi-regular. All four still managed to play the role of heterosexual troglodyte to a T.

Tag leaned forward with a toothless smile. "Apologies, gentlemen. Would you mind turning the volume down? It's important that I meditate for a bit."

"Get bent."

The bromides howled uproariously at Tim's witty rejoinder. Tag could already tell he was the Oscar Wilde of the bunch. His smile only broadened at the insult. "I'll remember that directive when we meet again down the road."

Tim's expression deadened instantly when he was provided a telepathic slideshow. The comedian saw himself flattened chest first against a superheated metallic box with his arms pulled taut and tied down on each side. When he glanced back, he could see the cherry-tipped end of the fireplace poker as it headed toward his backside. Pledge week was mere preparation. The metallic rapier screeched upon insertion. It sounded the same as a blacksmith quenching his blade in a vat of ice-cold water.

When Tim let out a startled scream his friends went quiet with concern.

Tag leaned back against the wooden slats with a placid grin plastered across his face. He placed a hood over his head using the spare white towel sitting beside him. "Your friend got the point loud and clear. Now shut your mouths before you're all forced to follow suit."

Tim was lightly blubbering with his eyes locked on the prim reaper. Jack and Jim took turns softly consoling him while exchanging concerned looks. Paul was always itching for a fight. Kegs tapped by uninvited male strangers back in college gave way to inadvertent bumps on Broadway when he was already five minutes late for the boardroom. With a gram of cocaine in his system since this morning, he was raring to go. "Hey asshole, why you don't mind your own business? Or better yet, just get the hell out of here before I beat the shit out of you."

"Yeah, I'm not your wife Paul, so that's not going to be possible," Tag responded with utter nonchalance. "Other than Karen and that couple you gay-bashed from behind in the Meatpacking District, you haven't struck anyone since sophomore year. And I'm pretty sure Patrick kicked your ass. Dotted your eye red like a T-800 if I recall correctly."

He was on his feet and headed the Congressman's way. "Who the fu—"

Paul never had the chance to finish his sentence. With a pair of movements from Tag's index finger, he was forced to retake his seat. All the friends were instantly soldered into place in the same fashion.

The Anti-God sat back up and tossed his head covering aside. He slid both palms down the length of his thighs before cupping each kneecap. His positioning gave him the regal air of The Great Sphinx. He decided to make time for one last riddle. "I was really looking forward to some peace and quiet before all the clamor and clang, but since you couldn't be polite, let's play a game instead. I want you to somehow convince me not to kill all of you—along with the rest of humanity. Consider it a two-fer."

Tag granted them full freedom of movement from the neck up. Each of the friends took turns looking at one another, and then back at their interrogator. Paul finally spoke up on behalf of the entire group. "What are you talking about?"

"You gentlemen are always on the lookout for the opportunity of a lifetime, and the only thing you want in this world is more of what you already have. So, let's put two and two together. There will be no more members of your forever fraternity. It's the apex of exclusivity. The ultimate champagne room. You will either be the saviors of all humankind, or its four headsmen. Apologies for springing the fate of the entire universe on you like this, but the element of surprise is kind of the whole point."

The perspiring pledges began sweating bullets.

Tim managed to eek out a stuttering response. "Maggie and Meggie. My daughters."

"Ah, yes, the twins. But fraternal, right? Thank God. They're the only kind I can stand. Identical twins are born under a bad sign. Amongst the twelve celestial seraphim, Gemini has always been one of the most insufferable. The only thing worse is Cancer. I don't think I need to tell you what he created."

"Just don't take their father away from my baby girls. Please."

"Oh, there won't be any need for that, really. Maggie will be struck by a drunk driver at the bus stop in a few years. The pain and anguish will ultimately drive you and Danielle to divorce. And poor, poor Meggie." Tag let the words hang as he shook his downturned head. "Sadly, she'll never recover from the loss of her sister. Falls in with the wrong crowd. Takes her first non-prescribed pill when she's thirteen. You'll find her in the basement of your McMansion four years later. She'll never stop being blue. Seems fitting to leave things on the same note."

Tim's tears couldn't be distinguished from the sweat covering his face.

Tag's smile was easy to see. "Who's next, then? How about our resident tough guy?"

Paul was hyperventilating for different reasons now. His eyes darted side to side while he searched for a viable response. He finally offered the best he could come up with under the circumstances. "Our firm employs dozens and dozens of people. You'd be destroying livelihoods. Entire families. We're part of the engine that drives this country."

"Yes, and you fuel the thing with nothing but methane," Tag countered with accompanying flatulence. "You utilize the analytics of insolvency purely to improve your own profit margin. Think about that—your wealth derives entirely from owning poor people and bringing the middle class down a peg. Credit card companies created a financial pandemic out of whole cloth and then you came along to offer an anti-booster. Reprobates like you think the cure for skin cancer is to stick them out in the sun a little bit longer. But hey, at least you got your second home on the coast. All it cost was a thousand foreclosures in Connecticut."

With two down, that only left the unambiguously gay duo to go.

Jack went up the hill first, but he didn't have the high ground.

"We've invested millions into our online college. *We Educate U* is growing by leaps and bounds every day. Based on projections, we're going to have a hundred thousand students enrolled by the end of the decade. Doesn't educating America mean anything?"

"Sure, if that's what you were doing," Tag acknowledged. "Unfortunately, WEU is a non-accredited diploma mill that specifically targets ESL citizens on Spanish language TV and radio. You offer degrees in *cashiering*. If someone pays you five hundred bucks and takes a selfie with a graphing calculator, that's sufficient to make them an engineer overnight. The distance between actual learning and what you're providing the people can be measured in light years. You might as well be running a tax-exempt clown college."

Jack dropped his head in defeat. The Anti-God slowly rotated his own toward the final contestant. When he arrived at the destination, he simply lifted his chin as an imprimatur to speak.

Jim was at a loss for words. "Umm, uhh, I mean—we do pay a lot in taxes."

Tag rolled his eyes then snapped his fingers. Jim's head popped like a balloon. Bone, blood, and brain matter splattered across the faces of his three screaming friends. The Anti-God silenced them with a shoosh to keep the spa employees from dialing 911. "I apologize, but I think we officially reached the end of the line here, gentlemen. I really don't need to hear about all the brown friends you've accumulated over the years. For some reason, you always think that's relevant when you're wealthy and white."

The Anti-God stood up and straightened his arms out to each side with a theatrical yawn. "Thank you so much for the warm-up. A good stretch before strenuous activity is always wise. Ushering in the end of the world is going to take a lot out of me. Enjoy the vapors, vermin."

Tag broke the door lock on the outside of the sauna before telekinetically turning the temperature up to 270 °F. He envisioned the bloodied, wrinkled friends looking like beef smoked sausages by the time their corpses were pulled free from the carnage.

Luckily for them they wouldn't have to wait that long for absolution.

The apocalypse was right around the corner.

***

Tag's smile died as soon as he made the turn.

Normally, the sight of two beautiful women waiting for him in front of a hotel elevator bank would have been just another Tuesday. In this case, he couldn't decide which lady's presence he found more perplexing.

His fiancée was clad in a New York Yankees T-shirt she would have normally incinerated on sight. Stacey could have been forced to sit over a dunk tank filled with hydrochloric acid while someone tossed a medicine ball at the target. That still wouldn't have been sufficient persuasion for her sartorial choice. Tag fondly recalled developing *African Dodger* back in the day. If the carnival-goers threw knives at Ms. Darden's face, she would have gladly played Pinhead before putting on anything adorned with that logo.

He was taken aback, but it was only the second strangest thing he saw.

Torie Eaton was standing right next to her.

The pair were smiling and laughing like long lost friends.

It made him sick to his stomach.

"Hey you." Stacey began to wave him over. "Come here. I want to introduce you to someone."

Tag and Torie stared one another down with fake smiles as he closed the gap.

"Honey, this is Torie Eaton. We just ran into one another in the waiting room. She and I went to middle school together until her family moved away. It's such a small world, right? You're never going to believe this—Lyle Stephens was her first boyfriend. Before she grew up."

"I'm sorry to hear Lyle never did. I assumed he'd have a growth spurt at some point."

"Yeah, no. He always got the short end of the stick."

Cackling erupted from both ladies that Tag felt compelled to complement. He lightly chuckled along with them despite having no previous knowledge of the purported relationship. Given his proximity to all the parties involved, his omniscience should have rendered that impossible. The Anti-God chalked it up to the general fogginess clouding his thinking as of late.

"Small world, indeed," Tag said with barely cloaked skepticism. He directed his words at Torie. "At least you two didn't date the same man."

Their eyelids lowered simultaneously.

Tag continued. "I'm surprised I'm only hearing about your friend here for the first time."

Stacey leveled up the snark to redirect his attention. "Oh, my apologies, I didn't know I had to provide you with a complete breakdown of every acquaintance I've ever had since birth. You know what, after dinner I'll start a spreadsheet. Work my way up from kindergarten and go from there."

"Alright, alright." He sidled up next to Stace and hooked his arm across her shoulder as an admission of defeat. Tag knew it was in his best interest to keep the bait on the line. "So, Torie—what brings you here?"

He didn't mean the hotel.

She knew exactly what he was implying but maintained the ruse. "Oh, I got a gift card for my birthday and decided to treat myself. It's the anniversary of my sister's death." Her eyes never left the Anti-God.

He looked daggers back at her in response.

Stacey's smile departed. She lightly shook off Tag and moved toward her former friend. Stace grabbed Torie's right hand with both of her own and lightly nuzzled her head against her shoulder. The act made it clear to him that the two had a shared history. "I'm so sorry about Kim. She always treated me like family."

Torie lifted her available arm and began to massage Stacey's elbow. "Thanks, babe. Anyway, I like to spend the day alone."

"Well, not this year," Stacey said with a step back. "We're heading upstairs for some kind of special acupuncture treatment, right honey?"

It was true that he planned to puncture her.

"You're coming with, Tor. Is that okay Tag?" It was barely framed in the form of a question. She looked at him like she was planning to ask for a puppy.

The Anti-God didn't require clairvoyance to know Torie intended to interfere with his plans, but he also understood a single misstep could leave Stacey marching back to the car before he had the chance to bleed her dry. Prophecy required her to ascend of her own free will, and a lack of social grace had always been one of her personal sticking points. He tried to thread the needle. "Stace, of course I'd love for your friend to come, but it required a bit of doing on my part just to get us access. It typically takes ages."

Lies mixed with truth.

Stacey pursed her lips and tilted her head to signal her discontent. "Tag Gottfried, you're a U.S. Congressman, for Christ's sake. Not one of the more well-liked ones at this point, but nevertheless. You're telling me if you pull that card, it won't push the turnstile forward for one more person?"

Torie kept her eyes to the ground without raising a hand or speaking a word to circumvent Stace's efforts on her behalf.

Tag wanted nothing more than to slap the taste out of the grieving girl's mendacious mouth, but he knew doing so would bring the world to a stop before he had the chance to accomplish the feat for real. Regardless, the Anti-God was bestowed with an inborn arrogance at birth. He decided whatever Torie might have in store was no match for his own might. "Fine. Let's head up. I'll see what I can do."

The Father of Perdition couldn't touch a Bible without

burning his fingers. A reading of the Book of Proverbs might have served him well in this instance.

Pride would prove to be his downfall.

Stacey gave him a kiss on the cheek in appreciation. "Thank you. Tor, you ready?"

"Hold on, one second." Torie appeared to be returning an urgent text. She was beaming by the time she hit send. "Okay. We're all set, Stacey."

Tag disregarded the elevator marked *Out of Order* and pressed up on its opposing number. When the doors chimed open, all three made their way inside. Torie's prediction was prescient. He was already too turned around to realize David Downey's ghost was nowhere to be found.

An elderly couple fresh from the beach began sandal-slapping in their direction with newlywed smiles. "Could you hold the elevator for us, please?"

"Sorry, it's at capacity," Tag informed them. He repeatedly tapped ▶|◀ until the doors smacked shut in their now-frowning faces.

"That was a little rude," Stacey chided him. "I don't think the additional hundred pounds between Maury and Maude would have caused the cables to snap."

"I'm sorry but it's going to take a little longer than normal to get to the top. We're on a tight schedule. Can't have any delays or we'll miss our appointment."

In 3-D, the hotel only had twenty-five available floors. When Tag placed Kim's halo against the control panel, an inter-dimensional LED readout appeared above it that only he could see. He tapped the numbered buttons in appropriate sequence until level 85,000 was selected. The ground beneath them suddenly seemed propelled by rocket boosters. The Anti-God dropped his head and exhaled before silently chuckling to himself. When he finally turned to face the ladies, he was grinning ear to ear. "Going up."

Torie knew that was her cue. "So, let me ask you shithead—have you told your fiancée here how you killed my sister in cold blood? Or snuffed out her soul, anyway. I'm not sure what the appropriate nomenclature is when you end an angel's everlasting existence."

Stacey took a step to the side in concern while shifting her eyes from friend to foe. "What's she talking about, Tag?"

The Anti-God did his best to feign both ignorance and outrage. "I have absolutely no idea, Stace. I'm sorry Torie, but I think you must have me confused with someone else."

"Not possible." Torie shook off the suggestion. "Your dickishness is indelible. Anyway, you think I'd ever forget the face of the man who extinguished my sister? Matter of fact, you did it right across the street there. Figures a monster like you would come back to the scene of the crime. It's a common trait among serial killers."

Tag wasn't sure if he should make a move to comfort Stacey or strangle Torie. He correctly surmised the latter would do little to fulfill the former. "Honey, I'm not sure what's come over your friend here, but I promise you I have not murdered anyone."

"In the last five minutes you mean?" Torie crossed her arms and smirked at him as a dare to do something about it.

In Tag's defense, any denial on his part would have been technically accurate. It had been over ten minutes since his little steam room slaughter.

Stacey matched her friend's posture from the opposite corner of the elevator. The Anti-God couldn't decide which of the two presented the more imminent threat. His fiancée was next to speak. "Torie's never given me any reason to think she would lie to me. You on the other hand are a known prevaricator. Two hours ago, you took off your mask for me, remember? You're not a compassionate progressive. You're a flamethrowing firebrand who was screwing my ex-best friend behind my back along with half the female pages and reporters in DC. Every move you've made since you arrived in New York City was designed to destroy it, and then take the rest of America along on the same ferry ride to Hell. You turned the entire country into a Satanic concentration camp. Skin tags and all. Suddenly it's not that hard envisioning you with blood on your hands. Speaking of which, what really happened to Adam Willco that night? Did you kill him, too?"

He briefly flicked his eyes between the two ladies and then over to the control panel. They still had miles to go before they would see the sunrise. Tag just needed to buy himself some time. He decided to direct his ire toward Torie. When he took a step forward, she didn't flinch. "Listen to me. I don't appreciate you showing up here and filling Stacey's head with lies. This is our time together. I'll give you a few minutes to reconsider your actions, because once those doors open—"

"*All bets are off.*" Tore finished his sentence with a sneer.

"That's right," he acknowledged with palpable uncertainty. Torie's lack of fear put him on edge. No matter how hard he tried to batter and bully his way into her subconscious mind, he was unable to gain access. Instead, he saw a single image projected back to him on repeat.

A ring of anti-hellfire. Glorious golden light that could only originate from one source.

The pieces began to fall into place.

"Hey, don't you dare threaten her." Stacey's warning snapped him out of his stupor.

Before he had any further chance to respond, a blast of heavenly trumpets signaled their arrival on the top level. This time it was the ladies turn to be caught flat-footed. A doorway appeared on the opposite side of the elevator that wasn't there when they first began to ascend.

"We're here," Tag said with a smile. The metallic slabs receded to reveal an endless hallway of black doors on each side stretching out before them into infinity. When the Anti-God unsheathed his blue blade, Torie knew what was coming next. She grabbed a wide-eyed Stacey by the wrist and pulled her backward into the corridor while Tag followed after them.

"Where is it, Ms. Eaton?"

She played dumb. "Where is what?"

"The Tether you've been keeping in your back pocket." He raised the tip of the blade until it was level with the bridge of her nose. "There can't be anything standing in the way of my transcendence. You can hand it over, or I can take it off your corpse. The choice is yours."

Stacey decided to play peacemaker. "Tag, what are you doing? Put the knife down."

The blade was suddenly redirected. "Your friend and I have unfinished business, Stacey. Keep your mouth shut until it's concluded, or I'll take your tongue. Before I have your head."

The ladies shared a look before sprinting in the opposite direction. Tag made no effort to give chase. He remained in the same position a few feet from the elevator bank and began to lightly chuckle to himself. "Why don't you ladies see what's behind Door #2?"

Running at full speed put thirty yards between themselves and the Anti-God. Taking his advice, Torie reached for the handle of the nearest exit point to her right and dragged Stacey through it by the hand.

The door ten feet to Tag's left opened abruptly and the pair came spilling out.

He laughed in their faces.

"Welcome to the Star Gate. The 10th Dimension provides access points to anywhere in the universe. Unfortunately for both of you, I'm in charge of the ticket counter now. Run as much as you want. You'll always end up in the same place. Back here. With me. There is no escape."

They gave it another go, and another, and another. By the fourth effort they were fully exhausted. Stacey was too tired to avoid her fiancée's clutches when they both bounded out of the door directly to his right.

With a single motion he lifted her up and impaled her right shoulder with his blade until she was pinioned against the wall. Tag had her pegged three feet above the floor. Her howls of pain echoed down the hall in a continuous loop.

Torie's attempts to slap his shoulders into submission from behind only served to place her within easy reach. A no-look flick of his wrist met her forehead and bounced her backward onto the floor. She shuffled away from him on her hands and heels further down the hallway. Tag leaned down and encircled her throat until she was hovering against the flickering fluorescent office lighting above them. Stacey's screaming was the only soundtrack.

It covered the creak of the elevator doors opening behind them.

"Now tell me where you buried your little treasure before I break your neck."

"It's right here, asshole."

Tag didn't even have time to register the sound of Stacey's voice before the click of the golden Tether being locked around his ankle rang out in his ears. The diversion caused him to drop Torie's crumpled body and turn around.

There were now six identical versions of Stacey Darden semi-encircling the Anti-God.

"I know what you're thinking." David Darden spoke the words from the wall as he removed the carving knife. He fell to the floor feet first and brushed the dirt off his shoulder. "This is every man's worst nightmare."

The real thing was currently fourth in line. Stacey had to force her mouth closed to avoid telling David to shut his own.

Tag literally didn't know who to kill first.

"Say hello to your anti-halo," Torie confirmed from behind him. "You're not going anywhere now. Tethered just like the rest of us. And the only thing capable of sawing it off is hanging over your head. Can't have it both ways. Something's gotta give. So what's it going to be, Old Scratch?"

"You're stuck in a celestial *Saw* trap," Stacey added. "That's what you get for being diabolical. Consider your visitation rights hereby revoked."

Tag made a move toward the fourth in line of succession.

She didn't budge. "You think I'm scared of you? Daphne over here gave us the skinny. You're just a *man* now. I've had plenty of those for breakfast. Hey, you want to see a neat trick?"

On cue, all six Staceys raced through different doors before reentering the hallway. They did it once more for effect until Tag was surrounded on all sides.

"Good luck sorting us out."

He reddened to reveal his true nature. His head rotated around the circle of life. "You're nothing without me, Stacey. You were nothing before me, and you'll be nothing after. You'll *have* nothing."

"That is not entirely accurate," Daphne Darden said. "You would have added a note to your ledger of names upon the birth of your baby. Everything to be left to the Prince of Darkness should your everlasting light be snuffed out. Interim administrator planning is mandatory in all divine contracts. Dreadful or otherwise. True or false?"

The scowl forming across his face served to confirm the veracity of his statement.

"Stacey may not receive anything, but young Nicky will inherit your entire kingdom."

"You really should have taken a closer look at all four corners of the document," Stacey said. "Speaking of which—show him the scroll, Daffy."

The glowing tube he pulled out of thin air caused Tag's face to emit fear for the first time in his entire existence. "What the hell is that?"

"A heavenly how-to guide on how to destroy you," David confirmed. "Thing's pretty cool. The Greys even drew pictograms. It's like an Ikea instruction manual." He leaned over Daphne's shoulder to take another look and shook his head with mock approval.

"Stacey is the key master," Torie added. "She opened the door, but she's also the only one who could lock you out. Yin and yang, right? Having to keep her alive all this time also sealed your fate."

"And your final eradication requires the same angelic blood you shed to arrive here in the 10$^{th}$ dimension," Daphne offered in further corroboration. "It's a contractual loophole that typically inures to your benefit. It makes it almost impossible to destroy you."

"*Almost*," Torie said while slipping the tip of his own blade against his jugular. David passed it off to her behind his back. "Last time I checked, Kim and I share a bloodline. You should have killed me when you had the chance, you bastard."

"In any event, I only need my son," Stacey hissed into his left ear. "You can go to Hell."

"For good measure," Torie whispered into the other before slitting his throat. Tag fell to his knees while blood poured free from the gaping wound. Both ladies grabbed a handful of the halo hanging over his head and used his lower back for leverage. They each shoved a separate shoe into his spine and ripped backward with as much violence as they could muster. The crown tore free and he fell chest down into a puddle of his own blackened plasma. His body charred over like smoke pit pork and then exploded into a cloud of dust.

The two ladies held the golden hoop in each hand as their five almost-female companions rejoiced in victory.

Daphne reverted to his true form and slowly stepped forward. "May I see that halo?"

Without a thought the ladies handed it over. The alien

proceeded to bend over and rinse it in the blood of the damned. He held the dripping ring aloft next to him with an outstretched arm.

Torie looked disgusted. "What the hell are you doing, Daffy?"

"There was one final clause in the scroll I failed to mention. *To the victor go the spoils.*"

Following a flash of blinding light, Kim Eaton stood before her sister once again.

"Oh my God," Torie exclaimed. Roar bum rushed Lor and they toppled over to the ground in reunification.

David Darden looked like she had never been happier.

"Jesus, lady," her sister responded with sore laughter. "Go easy on the goods. I've been doing hard time in purgatory. Let me get a stretch in before you squeeze the afterlife out of me."

Once Torie concluded bear hugging her almost back to death, the Eaton sisters helped one another to their feet.

Kim stared down the line at each version of Stace. "Who are the sextuplets?

David couldn't let the opportunity pass. "Has there ever been a more appropriate designation for Stacey Darden?"

"*Downey.*" The real Stacey was not amused.

"I'm sorry, Stace. I swear, it's the last time."

"Trust me, the last time was a long time ago," she responded.

"This is David's ex Stacey," Torie explained to her sister. "The rest of these idiots were just cosplaying to sew a bit of confusion. Everyone say hello to my big sis."

The Eaton sisters received the strangest group hug in history.

"I'd still like to know who was looking out for us from up above," Torie said as the crowd dispersed.

"Oh, shit. That reminds me," Kim responded. She shuffled over to the golden Tether laying flat on the ground and lifted it beside her in the same manner as Daphne. "Abracadabra—just kidding."

Another flash and this time Bobby Kennedy was standing before them.

Everyone save Kim was awestruck.

He could see right through David's disguise. "Well, if it isn't Mr. Downey. Glad you finally made it out of the fourth dimension."

The two shook hands like old friends. "How did you get here, Senator?"

"You think you people are the only ones capable of pulling off a body swap? Your old friend Harley Mike got to go to Heaven three years early, and I took his place in exchange. Sorry for the cloak and dagger. Orders from above. Anyway, that's how you all got hold of that heavenly Time Tether. Jesus carpentered the thing himself for me."

"Guess it almost makes sense now," David said. "I am sorry you had to descend back down to the land of the semi-living in order to get the job done, though."

"Eh, 4-D was fun for a few months, but I'm ready to go home. Purgatory was definitely no picnic. Kim and I played a crazy amount of Pinochle to pass the time."

"I'm up by over four thousand games, by the way," Kim confirmed.

"No one cares for a braggart, Kimberly."

Thomas Eaton was the only man she every allowed to call her by her full name.

Torie could see a paternal relationship had grown between the two.

For Kim, it would always be something more. Unrequited for the rest of eternity.

She would never love another man as much as Bobby Kennedy.

David took up a position between his former and current

girlfriends. "What would you two have done if you'd been stuck in Purgatory in perpetuity?"

"I don't know. *Uno*, I guess." Kim stated it a matter of fact rather than a question posed.

Torie gave her sister a lifeless punch in the shoulder before they both started laughing.

Although it was tough to tell in his current feminine disguise, Wes posed a question to Darrell. "What the hell is Daphne doing right now?"

The alien was busy jerking his spindly limbs in every direction.

"He's dancing—or having a stroke."

While the ladies were distracted, RFK tapped David's elbow. "I think it's time we get you to Heaven, young man. Kim and I can show you the way. Would you say he's finally earned the right, Stacey?"

She narrowed her eyelids and stared him down with a flat expression. A smile finally broke the plane. "Yeah, I think he's suffered enough. *I release you, David Downey.*" The mask dropped and her ex-boyfriend was standing before the assembled group once again. Without warning, she reached across the aisle and gave him a bipartisan embrace. Her voice barely cracked a whisper. "No matter what dimension you're in, I'm going to miss you, kid. I'm sorry about Lyle. I'm sorry about a lot of things."

"I'm sorry about everything," David responded. "You're singular, Stace. I never took anything more for granted. I didn't earn the right to be with you. Someone will, though—and they'll be the luckiest man alive."

"Agreed." She sniffled and laughed at the same time. "Hey, one day when I make my way up there, let's have lunch. See if we can make this friendship thing finally work in the great beyond."

"Deal. You won't have to come looking. I'll find you."

They hugged for a few more seconds. It felt like forever.

She took a step back with a few tears trickling down her

face. Stacey wiped away the evidence. "Well, you've been released, dummy. Get a move on, already. I hear the Detroit Lions are looking for a waterboy."

"That's very funny."

He could see his girlfriend was the only one who wasn't laughing.

David Darden matched her expression. "Actually, can Torie and I have a second?"

He pulled her aside. Everyone but Kim pretended not to pay attention.

"Do you want to spend eternity with me?"

She lit up. "What?"

"It doesn't have to be forever," he assured her. "I know that doesn't make any sense, but you know what I mean. I just need to hear that's what you want before I tell Bobby Kennedy to go pound sand."

"I heard that," RFK said.

"I know you did," David responded. "Look, you have your faults, Torie. I certainly do. But that doesn't make you any less perfect. How can that place be Heaven if you're not there? I don't want—"

She clasped both hands behind his head before he could finish and kissed him. It took a moment before they came up for air. "Forever ever. That's how long I want to be with you."

Stacey smiled at the sight.

"Okay." David turned to his angelic escorts. "I think I'm going to stick around in the fourth dimension for awhile. At least until the missus here is ready to ascend, too. That doesn't preclude me from entering the holy kingdom at a later date, right?"

Bobby and Kim looked at one another in mock contemplation before he turned to respond. "I think helping to save the universe grants you a special exemption. I'll let God know your flight's just going to be delayed for a few years. I'm sure she won't have any issue with it."

Kim made her way over to engulf them both in one clinch. "I'll check in on you crazy kids in a couple months. Take care of my sister, David—or I'll end you for real."

"Understood."

RFK held the door open for his companion and then followed after her. He turned and offered final words before it closed behind them. "Until we meet again, everyone. If you stop by Hyannis Port, please try not to burn the place down. Sentimental value and all."

The crew took the elevator back to Earth. In the lobby, Stacey had a sudden epiphany that caused her concern level to jump through the roof. "Oh, shit—is Ms. Kolyab going to try and kill me when I get back and she sees I'm Tagless? That bitch can bench press a bison."

"No need to worry," Daphne reassured her. "She was returned to Hell when Tag evaporated. Little Nicholas is sound asleep. I'll use the Fabricator to teleport you home."

She exhaled. "Appreciate you, Daffy. Well, I guess this is goodbye for now."

Torie palmed her elbow. "So, what are your plans with the Anti-God out of the picture?"

Stacey smiled. "You know, I've been thinking lately—anything Tag can do, I can do better. This world's going to need a woman's touch to get things back on track. Until we meet again." Daphne blinked out and a moment later Stacey followed suit.

David admired her from afar for the rest of her life.

The same as always.

# THE AFTERGLOW

"Senator, what are your plans for your first day in office?"

"Well, as I made clear to everyone when I took Tag's place on the ballot, my first order of business is ensuring AMPA is immediately repealed. ID Tag removal for every person in this country, citizen or not, that's next up on the docket. After that, I don't know. I thought scuttling the Staten Island Ferry in Upper Bay might be the quickest path to goosing my approval ratings. What do you guys think?"

The assembled reporters laughed. Stacey smiled back in response.

"No, in all seriousness, while my affection for Congressman Gottfried the man will always remain, the fact is he lost his way politically in his final months. We all saw it clear as day. That he felt the need to take his own life speaks to his own recognition of that reality. I'm here to do penance, and to put our house back in order. My own, New York City's, and America's. I plan to work tirelessly on behalf of all three until that's been accomplished. Now, if you'll excuse me ladies and gentlemen, I've got a puppy upstairs to house train and a lot of packing yet to do. I'll see you all in Washington."

Flashbulbs and shouted final questions followed as Carol ushered her through the building's Christmas light-adorned front entrance and into the elevator. The newly elected Senator smiled and waved back at them the entire way until the doors closed behind them.

"That went really well, Stacey," Carrie beamed. "You're a natural. Like Tag Gottfried, but without the sadomasochism."

"Think you just stumbled on my next campaign slogan there, Care-Bear."

"You know what I meant," she offered apologetically.

"It's totally fine, Carrie," Stacey said. "And I'm not the only one who's a natural. You're my ride-or-die chick. Always. I'm not going anywhere in this political life without you on my hip. It's a promise."

They shared a hug.

"Alright, easy there, Carrie, I'm not your wife." She leaned away with a smile.

"No, you'd need a KD Lang haircut and a shoe rack full of Vans to make that work for me."

A quartet of Tag-appointed bodyguards in black Armani hand-tailored suits awaited their arrival as soon as they stepped off the lift. Their earpieces kept them in perpetual contact with the other six of their number stationed on the first floor at various intervals around the building. The nine-figure fortune left to her son by Tag ensured their permanent placement.

Team leader Victor broke down their individual bona fides for her over morning coffee a month back. Each one of them was a cold-blooded murderer in his own right fully capable of dispatching an entire crew of assassins if it came to that. It made her feel safe when that feeling was in short supply.

She and Vic had been sleeping together for the past three weeks, but Stacey made it abundantly clear it was nothing serious. The Senator just needed to take a breath.

Plus, he was great in bed.

Prior to Tag's death, the only half of the couple not being sexually gratified on a regular basis was Stacey Darden.

Victor remained a total professional. He addressed her as Senator and nothing more before she and Carol entered the penthouse.

Tonya and the rest of her team were seated in various positions around the TV. When they saw Stacey reenter the room, they all rose to their feet and began clapping.

"You were fantastic down there, Stacey," Tonya beamed. "You're making our job a whole lot easier."

"Well, that's no good." Stacey's response elicited more laughter from the entire group. Truthfully, she could be reading last night's Powerball numbers at this point. Her boot-licking underlings would find a way to laud her elucidation. "No, I want to thank all of you. I'm not in this position without you guys working tirelessly on my behalf these last few months. Back in August, I was just a grieving widow with no political name recognition. The nameplate might say Senator Darden, but this is never going to be a one-woman operation. I have a lot of ideas for where we go from here, but whatever comes next, I can't get there without you."

Smiles and manufactured tears quickly spread throughout the room.

"With that said, I'm not springing for any more pizza, so get the hell out of here and go home to your families. You officially have the day off work. We're back at it bright and early in the AM."

Hugs and high fives were dispensed to the row of fleeing subordinates as they made their way out of the penthouse.

Tonya and Carol implicitly understood their presence would still be required and remained in their seats.

Stacey eased herself into the couch across from them and took in the CNN ticker for a few seconds. The Senator decided to platform actual compassion for America's migrants. Many already stationed in the city were now being gainfully employed to help clean up Tag's mess and restore Manhattan to a place fit for man rather than beast. She raised a finger toward the flatscreen. "Looks like the FBI's almost done rounding up those Patriot's Sword assholes. I'll look forward to not having a bomb-sniffing dog sorting through my mail."

"Yeah, apparently they're on their last legs," Tonya confirmed for the two of them.

"Their command and control seemed to collapse after Tag's

death," Carol continued. "All I see now are a bunch of zit-faced thirty something castration candidates being dragged out of their mom's basements."

A male voice interrupted their colloquy. "Stacey, I put Nicky down for his nap and I fed Copper for you. He's sleeping in Nick's room. Do you mind if I run home and shower?"

The Senator finally discovered the perfect position for Evan.

Manny.

Whether it was his presence or Tag's absence, day by day the boy seemed to have less of the devil in him. Either way, she was grateful.

"Why don't you all take the rest of the day off, actually? I've got things handled here. I think I might lay down with the little one for a few hours myself. I'll call you ladies at three and we can go over the agenda for the rest of the week."

The trio thought better than to offer any further resistance. Their boss walked them to the door and then bid them each adieu. Next stop was the refrigerator for a bottom shelf Sprite that was kept one degree above freezing at all times. She admired the city through the floor to ceiling windows while she sipped on her elixir. It appeared all the fires had finally been put out. Although she would be spending most of her time in DC moving forward, New York City would never stop being her home. The damage Tag did seemed to evaporate overnight along with him. Things were almost back to normal.

For the first time in months, she let herself yawn. The Senator was tired as hell, but she had never been happier.

After emptying the can, she made her way to Nicky's bedroom and pushed the door open.

When Stacey saw what he did to the dog, she screamed.

***

The Anti-God was in misery.

His heavenly oppressors found new and more creative ways to torture him each day.

Serving as referee at the Puppy Bowl.

DJing a Molly-fueled EDM rave in Ibiza.

Squirrel-suiting through Sun Valley.

This month, the assholes upstairs really topped themselves.

He was being forced to silently observe each new birth in the Mount Sinai Hospital maternity ward. One baby after another. An assembly line of little bastards.

It was a place of endless joy.

Their bliss made him want to barf.

Swimming all alone in a pool of anti-matter for eternity suddenly seemed like Heaven.

In the final analysis, Sartre's thesis proved almost accurate.

For Tag Gottfried, Hell was other happy people.

***

Darrell and Daphne decided to honeymoon in the Quarton galaxy.

The beaches there were unbelievable. Watching the space whales breach each evening became their new favorite activity.

"I've never been happier," Daffy declared one night while they walked hand in hand through the violet sands of Exogis-3.

"Same," Darrell responded. "I've been thinking, though. Would you have any interest in adopting one day? I think I might be ready to be a dad."

"I can offer you something even better," the alien said with a smile.

"What's that?"

"Let's start a construct. Instead of one child, we'll have five trillion."

Their decision was sealed with a kiss. The greatest foster family in the history of the universe was born that night.

When the Sun finally burned out five billion years later, Darrell and Daphne's Star Children would be there to wish it a fond farewell.

The end of all things was just the beginning.

***

*For every Anti-God…*

"Hey, Daredevil! Can you come inside for a sec? I need to show you something."

Torie and David emigrated to Stockholm in the aftermath of Tag's undoing. He wanted nothing more than to give her the home she always wanted.

David put down the shovel and trudged up onto the wraparound. His dirt-caked boots were discarded in turn onto the *Welcome* mat. Despite her urgent request, she was nowhere to be found when he entered the ten thousand square foot abode. The indoor waterfall made pinning down her location even more difficult. "Baby, where are you?"

"Famous last words. I'm in the bathroom. The one next to the kitchen." Her voice was smiling. He could see it from where he stood.

It took him thirty seconds to make the trek. When he finally arrived at the destination, he found the door ajar in anticipation. He pushed it all the way in with an index finger.

The Queen was biting her lip and holding the scepter aloft from her seated position when he entered the throne room.

It was positively blue, but she was anything but.

"Read it and weep, sucker. I'm pregnant."


*-THE END-*

Jason Anderson enjoys A24 films, ufology, EDM, Peloton (#TeamLovewell), Victor Wembanyama, female pop stars on the verge, and the collected works of Jessie Buckley. Make it make sense. He resides in Parts Unknown, Michigan—which is totally a place, and you should actively try and locate it. In his spare time, the author is a consumer defense attorney.

All appropriate inquiries are being made.

# MORE ROADSIDE PRESS TITLES:

*By Plane, Train or Coincidence*
Michele McDannold

*Prying*
Jack Micheline, Charles Bukowski and Catfish McDaris

*Wolf Whistles Behind the Dumpster*
Dan Provost

*Busking Blues: Recollections of a Chicago Street Musician and Squatter*
Westley Heine

*Unknowable Things*
Kerry Trautman

*How to Play House*
Heather Dorn

*Kiss the Heathens*
Ryan Quinn Flanagan

*St. James Infirmary*
Steven Meloan

*Street Corner Spirits*
Westley Heine

*A Room Above a Convenience Store*
William Taylor Jr.

*Resurrection Song*
George Wallace

*Nothing and Too Much to Talk About*
Nancy Patrice Davenport

*Bar Guide for the Seriously Deranged*
Alan Catlin